THE LUCKIEST MAN ALIVE

IAIN RONAYNE

LUKE817 PUBLISHING

CONTENTS

PROLOGUE

In the business-class cabin of Vivair Flight 002 to London, Chloe Mitchell, a lawyer for a group of exiled African politicians, glanced at the man beside her.

His face, etched with anguish, communicated the news before any words left his mouth. "They murdered Viktor. It's confirmed."

Chloe stared at him for a few seconds, her mind trying to process the revelation. They'd killed Viktor Malaba, the beacon of hope for the country of Njala, the man who vowed to dismantle corruption and champion an equal wealth distribution in their oil- and mineral-rich homeland. *Murder?* A cold wave of panic washed over her.

The politician leaned in closer. "It was an assassination, Chloe," he whispered urgently. "The crash that killed Viktor . . . It was orchestrated." He produced a USB stick from his jacket and held it to her with a trembling hand. "Everything is on here —evidence, names, plans. It's all we have now."

Chloe took the USB stick, her fingers brushing against his. "Is there another copy?" she asked, her voice barely above a whisper.

"No, there was no time. You must keep it safe," the politician replied, his eyes darting nervously.

Chloe's face contorted as she realized what a precarious position she was in. She was now an even bigger target, carrying the only evidence of a conspiracy that could topple a regime. She grasped the USB stick, which suddenly felt heavier.

Chloe hurriedly grabbed her laptop and connected the USB stick. With a few clicks, she had password-protected the device, using a password she knew was memorable and hoped was secure, momentarily quelling her rising anguish. Chloe returned her laptop to its bag and slid it under the ottoman in front of her. She then looked at the USB stick in her hand, turning it over before clasping her hand around it tightly.

Her gaze shifted to the screen in front of her, with its anodyne welcome graphic on a loop. Covering her mouth with her hand, she tried to calm the thoughts speeding through her head, but her heart now joined the race. Every day, she seemed to get deeper into something, and now this.

Her attention snapped to a disturbance behind her. Peering around the seats, she saw a man being escorted off the plane by the police—a drunk passenger, by the looks of it. An impulsive plan formed in her mind, risky but potentially lifesaving. Without a second thought, Chloe stood up and moved into the aisle, pretending to look for something in the overhead compartment. As the police officer pushing the man reached her, she stopped and turned. Then, as she mumbled an apology and moved aside, she deftly slipped the USB stick into the outside pocket of the drunk man's jacket.

Returning to her seat, Chloe watched the entourage with the drunk depart the aircraft. She pulled out her phone and composed a message to her grandfather, sure he'd know what to do.

> Urgent. A man removed from Vivair Flight 002
> to London. In police custody. Gave him USB
> with vital info. He doesn't know he has it.
> Please track him down, keep USB safe. Will
> explain later. Love you.

She sent the text, feeling both relief and anxiety, then turned off the phone. Her eyes returned to the politician, who looked at her confused, before looking away. Chloe knew he trusted her. They all did. She also knew trust was the only currency in the dangerous landscape she now inhabited. She heard the forward door close with a thump and fastened her seat belt.

CHAPTER 1

S ilas Knox, the founder of luke-817.org, sat in his dimly lit, dusty office in London's Soho, surrounded by multiple monitors, piles of papers, and boxes of files. His eager eyes scanned his inbox, searching for the next big story.

There was a sexual scandal involving a famous TV presenter, and he'd been investigating the subsequent whitewashing by the TV company. The presenter, a well-known figure with a squeaky-clean image, faced multiple accusations of inappropriate behavior, and several of his alleged victims contacted the website to share their unpleasant experiences. Silas had been collecting evidence, interviewing, and piecing together the puzzle of cover-ups and conspiracy. He knew the police had interviewed several of his whistleblowers but had not taken their investigations further. Despite his work, the presenter's damaging story did not appeal to Silas. He wanted something substantial he could sink his teeth into, something earth-shattering.

A light tap on his office door made him look up. His assistant, Sue, cracked the door and stuck her head through the gap.

"The reporter from *The Guardian* is here."

Silas screwed his face up. *She's early.*

"OK, send her in, thanks."

Silas sighed and looked down at his scruffy "Free Nelson Mandela" T-shirt. He'd put in zero effort at sprucing himself up for this interview. He knew the reporter—a tough cookie who covered war zones, political scandals, everything. Now, she wanted to write a feature on him. He would be lying if he said it did not flatter him.

Jenny Slater stepped inside, the weight of her large bag pressing against her shoulder. She clutched her notebook close, and he watched her eyes scan the chaotic landscape of his office. Silas could almost hear the cogs turning in her head, cataloging the details.

Her sharp eyes met his.

"Thanks for agreeing to meet me." Silas detected an edge to her voice.

"Would you like some tea?" he said in an upbeat tone, grinning.

"No, thanks. Alright if we get down to business?"

His smile faded as quickly as it had appeared. Silas understood the shift in tone—this would be a no-nonsense exchange. He settled into his chair, bracing himself.

"What are you working on?" Jenny asked, nodding toward his cluttered desk, sounding casual.

Silas wrinkled up his nose as he replied in a flat tone, "A celebrity douchebag."

"Ten a penny?" Jenny quipped.

"You could say that," Silas responded, unsmiling.

As the interview progressed, Jenny's questions wove through his past, trying to discover what made him tick.

"Your journey to this point is quite a story. Cornwall to Cambridge, and from the BBC to luke-817.org. Tell me more about that transition?" Jenny asked.

Silas leaned back, relaxing into the subject matter. "Cornwall was a different world," he began, his voice softening. "My dad was a fisherman, my mum a schoolteacher. They worked hard and believed in hard work. Cambridge was, well, a leap in education and worlds."

Jenny nodded, encouraging him to continue.

"At Cambridge, literature wasn't just about words. It was about the power they wield and the realities they create. That understanding shapes you. Then, at the BBC, it all came to life. Investigating, unearthing the truth, often hidden in plain sight."

"You've always sought to reveal the deliberately hidden, buried stuff," Jenny observed. "What drives that?"

Silas's expression hardened slightly. "Truth is a powerful tool, often wielded selectively. At the BBC, I learned the ropes but needed the freedom to chase the stories that mattered, the ones slipping through the cracks."

"So, you were hamstrung? Is that what you're saying?"

"Not exactly. I wanted to be an editor; that's the reality."

"And your books," Jenny interjected. "They've won awards. Do you see them as extensions of your journalism? Sidearms? You wrote *Whistleblower* and quickly followed it up with *Digital Revolution*. Did you feel compelled to write them somehow?"

"Absolutely," Silas replied. "They were narratives that needed to be told, honestly. Books have a permanence, an impact that transcends the immediacy of the news."

Jenny's gaze briefly swept over the modest office. "And Luke, the website—how does your creation fit into your vision?"

A deep smile spread across Silas's face. "Luke is more than a project; it's my ethos, my dedication to unveiling the truth. Luke 8:17: 'For nothing is secret that will not be revealed.' It's biblical!" He laughed before continuing. "It began small, but it's grown to define my life's work. It's a relentless balancing act. The third book I'd planned on writing, *Senator Connelly*, has had to take a back seat, but it's still on my to-do list. I'll write it."

"You're bankrolled, though, aren't you? Someone else foots the bills?" The directness of her question didn't surprise him; he sensed she already knew the answer.

"It's no secret," Silas admitted, maintaining an even tone. "His lordship has been a steadfast supporter of both Luke and me personally."

Jenny scribbled something in her notebook and then flipped back a few pages. "I have always seen you as a lone wolf. What drove you to collaborate with Sarah Reynolds on the Connelly story? It's different to how you usually work."

Silas leaned back again, lacing his fingers behind his head, thinking hard about her question. It wasn't just a query about his work style but a deeper probe into his personal choices and career evolution. The shift from solitary work to collaboration wasn't a decision he'd made lightly, and he could see Jenny's keenness to understand his rationale.

The corners of his mouth lifted into a faint smile. "You're right. I do prefer to work alone, but the Connelly story was different. Sarah had initially gotten on to it. A woman from the senator's office had contacted her after her article in *Vanity Fair* on Washington sleazebags."

He recalled the first time he'd spoken with Sarah about the story. "She called me one evening, all breathless with excitement. She told me about the allegations against Connelly—his misconduct with young interns. It was a bombshell story."

Jenny leaned forward, her eyes not leaving his. "So, you joined forces?"

"Yes." Silas nodded. "The story's scope was growing, and Sarah realized we needed to pool our resources and expertise. I've always admired her as a journalist. Working together, we unraveled a network of sexual assault, bribery, and embezzlement. It went much further than the senator, including several high-profile figures."

Jenny scribbled in her notebook again, then looked up, pointing her pen at him. "What was the biggest challenge you faced?"

Silas's expression changed, his face clouding over. "The backlash was intense. Threats, smear campaigns, every effort made to silence us . . . they pulled out all the stops. But we stuck it out. The story might have never come out without Sarah's sheer determination."

"And the publication?" Jenny asked.

Silas nodded, a sense of pride evident as he spoke. "We coordinated the release in New York and London. The fallout was immediate and massive. They were scrambling for cover like cockroaches with the lights on."

Jenny closed her notebook, her expression thoughtful. "So, did this story change your perspective on working with others?"

Silas took a long look around his office, then back at Jenny. "It did. I value my independence, but I learned that sometimes collaboration can bring out the best in a story. Working with Sarah was a testament to that. You can teach an old dog new tricks."

"Your personal life, if you don't mind me asking?"

Silas hesitated, his face momentarily clouded by a flicker of emotion. "I'll keep it simple," he said, a touch of wistfulness in his voice. "Married and divorced twice. Now, it's just me in my flat in Ealing. My work, well, it consumes everything else."

Jenny gazed at him. "Was your relationship with Sarah Reynolds ever anything more than business?"

Silas felt his face flush, the question catching him off guard. She must know something, he thought, or she wouldn't have asked. "A gentleman never tells," he replied, his only response. He cringed, imagining Jenny interpreting his words in her write-up.

Jenny's next question about Lord Worthington came softly, yet it tugged at something deeper within him. "Tell me more about Lord Worthington?"

He didn't hesitate this time. "We've been friends since Oxford. Jonathan's been a lifeline." He leaned forward slightly, reflecting on Jonathan's profound impact on his life. "Without his support, Luke might have remained a dream. He's been more than a benefactor. He's a loyal friend," he said, genuine appreciation resonating in his words. Jonathan's role in his life was as a supporter and a pillar of strength and companionship, something rare in his line of work.

Jenny smiled. Her eyes warm. "Thank you. I have to say, your story is every bit as compelling as the ones you uncover."

"I don't know about that," Silas said.

After Jenny's departure, Silas remained in the quiet aftermath of the interview, feeling satisfied but uneasy. Recounting his journey brought him a sense of accomplishment, but an unsettling feeling ate at him. His office, cluttered with evidence from ongoing investigations, seemed to taunt him with its disorder. The excitement of past discoveries, documented in his books, now felt remote and insignificant beneath the shadow of his growing frustration. Silas always pursued the next big story as a natural hunter, relentlessly uncovering new truths capable of shaking foundations. However, the stories reaching his desk lately appeared trivial and insignificant. The world had evolved, and the meaningful stories, the "big fish," were diving deeper, eluding his grasp. For Silas, it wasn't merely about uncovering any story; he sought one that would make a difference, one that could stir the waters and create ripples. This yearning for a groundbreaking discovery and his disillusionment with the current state of affairs left him restless and eager to pick up the scent of a fresh lead. The fleeting nature of past accomplishments only fueled his drive for future challenges.

Silas drifted to the small window overlooking Soho, his eyes squinting to make out the street below through the dirt-streaked glass. He ran a finger across the dust-laden windowsill, his long sigh echoing in the room—a sound of frustration born of a deep-seated belief that a significant story had its feet up out there, just waiting for him to notice it.

His train of thought shattered as the shrill ring of his desk phone sliced through the office's dusty silence. He strode across the room, snapping back into the moment. Picking up the receiver, he felt its familiar coolness against his ear.

"I have Sarah Reynolds on the line. Can I put her through?" Sue's voice crackled over the line.

"Sure, thanks," Silas replied, his voice controlled and calm, which belied the flutter of excitement Sarah's name stirred in him. His grip on the receiver tightened, and his heart quickened slightly as he heard the click of the call connecting. "Hello, petal, how are you?"

"Hi, Silas." Sarah's voice, familiar yet urgent, filled his ear, sparking a keen sense of alertness in Silas. Something in her tone told him this might be more than a casual check-in. "Have you seen the news?"

CHAPTER 2

Mike Anderson slouched at Hub 51's bar in Chicago's O'Hare Airport, his gaze fixed on the boarding pass resting on the counter. The smart gray suit now crumpled, his forehead creased. With a heavy sigh, he took another long gulp of beer. "Fucking coach," he muttered under his breath.

Each sip seemed to untie a knot in his mind. His firm sending him to London on a client rescue mission and then booking him in economy class was the final straw. Resentment bubbled over the manipulation at work, derailing his career and life.

Restlessly, Mike loosened his shirt collar and caught the bartender's eye, signaling for another round.

He replayed the last two years since the new boss, Nathaniel Cooper, had taken the helm at his firm. Mike had been the top gun, the star performer everyone turned to, the one who handled the most prestigious clients. But Cooper's arrival marked the end of his reign. Now, he found himself sidelined, assigned to tasks that barely scratched the surface of his abilities. His suggestions and input, once sought after, were now brushed aside. Previously spread wide in the corporate skies of brand marketing, Mike's wings were now clipped, leaving his career grounded and him seething at the injustice of it all.

Mike caught the bartender's eye again and ordered a house margarita. *Fuck it.*

Two margaritas later, Mike glanced at the airport clock, noting the dwindling time before his London flight. He pulled out his wallet, leaving cash and a tip on the bar. A wave of dizziness hit as he stood and gathered his coat, laptop bag, and trolley case. He steadied himself against the bar. *Shit, those margaritas were strong. Hold it together, Anderson.* He focused on each step as he walked from the bar into the busy concourse.

Mike navigated through the crowd of travelers and ducked into the nearest restroom, lugging his bags into a stall. He locked the door and relieved himself with a long, noisy stream. Afterward, he clumsily lowered himself to sit on the closed toilet seat, misjudging the distance and landing with a thud. He leaned forward, put his face in his hands, and sighed. *What a fucking mess.*

After a few minutes, he stood unsteadily, grabbed his bags, and moved to the sink. He washed his hands and splashed cold water onto his face to shock some sobriety back into his system. Grabbing a handful of paper towels, he patted his face dry and examined his reflection in the mirror.

Staring back at him was a man who looked like he'd let himself go. His shirt strained slightly over a growing belly, his flesh spilling over the waistband of his once well-fitting trousers. He felt the pinch of his belt, a constant reminder of his expanding waistline. *Comfortable clothes, that's what you need in economy class.* Despite the numbing effects of the alcohol, he couldn't shake off the discontentment.

He figured he'd take his belt and shoes off when he got on board. *Try and sleep. Get one of those neck pillow things.*

Leaving, Mike staggered to the side as the restroom door rebounded with a vengeance, slamming against his shoulder. Swearing under his breath and clutching the doorframe briefly, he regained his footing, his bags swinging awkwardly in his grip. He moved slowly toward the departure board and, with a squint, peered up at the screen, the numbers and letters blurring slightly. Taking a hesitant step, he shuffled toward Gate M11, each movement betraying the struggle for balance.

On the way, he stopped at a kiosk, where he bought gum to hide the smell of alcohol on his breath. He eyed a neck pillow and bought it, along with flight socks and a "luxury padded" eye mask. *Fucking coach.*

Drunk and irritated, a sense of paranoia hit him. *Keep it together. Don't let them think you're too wasted to fly. That would be a fucking disaster.*

Mike reached the gate and lingered just outside the entrance, carefully avoiding the ground staff's gaze. He looked again at his crumpled boarding pass, 43J—the middle seat. Under normal circumstances, he might try to change his seat assignment, but he thought he should steer clear of potential confrontations in his inebriated state. He could almost taste the brewing argument, which he knew could escalate quickly.

The familiar ping of his phone broke Mike's train of thought. He fished it out of his pocket, his movements slightly sluggish. The screen lit up with a message from Cooper:

> We need to talk ASAP. Strategy discussion needed to rectify London situ. Don't delay, call me as soon as you land. NC.

"Fuck you." Mike was surprised to realize he'd said it out loud.

He noticed a young mother with her baby seated near him in the gate waiting area. Sensing her glare, he offered a sheepish smile and a half-hearted wave of apology. Unimpressed, the woman merely shook her head and redirected her attention to her baby. He observed her casual attire—a hoodie and beige sweatpants, her blonde hair pulled back into a loose ponytail. *Dressed for comfort.*

Mike pocketed his phone, his mind churning. He decided he wouldn't contact Cooper after landing, not during the cab ride, and certainly not once he'd reached his room. *Fuck him*, he thought. But he didn't say it this time.

The crowd at the gate dwindled as passengers filtered through to the air bridge. Mike joined the flow, stepping up to the desk with his passport and tattered boarding pass. The airline operative—"Emilio," from his name tag—took both, smoothing out the boarding pass before scanning it and examining Mike's passport closely. His scrutiny lingered long enough for Mike's heart to start pounding, the sound echoing in his ears like a bass drum. "Have a pleasant flight," Emilio finally said, returning the documents.

Before he could stop, Mike blurted out, "Is there any way I can change my seat assignment?" He stood rigid, staring straight ahead. He hadn't planned to ask; he'd intended to get on with it, but the words tumbled out anyway. "You gave me a middle seat," he continued, with a hint of desperation. "I was hoping for an aisle seat or even a window?"

"Sorry, sir, the flight is full; we can't change any seat assignments," Emilio said, gesturing at the next passenger to come forward. Mike's face turned hot with embarrassment and rising anger. *Emilio wouldn't dismiss me like this if I were in business class. He'd have shown some damn respect.* It seemed respect eluded him everywhere, both at work and now here.

Frustrated, but biting his tongue, Mike stumbled toward the air bridge, his movements clumsy. He wrestled with his trolley case, the laptop bag slipping off his shoulder and the bright blue neck pillow he'd tied to his laptop bag swinging awkwardly. The resentment percolated as he joined the line, swallowed up by the crowd.

Mike's gaze trailed over the lengthy queue of economy-class passengers, everyone shuffling forward every few moments. The space buzzed with chatter, punctuated by the cries of babies and a constant chorus of coughs. *God, the coughing!*

He watched the bobbing heads before him as the crowd inside the air bridge continued inching forward. He dreaded the cramped conditions on the plane, but he couldn't help but feel it would be a welcome relief from the air bridge's oppressive heat, stuffy air, and discordant noise.

Mike eventually approached the forward door, where the air bridge met the aircraft, a portion of the vibrant crimson and royal blue of the Vivair livery coming into view. He put some fresh gum in his mouth and crossed the threshold.

CHAPTER 3

As Mike entered the aircraft, the cabin air hit him, bearing the distinct aroma of a peculiar blend—old cooking smells and disinfectant, the signature scent of commercial planes. It stirred a faint lurch in his stomach, a reminder of countless flights past. At the entrance, a flight attendant greeted passengers with mechanical precision. Her lips curved in a well-practiced smile, yet her eyes remained unengaged.

"Good afternoon, sir. Welcome aboard," she recited as Mike handed over his dog-eared boarding pass. Her name tag read "Joy," but her demeanor suggested otherwise as she briskly gestured toward the plane's rear. Mike squeezed past her with his trolley case, his attention briefly caught by Joy's subtle exchange of pained glances with her colleague when she eyed his bag.

Mike navigated through the business-class cabin, his eyes scanning the privileged scene. VivaSuites' occupants reclined in comfort, engrossed in newspapers or books, their champagne glasses resting on nearby consoles. Some had their feet up, earbuds in, and eyes closed in serene detachment. A few, however, cast annoyed glances at the steady stream of economy passengers shuffling past.

To Mike's relief, he detected no hints of pity on their faces. He tried to maintain a forward focus, but his gaze inevitably wandered. He couldn't help but notice a group attired in vibrant traditional African clothing, their colorful garments standing out in the subdued business-class surroundings.

Stepping into the spacious premium economy cabin with its two-four-two seating configuration and mood lighting, Mike found several vacant seats. Either Emilio lied to him about the full flight, or other passengers hadn't yet boarded.

This brief respite gave way to the bustling VivaFlex economy class, where chaos and noise prevailed. The harsh lighting accentuated the bright red-and-blue airline seats, contrasting the muted elegance of the preceding cabins.

Navigating the narrow three-four-three aisle proved challenging, as Mike's laptop bag grazed against every seat, its attached pillow bouncing with each step. Amid this struggle, the PA system chimed in with a curt reminder: "Please keep the aisle clear." Glancing up at the crowded overhead compartments, Mike cursed under his breath.

He forged ahead, finally reaching his assigned row, where the young woman from earlier sat, cradling her fussy child in aisle seat 43H. Recognition flitted across her eyes, and she quickly averted her gaze.

"Great," Mike muttered under his breath, bracing himself for the ordeal of sitting next to her and her unhappy baby. *Could this situation possibly get any worse?*

His attention shifted back to the overhead compartments, which still had no room for his bag. "Fuck it," he hissed, frustration simmering within, earning him another icy glare from the woman in 43H.

Mike stood in the aisle, surveying his surroundings while ignoring her intense gaze. His presence created a bottleneck, inconveniencing fellow passengers attempting to find their seats. A flight attendant approached, inquiring about the situation. Mike's gaze shifted between her and his bag.

"What should I do with this?" he asked, his tone sharp and loud.

She explained that they'd need to check his bag due to the full flight and assured him there'd be a claim ticket. Mike's frustration boiled over. "You've got to be kidding me!" he exclaimed, his voice rising involuntarily.

"Please, sir, lower your voice," the flight attendant retorted firmly.

"I am not shouting," Mike seethed through clenched teeth.

"We need to check your bag, and you'll receive a claim ticket." The flight attendant turned around, dragging Mike's case behind her, navigating through the oncoming passengers with difficulty.

"For fuck's sake," Mike muttered.

Once again, the woman in 43H shot him a withering glare. Mike couldn't help but react. "*What?*" he demanded, locking eyes with her.

She turned her head away, choosing not to dignify his question with a response, her baby now pacified over her shoulder.

Determined to take his seat, Mike attempted to maneuver himself into the row. The woman sighed and fumbled with her extended seat belt. *Why the fuck has she got her seat belt fastened already?*

As he swung his laptop bag around, he accidentally bumped the woman's arm with his neck pillow before settling into the middle seat, 43J—a seat he had come to despise.

The woman tutted and rubbed her arm in response.

Mike rolled his eyes. *It's just a fucking pillow.*

Struggling in the cramped space, Mike tried to wedge his bulky laptop bag under the seat in front of him, only to find it futile. With a frustrated huff, he stood up again.

Beside him, the woman emitted another disapproving tut as she grappled with her seat belt. "What the fuck?" he whispered, his thoughts seething. *She's put that fucking belt on again.*

The baby had awakened, the cries echoing through the cabin

as Mike, back in the aisle, wrestled with his laptop bag, determined to secure an overhead spot. After three vexing attempts at shutting the compartment door, he finally succeeded and returned to his row.

"Excuse me?" he hissed at the woman beside him.

She fumbled with the seat belt again, stepped aside to accommodate Mike, and attempted to soothe her wailing baby. As Mike settled into his seat, he couldn't resist sharing a piece of advice. "You know you don't have to fasten your seat belt until they announce it," he remarked.

Meeting his gaze, the woman remained silent, fastening the seat belt once more.

Mike shook his head and sighed.

Three rowdy teenagers in the row immediately behind him were bursting with laughter and unrestrained energy. Their antics turned his seat into a makeshift punching bag as they playfully fiddled with the in-flight entertainment touch screen, bony knees jabbing into his back. He silently yearned for a moment of respite, hoping their frenetic enthusiasm would ebb or he could muster the nerve to confront them.

Like an octogenarian weighed down by the burdens of life, the many years etched into every crease of his existence, he simmered. *God, I feel like shit.*

Mike stole a sideways glance at the unoccupied window seat beside him. A vague sense of optimism tickled him, a small glimmer of hope amid the mounting chaos. He clung to the possibility that Emilio had lied. His gaze followed the dwindling stream of passengers descending both aisles, silently praying for a stroke of luck.

Please, give me this one break.

Casting a brief look over his shoulder at the few remaining vacant seats behind him, Mike locked eyes with one of the teenagers, who shot him a disdainful glare from beneath a curtain of unruly fringe.

Returning his gaze forward, he couldn't help but notice an

overweight man in an uncomfortably snug T-shirt. The word "moist" stretched across the fabric in bold letters. Mike's features contorted. *Please, not him.*

He let out a long breath as the portly man squeezed past their row, heading farther down the aisle. "Thank you," he whispered under his breath.

Just when Mike dared to believe that the window seat next to him would remain vacant, his hopes were dashed. Another man approached, his tall frame towering above the rest of the passengers. Mike estimated he had to be at least six feet five inches tall.

The newcomer halted at row 43, glancing down at his boarding pass and then back up at the seat numbers. Finally, his eyes met Mike's.

"This is me," he said with a self-conscious smile, gesturing to the empty window seat.

Mike stood, his lips curving into a frail, forced smile as he glanced at the towering man. His attention shifted to the woman in the aisle seat cradling the fussy baby in her lap, once more grappling with the seat belt. In disbelief, he gave a subtle shake of his head as they waited for her to get up.

Mike and the woman entered the narrow aisle to let the tall man pass. The man deftly stowed his compact purple backpack with practiced efficiency beneath the seat. Mike squeezed back into his confined space, and the woman and her restless baby followed suit. A grimace etched itself onto Mike's face as he keenly felt the sharp jab of the man's bony elbow against his side.

Mike's desperation gnawed at him, his fingers tugging at his shirt collar as he sweated, and his headache throbbed. His spirit sagged, unease and discomfort clinging to him like a second skin, the airplane still tethered to the gate.

Restlessly, he shifted in his seat, trying to get comfortable. Then, like a forgotten lifeline, he remembered his pillow.

"Fuck it," he muttered. From beside him, the woman emitted an exasperated huff in response.

With deliberate care and a sigh, Mike pushed on the armrests and rose, his eyes darting upward to avoid accidental collisions with the overhead compartments. His gaze found the woman, and their eyes locked.

"Seriously?" she whispered, her voice tinged with exasperation as she reluctantly undid her seat belt again and stood up.

Mike squeezed past her and returned to the overhead compartment where he'd stowed his bag, opened it, and retrieved the pillow. Once again, it took three attempts to close the compartment.

Returning to his row, he was surprised to see the woman still standing in the aisle, baby draped over her shoulder as she gently patted its back.

Mike slid past her. His muscles tensed as he gripped the seat in front of him and tried to lower himself. Before he managed to regain his seat, he felt sudden warmth as the infant, now facing him, vomited. It cascaded down the woman's back, splashed his armrest, and seeped into his space, sliding onto the seat cushion. His heart raced, adrenaline spiking, as he jerked to standing, crashing his head on the overhead compartment. The tall man's firm grip steadied him from a backward fall. A surge of anger bubbled up within him. "What the fuck!" Mike shouted, his voice loud and harsh, his hand instinctively going to the sore spot on his head.

Laughter echoed from the three teenagers. Their mirth stopped abruptly as one gagged, the stench hitting them. Tears streaked down the woman's cheeks, her distress evident.

Joy, the senior flight attendant, approached with an expression of concerned professionalism. "What's going on here?" she inquired, eyes darting between Mike and the chaotic scene.

Exasperation laced Mike's reply. "Her kid . . . just threw up on me. And I hit my fucking head." He was still rubbing the throbbing spot.

Joy narrowed her eyes. "Please, mind your language, sir. There are children here."

Mike sneered. "Yeah, I know that. One of them just fucking vomited on me," he retorted, eyeing the child responsible for his discomfort.

A mischievous glint sparkled in one of the teenager's eyes as he stealthily slid his phone from his pocket. He aimed it toward the unfolding drama with a swift, practiced motion, his fingers dancing over the screen to capture every moment. A partially suppressed chuckle escaped his lips, his shoulders shaking with barely contained glee at the spectacle before him.

Another flight attendant, with an empathetic expression, gently guided the young mother through the aisle. The mother's eyes brimmed with tears, her shoulders trembling as she cradled her wailing baby close to her chest. They moved slowly toward the restroom at the back of the plane, the attendant's reassuring hand on her back.

Joy stood firm, her gaze steady on Mike. "Please stay calm, sir," she said, her voice firm.

Mike's frustration and anger continued to simmer. "That kid vomited on my seat, and I banged my fucking head," he growled, struggling to keep his voice level. "Staying calm isn't exactly easy right now."

Joy's response was immediate, still professional, but more firm and slightly shrill. "Sir, I must insist that you refrain from swearing," she said, indicating no room for negotiation.

Mike glanced at her name badge. "Joy," he said, a hint of sarcasm in his voice. "Look, just move me to a premium seat, alright? I can't sit here like this."

Her reply was unwavering. "I'm sorry, sir. The flight is fully booked. There's nowhere else for you to sit."

"So, what, I'm supposed to just sit in a pile of vomit?" Mike's voice rose, his disbelief evident.

Joy leaned closer, her eyes scanning the soiled seat before returning to meet his gaze. "Sir, it's not that bad. We can lay out some air-sickness bags for you."

Mike's eyes were wide, his face red. "You're joking, right? I can't sit here; it fucking stinks!" His voice became shrill.

"Sir, I won't tolerate any more foul language." With a swift motion, Joy grabbed a handful of air-sickness bags and thrust them into his hands. "Use these, and please return to your seat."

Mike's frustration boiled over. "And who's going to pay for my ruined fucking suit?" he snapped.

Before Joy could respond, Mike cut in, his tone bitterly sarcastic. "Isn't it ironic, Joy? Your name? I bet you've brought no one a moment of fucking joy in your entire life, you miserable fucking bitch!"

He hurled the sick bags to the floor, his face crimson, his teeth showing.

"I'll be speaking with the captain," Joy said, her voice tight with restrained anger as she turned and walked briskly away.

Mike suddenly felt some hope amid the chaos. *This might work out. Once the captain steps in, he'll get me moved, especially now that things are escalating.* Deep down, Mike knew they had lied about the flight being full. To Emilio, he was just another face in the economy crowd, unworthy of attention or, seemingly, the truth. He remembered the vacant seats he had spotted in premium economy, even a few empty VivaSuites. *Jesus, what if this kid gets me bumped up to one of those?* The possibility ignited a spark of excitement. The thought of luxuriating in a VivaSuite, far from the cramped economy cabin, was intoxicating.

An older man in row 42, craning his neck from his window seat, snapped at Mike, "Hey, buddy, why don't you just sit down? You're going to delay the flight."

Defiantly, Mike shot back, "Hey, how about we swap seats?" The man just scoffed and turned away, dismissing Mike's suggestion. "Yeah, I didn't think so," Mike muttered.

Moments later, his heart sank as he spotted Joy returning, this time with a dispatcher clad in a bright yellow high-visibility jacket. The seriousness of his situation hit him as Joy delivered the captain's decision. "Sir, the captain has requested your removal from the aircraft. We believe you're intoxicated and may pose a serious risk to other passengers," she announced, her voice firm and unwavering.

The dispatcher stepped forward, his tone authoritative yet neutral. "Come with me, please, sir." Mike felt a rush of disbelief and panic. This wasn't how he had envisioned events unfolding. Instead of an upgrade, he faced the humiliating prospect of being escorted off the plane.

The young mother, clutching her child, returned from the restroom, her face displaying relief and anxiety in unison as she grasped the unfolding scene. "His bag's in here," she blurted out, juggling her child while pointing to an overhead compartment a few rows from where Mike stood.

Joy, focused and determined, moved past Mike to retrieve his bag. Mike's mind reeled in shock. "Whoa, what's happening? I didn't do anything! I can't miss this flight; I'll lose my job!" he pleaded to Joy, his tone desperate. "I'm sorry for what I said earlier."

"The captain's decision is final; you need to disembark the plane," Joy replied, unsmiling, unmoved by his pleas.

Meanwhile, the teenagers in row 44 watched, fascinated. The one on the end, phone in hand, captured every moment. "You getting all this, Josh?" asked his friend. "This is totally going to go viral!"

"Yeah, I've got it all," the teen with the phone replied eagerly. "Can't wait to upload this once they kick this loser off!"

Panic surged through Mike, his eyes wide with desperate urgency. "No, I can't go!" he exclaimed, his voice cracking. "You don't understand; I must be on this flight!" His hands shook slightly as he gestured emphatically.

The dispatcher was resolute. "Time's up," he declared, signaling Mike to quit his frantic appeals.

As Joy instructed the dispatcher to radio for law enforcement, Mike's heart sank. He overheard the dispatcher's call, "We need law enforcement to come help to remove a drunk and dangerous passenger." The terse response from operations only amplified Mike's disbelief.

His gaze darted between Joy and the dispatcher, his mind racing with frantic thoughts, backpedaling wildly. *I'll sit in the vomit, write an apology, buy flowers, whatever it takes.* "Is all this necessary? Can't we, you know, work something out?" he stammered. He could tell his pleading sounded pathetic.

Joy, her eyes unyielding, offered a cold and firm response: "You're not traveling to London today. The captain's decision is final."

"But he's only heard one side! Let me talk to him," Mike protested, his voice rising in desperation.

"For God's sake, get off the plane," the man from row 42 yelled, his frustration echoed by applause and cheers from other passengers. A different kind of heat flushed Mike's face as he felt the cabin's collective judgment bearing down on him.

At that moment, two airport police officers arrived, their presence sealing his fate. "This the guy?" one asked Joy, pointing at Mike. Joy nodded, and with an efficient twist, an officer cuffed Mike's hands behind his back, ignoring his protests. One of the officers took Mike's bag while the other pushed him from behind.

The teenage amateur cameraman in row 44 entered the aisle and, still filming with one hand, suddenly picked up and flung Mike's pillow at him, missing the officer but hitting Mike's ear. "Hey, douchebag, you forgot your stupid pillow!" the teenager jeered. Laughter and applause filled the cabin, a stinging slap to Mike's dignity.

One of the officers marched Mike back through the cabin. Mike bowed his head, drowning in waves of humiliation.

As Mike was escorted through the business-class section, he could feel the eyes of all the passengers on him, their glances laden with discomfort and curiosity about his humiliating exit. Among them, a tall, well-dressed woman momentarily blocked their path, standing in the aisle to grab something from the overhead compartment. Their eyes met briefly, hers holding a hint of something . . . Was it pity? Desperation? He couldn't quite decipher it before she murmured an apology and retreated to her seat.

Reaching the forward door, the police officers firmly guided Mike back onto the air bridge. Behind him, Joy politely thanked the officers and the dispatcher, her voice a distant echo in Mike's ears. Then, the aircraft door closed with a definitive thump, sealing off the world he had just been ejected from.

As they marched him back to the gate, the reality of his situation sank in. London now felt impossibly distant.

CHAPTER 4

Mike sat in a windowless, whitewashed interrogation room. Overwhelmed by the day's chaos and the deep humiliation that still clung to him like a grimy veneer, his hands trembled against the cold metal table. The airport officers had left him in this isolated space seemingly hours ago, stripping him of any way to track time.

They had confiscated his belongings—his laptop, his suitcase, phone, watch, jacket. His thoughts lingered on his toiletry bag, especially the cologne his mother had given him, and it brought an unexpected surge of emotion, almost enough to make him cry. "What a fucking mess," he whispered to himself, not for the first time that day.

Being marched, still cuffed, to this secluded part of the airport had felt like an endless journey through a maze of corridors. Sitting alone with a throbbing headache and his mind spinning, Mike tried to piece together what had happened. *How much time has passed since that officer came in? Thirty minutes? An hour?* She had asked if he needed anything. Water and Advil, he had said, but she had never returned. The growing urge for the bathroom added to his discomfort.

Fear crept in as he contemplated the seriousness of his situation. His thoughts oscillated between scenarios—potential felony charges for endangering an aircraft or perhaps escaping with no charges. *What have I done?* he questioned himself. *Drinking too much isn't a crime, surely. And verbally abusing a flight attendant doesn't warrant all this, does it?*

As time passed, Mike started to believe this might be an intimidation tactic, a way to teach him a lesson before releasing him. Yet, as he sat there, doubts and uncertainties continued to trouble him, leaving him restless in the bleak surroundings.

Mike tried to assemble potential excuses to tell his boss as he sat in the sterile interrogation room. *Maybe I can tell Cooper I caught some bug at the airport.* If there were no charges, this embarrassing episode might stay under wraps. This thought brought him some slight relief, a sense of regaining control. Yet, embarrassment from the onboard fiasco lingered, though he hoped it would fade with time and distance.

The oppressive silence of the room nibbled away at his nerves, stretching each minute into what felt like an eternity. The officer returning with a bottle of water and two tablets broke the monotony. "Here you go," she said, apologizing for the delay.

"Thank you. How much longer will this take?" Mike asked, his voice betraying a hint of desperation.

"The detective needs to question you," she informed him before she left the room.

Mike's brief sense of relief vanished at the mention of a detective. *They're taking this seriously.* His heart pounded in sync with his throbbing headache. He quickly downed the tablets and gulped the water, hoping for physical relief.

He rested his head on his folded arms atop the table, trying to steady his thoughts. The door opened suddenly, jolting him. In stepped a stocky, balding man in his fifties, clad in shirtsleeves and dark trousers. The man's stern gaze met Mike's, intensifying his sense of vulnerability. Mike tried to maintain a blank expression to mask his fear, but it seemed futile beneath the detective's scrutinizing look.

"Mr. Anderson," the man said in a firm, no-nonsense tone, dropping a notepad on the table that made Mike flinch. "I am Detective Johnson. Please remain calm and answer my questions. Do you understand?"

Mike managed a nod, whispering, "Detective, I . . . I'm sorry for causing a scene. I didn't intend for things to turn out like they did."

Detective Johnson's expression softened slightly, his eyes holding Mike's steadily. "We'll get to that, Mr. Anderson. Before we proceed, I need you to walk me through what happened on the flight."

Mike drew in a shaky breath, the reality of the situation settling on him like a heavy overcoat as he prepared to go over the events that had led directly to his current predicament.

As Mike began recounting what occurred on the flight, he felt weighed down by every word he uttered. He strived for composure, attempting to narrate the events matter-of-factly without letting the overwhelming emotions he had felt on board consume him. Across the table, Detective Johnson listened intently, his pen moving steadily across his notepad.

Desperately, Mike tried to explain his preflight emotions and the turmoil at work, seeking to provide context for his actions. But Detective Johnson cut him off each time. "Please, just stick to the facts, Mr. Anderson; we are only concerned with what transpired, not your state of mind."

This restriction frustrated Mike, as he knew that his actions seemed even more strange without the context of his mental state. A realization dawned: his behavior had, indeed, been deplorable. Shame washed over him.

As he finished, a heavy silence descended over the room. Mike returned Detective Johnson's contemplative gaze. He felt exposed under the detective's scrutiny, his vulnerability laid bare.

"You understand, Mr. Anderson, that your actions were disruptive and could have endangered the safety of the flight," the detective stated, his voice a troubling concoction of concern and sternness. "We treat incidents like this with the utmost seriousness."

Mike's throat tightened as he struggled to respond. "Things went further than I intended. A moment of frustration led me to a serious lapse in judgment. I regret my actions," he managed to say, his gaze falling to his hands as the detective made a final note.

Detective Johnson then stood up, the metallic scrape of his chair echoing in the small room. "I have to verify a few things. I'll be back as soon as possible. Just sit tight."

Feeling a sudden urgent need, Mike mumbled, "I need to use the bathroom."

"Sure, of course. My colleague will be along shortly to escort you," replied the detective before he exited the room and closed the door behind him.

Left alone, Mike's thoughts turned to the term "shortly," still hanging ambiguously in the air. He squirmed in his seat, hoping he wouldn't embarrass himself further.

A few minutes later, led by a uniformed officer, Mike trudged down the hall to the restroom. Inside, he exhaled a long, heavy sigh, the sound echoing off the tiled walls as he stood at the urinal, the relief both physical and mental. He lingered at the sink, splashing water on his face, the Advil starting to dull his headache.

The officer, a silent sentinel, waited outside. As Mike stepped out, she escorted him back to the interrogation room. Along the way, Mike couldn't resist a glance into what looked like the main squad room. There was a whirlwind of activity—officers bustling around, some barking into phones with furrowed brows and tense expressions. The obvious urgency intrigued him, but he chose not to ask. Something big was happening, but he had his own problems to deal with.

Back in the confines of the interview room, Mike slumped into the chair, his head cradled in his arms. Weariness blanketed him, and he closed his eyes, hoping for a brief escape from consciousness.

Sleep, however, remained elusive. His mind had welcomed a cyclone, his thoughts swirling relentlessly. He longed for the end of this ordeal.

A sudden burst of shouting and running footsteps in the corridor jolted him from his restless half-sleep. His heart raced for a moment, but then silence returned, save for a faint hissing in his ears. Leaning back, he let out a resigned sigh. *How long has it been? Four, maybe five hours?*

He contemplated his predicament. They should either charge him or let him go. Doubts crept in. Had his rights been read to him? He couldn't recall; his arrival had been a blur of confusion. *Should I ask for a lawyer?*

In his head, he clocked it as around ten p.m. If they released him, his first steps were clear: recover his belongings, call an Uber, and retreat to the comfort of his home. A pizza, a few beers, and his own bed. *Things will look better in the morning.* He could concoct a story for Cooper, then.

Right now, all he yearned for was the sanctuary of home.

Minutes dragged on endlessly for Mike as he sat with his head leaned back and eyes closed, trying to find solace in the quiet. The sudden sound of the door opening again jarred him awake, and he jolted upright, eyes snapping open. Detective Johnson walked in, his notepad clasped in his hand. As he sat down and tossed the notepad onto the table, Mike couldn't help but notice the change in the detective's demeanor—he seemed distracted, almost preoccupied.

The detective's fingers tapped rhythmically on the table, his gaze elsewhere, lost in thought. Mike watched those fingers, a growing sense of unease settling in his stomach. The prolonged silence, the detective's apparent distraction—it all compounded Mike's anxiety.

Clearing his throat to break the silence, Mike watched the detective snap out of his reverie and return his attention to him.

"Sorry you've had to be sitting here so long, Mr. Anderson," the detective finally said. "Some unforeseen circumstances have diverted resources."

"Ah, that's OK," Mike replied, uncertain, not knowing what else to say in response to the detective's vague explanation.

Detective Johnson's gaze drifted past Mike, focusing on the wall behind him. Mike's mind screwed itself up with worry. Maybe the higher-ups wanted to make an example out of him, and the detective was struggling over how to break the news. Mike just wanted this ordeal to end, one way or another.

The detective absently flipped through his notepad, then pulled a pen from his shirt pocket and scribbled something down. Closing the notepad with a snap, he began tapping the table's edge with the pen, his eyes finally meeting Mike's again.

Mike felt a lump in his throat as he swallowed hard, bracing himself. Every tap of the pen felt like a countdown to a verdict he didn't want to hear.

Relief washed over Mike as Detective Johnson announced, "We will not charge you with any felony or misdemeanor today, Mr. Anderson."

He exhaled a long breath, feeling a wave of relief. "Thank you, Detective. I'm sorry . . ." he began, but the detective raised a hand, halting his words.

"There are some things you should know. Some of them may be upsetting." Confusion wrinkled Mike's forehead. His heart rate ticked up, a sense of foreboding creeping in again. *What now?*

"Katherine will join us shortly for a discussion. We must follow procedure. Your belongings are ready to be returned to you." Detective Johnson's words were delivered with a practiced calm, each syllable measured and deliberate. Yet, beneath his steady tone, there was an unmistakable firmness.

"My suitcase? Did you retrieve it?" Mike asked, clinging to a thread of hope.

"Yes, we have your suitcase. It was left at the gate." Relief flooded through Mike again, so intense it brought tears to the corners of his eyes. *Hold it together. This is almost over.*

"Please wait ten minutes while I fetch my colleague and your belongings. Thanks for your patience; I know it's been hard," the detective said before standing and leaving the room, his chair screeching against the floor again.

Left alone, Mike stared at the door, his thoughts a bubbling whirlpool of questions. *They aren't charging me, but what else could there be? Why would it be upsetting? And who the fuck is Katherine?* His thoughts raced, yearning for freedom from this nightmare of his own making.

The door opened again, and the uniformed officer from earlier entered, carrying Mike's bag, and wheeling his suitcase to a corner. She took a small plastic bag from her pocket and slid it across the table to Mike. It was his watch: 10:45 p.m. He had guessed the time right. She passed him his suit jacket, which he slipped on, instinctively checking the pockets. He felt a USB drive, and his forehead creased. *What is that?* He didn't think it was his. He fingered it in his pocket but didn't say anything. He removed his hand and strapped his watch to his wrist.

As Mike looked up at the officer, he noticed something different about her. *Has she been crying?* Her eyes looked red, and he detected a sadness in her expression that hadn't been there before. Mike's confusion deepened, his heart pounding in his chest.

"Um, do you have my phone?" Mike asked, his voice uncertain.

"Detective Johnson has it. He's just trying to locate Dr. Sanders. I promise it won't be much longer," she replied with a faint, forced smile before leaving the room.

Mike watched her go, her demeanor etching a deepening confusion in his mind. *She's definitely been crying*—the realization adding another layer to the puzzle. *Wait, Katherine is a doctor? A shrink, maybe? Are they thinking of recommending treatment or, worse, a court mandate?* The thought of explaining any of this to Cooper made his stomach churn. *Maybe this isn't over.*

As these worries feasted on his psyche, the door swung open again. A slim woman walked in with an air of elegance, her blonde hair cascading to her shoulders. Detective Johnson followed, closing the door behind them. He pulled an extra chair up to the small table, and they sat opposite Mike.

Dr. Sanders leaned forward, extending her hand. Mike shook it, noting the warmth and dryness of her palm. "Good afternoon, Mr. Anderson. I'm Dr. Katherine Sanders," she introduced herself with a calm, measured tone. "Brett here has asked me to speak with you about your well-being after what happened on the flight. How are you feeling today?"

Mike hesitated, trying to marshal his thoughts amid this sudden shift to a more personal manner. *Why this sudden concern? Do they think I'm some VIP?* The surreal turn of events left him grappling with a feeling of skepticism and a growing unease about what was really going on.

Mike grappled with the description of his actions, his voice tinged with disbelief and regret, his features contorted. "It's my first time being arrested. I've never been that rude to anyone," he confessed, a fleeting half-smile melting under the unyielding gazes of Dr. Sanders and Detective Johnson.

"I'm not using my drinking or stress as an excuse," he said firmly, his expression earnest, palms open, trying to take responsibility for his behavior.

With a compassionate yet probing tone, Dr. Sanders urged him to recount the events on the flight. "Could you walk us through what happened on the plane, Mike?" she asked gently.

Mike sighed, his voice shaky. *Again? OK.* "Before boarding, I was anxious, more than usual. It's been building up lately." He detailed his escalating tension and reliance on alcohol to cope with the mounting stress in his life.

His voice trembled as he described the overwhelming feelings on board—the anger, frustration, and a sense of entrapment.

"I lost control. The frustration, being in coach, the kid throwing up on me, and then being asked to sit in it felt like a metaphor or something. I just snapped. I'm really sorry," he concluded, a deep sense of remorse evident in his tone.

Dr. Sanders nodded, her voice soothing. "Acknowledging these feelings is important, Mike. But let's focus on understanding them."

Mike felt isolated and overwhelmed thinking about it. "Work's been a nightmare," he admitted, suddenly feeling very alone.

Then, Detective Johnson interjected, shifting the conversation to a more serious tone. Mike's heart raced with apprehension as Dr. Sanders and the detective exchanged a glance. *What was that look?*

"The flight you were removed from, VA002 . . . There has been a tragic incident," Dr. Sanders began, the words heavy. "About three hours into its journey, the plane crashed into the Atlantic Ocean. Rescue teams are at the scene, but the situation looks dire. I've seen the news reports, and there's a large debris field, and . . ." She trailed off.

Mike sat frozen, his mouth agape, his mind blank. "I was supposed to be on that plane," he murmured, disbelief and shock snaking through him.

Dr. Sanders continued, her tone gentle yet somber. "It's OK to feel overwhelmed by this news. Survivor's guilt is a common reaction in these situations. It's not your fault, and it's important to process these emotions."

"Survivors?" Mike whispered his question, his hope faint.

Dr. Sanders shook her head softly. "At this stage, it seems unlikely. The crash was catastrophic."

Mike's thoughts spiraled into chaos, tears pricking his eyes as he struggled to comprehend what he'd just learned. The burden of being a survivor, the guilt, and the what-ifs all smashed into him like relentless waves.

"It's a significant loss," Dr. Sanders added, her voice echoing the collective grief. "We're here to support you through this."

Mike's profound sense of isolation had grown, his desire to escape the room now unbearable. Standing abruptly, he sent his chair flying back. "I need to leave," he said, his voice urgent.

Detective Johnson quickly arranged a ride home, a route avoiding the terminal where grieving families gathered. Dr. Sanders offered her business card in case he needed support, which Mike accepted without a word, slipping it into his pocket.

"Can we leave now?" Mike asked, his voice barely a whisper.

CHAPTER 5

Silas Knox circled his desk; the phone receiver clutched tightly against his ear as he sank into his chair. His grip on the receiver tightened, anticipation and trepidation rising up.

"No, I haven't seen the news," he said, his voice wary. "Just had an encounter with Slasher Slater from *The Guardian*. Fingers crossed she doesn't tear me to shreds in her piece."

The voice on the other sounded somber. "There's been a plane crash, a bad one. Vivair flight from Chicago to London. It went down in the Atlantic, no survivors."

A cold wave of shock washed over him. "Shit, that's terrible," he muttered, the news coming from out of the blue. The distant tragedy suddenly felt uncomfortably close, forming a strange, unsettling connection between Sarah in Chicago and him in London.

"Any word on what happened?" he asked.

"No word yet on the cause. They're still hunting for the black boxes," came the response, her tone businesslike.

"They're orange, actually," Silas corrected reflexively, his mind forcing him to blurt out that small, factual detail, almost unbidden.

"They're what?"

"The black boxes—they're orange, not black." Silas felt his nose wrinkle involuntarily, a physical manifestation of his inner annoyance, berating himself for focusing on such a minor detail amid a serious conversation.

"OK, whatever." Sarah brushed the comment off. "Listen, watch the news, then call me back. There were some interesting people on that flight."

"Really? Sure, speak soon," Silas said, his curiosity thoroughly piqued, his journalist's instincts kicking in. The conversation ended, leaving him with a newfound urgency to piece together the story.

He returned to his computer, pulled up the Sky News website, and clicked the "Watch Live" link. The crash was headline news. He watched footage of the arrivals hall at London's Heathrow Airport and listened closely to the reporter's words.

"In the bustling Heathrow Terminal 3, the arrivals board listed flights from Houston and Miami as 'Arrived,' but Vivair 002 from Chicago starkly stood out with its status blinking 'Delayed.' The uneasy atmosphere was tangible, with airport staff gently guiding the anxious relatives of passengers to a private area, silently communicating the grim reality: flight VA002 would never reach its destination.

"The flight, bound for London from Chicago with three hundred and twenty-four passengers and crew, had disappeared from radar around three hours into its transatlantic journey. The aircraft, renowned for its reliability on long-haul routes and carrying a mix of business travelers and vacationers, last checked in over the Atlantic. A vast debris field was located west of Musgrave Harbour in Newfoundland, extinguishing any hopes of finding survivors.

"Rescue and recovery teams have been deployed to the crash site, focusing their search on retrieving the aircraft's cockpit voice recorder and flight data recorder. These devices are crucial for unraveling what led to the catastrophic end of one of the world's safest jets. As the search continues, the aviation community and the families of those on board await answers about this tragic incident."

Silas called Sarah straight away.

"Hey, Sarah, I'm looking at the crash coverage now. They're tight-lipped about the details. What's the angle here? What do you know about the passengers?" Silas's voice brimmed with curiosity.

There was a brief pause on the line before Sarah's voice came through, tinged with urgency and a hint of disbelief. "One of the passengers on that flight was Chloe Mitchell. She's a high-profile lawyer working with the Njalian delegation. They were heading to London to set up a government in exile, to challenge the regime back in Njala. It's big, Silas. Her involvement with the delegation has been making waves in diplomatic circles."

Silas's eyebrows shot up in surprise. *Chloe Mitchell.* He had heard about her. A lawyer who had made a name for herself getting justice for the underdogs, often appearing on CNN as a legal talking head. Somehow, exiled Njalian politicians had her on a retainer to help them set up their parallel government. He started connecting dots, forming a picture larger and more complex than a tragic plane crash. This resonated with his journalistic senses. *This could be huge.*

"If Mitchell and the Njala delegation were on that flight . . . it would be very convenient for a lot of people, let's put it that way. Maybe this is bigger than we think," he said in an excited yet serious tone.

"Exactly," Sarah agreed. "This is making the hairs on my neck stand up. We need to dig deeper, that's for sure. There's a story here, and it's not just about a plane crash."

Silas leaned back in his chair, excitement surging through him. He thrived on stories like this, ones capable of shaking foundations. More than just uncovering scandals, he wanted to shine a light into the dark corners of power and influence.

"Keep me posted, Sarah. I'm on it," he said, a determined glint in his eye. Silas Knox was all in.

CHAPTER 6

The unmarked police car glided to a stop outside Mike's apartment complex, the silence inside heavy. Seated in the back, he had ridden home in a daze, the officer who had given him the Advil at the wheel. Neither had spoken during the journey; words felt pointless, inadequate.

Throughout the ride, Mike gazed numbly out the window, his mind a maelstrom of thoughts and emotions. Up front, the officer's downcast expression in the rearview matched his inner turmoil. A mutual, unspoken agreement hung in the air—a journey best made in silence.

Mike's departure from the airport had been a blur, fueled by a desperate need to escape. Detective Johnson and Dr. Sanders had expressed concern over his state, but Mike couldn't stay. Passing the media trucks, he had thought of the families gathered at the terminal, searching for answers he knew they wouldn't find. The irony that his drunken outburst had saved him while so many others perished was a bitter pill to swallow. He couldn't swallow it. He thought it might choke him.

Mike muttered a terse "thanks" to the officer as the car stopped. He retrieved his bags from the trunk and closed it with a hollow thud. Standing at his front door, he watched the car drive away, feeling isolated. Everything around him looked the same, but nothing felt the same. He stood in the still night air, staring numbly at his feet. He then looked up, retrieved his keys, and opened the door to his apartment.

Once inside, he dropped his bags in the hall, the thump echoing. The place was exactly as he had left it, the air-conditioning still not working. He'd meant to fix it, but the trip had gotten in the way. The stale, warm air seemed to cling to him. He threw his jacket over the back of one of the dining table chairs and slumped onto the couch, his eyes vacant, his thoughts racing, and his mind numb. *What just happened?* It was going to be a struggle to come to terms with the surreal events that had unfolded, events that had spared his life but left him in tatters.

A sudden realization struck Mike like a lightning bolt. Cooper, unaware of the turn of events, would believe he had perished in the crash. The news would inevitably reach his boss, painting a picture of a tragedy for the company. He was hit by the twisted irony of his London client offering condolences, possibly even attempting to mend their strained relations posthumously.

Mike's thoughts drifted back to the people on the plane. The petty office politics, his job concerns, and the demanding London client seemed so insignificant now, so utterly pointless. He winced, remembering Joy, the flight attendant. His disgraceful behavior had tainted her final professional memory. And the young mother with her baby, diligently fastening her seat belt, an utterly futile gesture in the face of such a catastrophe.

He recalled others—the man in the "moist" T-shirt, the tall guy with the purple backpack, possibly relieved there was an empty seat next to him despite the splatter of vomit. Now, they were all just memories, lives extinguished in an instant.

His thoughts turned to his neck pillow, the one thrown at him during his humiliating exit. He pictured it floating in the Atlantic, slowly absorbing water and sinking, journeying to the ocean floor, nudged by curious fish. It was a surreal image, a jarring contrast to the sudden resurgence of his work worries, which now seemed trivial yet overwhelmingly urgent. How could he reconcile these conflicting feelings? The reality of the crash, juxtaposed with the mundanity of his job concerns, left him in emotional turmoil, struggling to find clarity.

Intrusive thoughts and memories trapped his head in an endless loop, replaying uncomfortable moments from his short time on board, mixing with the horror of what would happen to the flight and everyone on board and projecting it onto every aspect of his life. The boundaries were blurred, leaving him trapped in perpetual heightened anxiety.

A sudden recollection jolted Mike—the USB stick he'd discovered in his pocket. He rose with a newfound sense of urgency and moved to the jacket draped over the chair. His fingers delved into the pocket, fishing out the small device. He didn't know why, but a wave of relief washed over him as he held it; it was still there, a puzzling artifact of this terrible day.

He turned the USB stick over in his hands, examining it closely. It wasn't his—its unfamiliarity was unmistakable. Confusion swirled in his mind. *Where did it come from? Did someone slip it into my pocket? But why?* The urge to uncover its contents became overwhelming.

He contemplated plugging it into his laptop, only to be halted by the memory of the company's strict security policy— no external devices allowed. They were prohibited, and it wouldn't work. With a resigned sigh, he placed the USB stick on the coffee table, his eyes fixed on it. It lay there innocently, yet it seemed to pulsate with secrets, beckoning him to delve deeper. Mike sat back, his gaze not leaving the small object, thinking about what mysteries it held and how it had come to be in his possession.

He then recalled his old Dell laptop, a refurb he had purchased from work a few years back. He felt confident it still worked. Going to his bedroom closet, he rummaged for a few

minutes and discovered it under a pile of *Rolling Stone* maga-
zines down the back.

He returned to the kitchen table, plugged the computer into
the power socket, and pressed the power button; a small smile
emerged on his face as the old unit sprung to life, lending a soft
glow to the dingy surroundings.

Sitting down, Mike hesitated for a moment before connecting
the USB stick. His heart pounded faster as he watched the screen
light up, revealing the drive icon. He double-clicked, only to be
met with a prompt for a password. Staring at the screen, the
blinking cursor in the password box seemed to mock him, a
digital barrier to the secrets it held.

*Why do I have this? What is on it? Why was it given to me, of all
people?* These questions spun around his head as he unplugged
the USB stick. Its contents were not meant for him—yet there it
was, in his possession.

Closing the laptop, Mike sat in silence.

He picked up the USB stick again and took it to the kitchen.
He felt he had to keep it safe, so he started looking in the
cupboard for a suitable hiding place.

Rummaging, his eyes landed on an old pickle jar he used for
collecting odd bits and pieces—coins, tokens, ticket stubs, and
the occasional paper clip. Opening the jar, he gently placed the
USB stick among the assorted trinkets—its digital secrets, whatever they were, now nestled among the mundane relics of
everyday life. Screwing the lid back on, the jar, with its new
secret occupant, went back to its usual spot, blending seamlessly
with the other containers.

Mike instinctively ambled to the fridge and yanked out a can
of beer. The metallic click as he popped the top briefly pierced
his fog of emotions. He gulped down the beer greedily, feeling
the cold liquid slide down his throat. The belch that followed, a
raw sound in the quiet room, prompted a brief moment of self-
reflection. *Is this helping? Hardly.* He reached for another can
anyway, the chill of the aluminum momentarily grounding him.

Standing in the kitchen, he finished his second beer, and the empty can hitting the counter echoed in the silence. He grabbed a third from the fridge, its weight and coldness familiar and oddly comforting in his hand, and trudged back to the couch. As he collapsed onto it, a sense of inertia overwhelmed him, the slight buzz from the beers doing little to combat the storm of emotions inside him. Instead, it seemed to amplify his turmoil, deepening his sense of despair.

He put the can down on the side table, and his eyes fixated on the blank TV screen, gripped with a reluctance to face the world outside his apartment. He dreaded seeing news about the crash, the reality of it all. He yearned to escape, to forget about the disaster, about everything.

Gradually, his relentless thoughts began to ebb as the day's exhaustion took over. The beers, the emotional drain, and the unyielding weariness all converged, pulling him into a deep, albeit uneasy, sleep. For a few hours, at least, he could escape the horror of his new reality.

Mike stirred from his restless sleep, not because of the morning sun filtering through his living room in Chicago's Rogers Park but from the insistent buzzing of his phone on the kitchen countertop. The sound drilled into his consciousness, pulling him back to a reality he wasn't ready to face yet.

As he opened his eyes, he took in his surroundings, and the fact he was still dressed in yesterday's clothes, bent up on the sofa, the insistent vibration from his phone forcing him to move. By the time he reached it, the vibrating had stopped. He picked it up just in time to see the voice-mail notification.

Mike hesitantly dialed his voice mail, his heart thudding heavily in his chest. As the phone connected, it surprised him to find eight new messages waiting. He braced himself as the latest message began to play.

"Mike, it's Mary," said Cooper's assistant without her usual cheeriness. The normal singsong quality of her voice had been replaced with an urgency that troubled him. Mike usually got on well with her, so this change in tone was enough to send in a fresh wave of anxiety.

"Mr. Cooper has called a meeting this morning at ten a.m. sharp in meeting room 7C3. Do you know where that is? Anyway, I hope you get this. It's serious, Mike, critical. Please make sure you attend. Thanks, we'll hopefully see you later." The click of her receiver punctuated her words.

Mike's hand trembled slightly as he ended the call and slowly returned to the couch. He sat down heavily, a sense of foreboding enveloping him. With a sudden, frantic motion, he switched off his phone and tossed it beside him as if it were scorching his skin. He sat frozen, his heart continuing to race, the seriousness of Mary's message echoing in his mind. *So, they knew he hadn't made the flight, but how?*

Mike glanced down at his watch, still strapped to his wrist. Eight a.m. He rose, every muscle protesting the movement, and trudged toward the bathroom. With each step, he shed his clothes, discarding them into the hallway as if they were contaminated, their very fabric holding the remnants of yesterday's chaos.

Under the shower's cascade, he stood motionless, letting the rhythmic drumming of the water wash over him. Each drop felt like a balm to his frayed nerves, the warmth seeping into his skin and offering comfort. Time seemed to stand still as he lingered there, lost in the soothing embrace of the water.

By nine a.m., he had dressed and looked outwardly composed, ready to face whatever the day held. But inside, the turmoil still simmered, bubbling just below boiling point. It felt uncomfortable, like wearing a suit made of nettles.

CHAPTER 7

Mike stood in line at the Starbucks near the offices, feeling increasingly uncomfortable under the scrutiny of two teenage girls nearby. Their giggles and lingering stares made him feel self-conscious. He subtly glanced down at his shoes, half expecting to find toilet paper trailing behind him, then surreptitiously checked his fly—all clear. Although he tried to dismiss their behavior, a nagging sense of unease twisted in his stomach. What did they find so amusing about him? The thought lingered, unsettling and persistent, as he waited for his coffee.

Mike's steps faltered as he approached the BrandWizards offices on West Washington Street, a place that used to fill him with pride and excitement. The once impressive aesthetics and clever functionality now seemed hollow, depressing even. The murals adorned with brand logos and quotes, which he used to admire, now felt alienating, emphasizing his growing sense of disconnection.

He entered the softly lit reception area, where the polished marble desk and the softly illuminated company logo on the wall now seemed to mock him. Molly, the receptionist, appeared busy on her headset. Mike approached, his legs weak, and attempted a casual, "Hi, Molly."

Molly looked up, surprise widening her eyes. She signaled for him to wait. Mike was about to head to the offices, but her response halted him. "Sorry, Mike, um, you can't go up. Someone will come for you. Please wait over there." She gestured toward the plush sofas by the big windows, looking out onto the street.

Mike was confused as he went to the waiting area, unable to distract himself with his phone, which he'd left at home, still powered off because his anxiety had turned it into a foreign object that he believed only brought him bad news. The foyer buzzed with activity, but the lively atmosphere only deepened his sense of isolation and anxiety. Memories of yesterday's chaos and horror mingled with his current trepidation, creating an unstable blend of emotions.

He considered leaving, the urge to escape battling with his need to stay put. He felt like a deer caught in headlights, frozen in uncertainty. Not a deer, more like a rabbit.

The sound of approaching high heels snapped him out of his spiraling thought pattern. Amanda Lowry from HR was headed his way. Their cheerful past interactions seemed a world away now as she approached with a businesslike severity. Mike sensed this wasn't going to be a friendly encounter.

"Good morning, Mike," Amanda said, her face devoid of her usual charm. "Would you come with me, please?"

He followed her question with his own: "What's this all about?" His voice betrayed a tremor of unease.

Amanda's brisk reply confirmed his fears. "They'll get to all that upstairs." This was indeed serious.

Resigned, Mike followed her to the elevator. Inside, Amanda pressed the button for the seventh floor, and Mike retreated to the back. Her citrus perfume filled the small space, contrasting sharply with the dense atmosphere. He thought about the cologne his mother had given him, wondering if it might have brought him luck today. He pushed down the surge of emotion, determined to stay composed.

The elevator dinged at their destination, and Amanda led the way down the corridor. Mike followed her, caught up in a chaotic amalgam of apprehension and desperation in anticipation of what awaited him.

Upon reaching meeting room 7C3, Amanda gave a cursory knock and entered, Mike trailing behind. The sight that greeted him set his nerves on edge. A lineup of familiar and unfamiliar faces was seated at an enormous mahogany desk, all waiting for him. Cooper sat smugly in the middle, exuding his usual air of arrogance. Mike's gaze swept over the group. He recognized Rebecca Stanford, the HR director, and noticed an unknown woman beside her. To Cooper's right sat a well-dressed, portly, balding man, and next to him sat Mary Steen, Cooper's PA, likely there to take notes.

Amanda gestured to a lone chair facing the panel. As Mike took his seat, she offered him water. "I'm fine, thanks," he managed to say with a quivering voice. *Get a grip, Anderson. Don't let them see you're rattled.*

Cooper scribbled away on his legal pad while the others stared at Mike, their gazes like spotlights on a stage. Feeling the collar of his shirt tighten around his neck, Mike discreetly loosened it, the room's temperature suddenly oppressive. *Typical Cooper, using discomfort as a power move.*

Impatience bubbling inside him, Mike broke the silence more sharply than he'd intended. "Well?" The word shot out like a bullet, making Cooper glance up, visibly caught off guard.

Mike felt a flicker of satisfaction. He had momentarily unsettled the tormentor-in-chief, and it felt good.

Mike's eyes narrowed as he observed Cooper, the man's slicked-back black hair and penchant for pinstriped suits and vivid silk ties as apparent as ever. Today, Cooper had chosen a pink and pale blue tie, contrasting with his crisp white shirt. His gaunt face made his dark eyes all the more piercing.

"Mike, thank you for coming in this morning," Cooper started, his voice smooth yet devoid of warmth. "I'm glad Mary was able to reach you, given the . . . circumstances." His eyes briefly flicked back to his notepad, avoiding direct eye contact.

Feeling a knot of apprehension in his stomach, Mike asked, "What's this about?"

Cooper raised an eyebrow, his expression suggesting Mike should already know. "We'll address that shortly. First, introductions." Cooper's tone held a tinge of frustration, revealing a slight crack in his impeccable demeanor.

He gestured toward the woman beside him. "As you know, this is Rebecca, our HR director, and beside her is Charlotte Becker from the PR firm we work with. On my right is Samuel Hoffman, our legal counsel. And Mary will be taking notes." Mike's polite smile at Mary was met with indifference, her focus immediately returning to her laptop.

Cooper's spiel continued, with his enjoyment of the situation thinly veiled. Mike felt anger and uncertainty rise as Cooper elaborated on the purpose of the meeting, discussing allegations against him that Mike had not prepared himself for.

Cooper emphasized the need for open and honest communication, but Mike could sense the underlying satisfaction Cooper derived from the power he wielded in the room. The meeting, supposedly a chance for Mike to explain why he'd gotten off the flight, felt more like a carefully orchestrated tribunal, with Cooper relishing his role as the ringmaster—or, Mike feared, executioner. As Cooper outlined the proceedings, Mike's forehead creased with worry as he wondered how all this would play out.

Cooper gave Rebecca a nod, and she took a deep breath, her gaze fixed on Mike. "Mike, earlier you asked what this is all about. Given the incident involving you on that flight and it being recorded, I believe you might have an idea."

Mike's confusion deepened. "I seriously have no idea what you're talking about."

Rebecca's voice sounded steady, but her expression conveyed seriousness, making Mike's stomach churn. "There's a video recording of an incident involving you. It's online, attracting a lot of attention. We're treating this very seriously and must investigate its implications thoroughly."

Mike's expression morphed into disbelief, his voice escalating in a tumultuous brew of confusion and burgeoning panic. "Wait, what video? What the hell are you talking about?" he exclaimed, the words tumbling out in bewilderment and rising alarm.

Cooper cut in, his tone dismissive. "Mike, let's skip the act. It'll be easier for everyone."

Mike's face started to burn, and his frustration boiled over. "It's not an act. I honestly have no fucking clue what you're talking about!"

The lawyer, a corpulent figure, interjected with a stern rebuke about Mike's language.

Mike felt like he was back on the plane, his emotions a whirlwind of panic and confusion. He struggled to grasp the situation, his heart pounding in his chest.

Rebecca continued, her voice calm but insistent. "Our goal is to understand this video's context and implications fully. We need your perspective, Mike. We must make informed decisions."

Mike listened, his thoughts a jumble. The reality of the situation started to sink in, yet it felt surreal, like being trapped in a nightmare he couldn't wake up from.

Mike's face twisted into a mask of disbelief and irritation as he stared at her. Her words about the video's impact on his professional reputation and public perception felt like a distant echo that barely registered.

"What fucking video?" he blurted out. The idea of a video, unknown to him yet infamous to the rest of the world, sent his emotions into a tailspin.

Mary's soft voice tried to pierce through his confusion.

"Mike, how can you not know? It's been all over the news, online, everywhere."

Mike's thoughts raced, his pulse hammering in his ears. *I wish I'd watched the fucking news instead of staring at a blank screen.* The revelation that his actions had been broadcast widely, scrutinized, and discussed by strangers hit him like a physical blow. Fear gripped him, a cold, sinking sensation that threatened to overwhelm his senses.

Cooper's words sliced through the tense air. "OK, I'm going to cut to the chase. The aircraft incident was regrettable; we know you were meant to be on that flight. It's hard to accept what happened. However, today focuses on the video and its impact on BrandWizards, Mike, nothing more."

Mike's response came out shaky, his disbelief coloring every word. "I know nothing about any fucking video."

He noticed the lawyer shaking his head in silent disapproval from the corner of his eye, but no words followed.

Mary's gaze fixed on him, and her head tilted slightly, a look of uncertainty in her eyes. "Mike," she began softly, almost with a hint of sympathy, "someone uploaded a video to social media. It showed you in an altercation, then being arrested and removed from the plane. You seemed pretty drunk and out of control, to be honest. Because of subsequent events, the video has gone viral. Everyone's talking about you and calling you the Luckiest Man Alive, considering what happened to everyone else on the flight."

Mike was reeling, each word hitting him like a physical blow. The revelation that his worst moment had been captured, shared, and now dissected by the world felt like a nightmare come alive. The irony of the nickname the Luckiest Man Alive stung bitterly—a title born from a moment he desperately wished to forget.

A tsunami of shame surged through Mike, a tangible force coursing through his veins. His sudden understanding anchored him to his seat, his stomach churning. He felt like he was going to throw up, just like the kid on the plane.

His earlier annoyance, ignited by the lawyer's reprimand, now swelled into a fiery anger that burned away the nausea. It dawned on him with piercing clarity: this meeting was about safeguarding the company's image. The so-called concerns of HR were nothing but a facade, a strategic play in a game he had no desire to participate in. His pulse quickened with indignation, a hot, righteous anger simmering in his chest.

The shame and rage within him had become volatile, a dangerous cocktail threatening to overflow. Once shaky with emotion, Mike's voice now carried a chilling steadiness. "You know what happened to everyone on that flight, right?" he asked, the coldness in his voice a blunt contrast to the turmoil raging inside him.

Mike stared daggers at Cooper, unflinching and piercing. "Look, Mike, we're well aware of—" Cooper's voice faltered as Mike cut in sharply.

"And you know why I wasn't on that flight," Mike said bitterly.

The lawyer chimed in, his tone accusatory: "Your actions have brought this company into disrepute; it's very damaging."

Mike retorted swiftly, his eyes still locked with Cooper's. "The actions that saved my life, you mean?" His voice had a defiant edge, a challenge laid bare.

Cooper's response was clipped, the words slicing through the air with finality. "Mike, it's irrelevant." His words left no room for debate, a clear dismissal.

"Irrelevant?" Mike's voice cracked like a whip, his words dripping with scorn. "Me not being on that flight is the only reason I'm still here. Isn't that relevant?" His question hung in the air.

Rebecca, her voice wavering, attempted to interject. "Mike, of course, we're relieved you're alive, but . . ." She trailed off, lost in the enormity of what had unfolded.

Mike's question had an accusing tone. "So, you think I should have just stayed on the plane?"

Rebecca faltered again, unable to articulate the company's stance in such an unprecedented situation.

Cooper, visibly exasperated, turned toward Rebecca, his expression contorted with frustration and desperation. The tension in the room reflected the unprecedented and delicate predicament they all found themselves in.

The lawyer, taking control of the conversation, leaned forward with a stern expression. "Look, what we're saying is, the manner in which you exited the aircraft is problematic for the company. Your identity being public, especially under these circumstances, and linked to BrandWizards has created a significant reputational issue."

Mike spoke, his voice rising in pitch. "If I hadn't left the plane the way I did, I'd be dead. Is that preferable to you?" The question came out sharp and piercing, his tone morphing into something shrill and accusatory, each word a pointed jab that seemed to hang between them.

"The video is quite damaging," the lawyer responded, visibly flustered by the direction of the conversation.

Mike's confusion and anger intensified. "Wait, you're saying they publicized my name?" He could feel his throat tighten. "Who did that? What about my reputation?"

Cooper, attempting to interject, hesitated. "You should have considered that before—"

"Fuck you, Cooper," Mike interrupted sharply. "Who released my name? Who did that?" His demand hung in the air, frustration, and betrayal etched into his features.

Cooper opened his mouth to respond, but Rebecca cut in quickly. "Mike, no one here disclosed your name. The media, they do their thing. They probably got the flight manifest from the airline, found your name, and started digging. It's not hard for them." Her voice conveyed a resigned tone, acknowledging the harsh reality of media scrutiny.

Mike's head spun from the information overload. The situation seemed to be spiraling out of control. *Jesus, what's next?*

"So, what's the plan?" he asked a note of sarcasm in his voice.

The lawyer laid out their proposal. "We suggest you take some time off, administrative leave. There's significant media attention, and we believe it's best if you avoid any interactions with the press."

"So, I'm not fired?" Mike asked, surprised.

"Not at this point, no," Rebecca confirmed, her face unreadable.

Mike's anger grew as he pieced together their strategy. "Let me get this straight. I lay low, sign something to keep quiet, and then, once this blows over, you'll let me go. All neat, right?"

The lawyer subconsciously rested his hand on the folder in front of him, sliding it closer to him.

"That's quite a cynical view, Mike," Rebecca said, attempting to soften the blow. But Mike could see through it. The veiled intentions, the corporate maneuvering—the picture was clear.

Charlotte's voice broke through the tension, her hand raised like a student waiting for permission to speak. "We all want what's best for BrandWizards. This proposal is about protecting everyone. You get a break, Mike, without financial worry, while the company addresses the situation."

"Screw BrandWizards," he declared, his voice dripping with disdain. Rebecca cautiously tried to interject, but Mike hadn't finished. "No, really, fuck all this. I'm not signing anything. No agreements, no deals."

Rebecca leaned in, her voice softening in an attempt to reason with him. "Mike, please, take a moment. Think about your future here. You still have a place at BrandWizards, I assure you."

Mike felt the hollowness of her words. Their "reassurances" sounded like veiled threats, their concern for him nothing more than a facade to protect the company's image. He saw through the corporate veneer to the cold calculation underneath. It represented a strategic play; he was just a pawn in their game. The realization fueled his resolve to stand his ground, no matter the cost.

Mike's fury reached a boiling point. "I used to have a future here until he"—he jabbed a finger at Cooper—"destroyed it." Cooper's mouth hung open, shock and anger jostling for position on his features.

Staring at Cooper, Mike spoke icily. "I'm sick of your arrogance, your manipulative schemes. You're a nobody to me, Cooper. Your twisted idea of success? It means fuck all."

The lawyer tried to calm the storm, but Mike couldn't be reached.

"Fuck you," he spat out. "I'm done. I quit." In a defiant gesture, Mike yanked his ID card from his pocket and hurled it at Cooper. Cooper dodged, a look of shock and disbelief on his thin features.

Mike's frustration had reached a crescendo, leading to a final, resolute act. He stood tall, feeling a momentary rush of empowerment. He'd broken free from their control, their games. The room fell silent, everyone stunned by the display of defiance.

Turning on his heel, Mike stormed out, leaving the echoes of his departure reverberating in the stunned silence he left behind.

Mike, his heart racing, spun on his heel and threw one last defiant remark over his shoulder: "I'll give the *Tribune* a call, see if they want my story!" His voice echoed as he slammed the door behind him, the glass walls of the meeting room quivering from the force.

In a daze of triumph and confusion, Mike took a wrong turn, striding into the main office space instead of exiting. Heads turned, eyes wide with shock and recognition. Whispers and murmurs filled the air—some had heard the uproar, and others had seen the viral video. To them, Mike had become infamous.

As he retraced his steps, two security guards approached him. They were courteous but firm, relaying instructions to escort him out. Mike could sense their readiness for this scenario, perhaps anticipating his outburst.

Despite his dilemma, a strange euphoria rose within him. He felt liberated, almost giddy, as if a great weight had been lifted. A wry smile crossed his face. *Everyone should make an exit like that at least once.*

Accompanied by the guards, Mike visited his desk on the third floor for the last time, collecting his items in a modest cardboard box. The final walk through the foyer felt surreal, the familiar halls now tainted.

At the reception desk, one of the guards inquired about his identity card. "Tossed it at Cooper," Mike said, a hint of mischief in his tone. The younger guard suppressed a chuckle. The senior security guard told Mike they would send a car to collect his laptop and phone, a reminder of the finality of his decision.

Stepping out of the building, the reality of his actions started to sink in. Mike had gained freedom from BrandWizards, but at what cost? For now, though, he relished the sensation of breaking free, but already, the doubts were starting to make themselves known.

CHAPTER 8

As Silas scrolled through the bombardment of news feeds, a particular video caught his eye—raw and chaotic footage from inside a plane. He peered closer at the scene unfolding on the small screen. A clearly intoxicated man was being unruly and causing a commotion. The reason for the video's newsworthiness soon became apparent: someone had recorded it on board the doomed Vivair flight moments before its departure.

The footage started with the intoxicated man in a crumpled gray suit arguing with a flight attendant. It looked like he refused to take his seat, and things escalated quickly. Silas heard giggling from the person filming, the footage jumping around while they tried to get a better shot of the action.

Watching it made Silas uneasy, especially knowing the fate of everyone on the flight. He shook his head as he watched, thinking about the giggling cameraman and his impending doom.

He continued watching as, eventually, two uniformed police officers marched down the aisle. Moments later, they handcuffed the drunk and frog-marched him off the plane. The person filming seemed to follow them, and then someone threw a pillow at the drunk, bouncing off his head. Cheers and claps filled the cabin, celebrating a humiliating spectacle. The camera then stopped in the aisle, apparently entering the business-class cabin. Silas heard a flight attendant ask the person filming to return to their seat, but before complying, the camera captured a woman standing in the aisle, blocking the path. Zooming in, Silas recognized her as the lawyer Chloe Mitchell. She appeared to be reaching for something in the overhead compartment, but her posture struck him as odd. *What was it?*

She muttered something indistinct, possibly an apology, and then slipped back into her seat, moving oddly. Silas rewound the video, zoomed in, and played it back at half speed. That's when he spotted it. Rewinding again and pressing play, he saw it clearly. As Chloe Mitchell turned to return to her seat, she'd looked directly at the drunk man and made a subtle hand movement.

His focus narrowed while watching her deftly, almost imperceptibly, slide something into the guy's pocket. She executed it with such finesse that nobody, not even the drunk guy, appeared to notice, but Silas caught it. His heart pounded, realizing the significance of what he was witnessing. This video wasn't merely a record of a drunken outburst and a degrading exit; it was potentially a key piece of evidence.

Silas leaned closer to the screen, his thoughts spinning. Why would Chloe Mitchell, a lawyer embroiled in high-stakes political drama, discreetly pass something to a drunk? The only plausible reason was that she knew they were taking the drunk guy off the flight. *What did she know? What did she give him, and why?* Silas furrowed his brow, struggling to piece it together. *She couldn't have known what would happen.* The implications intrigued Silas. To him, this video transcended being just a viral sensation; it opened a window into a mysterious covert action, a breadcrumb on a trail that might lead to explosive material. Maybe he stood on the brink of uncovering something monumental. His thoughts spiraled as he assembled this intricate puzzle, determined to find the truth.

His gaze remained on the laptop screen as he instinctively picked up his desk phone and called Sarah, pressing the speed-dial button without looking. She picked up after one ring.

"What you got?" she said, sounding enthusiastic.

"You are not going to fucking believe this, petal," Silas said, sounding breathless.

"What is it? Something about the crash?" she replied, her excitement now rising.

"Yes, have you seen the video of the drunk guy?" Silas asked.

"The one kicked off the flight? I sure have; it's all over the news stations. They are calling the guy the Luckiest Man Alive. Saying that getting wasted saved his life, the fickle finger of fate, and all of that. Why are you asking?" Sarah said, intrigued.

"Did you see Chloe Mitchell in the video?"

"Wait, she's in it?" Sarah's surprise mirrored his initial reaction.

"Oh, she's in it, all right, and I have noticed something pretty mind-blowing," Silas declared, combining intrigue, revelation, and pride in his tone.

"I'm listening," Sarah urged.

Silas leaned closer to the phone and lowered his voice. "She passes something to the drunk dude. She puts it in his jacket pocket. You can see it clearly in the video if you zoom in and slow it down."

"What? Are you serious?" Sarah's voice crackled with disbelief.

"Absolutely," Silas affirmed. "There's more to this video than meets the eye, and I'm determined to find out what this all means. Do you have a name for the drunk guy?"

"Yeah, it's Mike Anderson. The media's all over him. They won't let up until they milk his story dry." Sarah's voice crackled with an electric enthusiasm and urgency.

"Right, we need to beat them to it. Sarah, please find him, and fast. Use your contacts, whatever it takes. We need to know what Mitchell passed to him," Silas urged, his voice steady but intense.

"I'm on it. I'll keep you posted," Sarah responded, her tone matching Silas's seriousness.

As Silas hung up the phone, adrenaline surged through him. His heart pounded against his chest, the enormity of the discovery racing through his veins. The grubby celebrity story he'd been chasing now seemed beyond trivial; he had reentered the realm of real investigative journalism. Leaning back in his chair, he buzzed with possibilities and plans. This could be the big break he had been waiting for, and he knew he couldn't let this opportunity slip away.

CHAPTER 9

M ike stumbled into his apartment around noon, the aftermath of the meeting making the trip home feel like a blur. He had just watched one of the security guards from earlier drive away with his laptop, phone, and a client file he'd been working on. Standing in the doorway, he watched the van disappear from his apartment complex, feeling hollow inside.

The hot and stuffy air in his apartment had become a familiar discomfort. He considered calling the air-conditioning repair service, but without his phone, this plan quickly evaporated.

After unpacking his few belongings and tidying up the remnants of the previous night's turmoil, he sat at the small dining table, trying to chart a practical course forward. A trip to the store topped his list—he needed food and, more urgently, a phone.

Sitting there, the severity of his situation pressed him into his seat. The anger that had fueled his outburst at the meeting had dissolved, leaving a gnawing insecurity in its wake. He replayed the events in his head, questioning his impulsive decision. He mulled over his finances, a dismal picture; he knew he could only stretch his resources for a few weeks. The option of three months of paid gardening leave, a notion he'd scoffed at, now seemed like a sorely missed lifeline. He cursed himself for squandering it due to his pride.

His job prospects seemed bleak, especially if the video had spread as widely as his colleagues had claimed. He remembered the giggling teenage girls at Starbucks. Had they recognized him? Were they laughing at the man from the viral video? The thought sent his pulse racing with dread over the prospect of stepping outside, of being labeled as "that drunk plane-crash guy."

Lost in his spiraling thoughts, Mike's heart jolted as a loud knock at the door pierced the stuffy silence of his apartment. He sat frozen, staring at his hands until another knock amplified his anxiety.

Mike's heart pounded in his ears as he stood, paralyzed for a moment, wondering who could be at his door. Could it be the security guard returning for something else? He cautiously approached the door, his legs trembling slightly.

Peering through the peephole, Mike's breath caught in his throat. Outside stood a familiar-looking woman, poised and professional, flanked by a cameraman hoisting his equipment.

"I'm not feeling well," he called out, his voice muffled by the barrier of the door.

"Hello, sir, it's Jenna Paynton from WGN-TV; we'd like to ask you a few questions." The reporter's voice sounded clear, even through the door.

Mike's thoughts scrambled. "I think you have the wrong address," he said, trying to sound convincing, but his voice wavered.

"Are you Michael Anderson?" she persisted.

Mike hesitated, his throat tight. "Yes. I mean . . ."

"Then we have the right address, sir," she said firmly. "Mr. Anderson, we understand you're struggling, but we'd like to talk to you. Our viewers are eager to hear your perspective on what happened. The story is gaining momentum and public interest. You can share your perspective with our viewers and the world."

Anxiety weaved through him. Being thrust into the spotlight filled him with a cold dread, especially now. "I want to be left alone. I just quit my job," he managed, his voice barely above a whisper. The idea of facing cameras, broadcasting his story and pain to strangers, seemed unbearable. He yearned to retreat.

Mike's thoughts spun as the reporter's persistent voice filtered through the door. Her words, intended to be reassuring, felt like a siren call to a world he wasn't ready to face.

"I need some time," Mike managed to say, sounding weary and cautious.

"We get it, Mr. Anderson. You're at the heart of a big news story. People are waiting to hear from you, to understand your experience," the reporter insisted, her tone earnest.

A tiny part of him did find the idea of sharing his story intriguing, but mostly it sounded overwhelming. He craved solitude. "Not now. Maybe later, but not now," he said, striving to project firmness.

There was a pause before the reporter agreed, hope still coloring her voice. "When you're ready, please call me. I'll leave my card." She slid her business card under the door, a tangible reminder of the outside world's interest in him.

Mike peered through the peephole, watching Jenna Paynton and the cameraman retreat to their van. He leaned against the door, his emotions on overdrive. He couldn't help but feel an undeniable thrill at being the center of attention, but it quickly soured as he remembered why.

Eventually, Mike found the strength to move. He needed to see the video. He retrieved his old Dell laptop, its familiar hum offering some comfort. He connected to the Wi-Fi and typed "Vivair 002" into YouTube. The search results were overwhelming, but one video stood out and made his heart race: "Luckiest Man Alive."

He clicked on the link with hesitation. No hiding now. The

video showed him arguing with Joy, his swearing censored, but his red-faced agitation clear. The footage of his removal, the clapping, the cheering—it all played out, an indelible stain on his life.

The reality of his predicament felt like a millstone around his neck. He was not dead, but he didn't feel lucky. He was a viral sensation. *What the fuck?* His career, his reputation—everything —now in jeopardy.

He needed to think practically: the groceries and a new phone, but the fear of recognition, of being hounded by the media, scared him. He felt trapped in a paradox—a man saved by fate yet ensnared by its consequences.

Mike decided he needed a disguise. He rummaged through his closet, retrieving his Chicago Bulls cap, and then fished a pair of sunglasses from the bedside cabinet. Donning both, he scrutinized his reflection in the bathroom mirror. It was a mediocre disguise at best. Then, a crucial detail struck him—he needed to lose his beard.

With determination, Mike set to work. He trimmed it down with clippers and followed up with a wet razor. The process wasn't smooth; a few nicks and cuts marked his skin, which protested with irritation after being hidden under facial hair for so long. Yet, when he reassessed his appearance, cap, and sunglasses in place, he was almost unrecognizable.

He sat on the couch, considering his next move. The grocery store two blocks down seemed like a manageable target. He just had to make sure the coast was clear.

Peering out the door, half expecting to see Jenna Paynton crouched in the bushes, Mike felt relieved as he found the path clear. Stepping out, he cautiously closed the door behind him and set off briskly, only to consciously slow down moments later. *Act natural.*

Upon reaching the store, he prioritized buying a phone—a prepaid, no-contract burner, like drug dealers used in movies.

Nothing fancy, especially considering his dwindling finances. He knew he needed to contact Dr. Sanders and seek her insight on the disturbing video and his disastrous work meeting. He planned to put his new phone to good use.

He quickly picked up the cheapest prepaid phone, adding it to his basket, along with essential groceries, a six-pack of Miller Lite, and a bottle of Jack Daniel's. As he stood in the checkout line, trying to appear inconspicuous, a female voice behind him snapped him back to the present.

"Michael Anderson?"

Mike froze as he heard his name, his heart skipping a beat. "What? Um, who?" he stammered, feigning ignorance.

"You're Michael Anderson, aren't you?" the woman persisted, her tone confident.

"Who's asking?" Mike replied, cringing internally at how defensive he sounded.

"I'm Sarah Reynolds." She extended her hand confidently.

Without thinking, Mike shook her hand, his mind trying to catch up. "What do you want?"

"Mr. Anderson, I'm a freelance journalist. I cover major stories for several publications. Your story is something I want to write about," she explained, her voice steady and persuasive.

Mike's mind whirred. "How did you find me? I've been trying to keep a low profile," he protested, disbelief and unease churning.

"You weren't hard to track down," Sarah admitted casually. "I just waited for you to come out and followed you. By the way, nice work with the disguise."

Mike scrutinized her, taking in her long brown hair and striking eyes. She looked to be in her mid-thirties. Her casual yet chic attire spoke of a professional used to blending in. "Give me a moment to pay for these, and we can talk outside," he said, almost against his better judgment.

"Perfect, I'll wait for you by the exit. I can give you a ride home," she replied, smiling warmly before heading toward the door.

After paying, Mike approached Sarah, who offered to stow his groceries in her car. "How do I know you're a journalist?" he asked, eyeing her sleek black Audi and not considering what else she might be if she wasn't a journalist.

Sarah handed him her business card. "Here's my card, and if you need more proof, I can show you my press accreditation."

"No, this is fine," Mike responded, studying the card before getting into her car.

"As I said, the disguise is effective—you look different enough that most people wouldn't recognize you," she commented reassuringly as they made the short trip.

"Didn't seem to fool you, though," Mike replied, a hint of resignation in his voice.

"I had the advantage of stalking you," she admitted with a smile. "How about we talk at your place? Just some background information."

Mike realized he had been effortlessly reeled in for an interview. He hesitated but ultimately agreed, feeling trepidation and curiosity.

As they arrived at his apartment complex, Mike scanned the area, half expecting to see Jenna Paynton lurking nearby.

"Looking for Jenna?" Sarah asked, noticing his nervous glances.

Mike sighed, realizing how quickly his life had spiraled into a public spectacle, with journalists like Sarah Reynolds and Jenna Paynton part of his new reality.

Mike's nerves jangled as Sarah's words hit home. "They'll be back, as will others. You're big news now, Mr. Anderson." Her voice, matter-of-fact, scared him.

"Just Mike, please," he murmured, seeking a sliver of normalcy amid the chaos.

"Of course, Mike. Here, let me help," Sarah offered, reaching for a grocery bag.

THE LUCKIEST MAN ALIVE   73

As they entered his apartment, Mike reflexively glanced around, his nervousness stemming from his new sense of exposure. "Please, have a seat. I'll just put these away," he said, gesturing toward the dining table.

Sarah settled in at the table, pulling out a notepad from her bag, her professionalism evident. "They won't leave you alone, you know. The media . . . they're relentless. They're like sharks, and they sense blood in the water."

Her words echoed ominously around the room. Mike had a visceral reaction as he was flooded with grim images from the crash that he couldn't shake off. "Shit," he whispered, the horror of his thoughts breaking through.

"You OK?" Sarah asked, her voice tinged with genuine concern.

He forced a smile, trying to push away the dark thoughts. "Yeah, just . . . it's hard, you know? These memories just hit me out of nowhere. Your phrase, 'blood in the water' . . . it was too real."

Sarah's pen paused, and she offered him an apologetic look. "I'm sorry, that was thoughtless of me."

Mike's attempt at hospitality felt like he was clinging to a lifeline. "Can I get you a drink? Beer, or maybe coffee?"

"No, thanks. I'm ready to start whenever you are," she replied, her gaze steady.

He needed something to calm his jittery nerves. He reached for a beer. "Do you mind if I . . . ?" he asked, not really seeking permission.

"Go ahead," she encouraged, her attention fixed on him.

Mike sat opposite her, the table feeling like a barrier and a bridge. He took a long drink, the cold beer offering a brief respite. "OK, I'm ready," he said, more to himself than to her, bracing for whatever came next.

"Before we start, I want to let you know I don't need the lowdown on why you got kicked off the flight, Mike. I've watched the video many times."

"I'm guessing it doesn't get better the more times you watch it?" Mike said, screwing up his face.

"Nope, it doesn't. But I need to ask about something that happened during your removal from the aircraft," Sarah pressed on.

"Sure, ask away," Mike replied, albeit hesitantly.

"Did anyone give you anything as you were escorted off the plane?"

A chill swept through Mike at her question. The USB stick he'd found in his jacket pocket flashed in his mind. *How does she know?* "I'm not sure I follow," he said cautiously.

"Let me level with you, Mike. I have watched the video very closely, and it is clear that, as you were leaving, a woman named Chloe Mitchell slipped something into your jacket pocket."

"Oh, that." *There's no point in lying about it.*

"So, you found something?"

"Yeah, when they returned my jacket in the police interview room, I checked the pockets and found it. It's a USB stick. I didn't mention it to anyone. Just didn't know why it was there." He pointed his thumb over his shoulder at the kitchen cabinet. "I put it in an old pickle jar for safekeeping." He smiled, but it soon faded when he saw the look on Sarah's face.

"Can I see it?" Sarah asked urgently.

Mike paused, confused and curious. "Sure, but why? What's this all about?"

Sarah hesitated. "We think it's important. Otherwise, why would she–"

"We?" Mike's suspicion spiked. "Who's 'we'?"

Sarah seemed taken aback. "Sorry, I meant my colleague, Silas Knox, in London. He's the one who first noticed the handoff in the video."

Mike stood up, went to the cupboard, and retrieved the USB stick from the pickle jar. He handed it to Sarah.

"It won't be much use to you. It needs a password."

Sarah's expression shifted to frustration. "Can I keep this?"

"Sure," Mike agreed, his head spinning with questions. "But why do you need it?"

Sarah hastily gathered her things. "I need to check on something. I'll be in touch."

Mike's hope of sharing his story deflated. "But, the interview?" he asked, his voice colored with disappointment.

"I'll contact you," she reassured, but her swift goodbye left him feeling used and unsure.

As Sarah's car disappeared down the street, Mike's new reality began to sink in, his thoughts bouncing around all the day's events. He felt out of his depth, lost in an alien landscape.

He returned to his apartment, picked up his new phone from the kitchen counter, unpacked it, and switched it on. He thought about how the day had gone, how Sarah had done a slick bait-and-switch job on him. He felt naïve and a little shell-shocked when he realized she had no way to contact him, as he hadn't given her an email address or his new phone number. Mike felt a cold shiver run through him, thinking she may have duped him. He sat back, anxiety rising again.

He took a few deep breaths and tried to calm down. Then the new phone rang.

His heart racing, he stared at it. *What the fuck.* He picked it up and pressed the answer button.

Mike's voice wavered as he spoke, "Hello?"

"Hi, it's Sarah. I'm just making sure your new phone works," came the casual reply.

Mike's confusion spiked. "Wait, how did you get this number?"

Sarah's voice had a playful lilt. "I'm a journalist, Mike, a real one. I'm not Jenna from the station. I noted down the number from your phone box. Just a precaution."

Mike felt a swirl of emotions: admiration, relief, and unease. She was thorough, no doubt about it. "Oh," he managed to utter, surprised by her resourcefulness.

"And, Mike, try to avoid talking to anyone else, OK? Especially the press. You can reach out to me on this number if you need anything," Sarah advised, her tone shifting to one of concern.

"Got it, thanks," Mike replied. The line went dead, and he stood there, phone in hand, now thankful while still feeling vulnerable.

Sarah's call made him feel paradoxically more isolated and more connected. Alone, yet under the watchful eye of a journalist with an agenda, Mike realized he wasn't just a bystander in this unfolding drama; he played a part in something bigger, something he didn't yet understand.

His heart pounded as he absorbed his newfound notoriety. He lay sprawled on his couch, staring blankly at the ceiling. The irony that his drunken antics had saved him from a fatal crash gnawed at him. He envisioned the plane's horrifying plunge, the terrible dread and chaos that must have engulfed the passengers, his fellow travelers, in their final moments. A cocktail of relief, fear, guilt, and anger surged within him.

After staring at the ceiling, he closed his eyes and drifted asleep.

Startled awake by a loud banging on his door, Mike stumbled to check the time: 8:30 p.m. Peering through the peephole, he saw no one and cautiously opened the door, only to be blinded by a camera light. A reporter's voice began bombarding him with questions: "Mr. Anderson, you're the Luckiest Man Alive. How does that feel?"

Mike recoiled and slammed the door shut. "Fuck off!" he yelled, his frustration boiling over. He cringed at his harsh response as the reporter slid a business card under the door. Mike picked it up and added it to his growing collection of media contacts.

Mike collapsed back onto the sofa and shut his eyes, overcome. The same question circled in his mind relentlessly: *What have I done to merit such chaos?* He knew the harsh truth: his drunkenness, abusive behavior, and ejection from the flight had brought all this upon him. But what if he hadn't left the plane? The thought of the plane's fate chilled him. Amid his current turmoil, he feared that the tragic outcome, the alternative reality where he had stayed on the plane, might begin to seem preferable.

CHAPTER 10

Sarah called Silas from her car. "It was a USB stick," she recounted feverishly. "Chloe dropped a USB stick into Mike's pocket."

"So, you met him? How did it go?" Silas couldn't hide his excitement.

She drummed her fingers on the steering wheel, her mind racing with the implications of her meeting with Mike. "Yes, I met him. He's quite a mess. I mean, the guy's on edge—looks like he's barely holding it together." She sighed, the image of Mike's anxious face still vivid in her memory.

Silas's tone softened slightly. "Keep an eye on him."

"I got the USB stick. He said he found it in his pocket while in detention at the airport, thought it was odd, and didn't know how it got there. Anyway, he gave it to me. He was keeping it safe in an old pickle jar." She laughed.

"So, you have it?" Silas asked breathlessly.

"Yes, I have it," she confirmed, glancing at the small device on the passenger seat. "But there's a catch. It's encrypted. Needs a password. I tried to access it, but no dice."

"Damn," Silas muttered. "Any idea what's on it?"

Sarah shook her head, even though Silas couldn't see her.

"No clue. But it won't contain holiday snaps, given Chloe Mitchell's involvement."

Silas's voice crackled with urgency through the phone. "We need to get that USB checked out ASAP. Can you find someone trustworthy in Chicago to crack the password? We can't just take it to any tech shop."

Sarah's eyes narrowed in thought, scanning her mental Rolodex for contacts. "I might know someone. There's a tech guy who used to work with some journalists. Discreet and knows his stuff."

"That sounds promising," Silas replied. "But be cautious, Sarah. We don't know what we're dealing with here. And keep in contact with this Anderson guy; we may need him."

She nodded to herself, a plan forming in her head. "I'll handle it."

CHAPTER 11

Mike stayed in his apartment for three days, eating and drinking through his provisions and startling at every knock on the door. He became a recluse, dodging the persistent media camped outside. Despite Sarah's progress messages and encouragement, he felt increasingly isolated and desperate. Finally, overwhelmed and craving a break from the oppressive atmosphere of his apartment, he decided he would venture out.

But Mike's head filled once again with desperation and panic. He knew he couldn't stay cooped up in his apartment anymore; it felt like a cage, and every knock at the door sent his heart racing and his nerves ablaze. But where could he go? His whole world revolved around his job; even his social life was entwined with work.

He thought of reaching out to Doug Richards, a colleague who might understand and offer him a couch to crash on so he could escape the unwanted attention. But then reality hit—he didn't have Doug's number anymore, only his email address from memory, and reaching out via work felt like opening a can of worms he wasn't ready to deal with. *What about a hotel?* He discounted the idea almost immediately. The thought of using his credit card and being easily traceable made him uneasy.

He knew he didn't want to stay in his apartment, which now felt more like a prison than a home. He needed to escape, even if just for a few hours, to breathe, to think.

In the darkness of his bedroom, Mike rummaged for his disguise again. He pulled out a black hoodie, but seeing his reflection in the mirror, he realized it screamed *suspicious*. He swapped it for a less conspicuous blue sweatshirt. He needed to blend in, not stick out.

Back in the Chicago Bulls cap and sunglasses, despite being dark, Mike peeked out the front door and stepped into the cool night air, the street quiet and unwelcoming. He didn't head for his usual bar, The Hideaway. Instead, he aimed for The Brickyard Saloon, a few blocks away, a place he'd never been to but always noticed as he passed. He needed a change of scenery. Somewhere to sit unnoticed, just another face in the crowd.

The walk to The Brickyard Saloon took about fifteen minutes. He adjusted his cap as he entered the dimly lit bar. The atmosphere seemed relaxed, a welcome change from the tense air of his apartment. The TV screens at either end of the bar played country and western music videos, and no news channels were in sight.

He ordered a beer, and the frosty pint glass was a small comfort. Mike found an empty booth near the window and settled in, casting wary glances around the bar. Taking a long sip of the cold beer, he felt his anxiety slightly ease. Removing his sunglasses, he leaned back, trying to enjoy this brief respite from the chaos that had become his life. In this small, anonymous corner of the city, he could think, plan, and maybe find a semblance of peace, at least for a little while.

CHAPTER 12

Mike fidgeted, his gaze darting to the server bringing over another beer. An older man entered the bar, a striking figure with a straight posture belying his age, which quickly diverted his attention. Wearing a worn red trucker's cap, the man confidently strode to the bar, ordered a beer, and turned toward Mike's booth.

Mike tensed slightly as the man neared. "This seat taken?" the old man asked, nodding toward the opposite bench.

"Sure, go ahead," Mike responded, his eyebrows knitting in confusion at the man's choice, given the abundance of empty tables elsewhere.

The old man introduced himself. "Henry Mitchell." His sharp blue eyes locked onto Mike's with an almost invasive intensity.

Caught off guard, Mike stumbled over his ill-thought-out alias. "Um, Brett, ah, Sanders," he managed.

Henry's gaze never wavered, the silence between them stretching out uncomfortably. Mike cleared his throat. "Is this your local, Henry?"

"Nope. I'm from Wisconsin. Sheboygan Falls," Henry replied.

Curious, Mike asked Henry what brought him to Chicago.

However, Henry pivoted to a question that chilled Mike. "Did you hear about the plane crash? The Vivair flight?"

Mike's heart pounded in his chest as he acknowledged the news that had been unavoidable. The older man's scrutiny intensified, making Mike squirm in his seat.

"There's something you need to know, Mr. Anderson," Henry finally said, his tone serious.

Mike felt his face flush. "How do you know my name?" he blurted out.

"I made it my business," Henry said, the smile disappearing from his face.

Mike's thoughts scurried around his head as he tried to piece together what this curious stranger wanted. "Are you another reporter?" he ventured, though Henry's demeanor suggested otherwise.

"Do I look like one?"

"No."

"Well, you're right, I'm not a reporter."

Henry's reassurance did little to ease Mike's rising anxiety. When asked how he'd like to be addressed, Mike said, "Mike."

"Great, Mike, it is," Henry said, a smile returning to his face.

As Henry hinted at a mutually beneficial relationship, Mike assessed the older man. There appeared to be something about Henry's poise, a hint of military discipline, that suggested he wasn't a man to be trifled with.

The conversation returned to the flight, and, feeling deflated, Mike acknowledged the viral video. "I take it you've seen it?"

Henry dismissed the video. "It is what it is. Maybe things happen for a reason."

Mike's eyes dropped to the table, his gaze lingering on the scuffed edge. "The reason being I got drunk and called the flight attendant a stupid fucking bitch and got dragged off the plane by the cops," he confessed, his voice thick with remorse.

Henry's response seemed matter-of-fact, nonjudgmental. "Yeah, well, that too," he said, devoid of emotion.

Mike's confession poured out. "I'm not proud of what I did. This isn't a high point for me. I'm alive because of my bad behavior. All those people had to die, and the flight attendant— Joy, her name was. Anyway, I get to live; the douchebag gets to live. Do you know what that feels like?"

At that moment, Mike felt the full impact of survivor's guilt, coupled with the surreal nature of sitting across from a stranger who seemed to hold some unknown key to the unfolding mystery of his life.

"Can't say I do, no. But I know a bit about redemption," Henry replied, looking up from the table and catching Mike's gaze.

Mike leaned back in his booth, a troubled look crossing his face as he contemplated his next steps. His voice, when he spoke, carried both resignation and a faint hope for respite. "So, I'm trying to lie low until all this blows over; tomorrow, I think I'll skip town, as I'm getting hounded by the press. I met with a journalist who wants an exclusive interview, and I'll hide out until that's done. Oh, and I'm going to see a shrink." He paused, slightly taken aback by his openness about seeking therapy. He glanced at Henry, trying to gauge his reaction.

"Well, that's good," Henry responded, prompting Mike to let out a weary sigh. He lifted his beer, the cold glass momentarily distracting him from the chaos of his thoughts. "Who's the journalist?" Henry asked.

"Her name's Sarah Reynolds. She's cool and knows her stuff," Mike said with slight uncertainty, betraying his mixed feelings about trusting Sarah.

"Mike, your situation is tough, but you're still alive, and there's hope, right? And I'm going to offer you a shot at redemption. What I want to discuss is more important than getting drunk and feeling ashamed. Do you think you can trust this journalist?"

Mike shifted uneasily in the booth as he processed Henry's words, thinking about the USB stick he'd handed Sarah. "Trust her? I guess so. She gave me her number, and I left my phone at home, so I can't call her now, but . . ." He trailed off, his voice still uncertain. Trust, especially in his current predicament, felt like a luxury he couldn't afford. Yet something in Henry's demeanor suggested he wasn't just another person looking to exploit Mike's story. "Why do you ask?" Mike's voice held a note of cautious curiosity, and he narrowed his eyes slightly as he tried to decipher Henry's intentions.

"I'll level with you; I need your help, and you and I will need a journalist friend."

Mike laughed nervously. "Help? What do you want from me? I can't even help myself."

"Well, Mike, you may have noticed that I'm an old man. I'm completely alone. I'm a ghost, and I've now latched on to you."

Henry's demeanor was simultaneously comforting and unsettling. Declaring that he was a ghost clinging to Mike stirred up emotions. Mike's gaze locked onto Henry's, searching for answers in the craggy landscape of the older man's face. "You think I can help you? With what?" he asked.

"Let's grab another couple of beers, and I'll tell you."

Henry summoned the server and ordered two more beers. He also ordered nachos. "Want anything to eat?" he asked. Mike had misgivings about eating in these establishments but didn't voice his concern. "Just a beer, thanks."

His posture, erect and commanding, possessed an air of unwavering focus. His arms were crossed over his chest like a physical barrier, withholding the answers. Sharp and perceptive, his eyes scanned the bar over Mike's shoulder as if every patron held a piece of the puzzle they were discussing.

Mike leaned in. "Well? Are you going to spill the beans?" he said, his voice barely above a murmur, a ripple of impatience breaking through. His words were a quiet demand in the dimly lit booth.

Henry's attention remained fixed on the room, his observant gaze never faltering. Mike shifted in his seat, the urgency of his question battling against Henry's deliberate patience. The tension between them hung in the air: a silent standoff, each awaiting the next move. Henry looked Mike squarely in the eyes. "Keep your voice down; we don't want anyone to hear us. Let's wait for our order. We'll talk when we have everything, and the server is gone. OK?" Henry removed his battered hat and placed it beside him on the bench.

Mike's head dipped slightly in agreement. He reclined into the booth, his posture easing as he waited. Henry's presence commanded a certain respect; the man had the air of someone who had navigated life's rough waters and had emerged with a hardened resolve. Mike couldn't help but wonder about the paths Henry had trodden, the experiences that had shaped him into this imposing figure. After the server had delivered their order and moved out of earshot, Henry started speaking again.

"I told you earlier, I'm a ghost. No family, no friends. Well, I had a granddaughter. She was everything to me. We were very close. After losing her parents, I took her under my wing." As Henry spoke about his life, a sense of solemnity enveloped them. Mike watched, almost hypnotized, as Henry deftly navigated a tortilla chip through the chili and sour cream. The mundane action contrasted sharply with Henry's words.

Henry stared at Mike for a moment before continuing. "Well, my granddaughter, Chloe, was on that flight." Mike just stared back at Henry. *Chloe? That's the name Sarah mentioned.*

"She sent me a message from the flight before it took off, and it has something to do with you." Henry held Mike's gaze as he reached into his pocket for his phone. He opened his messaging app and slid the phone across the table to Mike. "There, read it."

Mike picked the phone up and looked at the screen.

> Urgent. A man removed from Vivair Flight 002 to London. In police custody. Gave him USB with vital info. He doesn't know he has it. Please track him down, keep USB safe. Will explain later. Love you.

Mike looked back at Henry, who carried on staring at him. "Know anything about that?" Henry asked, nodding at his phone.

"Well, yeah, I do. I found it after the police returned my things; it was in my jacket pocket. I didn't know how it got there. I thought it might be something to do with work. Anyway, I put it in an old pickle jar in the kitchen, and I did try to see what was on it, but it asked for a password, so I just put it back in the jar."

"OK, can you go get it? Chloe wanted me to have it, and I think I need to see what's stored on it in light of what happened."

Mike shifted in his seat before speaking. "I haven't got it anymore."

"What?"

"I gave it to Sarah, the journalist, the one I told you—"

"Why?"

"She said she'd seen a woman pass something to me on the video—you know when I was arrested—and she thinks it could be important, so I —"

"I need that USB stick. Can you get it back?"

"I can call her, but I left my phone at home. I can–"

"I don't think you should return to your apartment. It's too risky. It would be best to avoid the press and anyone else who might be snooping around. I don't want to scare you, but if your journalist friend saw what happened, other people may as well. We can't be too careful. I have an RV parked up the street; you can stay there tonight. In the morning, I'll head back to your place, pick up your phone and some things for you, and then, later, we can call your journalist friend and invite her over for a chat. What do you think?" Henry said.

Mike wasn't sure what to say. Things were getting weird. He felt off-kilter, a player in something big, something dark, something he hadn't asked to be a part of. "OK," he said, reticent.

"Before we get going, I'll tell you what I know. Put you in the picture, as it were," Henry said before taking another sip of beer.

Mike didn't think he wanted to know; he felt like he was being sucked into something with nothing to hold on to.

"So, Chloe visited me before leaving for the airport to catch the flight to London. She's a lawyer. A specialist lawyer. She was outstanding, in demand, and had been on TV, and I was so proud of her. She worked for a group of African politicians in exile from their country. Forced out by what she told me were undemocratic means, but I think you can read between the lines. Anyway, she was going to London to help set up a government in exile to pressure the regime in power. These guys were serious people, determined to take their country back. Chloe worked with a team of lawyers to get everything started; she'd been working hard on it for months. So, she visits me before she leaves on the trip. She told me what was happening, how important it was, and—"

"What country?" Mike asked.

"Njala, it's in West Africa. Rich in oil and minerals, and where there's money, there's trouble."

"OK. So, what did she tell you?" Mike asked, his voice wavering.

"Bad stuff was happening in Njala. This is high-stakes stuff. Right, so there's a guy called Viktor Malaba. He's some up-and-coming politician in Njala, very popular. He vowed to stop corruption and redistribute the country's wealth. Chloe tells me this guy is the real deal, incorruptible. Despite being born into poverty, he studied in England on a scholarship and became a lawyer. He gained massive support, and any attempt to rig the election would lead to an uprising. The people in control felt scared. Interestingly, the people in control are not who you think."

"Well, who are they?" Mike asked.

"Let's talk about Viktor for a moment. I'll get back to that. So, this politician threatens to take power on a wave of popular support. He's in his hometown at a rally, promising to give back Njala to the people, and they're all going crazy. His next stop is the capital, where he will go on the nation's top TV talk show. This is a big-time speech for the masses. So, he boards a plane; it's about a two-hour flight. Can you guess what happened to the plane?"

"I'm guessing it crashed?" Mike said.

"Bingo! Well, that's kind of convenient. And fifty-three other innocent people died on that plane."

"I guess, but I'm not sure what—"

"Oh, we're not done. I'm just about to get to the scary part," Henry said.

"I told you the individuals in charge of Njala are not who you might think they are. You know, generals or a corrupt cabal of politicians? No, have you heard of Alithia Corp?" Henry asked.

Mike stared at Henry for a while and then spoke.

"The London client."

"The what?" Henry said.

"Alithia Energy? That's the name of the client in London I was supposed to be seeing," Mike replied, a note of doubt in his voice.

"I guess it's a subsidiary. Alithia is a massive multinational, multi-billion-dollar corporation that's into everything: security services, commodities trading, oil exploration, energy, the works. Chloe told me they run Njala, Mike. They control everything in that country from top to bottom. Alithia has its own goddam country, and it's bleeding it dry. I have a theory about what happened to poor old Viktor's plane."

Mike stared at Henry for a while. His now pale face betrayed his feelings of concern and confusion. "What?"

"Chloe grew suspicious after Viktor's death; as I said, the convenient timing raised questions. You should know that Alithia manufactures flight control systems for the military and private sectors. I found out they never recovered the black boxes from Viktor's plane crash. Can you connect the dots?" Henry said.

Mike opened his mouth, intending to speak, but Henry continued before he could think of anything meaningful.

"Now, when Viktor died, a few of the senior members of his party went down with him, so the key people that were left fled the country; some went to Europe, but a few of the leadership ended up first in New York and then Chicago. That's where they started work on the government in exile. These people knew what was happening but had to be careful; they still had family in Njala. They worked with Chloe and her team to get everything set up. The plan was to base themselves in London. First, it's closer, and second, the Chinese government was backing these people financially, and, well, let's say that prevented them from setting up in the US."

Mike grew concerned as it became more apparent which direction this conversation seemed to take.

"You have guessed who else was on the Vivair flight with Chloe, right?" Henry asked Mike.

"The government in exile?"

"Yup, six of them and three other lawyers, all wiped out," Henry said, shaking his head. "A few were already in London, but all the principal players are gone. Again, that's convenient, ain't it?"

"You're saying that . . ." Mike trailed off, trying to get a handle on his thoughts.

"Mike, I'm saying that Chloe was murdered, along with everyone else on board that plane, I'm certain of it."

Mike's thoughts were reeling as he stared at the table. After a while, he looked up at Henry.

"But you can't prove that, though, can you? I mean, it's just a theory, right? Speculation?"

"Well, what if Chloe had evidence to show they were behind the crash that killed Viktor Mabala? What if that is what's on the USB stick? If they killed him, then it's not a massive leap to think they would finish the job with the same methods—think about it. We will bring the guilty to justice with you and your journalist friend's help."

"But why did she give it to me? Why didn't she give it to you before the flight? I don't understand."

"I've been thinking about that. I read her message after the flight had departed, so I never got to ask her. My best guess is someone in her delegation gave it to her on board, and you provided her with a means to protect it. Stroke of luck, if you ask me."

Mike stayed silent for a while and then said, "If these people are capable of what you say, they're pretty much capable of anything, aren't they? Shouldn't you go to the police or the FBI?"

"This company is enormous; military contracts mean compromised politicians. I don't know who they control. I can't take the risk with this stuff. We're both targets if they discover what we possess. The best protection is daylight—to get everything out in the open."

Both targets? Mike didn't like the sound of that.

"So, let me get this straight. This Viktor—"

"Can I get you guys some more beer, nachos?" the server interrupted them.

"Margarita, please," Mike blurted.

"I'll have a beer, thanks," said Henry.

They both sat in silence again while they waited for the drinks. Once the server delivered them and moved out of earshot, Mike continued, in little more than a whisper.

"You're saying that the Alithia Corporation murdered this Viktor Mabala and fifty-three other people to stop him and his party from taking power in Njala. Then, when the remaining leadership was attempting to set up a government in exile, they wiped them out, too, along with hundreds of other innocent people on the Vivair flight. Jesus, that's fucked up."

"Sure is. I'm old. I've got nothing left to lose. I want to expose these scum or die trying," Henry said through clenched teeth.

Mike stared at Henry. *I don't doubt it.*

"So, with two plane crashes, they have wiped out almost all the opposition?" Mike said, blowing out a breath.

"Yes, likely, they see all the other lives lost as collateral damage."

"Henry, I don't know what I'm supposed to do with this information; it's freaking me out, if I'm honest."

"Well, I said I was going to offer you redemption, didn't I?" Henry said.

Mike nodded.

"So, here it is. You're the miserable drunk who got kicked off the plane that crashed. What a loser, a joke. Everyone wants to talk to you because nobody can comprehend why you are the only survivor. Where's the sense in that? Where is the natural justice?"

Mike could feel his face flush.

"Imagine being involved in telling the world what happened? Exposing the truth? You're no longer a douchebag. Do I need to spell it out for you? If you don't take this shot at redemption, I'm sorry to say, you're finished."

"You don't pull your punches."

Henry opened his arms out in a palms-up gesture.

"There it is: the truth."

Mike sat there deep in thought, taking the occasional sip of his margarita. It transported his mind back to Hub 51 for a moment. He felt dazed and more than a little confused. He'd become involved, whether he wanted to be or not. His fleeting possession of the USB stick had put him right in the center.

They finished their drinks and left the bar, Henry first, followed by Mike a few paces behind. They walked down the street without speaking until they reached Henry's big cream-and-brown-colored RV. It appeared to be in pristine condition.

"This is Big Bertha," Henry said, slapping the side of the vehicle. "She's a Minnie Winnie built to last."

Henry opened the door and let Mike inside.

Henry clearly took great care of Bertha; the interior was as immaculate as the outside.

"You can take that bunk down there," Henry said, pointing down the far end of the RV.

"OK, thanks, Henry, I appreciate—"

"It's nothing. Get some sleep; we've got a busy day ahead of us tomorrow."

Henry turned around and entered the bedroom, closing the door behind him.

Mike lay awake for a while, thinking about what Henry had revealed. It all felt so unreal. Just days ago, his biggest worry was traveling in coach. Shit, could that be true? Had someone intentionally brought the plane down? Then, a thought struck him: *Have they found the black boxes?* If they'd recovered them, it was likely just an accident, as a perpetrator would need to cover their tracks. He would mention it to Henry first thing in the morning. He felt pleased with himself, and after a long time staring into the darkness and wrestling with his thoughts, he drifted off to sleep.

The following day, the smell of fried bacon woke Mike up. He hadn't eaten properly for days and felt ravenous. He climbed down from the bunk and greeted Henry.

"That smells good," Mike said.

"Sit down," Henry replied, pointing at the small table.

It had just turned 8:30 when they finished breakfast; they sat opposite each other, drinking coffee.

"So, here's the plan," Henry said. "You'll give me your key, and I will take a bag back to your place, collect your phone and some clothes, lock up, and leave. I'll say I work for the landlord if I meet any press. When I get back here, you'll call your journalist friend, Ms. Reynolds, and have her come and see us; you'll tell her it's important and that she needs to bring the USB stick. When she arrives, we'll get her up to speed. She will either help us or she won't. I'm guessing she will; I checked her out last night, and she seems like the real deal. From there, we plan the next stage. Clear?"

Mike thought Henry must have done this sort of thing before. He seemed so in control, which he was relieved about because he felt close to being out of control most of the time.

"Clear," Mike said before continuing. "I told you about the password, though. I don't know what—"

"It's OK. I know what the password is," Henry replied, looking Mike straight in the eyes.

"But . . ."

"Trust me."

Mike didn't speak for a long while, then said, "Henry, you know how you said the black boxes never showed up in Africa? Have they found the black boxes from the Vivair flight? Given what you've told me, it seems important."

"Day seven, and no sign of them."

CHAPTER 13

President Jibril Abena's fingers drummed an impatient beat on the polished mahogany of his enormous desk, the irregular percussion punctuating the silent expanse of the presidential office in the heart of Jalaka, the capital city of Njala. Sunlight streamed through the tall windows, casting long, thin shadows that seemed to reach for the array of phones and red-leather-bound reports on the president's desk. His eyes flickered toward the ornate clock above the door—its hands creeping beyond the hour when the scent of strong coffee and sizzling plantains typically wafted in. A frown creased his forehead, and he glanced at the empty table by the patio doors, its gleaming surface untouched by the morning meal.

He grabbed a folder from his desk, flipping through the pages with a growing irritation. Each document seemed to amplify his annoyance. He felt keenly aware of his own presence, a towering figure that loomed over others, a fact often mirrored by the billboards scattered across the capital, showcasing his broad smile and imposing head. Hunger gnawed at him—not just for the delayed breakfast, but a deeper, more insatiable appetite for the myriad aspects of power and influence that came with his position and, lately, for escape. As he rifled through the papers, the hunger persisted, a constant companion in his life of grandeur and responsibility, annoyance rising higher within him.

A soft knocking at the oak-paneled doors snapped him to attention. "Come!" he said, his voice booming across the room.

The hinges of the grand door creaked as a figure in a heavily starched black dress and a lace-trimmed apron hesitated at the threshold. She balanced a tray that tipped under the weight of a porcelain coffeepot, steam curling up from its spout, and plates laden with the morning's fare. Her arms tensed, betraying the effort it took to keep the laden tray steady as she navigated the plush carpet. With a subtle tilt of his head, President Abena directed her toward the gleaming coffee table adjacent to the sheer patio doors, where daylight danced through the leaves of the lush presidential gardens and spilled into the room. The balcony beyond beckoned, a verdant escape framed by drapes that fluttered slightly in the morning breeze.

The tray rattled softly as it settled onto the coffee table, the delicate dance of china and silver announcing the long-awaited arrival of breakfast. President Abena's gaze lingered momentarily on the young woman's white-knuckled grip, which relaxed as she relinquished her burden. With a mere flick of his wrist, he dismissed her, his voice devoid of warmth: "You may go." As the maid retreated, her uniform whispering as she walked, the president turned his attention to the sunlit balcony, the garden's emerald arms reaching out as if to embrace the day's agenda. "Do not be late with my breakfast again!"

He sat briefly with his eyes closed and pinched the bridge of his nose. Stress nipped at his composure and had sharpened his words more than necessary. If the First Lady were there, she would surely have scolded him for such brusqueness. He made a mental note to offer the maid an apology later.

The tray boasted an assortment of his favorite breakfast items —fried fish, fufu, akara, and a generous serving of jollof rice, alongside a pot of the finest kopi-luwak coffee and a carafe of fresh orange juice. He settled into an oversized armchair, unfolding a napkin and tucking it into his collar, his eyes dancing over the feast before him.

President Abena felt a surge of annoyance as the shrill ring of his phone interrupted his meal before even a forkful had entered his eager mouth. As he stood up, discomfort washed over him, an unpleasant reminder of his increasing bulk. Each step he took toward the desk felt laborious, reflecting his growing frustration over the day's start. Settling into the creaking presidential chair, he let out a heavy sigh. Reluctantly, he reached for the phone, bracing himself for whatever issue lay ahead. Lifting the receiver to his ear, his tone combined weariness with authority. "Yes, what is it?" he snorted.

He heard the tremor in his assistant's voice, noting a nervous undertone that didn't bode well. "Mr. President, Mr. Rampton is on the line for you."

"Put him through immediately," he commanded with nervous surprise. As the line clicked, apprehension coursed through him.

"Mr. Rampton, what a pleasure to hear from you. How are you? And your family?" the president began, attempting a veneer of cordiality.

But Rampton cut straight to the point, his tone abrupt. "Jibril, let's talk about that infrastructure project. The asphalt for the cobalt mine roadway in Kasirga. What's happening there?"

President Abena started to interject, to offer some reassurance, but Rampton's impatience bulldozed through his attempt. "I need that road done, Jibril. You promised the work would have started by now. My sources say there's been no movement. What's going on?"

Struggling to maintain a facade of control, President Abena assured him, "We're on top of it, Mr. Rampton. Just a few minor setbacks, nothing to worry about. The project is very much on track."

Rampton responded with a thinly veiled threat. "I'll have my man check again tomorrow. If there's no progress, we will have a problem. Do you understand me?"

President Abena, feeling the walls closing in, managed a strained response. "Absolutely, Mr. Rampton. The work will begin shortly. You'll see progress soon and—"

Rampton had ended the call abruptly; Abena heard the click as he spoke. He sat staring at the receiver, a sense of foreboding settling in his stomach. He had a clear strategy: amass enough funds to escape Njala, first his family, then him, and do it swiftly. But Rampton's words presented a clear reminder of the tightrope he walked.

President Abena's gaze lingered on the phone, a distinct heaviness in his chest. A sheen of sweat glistened on his forehead, tension weaving through him. With deliberate movements, he plucked the napkin from his shirt collar and dabbed at his skin, attempting to erase the unease clawing at him. The rich aroma of his untouched breakfast hung in the air, now uninviting—his stomach, once growling with hunger, was now knotted.

Still grasping the phone but now with a decisiveness that belied his unsettled state, President Abena dialed his assistant. His gnawing hunger now lay forgotten, replaced by a hollow feeling that no food could satisfy. With a voice that masked his inner turmoil, he instructed his assistant, the words concise and clear: "Take it away, all of it. I cannot eat now."

The maid reappeared and collected the tray she'd deposited on the table moments earlier.

"Hurry, girl!" the President bellowed, and she hurried out of the room, the china clinking noisily.

The roadway issue, escalating through the ranks, had finally landed squarely on his and Mr. Rampton's desks. It now demanded President Abena's direct intervention. Reluctantly, he recognized the necessity to allocate substantial funds, dipping into reserves he had earmarked for future plans. This unwelcome decision ate away at him, a clear reminder of the constant high-wire act his position entailed.

So be it. He picked up the phone.

Within hours, the trucks rolled, breaking ground in Kasirga.

By the time the midday sun arched high over Jalaka, the rumbling in President Abena's belly had become fierce, demanding his attention. The unease he'd felt that morning had dissipated, replaced by a ravenous call to action that echoed through him with newfound authority. He pressed the intercom, his command slicing through the office's quiet: "Have my car brought around. I'll take lunch at the Jalaka Orchid Palace Hotel today." The declaration resonated with a sense of normality he craved, the prospect of the hotel's bustling atmosphere and finely garnished dishes sparking a rare flicker of anticipation in his eyes.

Many of the perks of the presidency delighted Jibril, and the luxury of bypassing restaurant reservations was among them. Yet, at times, being president lost its luster, particularly during dealings with Mr. Rampton and his cohort—encounters that left him feeling anything but presidential. And then there was Field Marshal Fatoumata Diallo, the formidable head of Njala's military forces, a constant thorn in his side. President Abena harbored a deep-seated loathing for the man, a puppet dancing on Rampton's strings, who consistently denied him any respect.

After a sumptuous lunch at the Orchid, President Abena returned to the palace and retired to his chamber to rest. His valet helped him change from his elegant, dark, tailored suit and silk shirt and helped him put on his casual boubou. He dismissed his valet, sat down at the end of the bed, and let out a long sigh. The money he had to release to get the roadway project moving had put a dent in his finances, leaving him vulnerable. Each day edged them closer to this crucial juncture, and today's setbacks only served to tighten the coil of anxiety within him. The urgency of his family's impending departure loomed ever more significant, a constant red flag waving in the back of his mind.

As President Abena lingered in his chamber, the echo of the day's chaos gave way to a heavy silence laden with unspoken truths, the relentless ticking of the clock marking his family's impending departure. He felt each second as a tightening spiral of anxiety, a reminder of the volatile path he was treading.

He barely registered the soft knock at the door. "Come in," he called, his voice weary and full of resigned authority.

Nia, the first lady, entered. Her presence was usually a calming balm, but it now mirrored his turmoil. Her eyes, searching his, brimmed with unvoiced questions. He'd told her they were in trouble and that they had to leave Njala soon, that she needed to be prepared. But he still had to tell her why.

"Nia," Abena greeted, her name heavy on his tongue. He hesitated, a pressure in his chest. "I have to tell you something." he looked down at the floor.

"What is it?" She said softly, sounding concerned.

He looked at her. "Viktor Malaba's death . . . It wasn't an accident. It was an assassination. And I knew . . ."

"You knew?" she whispered, her wide eyes echoing her feeling of betrayal.

Abena's eyes shifted away, the shame too much to bear. "I was aware of the plan, but I did nothing. They were convinced Viktor's influence threatened our position. My inaction, my silence. It was a choice, one I convinced myself was necessary."

"And allowed for his murder," Nia finished, her voice a cold blade.

"Yes," he admitted, feeling complicit. "But there's more, Nia. The Vivair flight, the one with the Njala delegation . . ."

Nia's eyes widened, her hand instinctively rising to her chest, her breath catching. "What about it?"

"It was connected. The same forces behind Viktor's assassination, they . . . they were involved in that too. It's all part of a larger plan, one that we're now involved in."

Nia's hand moved to her mouth, and she gasped. "But . . . why? How?"

Abena's face dropped. "Control, power, the usual motives. But they underestimated the consequences. The world's eyes will soon be upon us, on Njala. I promise you I will make amends. I will avenge all their deaths."

They sat together, the room's quiet opulence somehow pressing in on them, Nia's hand on his shoulder. Abena's heart ached for his childhood friend and the dreams they'd shared. Now, those dreams lay buried under layers of politics and greed. He thought of Viktor's last speech, his charisma, his vision for Njala, and how he, Jibril Abena, had stood aside and let his friend walk into the abyss.

The burden of his choices, the path he had chosen, lay heavy on his soul. He trod the path that benefited the Alithia Corporation and Mr. Rampton but not his people. The realization, a bitter truth he could no longer ignore, stung.

Silence enveloped them as each was lost in their thoughts, the sudden storm outside mirroring the one raging within.

Nia quietly exited the room, leaving Abena alone with his regrets. In his mind's eye, he revisited Viktor's final, powerful speech, remembering a leader he could never be. His thoughts circled back to his limitations as president, his inability to serve his people without serving the Alithia Corporation and Mr. Rampton first.

Lying back, Abena closed his eyes, Viktor's image and words lingering in his consciousness as he drifted into a restless sleep.

CHAPTER 14

At the dining table in his expansive Los Angeles mansion, Tyler Rampton exuded a sense of quiet control. His slender fingers clasped an antique china cup, a small indulgence amid the modern grandeur surrounding him. His eyes, clear and green, flickered with amusement as he watched a video on his laptop. A knock on the baronial doors barely registered in his preoccupied mind.

"Enter," he called out, his voice detached, his gaze still fixed on the screen.

The door opened, and a maid entered, her steps measured and silent. She carried a silver salver atop a small tray, presenting Rampton with a modest yet meticulously prepared breakfast. Without a word, he dismissed her, his attention already back to the video that had captured his interest.

A smirk played on his lips as he watched, his head shaking in amusement. Not a man of imposing physical stature, Rampton stood at five feet nine, his shoes subtly adding to his height. Keen alertness shone in his gaze, and his receding hairline appeared tinged with gray at the temples. He kept his hair short, accentuating a face with sharp, calculating features.

Despite his understated physical presence, Rampton had a

commanding aura, a byproduct of being accustomed to roles of authority. His tailored suits, a statement of his impeccable style, spoke of a man who understood the power of appearances. He moved with an almost hypnotic confidence; his charm concealed the brutality of his ascent, a path marked by manipulation and strategic betrayals.

In the quiet of his mansion, he sat alone, a man at ease with the darker facets of his nature, a fox keenly surveying the landscape, watching the henhouse, always poised, always calculating.

Rampton set his laptop aside with a fluid, practiced motion, focusing now on the sleek mobile phone in his hand. He used it with an air of casual authority. The phone pressed against his ear as he lounged in his chair, his demeanor portraying an image of relaxed power. His voice carried across the line with a light touch of amusement.

"Dalton, it's Tyler. I just watched the video; it's hilarious, honestly. They seem to be making this guy out as some hero. Tell me, is getting drunk, abusing people, and then getting dragged off a flight by the police what passes for heroism these days?" he said, his smirk evident in his voice.

Dalton's voice, calm and measured, came through the phone: "He's certainly a survivor. But there's more—did you catch the odd detail at the end?"

Rampton scoffed. "The whole spectacle is bizarre. What detail?"

"I am speaking specifically about the final moments. Something happens that could be of concern to us."

"What? I didn't see anything. Please elaborate—I haven't got time—"

"A woman in the final frames blocks the aisle in business class. We have identified her. She is Chloe Mitchell, a lawyer for the Njalian delegation," Dalton replied in a clipped tone.

A frown replaced Rampton's smirk. "And?"

"She passes something to the drunk. You can see her slip

something in his pocket. He likely didn't notice," Dalton continued.

There was a moment of silence as Rampton processed this. "Do we know what it was?"

"Negative. We're working on it."

"Well, OK, this changes things considerably. Find this man and retrieve whatever it is. I don't like this." Rampton's tone was unusually flustered.

"We're on it," came Dalton's brief reply.

"You better be. I want some time with you later. Drop by my office at three. We need to chat about our mutual friend, the president, among other things. Please make the arrangements."

"Roger that. Speak soon."

The call concluded; Rampton placed his phone aside, his movements deliberate, each action reflecting his methodical nature. He turned his attention to his breakfast, the eggs and toast now a mundane task. However, his mind had already shifted elsewhere, plotting his next move. Appetite gone, he pushed the food away.

A knock on the dining room door sounded again, and Laura, his PA, entered. She announced the car and driver were ready for Mr. Rampton's departure to the downtown offices at his convenience.

"Give me ten minutes. Wait in the car," he said.

Laura left without a word.

Rampton finished his tea. He wiped his mouth with a napkin, stood up, picked up his suit jacket from the back of his chair, and put it on. He put his mobile phone in the inside pocket and the laptop in his leather case, the initials "TBR" embossed in big gold lettering on the front.

He looked up at the large portrait of his father and grandfather. In it, his grandfather Randolph sat while his son, Seymour, stood behind him, his hand on the older man's shoulder. Thoughts of his grandfather, the all-powerful patriarch who'd built the company, filled Rampton's thoughts. He recalled their last conversation just a few months before his grandfather's death.

"In Mexico, they have this saying," the old man had said, his voice barely a whisper.

He'd continued in perfect Spanish: *"después de ahogado el niño, tapan el pozo."* He paused momentarily and said, "It translates to: 'After the child has drowned, they cover the well.' Do you know what that means?"

"I don't think so, Grandfather," the young Tyler had replied.

"Don't fix things after it's too late," his grandfather replied, his jaw set and face like granite.

The two figures in the portrait appeared to gaze out, their eyes intently locking onto him as if they could truly see. An unspoken truth emanated from their silent vigil, an earnestness transcending the image's stillness. Leaning in closer, Tyler noted that his grandfather's eyes reflected resolve and a hint of regret. "Don't fix things after it's too late," he murmured, his voice low. The moment felt suspended in time, reminding him that actions had consequences.

With one last look, he gathered his belongings and exited the room.

CHAPTER 15

I n Jalaka's presidential palace, within the grand expanse of the family room, President Jibril Abena reclined, embodying an intriguing combination of relaxation and strain. His eyes, usually clouded by presidential and other burdens, softened as he watched his children play. Their pure, childlike giggles offered a fleeting refuge amid the approaching political chaos.

However, Abena's thoughts were elsewhere. He knew his calls were now being monitored and his movements tracked. He also suspected they had recently bugged the presidential palace, causing him to tell the first lady they could no longer talk freely. He needed a phone that provided safety and couldn't be traced back to him. His thoughts seemed constantly plagued by the pressing need to accelerate his escape plan. He felt the walls created around his contrived presidency closing in, and the instinct to protect his family had become paramount. A race against time had commenced, and every second counted.

As his children's joyful noise filled the air, Abena's gaze wandered to the large picture window. From his vantage point, he could see the pristine gardens of the palace, a beautifully crafted display of order and splendor. But beyond that pristine facade, Abena knew that reality held far more complexity and peril. In the safety of this room, surrounded by the purity of his children's world, a blunt contrast remained between his public and private lives. At this moment, Abena found himself at the crossroads of his destiny, torn between love for his family and the unyielding demands of his paymasters.

Outside, a young gardener labored in the vibrant flower beds under the relentless early afternoon sun. Abena noted the young man's drenched uniform, testimony to his hard work in the sweltering heat. Leaning toward the telephone on the adjacent table, he dialed his assistant. "A young man is working in the garden among the flowers. Bring him to me," he instructed.

As he hung up, Abena's attention momentarily returned to his children, their innocent play a soothing balm to his troubled mind. Soon, a soft knock at the door heralded the gardener's arrival. Abena watched as his assistant ushered in the young man, who now awkwardly shuffled in, his usually bare, mud-stained feet encased in protective plastic booties. The gardener seemed out of place in the opulent setting of the room, his humble appearance contrasting sharply with the luxurious surroundings.

President Abena observed the young gardener with a benevolent eye, an unspoken recognition of the young man's diligence, and his obvious nervousness about being summoned by the nation's leader. The contrast in their worlds, within the confines of the same room, mirrored the diverse lives of those he governed—or at least pretended to.

The President watched the young gardener's unease as he walked farther into the opulent family room, his hands absentmindedly twisting the brim of his cap, which he held in front of him. The gardener's blue uniform, marked with the honest stains of soil, told a story of dedication and toil. Aware of the intimidating effect his presence could have, Abena gestured for the young man to approach, his smile warm and disarming.

"Thank you for coming," he began, his voice gentle yet resonant with the authority of his office. "Your hard work hasn't gone unnoticed. The gardens are a testament to your dedication. I wanted to thank you for that personally."

Reaching into his pocket, Abena retrieved a substantial wad of cash, clasped by a lion-shaped, diamond-encrusted money clip, symbolizing Njala's strength and pride. The young man's eyes widened at such wealth, dwarfing what he typically earned in a year.

Abena's gaze shifted to his children, who were carefree, playing in the room. "My children, please go to your playroom now," he instructed, his tone shifting to a fatherly directive. Sensing the shift in their father's focus, the children hurriedly exited the room.

Once alone with the gardener, Abena motioned toward the plush suede sofa. "Please, take a seat," he encouraged. Still visibly nervous, the gardener sat on the edge of the sofa, his hat clutched tightly in his lap.

Abena leaned forward, his demeanor shifting to one of seriousness. "I have a favor to ask of you. It's a matter of some importance. Do you think you could assist me?" He infused his voice with a seriousness that underscored the importance of his request.

"Of course, Mr. President," the gardener replied, trembling slightly with pride and apprehension. "I would be honored to help however I can, sir." His earnest, wide-eyed expression reflected his respect for the president and the overwhelming nature of the moment.

President Abena leaned further forward with an air of relaxed authority. His gaze fixed on the young gardener sitting opposite him. "Thank you for coming. What's your name?" he asked, smiling broadly.

The young gardener sat nervously, his hands twitching slightly. "Kwame, sir. Kwame Sankoh," he responded, his voice wavering.

Abena nodded, his smile broadening. "Kwame, you see, even as president, there are things I cannot do. The presidency means living under a microscope and sacrificing personal freedoms. Do you understand what I mean?" He leaned back, studying Kwame's reaction.

"Yes, sir, of course," Kwame stammered, his eyes darting between the president and the floor.

Abena chuckled lightly, easing the tension. "I need you to do something for me, something private, away from any prying eyes," he said, his tone now more serious, carrying a conspiratorial tone.

Kwame nodded, his eyes still wide with excitement and anxiety.

Abena's attention returned to the wad of cash in his hand. He counted three one hundred Njalian dollar notes and handed them to Kwame. The young man's eyes grew even wider, the amount representing a small fortune to him.

"Take this and buy me a box of cigars from the nearest store. My wife mustn't find out," Abena instructed, his voice low.

Kwame accepted the money, a puzzled expression crossing his face.

Then, with a conspiratorial gesture, Abena handed Kwame a folded piece of paper, pressing his finger to his lips. Kwame unfolded it, and his confusion deepened as he read the message:

I DO NOT WANT CIGARS; GET ME A THROWAWAY MOBILE PHONE.

Abena took the note back, ensuring the message remained secrecy. "Buy the cigars and return here directly. I'll inform my assistant to expect you. Oh, and keep the change. It's yours; you earned it," he said, his voice sounding assured.

Kwame, now a courier with clandestine instructions, nodded vigorously. "I'll give the change to my mother, sir. She'll be so proud. Thank you!"

"It's nothing. Now, move quickly." Abena dismissed him with a wave.

Kwame hurried out, and Abena stood, watching through the window as the young gardener mounted his bicycle and sped off. Abena's eyes followed him until he disappeared. He turned away from the window, a thoughtful frown creasing his brow. The stakes were high, and every move had to be calculated precisely. In the solitude of the room, all the possible consequences of his decisions and the clandestine nature of his actions hung heavily in the air.

CHAPTER 16

Tyler Rampton stood in his expansive office on the thirty-fifth floor of Alithia Corp headquarters, with his gaze fixed on an antique map of Njala adorning the wall. The map, a rare artifact from the early 1800s, acquired for over $15,000 at a prestigious cartography auction, usually brought a smile to his face. This represented a time before the world turned its covetous eyes to Njala's abundant riches. Today, however, pressing concerns preoccupied his mind, rendering a stern expression on his face.

Rampton paced before the map, his hands clasped behind his back. The revelation that President Jibril Abena had a close child-hood connection with Viktor Malaba unsettled him, and he bitterly regretted not receiving this critical piece of intelligence earlier. He considered loyalty a double-edged sword and now questioned where Abena's true allegiances lay.

Leaning forward, his fingertips brushing against the glass protecting the ancient map, Rampton contemplated the delicate balance of power. He had tolerated Abena's financial indiscretions, considering them a harmless side effect of power. But the prospect of Abena using his wealth to escape Njala introduced an intolerable level of risk.

Turning away from the map, Rampton walked to his large, polished desk, his reflection in the glass window mirroring his movements. He aimed to avoid expensive and inconvenient unrest in Njala at all costs. Such chaos could draw international scrutiny, complicating his carefully laid plans.

He paused, his eyes narrowing as he considered his next move. It had to be strategic and executed with finesse and discretion. The future of his operations in Njala depended on it. The stakes were high, and the path forward required careful navigation. In the intricate game of international politics and business, Rampton knew that subtlety and timing were everything.

Now seated behind his imposing desk, he urgently reached for the phone. He dialed swiftly, his expression focused.

"Laura, Dalton is imminent. No formalities; bring him straight in," he instructed, his tone cold.

"Understood, Mr. Rampton. Any refreshments?" Laura asked, her voice upbeat, a stark contrast to Rampton's.

"No." His terse response signaled the end of the conversation. He replaced the receiver, his thoughts shifting to the matters at hand.

Rampton stood and walked over to the enormous window, eyes taking in the expansive panorama of Los Angeles. Beneath, the highway buzzed, a live river of hustle and bustle.

Absorbed in the view, he remained lost in thought with his back to the door.

Without turning, he heard the door open and close. Dalton, Alithia's head of security, had entered the room.

"Afternoon, Tyler." Being in Tyler's private space and calling him by his first name signified their deep connection, a privilege few in the organization enjoyed.

Rampton turned smoothly from the window, his demeanor instantly shifting from contemplative to businesslike. Dalton settled into one of the plush leather armchairs as he watched Rampton approach his desk.

"Dalton," Rampton greeted his visitor quickly, his focus

already on the task at hand. He gestured toward an open folder on his desk. "We need to discuss our mutual friend," he said, his no-nonsense demeanor foreshadowing the serious chat about to begin.

Tyler Rampton looked closely at Dalton, a figure who certainly commanded attention. As the head of their lucrative security services division, Dalton had grown into more than just an employee; he had become vital to Rampton's ambitions.

Dalton, a former Navy SEAL with a shadowy past, had a build reminiscent of his military days that had hardly diminished with time. Now in his late forties, Rampton saw his impressive physique as a testament to his discipline.

Dalton's closely cropped dark hair and his small, piercing dark eyes painted a picture of a man who should not be messed with. He possessed a distinct aura of confidence and an underlying quality of menace. Rampton viewed this combination of qualities as ideal for his role.

Rampton couldn't help but think of Dalton's arrival at Alithia as fated. Dalton had come aboard at the infancy of their Njala operations when his particular skills and disposition were most needed. It seemed like the stars had aligned perfectly, presenting Rampton with the right person at the perfect moment. In Dalton, Rampton saw not just a head of security but a crucial ally in Alithia's strategic aims.

"The president is your typical loose end," Dalton said.

"Yes, Dalton, indeed. I know what he's up to. The work in Kigali didn't start due to his diversion of funds. He will run, you know that, don't you? What happened to Malaba has spooked him. He's now a problem, and I want him dealt with."

"I think things might soon come to a head."

"They already have. Our friend has been putting something aside for a rainy day, which means he plans to escape," Rampton said.

"Yes, that can't happen."

"Of course, it can't happen. I want you to have the president watched for now. When the time is right, you will know what to do," Rampton said.

"Understood. I will speak with Diallo."

"No. I don't want Diallo involved at this stage. We should call on him later if required, but I want Abena monitored for now. Your guys, Dalton—your best, understood?"

"Not a problem. If the president takes a shit, we'll know about it," Dalton said.

Rampton curled his lip at the thought.

"He will have an escape plan. Find out what it is. Find out where all his money is and ensure he has no insurance. If he does, destroy it. Then, we'll deal with the issue of succession. Understood?"

"Roger that," Dalton said and stood up to leave.

"That other thing? The drunk idiot and the mysterious hand-off? Where are we with that?"

"My guys are on it. I will report back soon," Dalton said, still standing.

"It worries me. Please give it full focus."

"Understood," Dalton said before exiting the room.

Rampton closed the file and stared out the huge window. He had complete faith in Dalton but worried about the number of moving parts. He did not have much faith in Field Marshal Diallo, the head of the Njalian Armed Forces. He relied on Dalton to handle the situation with the president without involving Diallo, known for his lack of subtlety. Rampton preferred staying a few steps removed from ground events, akin to Zeus observing from above, subtly influencing. However, he felt increasingly compelled to intervene directly, and his hands were getting dirty.

He believed it best if Abena died while in office of a heart attack or stroke, perhaps. There would then be a period of national mourning before they inaugurated a new president, a better president. That, to him, seemed like the simplest solution, and he didn't concern himself with how they might make that happen.

Rampton considered several candidates for the soon-to-be-vacant office of president. The current finance minister, Samuel Okafor, stood out as a strong possibility. Charismatic, ambitious, and an excellent communicator, Okafor's public image belied his true nature. Dalton's comprehensive dossier on Okafor revealed a litany of illegal financial dealings, embezzlement of public funds, and bribery. Recordings captured secret meetings with influential business figures, where Okafor promised political favors for monetary contributions. Photos and videos showed him in compromising positions with junior staff and captured drug use, all potent weapons to secure his loyalty. Despite his unsavory dealings, Rampton liked Samuel, even considering him a friend.

Aisha Bello presented a different kind of opportunity. Strikingly beautiful, cunning, and intelligent, she excelled in negotiation and had brokered significant deals. Serving as Njala's representative at the UN and residing in New York, her file revealed equally damning information. It contained evidence of shady international deals leveraged by her diplomatic position, benefitting Alithia while sidelining Njala's interests. Documents proved her acceptance of bribes and luxurious gifts from foreign entities, undermining her impartiality. Recordings of her private conversations with criminals and political rivals revealed a willingness to engage in covert activities for her gain. Video evidence of her intimate encounters with a Catholic bishop added to her vulnerability. Aisha had already advanced Alithia's interests significantly, making her Rampton's favored choice. Still, her inability to hide her disdain for those she disliked worried him. It was hardly a desirable quality for a potential head of state.

All this kingmaker stuff gave Rampton a warm feeling inside. Soon, Njala would be wrapped up in a pretty little bow. Abena had been a misstep, and once they had dealt with him, they would tie up the last loose end.

Rampton glanced at the ringing phone, his lips curving into a smile as he picked up the receiver. "Mr. Rampton, your son, Dexter, is on the line, saying it's urgent," Laura's voice came through.

"Put him through," he replied, the smile fading with a resigned sigh.

"Dad, it's Dexter. How's things?" Dexter's voice floated through casually, too casual for something "urgent."

"What's the urgency, Dexter?" Tyler asked, his brow furrowing, a sense of annoyance creeping in.

"It's pretty urgent; my buddies want to go to Cabo this weekend, and I said we could use your boat?" Dexter's voice carried a note of hesitance.

Tyler leaned back in his chair, his patience thinning. "Why would you promise that without asking first?"

"I thought it'd be cool, you know . . .?" Dexter's voice trailed off.

"Well, that is an expensive boat; a weekend down to Mexico and back with a full crew will stretch to over a hundred thousand dollars. Dexter, do you have any idea . . ."

"Fine, forget it. I thought you wouldn't mind." Dexter's voice bristled with resentment. "You can be such a douchebag."

Tyler's grip tightened on the phone as Dexter hung up. He stared at the handset, reflecting on his strict upbringing, a sharp contrast to Dexter's sense of entitlement. His family never tolerated disrespect; instilling discipline and understanding the value of money was paramount. He couldn't help but think Dexter's attitude stemmed partly from his mother's influence, Tyler's long-estranged wife.

He slammed the handset back in the phone cradle and picked it up again after a few seconds. "Laura, get the car sent around and cancel everything in my diary for the rest of the day. I'm going to my club."

"Yes, of course, Mr. Rampton."

CHAPTER 17

Mike hesitated before dialing Sarah's number, his finger hovering over the call button before hitting connect. His voice wavered as he greeted her: "Sarah, it's Mike. Um, Anderson?" He turned his name into a question, doubting whether she remembered him.

"Well, hello there, I was about to call you. Is everything alright?" Sarah replied, sounding upbeat.

"Ah, well, not exactly," Mike replied, his tone uncertain. "I need to see you. It's about . . . well, me and Henry."

"Henry? Who's that?" Sarah asked.

Mike glanced at Henry, who sat across from him in the RV, before continuing. "We'll explain everything when we meet. Can you come over?"

"Sure, sounds important. I'll head to your place," Sarah started.

Mike interrupted her. "No, don't come to my apartment. The press is swarming the place. Sorry, I know you're the press too. I meant…anyway, we're in Henry's RV, parked on West Greenleaf, across from the Baptist church."

Sarah chuckled lightly. "I'm guessing there aren't many RVs around there?"

"Just us," Mike said, trying to sound lighthearted.

"Got it. I'll be there around two," Sarah confirmed.

"Wait, Sarah," Mike said quickly. "Can you bring the USB stick with you?"

She paused. "Sure, but what for?"

"Once you're here, I'll fill you in on everything," he said, his pulse pounding.

"Alright, then. See you at two," Sarah replied cautiously before ending the call.

Mike set the phone down, exhaling deeply. "She's coming at two," he informed Henry, a sense of anticipation mixed with anxiety hitting him.

He shifted in his seat, feeling the heaviness of the silence that settled between him and Henry. He glanced at the older man, who seemed lost in his thoughts as he gazed out the small window of the RV. Mike seized the chance to find out a bit more about his host.

"Henry, could you . . . could you tell me more about Chloe?" Mike asked tentatively, watching Henry's face for a reaction.

Henry's features softened, a look of sadness overtaking his expression as he continued to look out the window. "Chloe," he began slowly. "She was smart, kindhearted, and brave. But the work with that exiled government consumed her, eating away her peace of mind."

Mike listened, sensing the pain in Henry's words as he continued. "She must've felt threatened to pass you that USB," Henry said, his gaze still fixed on the world outside, his voice low. "I just wish she'd known the extent of the danger she was in."

"Why was it just you two?" Mike probed gently, careful not to pry too much.

Henry turned to look at Mike. "Chloe lost her parents in a crash when she was just a kid. After my wife, Sandie, passed away, it was just Chloe and me. We were each other's world . . ."

Henry's voice trailed off, and his gaze returned to the window. "Now, there's just me," he added, his voice barely above a whisper.

Feeling Henry's loss, Mike decided to shift the conversation. "What did you do before you retired?"

Henry's response was enigmatic: "I navigated some pretty murky waters. It was a solitary kind of job."

"Sounds like you worked in a sewer or something," Mike joked, trying to lighten the mood.

Henry chuckled dryly. "Yeah, something like that." But then his tone shifted. "Sometimes, circumstances pull you back into the darkness."

Mike's brow furrowed, unsure of what Henry meant. He thought about working underground, maybe in sewers and their inherent darkness, but there seemed to be more to Henry's words. Perhaps, with Henry's experience and Sarah's confidence, Mike could find a way to reclaim his lost self-assurance. Could this odd pairing truly offer him a shot at redemption?

The silence returned, with each man lost in their thoughts. Mike found himself secretly wishing for Sarah to arrive, to laugh off their concerns and logically dismantle their fears with clear explanations. But until she did, he and Henry remained trapped in an uneasy quiet.

Without a word, Henry rose, his movements suggesting a need for escape, however brief. "I'm going for a walk," he announced, his voice carrying a hint of weariness. The door closed behind him with a soft thud.

Mike made his way to his bunk in the RV, lying down in a state of restlessness. The triviality of his job loss and the flight incident paled in comparison to the dark shadow of murder and conspiracies that now hovered over him. Heaving with unease, his mind, still exhausted, succumbed to sleep, drawing him into a vivid dream.

In his dream, Mike was alone in a small rowboat adrift in a

cold, still ocean. The unsettling silence was broken only by the soft sounds of water lapping against the boat. An ominous sense of dread filled him as objects began to hit the boat—softly, at first, then with increasing force. Mike didn't dare to look, his fear telling him they were bodies.

He awoke abruptly, bathed in sweat, as Henry reentered the RV.

"I went to the grocery store," Henry began, a touch of normality in his voice as he started unpacking the bags. "Did some research on our visitor. She likes chamomile tea and sushi, so I got some of that." Mike watched as Henry methodically unpacked the groceries.

"That's thoughtful," Mike said, thinking grocery store sushi probably wasn't what Sarah had in mind.

The remnants of his unsettling dream still clung to him, leaving a lingering sense of disconnection that was hard to shake off. He perched on the edge of his bunk, his breaths deep and deliberate as he attempted to anchor himself back to reality.

Glancing at his watch, Mike noted the time. Sarah would be arriving soon. He considered freshening up, the idea of a shower appealing as a means to wash away the lingering unease. With its surprising array of amenities, Henry's RV likely had a shower.

"Hey, Henry, is there a chance I could take a shower?" Mike asked, his tone hopeful.

"Sure, right through there," Henry replied nonchalantly, nodding toward the compact shower room.

Emerging refreshed in jeans and a black T-shirt, Mike felt a noticeable shift in his mood. The hot shower had brought back a measure of calm to his frazzled nerves. He settled across from Henry at the table.

Mike watched as Henry unfolded a newspaper, its pages rustling in the quiet. He stared at the front page from his seat. The Vivair 002 crash still dominated the headlines. He hoped the media had moved on from talking about him.

"Black boxes?" Mike ventured, his voice barely above a whisper.

Henry shook his head without looking up from the paper. "Nope."

Mike's heart sank a little more, a wave of fear washing over him.

"They stopped talking about me in there?" he asked, dreading the answer.

"Nope," came another clipped response.

Mike's stomach twisted. "Shit," he muttered under his breath.

Henry's voice cut through his thoughts. "New angle in the story. They interviewed a guy called Doug Richards. He's saying he worked with you. Calls you a 'fruit loop.'"

Mike's face twisted into a wry smile, his features combining a look of disbelief and resignation. "Great, thanks, Doug," he said, shaking his head slightly.

Henry stood up, folding the newspaper. "I'll make some coffee. You want one?"

Mike nodded, his expression clouded over with anxiety. "Yeah, sure, thanks." He longed for a beer to ease his nerves, maybe something a bit stronger, but he doubted Henry had thought to pick anything up.

Just then, three soft knocks echoed on the RV door.

Mike watched as Henry moved to answer it. The door swung open, revealing Sarah Reynolds standing outside, a large bag slung over her shoulder. She was dressed casually in jeans, a white T-shirt, and yellow desert boots, her hair in a ponytail, with sunglasses perched on her head. Mike found the calm way she carried herself reassuring.

"Gentlemen," Sarah greeted them as she stepped inside the confined space of the RV.

Mike got to his feet, his movements stiff from the nerves. "Hey, Sarah. This is Henry, the person I mentioned on the phone. It's his RV."

Sarah extended her hand toward Henry, who took it in a firm handshake. "Nice place," she commented, scanning the interior of the RV. "I'm Sarah Reynolds, journo."

"Thank you. I am pleased to meet you, Sarah. Take a seat. I read you like chamomile tea, so I'm just making a fresh pot," Henry offered, his voice calm and welcoming.

"Do I?" Sarah seemed surprised, a slight frown on her forehead.

"It's in your bio on that website," Henry explained, showing that he had done his homework.

"Then, it's true. OK, delicious, thank you," Sarah responded, her voice carrying a note of amusement.

"And if you're hungry, I have your favorite food," Henry added, trying to be hospitable.

"Meatloaf?" Sarah joked, glancing around the kitchen area.

"No, ah, sushi?" Henry corrected.

"Oh, yeah, sushi, lovely!" Sarah tried to sound enthusiastic, but Mike could sense her slight discomfort. She then pulled the USB stick out of the front pocket of her jeans. "Well, here it is. I have been trying to get the password cracked, but it's proving a challenge, so I'm not sure what—"

"I know it," Henry interjected confidently.

Sarah's eyes widened as she stared at Henry, clearly taken aback. "What, I don't—"

Before Sarah could finish, Mike cut in. "Sarah, Henry is Chloe's grandfather."

With a grave expression, Henry took out his phone, opened his messaging app, and slid it across the table toward Sarah. She hesitated momentarily before picking it up and reading Chloe's final message. A hand flew to her mouth as she absorbed the contents, and then she handed the phone back to Henry, her eyes reflecting shock and realization.

"Henry, do you know what might be on this thing?" she asked urgently, her expression serious, nodding toward the USB stick on the table.

Mike's mind reeled as Henry laid out his theory to Sarah, his words heavy in the air. "It was murder," Henry declared with a chilling certainty that shocked Mike.

Sarah, equally shocked, leaned in, her eyes wide with disbelief. "Murder?" she echoed, struggling to grasp the enormity of Henry's suggestion.

Henry nodded solemnly. "Murder. The passengers on that flight didn't die because of an accident. Someone murdered them all. I believe that drive may contain evidence."

Sarah remained silent for a while, sitting in her seat.

"Your tea, it's getting cold," Henry said after a while.

"Oh, yeah. OK, thanks," Sarah responded automatically, her voice distant as she reached for her laptop. She powered it up, her movements mechanical, still absorbing Henry's words.

Sarah picked up the USB stick and plugged it into her laptop. "SerenitySeeker53085," Henry revealed the password. He looked at Mike. "It's my boat. We used to go out on it all the time. The numbers are the marina zip code."

Sarah, absorbed in her task, typed the password into her laptop. The screen came alive with folders and files, and she delved into the digital depths of the drive. Mike and Henry sat in tense silence, exchanging uneasy glances, the only sound the distant hum of traffic and Sarah's methodical clicking.

After what felt like an eternity, Sarah broke the silence. "Flight control system," she murmured, her tone reflecting horror and realization. "It's all on this drive. Photographs, emails, videos. I don't know how they got all this stuff, but it is clear evidence of sabotage in the downing of the flight this Viktor Malaba person died on. This company, Alithia, appears to be behind it."

"Yes, I thought that's how they did it," Henry responded, his voice steady but carrying an undercurrent of anger. "So, I believe they did the same with Vivair."

"Yes, I mean, it is possible. No black boxes were recovered from Vivair. They haven't found them yet; I heard on the radio. I mean, I thought that odd. Guys, I don't need to tell you how big or serious this is or could be. If I am going to help you, we need to strategize. If they can bring down commercial airliners at will, then we're in grave danger and need to get to grips with our opposition. The consequences of speaking to the wrong person are obvious."

Mike sat there, suddenly feeling cold, looking at Sarah, Henry, and then back at Sarah. Henry remained stoic. None of this appeared surprising to him.

"Shit just got real," Henry stated, breaking the thick tension. His words, though simple, echoed the seriousness of their predicament. Mike sat there, feeling overwhelmed and out of his depth, the severity of their situation pressing down on him like a lead weight.

Mike fidgeted in his seat. "OK, what do we do?" he stammered, his voice quivering with nerves.

Sarah, leaning back in her chair, replied chillingly, "Not getting killed is our top priority."

Mike attempted a weak smile.

Sarah leaned forward, her expression serious. "This is huge, earth-shattering, but it's also dangerous. If they find out we have this information, they won't hesitate to silence us."

Henry nodded in agreement, his face stern. "She's right. We need to protect this data at all costs and trust no one. Alithia's reach is far and wide—lots of fingers in many pies."

Mike wrung his hands, feeling overwhelmed. "Shouldn't we hand this over to the FBI or something? They deal with this kind of stuff, right?"

Henry turned to Mike, his gaze intense. "We can't trust anyone. Not the FBI, not any law enforcement. The risk of this information being buried or used against us is too high. We need to keep it close until the time is right."

Sarah said, her tone firm, "We go public when we have enough to protect ourselves. Daylight is our best defense."

Mike sat in silence, his thoughts at full pelt. He reflected again on the routine life he'd had just a week ago, and now he was involved in a conspiracy that could cost him his life. He remembered Henry's comment about retribution and felt a newfound determination quietly begin stirring within him.

"So, what's next?" Mike asked, his voice steadier.

"We keep up appearances," Sarah stated. "To the world, you're still the Luckiest Man Alive. But we need to keep you safe. I don't want to scare you."

"It's a bit late," Mike whispered.

"And Silas Knox will help us," she added, explaining her trust in him.

"Who is this Silas?" Henry asked.

"He was an investigative reporter for TV in the UK, and we worked together on a big political story a few years ago. Anyway, he now runs the website luke-817.org. You may have heard of it. It helps whistleblowers publish classified information."

"This Silas guy, this stuff won't faze him. He's, like, been there, done that?" Mike said.

"Something like that," said Sarah.

Mike listened, his anxiety mingling with a sense of purpose. "I'm scared," he admitted, his voice barely above a whisper. "I wanted a simple life, not this."

"The thing is, you're already involved. Sarah here saw the handoff from Chloe in the video, so I'm guessing the bad guys did, too. They'll be coming for you, no doubt about it," Henry said.

Mike swallowed hard, his eyes darting between Henry and Sarah.

"Henry's right. We need to be very careful. They will want what we have, and they will kill us to get it."

"Shit," Mike whispered.

A new feeling struck Mike that felt like electricity. He remembered being back in his apartment, waiting for his Uber to take him to the airport, how he'd felt so low. Now, he felt scared, petrified, but there was something else—excitement, or purpose? He was unsure but felt more alive than he had in a long time.

Mike smiled. A weak half smile. He hoped a new version of himself might form, but he wasn't sure. He was desperate for that person to emerge before it was too late.

CHAPTER 18

Silas Knox sat at his desk in the dusty office in London's Soho. He drummed his fingers impatiently as he read the latest developments on the Vivair crash. They still hadn't recovered the black boxes, and there remained only talking-head speculation on what had caused the plane to crash into the Atlantic.

The office, though modest, held significance for Silas. His friend and benefactor, Lord Jonathan Worthington, a notable figure in the House of Lords, had provided it. Their friendship, rooted in their university days, had stood the test of time. Lord Worthington's generosity had become the lifeblood of Luke, the platform Silas ran, and his gratitude ran deep.

Lord Worthington's visits were frequent, each time brimming with curiosity for the latest scoop and offering unwavering support. "What's on your agenda, Silas? Do you need any bills cleared? New tech?" His questions were always coupled with a genuine willingness to help, whether covering travel costs, assisting with administrative tasks, or even making tea. Silas often wondered how he'd manage without such steadfast support.

Interrupting his thoughts, Sue, his assistant, tapped lightly on the glass door and stepped in, bringing with her the familiar comfort of morning routine—a steaming coffee and a ham-and-cheese croissant. She placed them before him with a knowing smile.

As he savored his breakfast, Silas's thoughts drifted to Sarah. He reminisced about their intense collaboration on a challenging investigation, the thrill of their successful publication day, and the fleeting, passionate affair that had followed. Their intense and brief relationship had burned brightly like a supernova, leaving a lingering afterglow in its wake.

Silas grappled with the reality of his situation, his thoughts a tangle of fear, disbelief, and a newfound sense of purpose. With everything up in the air, he couldn't help but think of Sarah. Her resolve, the apparent vulnerability beneath her tough exterior, and her courage had always struck a chord with him. The prospect of working with her again on an important, high-profile story brought a wave of excitement, a counterpoint to the superficial world of pampered TV stars and their sordid proclivities.

He contemplated reaching out to her, working out their next move; he didn't want to stand still; he needed to keep working, keep moving. The shrill ringer of his phone interrupted his thoughts. Grabbing the handset, he heard Sue's voice on the other end.

"Sarah's on the line. Shall I connect you?"

"Yes, please," Silas replied, a sense of anticipation building.

The line clicked, and Sarah's voice filled the room: "OK, this is serious."

"Sarah! I was just about to call you," he said, trying to inject a bit of lightness into his voice.

"I need to see you, Silas. It's urgent," Sarah's voice came through, laden with seriousness.

Taken aback by the urgency in her tone, Silas responded quickly, "Of course, I'll come. Let me check the flights and get back to you ASAP."

"Thanks. I'll wait for your call," Sarah said before the line went dead.

Silas set the phone down, a whirlwind blowing through his thoughts. He knew whatever Sarah had uncovered must be significant. With determination, he began making arrangements for an impromptu trip to Chicago. The stakes were high, and he sensed the burden of responsibility resting on his shoulders.

Silas leaned back in his chair, his mind turning over the possibilities of what Sarah's urgent call could mean. He knew all too well the significance of her reluctance to discuss details over the phone. Picking up his phone, he dialed his assistant, Sue.

"I need to get to Chicago ASAP. Something's come up; it sounds big. Can you find me the quickest flight out?" he asked.

Twenty minutes later, Sue entered his office, notepad in hand, with a selection of flight options. "The earliest I could get you out is tomorrow morning, first thing. Lufthansa via Munich. You'll be in Chicago by two p.m. Economy class, just over a thousand dollars," she briefed him.

"That's perfect, Sue. Book it and send the details to Jonathan. I'll let him know what's up," Silas said, his mind already zooming ahead to Chicago.

After wrapping up his workday, Silas headed home, ditching his evening plans with Lord Jonathan. He needed to be sharp for the journey ahead. At home, he sat in bed, the glow of his laptop illuminating the room as he scrolled through emails. He had already informed Sarah of his flight details, and she promised to pick him up. His attempts at gleaning more information from her had been fruitless; she remained tight-lipped about the situation.

Packing had been a hasty affair as he'd grabbed essentials and some cash, unsure of the duration of his stay in Chicago. After setting his alarm for the early morning, Silas closed his laptop and flicked on the TV, hoping for a distraction. But his mind seemed elsewhere, teeming with questions and possibilities. Once it arrived, sleep proved fitful, filled with anticipation of the unknown challenges awaiting him in Chicago.

The following day, the journey to the airport was uneventful.

He'd even had time to grab a coffee and breakfast before boarding the flight to Munich and changing planes for the Chicago flight. Luckily, with the flight half empty, he could move from his assigned seat to an empty row farther back, enjoying the ability to spread out. Traveling light, he avoided lingering at O'Hare's baggage claim. The flight's on-time arrival meant he'd made it to the other side forty-five minutes after touchdown, the inevitable holdup at US immigration only slightly delaying his progress.

Silas scanned the sea of waiting faces as he emerged through the doors into the arrival hall. He spotted Sarah straightaway. She looked stunning, and as Silas got closer, her sparkling brown eyes met his, followed by a smile as big as his own. They embraced for a long time, Silas dropping his bags where he stood, then remembering that one of them contained his laptop.

He greeted Sarah and scanned her face, asking how she had been.

"I've been good, a lot going on, but otherwise, I'm well. How about you? Still smoking?" she said, looking at him, her head tilted to one side.

"Well, you know, I have cut back."

"Thank you so much for coming out," Sarah said as she surveyed the crowd by the arrival hall doors. "Let's go to the car."

Silas picked up his bags and followed her as she headed to the exit.

Sarah popped the trunk when they got to the car, and Silas stowed his bags. He turned to Sarah as soon as they sat down in the car.

"So, what's the story, morning glory?"

Sarah looked back at him, and they locked eyes.

"This is serious shit, and I have to say I'm petrified. But I know it's a big story, huge. The implications are enormous."

Silas's heart skipped a beat. "I'm all ears."

Sarah delved into the details—the mysterious absence of the

black boxes, the tangled web of Njala's politics, Chloe Mitchell, Mike, Henry, and the enigmatic thumb drive.

"This is, well, I don't know what it is, but . . ." Silas trailed off.

"Yeah, that was my reaction: shock, excitement, closely followed by fear."

"I haven't got past the shock bit yet," Silas said.

"What do you think?" Sarah asked him.

"I think I need to see that thumb drive."

They pulled out of the parking lot and headed downtown.

"Where are we going?" Silas asked.

"The RV."

CHAPTER 19

In the opulent bathroom of the presidential palace, President Jibril Abena stood before a grand mirror, his reflection staring back at him. He scrutinized himself, seeing the image that he believed others perceived: a figure of inflated importance, lacking true merit. This realization, heavy and undeniable, pressed in upon him, giving him an uncomfortable feeling in his chest. The ticking clock of his presidency echoed in his mind, a relentless reminder of his dwindling days in power. The grandeur around him felt more like a fading illusion, a prelude to the impending collapse of his contrived position. The inevitability of his situation gave him an unmistakable sense of doom that seemed to permeate every corner of his being.

His hand delved into his pocket, retrieving his nondescript new phone, which he carefully placed on the countertop. His gaze lingered on it, understanding its significance in the precarious game he now played. This simple device, unassuming in appearance, would be his lifeline, a slender barrier separating him from the abyss.

Memories of his shantytown youth mingled with recollections of his days as a well-connected fixer, shaping his mindset for survival as he worked his way up from nothing. These experiences had honed him, preparing him for the treacherous path he now walked. His gaze remained fixed on the phone, knowing it would soon be time to reach out to an old, reliable contact—someone from his past whom he still trusted, luckily, with his life.

The president, the phone tucked inside his tunic, made his way out of the grand bathroom. He had a crucial call to make, a plan dependent on secrecy and a swift execution. But making the call from the palace would be too risky. Moving with purpose, he left a hastily written note for his wife, choosing not to speak out loud, his paranoia growing with every hour. Her understanding nod would be his only parting assurance.

He strode through the palace, ignoring the footman's attempts to attend to him, and headed straight for his wife's silver Toyota Land Cruiser. Slipping into the driver's seat, Abena fired up the engine, feeling unseen eyes upon him like he was a hen under the watchful gaze of foxes in the darkness.

Driving off, he noticed the two black SUVs tailing him, a silent confirmation of his suspicions. The forty-five-minute journey to his mother's farm seemed longer under their watchful presence. But as he turned onto the dirt track leading to the farm, the SUVs halted, content to wait at a distance.

The farm served as a haven, a place to momentarily escape the looming threats. The warm African sun, the scent of earth and grass, and the distant birdsong all grounded him and reminded him of simpler times. He parked near the entrance, casting a wary glance around before stepping out, the earth of home solid beneath his boots.

The embrace of his mother, her vibrant attire contrasting with the stark white walls of the modern farmhouse, offered a fleeting sense of comfort. The familiar aroma of home-cooked meals and the laughter of family inside provided a temporary refuge.

In this sanctuary, Jibril found a connection to his roots, a reminder of the simplicity and beauty inherent in his heritage. Amid the savannah's vast expanse and under Africa's endless sky, he found a fleeting sense of solace, a hint of his identity beyond the president's mantle. Here, he could briefly forget the coming storm and immerse himself in the comforting embrace of home.

In the warm glow of the setting sun, he walked through the fields of his mother's farm. He had come here to make a crucial, secret call, a lifeline for his family's safety. His brother, Cedric, accompanied him, oblivious to the true purpose of their stroll.

As they neared the barn, Jibril felt the familiar pang of nostalgia and a sense of urgency. He needed to act fast to utilize this brief window of opportunity to ensure his family's escape from Njala. He asked Cedric to wait outside and keep an ear out for their mother's dinner call.

Inside the barn, Jibril took out the new phone, checked for a signal, offered a quick prayer of thanks for three bars, and dialed a number etched in his memory. "Ezekial? Is it you, my brother?" he whispered, his voice both hopeful and desperate. Ezekial's affirmative response immediately soothed him. Jibril quickly made his request, speaking rapidly but clearly—he needed to get his family out of Njala immediately.

"I am in trouble. They are coming for me. My presidency will soon be over. I have a small window of time, an opportunity to act fast and protect my family. I must get them out of Njala—Nia and the children. It has to happen tomorrow; we can't waste time. I have money in Geneva; we have to get them there where they will be safe and cared for. Can you help me, Ezekial?"

"I can do it. Give me ten minutes, and I will call you back on this number," he said before disconnecting.

Jibril looked pained yet felt unburdened, glad to have taken action.

He pulled out a three-legged stool from the corner of the barn and stared at it, wondering if it would hold his weight. He hovered over it before sitting, the wood creaking but not giving out. He sat there with his elbows on his knees and the phone inches from his face, waiting for Ezekial to call back. If anyone could arrange a swift exit from the country, it was Ezekial. Known as the fixer's fixer, he had never let Jibril down in all their years of acquaintance, not even once. Jibril swallowed hard, knowing now was not the time to change that record.

After about ten minutes, which felt like an eternity to Jibril, the phone rang. He stabbed at the answer button.

"Hello? Ezekial?"

"Yes, Jibril, relax. I am making the arrangements. I will have a plane at Mkumbwa Airfield at dawn tomorrow. Do you know it?"

"Yes, north of the city. I know it."

"Correct. I will have a plane waiting there for you. It will fly you, Nia, and the children to Marrakesh. From there, another plane, a bigger one, will take you to Geneva."

"I am not going," Jibril said.

"What?"

"I want my family safe. I still have things to attend to. I will leave later."

"Well, if you are sure . . .?"

"I am certain. Now, this plane in Mkumbwa, is it safe? I want the best aircraft and the best pilot."

"It is safe, Jibril, trust me. It will have two pilots, both ex–air force. The best of the best. You do not need to worry about that, my old friend."

"Thank you, Ezekial."

"Tell your wife that she can bring no luggage, a handbag only. Same for the children. Nothing that isn't imperative. Is that OK?"

"Well, you know Nia, she will complain, but she can go shopping in Geneva, no problem."

"OK, then, it's all set, my friend. Tomorrow at six hundred hours. They will wait for us."

"Thank you, Ezekial. I will repay you, my friend."

"Please, it is my pleasure. Now, get everyone prepared. I will meet you at the palace tomorrow morning at five."

"We will need a diversion. They are watching everything. They will pursue us."

"We will have two cars. I will plan the diversion. Do not worry, Jibril. I will take care of everything."

Ezekial disconnected, and Jibril let out a long sigh. As he did so, the stool collapsed beneath him, and he hit the dirt floor with a thud accompanied by the sound of cracking wood and a plume of dust. Cedric rushed in, laughing, when he saw that Jibril was OK.

After Cedric had helped Jibril back to his feet and dusted him off they strode back to the farmhouse, Jibril's laughter mingled with his brother's, a rare sound of genuine joy. Each step toward the familiar warmth of home lightened Abena's heart, albeit fleetingly.

With its rustic charm and unspoiled vistas, the farm momentarily transported him away from his presidential woes. Here, amid the earthy scents and the honest toiling of the land, Jibril found a sliver of peace. Stepping through the doorway, he entered the embrace of homey aromas from a lovingly prepared dinner, with the chatter of family life enveloping him like a comforting shawl.

Yet, beneath this facade of normalcy, a storm of emotions raged within him. He couldn't shake off the deep-seated shame for his role in his country's plight. His once proud nation, now entangled in a web partly of his own making, scratched at his conscience. Ensuring the safety of his wife, Nia, and their children stood as his paramount task, the first step toward redemption. The thought of fleeing, of abandoning the land he loved, lingered in his mind, an unspoken plan waiting its turn. For now, he could only focus on getting his family to the safety of Switzerland, their unmentioned impending departure casting a shadow over the evening's familial warmth.

CHAPTER 20

Gathered around the modest dining table inside Big Bertha, Silas Knox, Sarah, Mike, and Henry sipped their coffee in the cramped space. Henry broke the silence first.

"Sarah's told us quite a bit about you, Mr. Knox," he said, eyeing Silas with curiosity.

"All good things, I hope. And please, call me Silas," he replied, offering a friendly smile to lighten the mood.

His gaze shifted to Mike, who recoiled under the attention. "So, you're the Luckiest Man Alive. Good to meet you, Mike." Silas said, smiling broadly.

Mike felt his cheeks redden, with embarrassment wafting over him. He looked down, stumbling over his words. "Don't feel very lucky, to be honest. You've seen the video?"

Silas nodded, his expression sympathetic. "Yes. It's unfortunate for you, obviously, but on the plus side, it's brought us all together." He said, opening his arms.

Henry interjected, his voice urgent, his disdain for small talk evident: "Has Sarah filled you in on everything?"

Silas leaned forward, his focus sharpening. "She has. Can I take a look at the drive?"

Without a word, Henry slid the USB stick across the table.

Silas pulled out his laptop, his fingers poised over the keyboard. "The password?"

Henry answered quickly. "SerenitySeeker53085, capital S's. No gaps."

Silas's fingers danced across the keys as he opened the files. The RV fell into a tense silence, punctuated once again by careful clicks and the occasional passing car. Mike watched intently, reading Silas's reactions as his eyes darted across the screen, his face a canvas of concentration and occasional disbelief.

Abruptly, Silas stood up, a hand brushing through his long hair. "I need a cigarette," he muttered, stepping outside into the fresh air.

Mike and Henry exchanged glances. Sarah, sensing their concern, reassured them. "Silas needs a moment when he smokes. It's his way of processing."

A few minutes later, Silas returned, the faint scent of tobacco trailing him. He resumed his work, his focus undisturbed by his brief exit. After an intense examination, he finally shut his laptop, making Mike jump. He was now facing the anxious eyes around the table.

Mike couldn't contain his curiosity. "Well? What do you think?"

Silas leaned back, his expression grave. "It's explosive. It's the biggest story I've ever encountered. But it's also incredibly dangerous. We're treading on thin ice here."

"So, what's the plan?" Henry asked, his voice firm.

"We need to talk about what we have here. I like to start with the basics and work outward. This is so potentially earth-shattering, so huge, that it could be difficult to get a handle on what we do with it. So, let's start with an overview."

Mike leaned forward, his gaze fixed on Silas as he spoke. The idea of starting with the basics resonated with him: first principles stuff. The structured approach he'd been trained in sparked a flicker of confidence in him. *I might actually be able to contribute something valuable here.* He nodded in agreement, ready to dive into the depths of this daunting, yet intriguing puzzle. Being part of something this significant felt both intimidating and exhilarating.

Silas spoke again, pointing at the USB stick. "The evidence points to persons unknown, affiliated with this Alithia Corp, being involved in bringing down a commercial airliner, the one carrying Viktor Mabala. It would appear they did this by interfering with the flight control systems on board the aircraft. Lansdown Aerospace manufactures and maintains flight control systems for the military and commercial sectors, and they are a subsidiary of Alithia Corp. Given the passenger manifest, we can assume that they were probably behind the downing of Vivair 002. So, they are the basics."

"It's a good theory, but we don't know the mechanism. How did they do it?" asked Sarah.

"Well, it would be sophisticated and require a team. There will be weak links if it's a conspiracy; you can count on it. So, let's brainstorm a little on the likely mechanisms. First is the infrastructure. They may have infiltrated critical positions within aviation, such as the control tower, maintenance crew, or the airline itself. This would provide them with access to essential systems."

Mike's eyebrows knitted together as he listened intently to Sarah's question and Silas's response. The idea of a sophisticated operation involving multiple players started to take shape in his mind. He imagined faceless figures lurking in the shadows of control towers, blending into maintenance crews and infiltrating airline staff. These were the people who could have access to the very lifeblood of the planes' operations, the ones who could turn a routine flight into a tragedy. Mike's grip tightened around his coffee mug, his sense of unease growing as he considered the terrifying implications of such deep infiltration.

Mike leaned forward as Silas outlined the second possible mechanism. "Cyber-intrusion," Silas said. "They could have compromised the airline's systems."

Mike's eyes widened slightly. "That seems a bit sci-fi, doesn't it?" he interjected. "Wouldn't there be obvious evidence of such an attack?"

Silas nodded, acknowledging Mike's point. "You'd think so. But last year at DEFCON, I saw what hackers can do with minimal equipment. Anything's possible." He then moved on to another theory involving aviation experts physically tampering with the flight control systems. Henry interjected, "But that would mean they all knew what they were doing . . . that they were OK with killing hundreds."

"That's why I think the covert installation of devices on the aircraft is more likely. Fewer people involved," Silas continued, his theory gaining momentum.

Henry, looking troubled, asked, "So, how did they cover their tracks?"

Silas paused, his expression turning grave. "A cover-up would involve manipulating evidence, silencing witnesses. It's why the black boxes haven't been found. They control the narrative."

Sarah leaned in, shifting the focus. "But it's a big conspiracy, right? We've got Viktor Mabala, eyewitnesses, and a video of the black boxes being stolen from the crash site. They must have known in advance where it was going to crash. That much is clear."

Silas nodded. "Yes, that video is crucial. We have evidence against Alithia, but is it enough? We need to find the weak link in their chain."

Mike sat back, absorbing the enormity of the task ahead. Theories about covert operations and conspiracies swirled in his head, each more alarming than the last. This situation transcended him being the Luckiest Man Alive; it involved unraveling a plot straight out of a Netflix movie.

Mike, feeling slightly out of his depth, listened intently as Henry asked the pivotal question: "So, how do we do that: find the weak link?" Mike's gaze shifted to Silas as he laid out his plan to set a trap. Silas talked about publishing an article on Viktor Malaba, leading readers to make their own connections. Send a tweet telling everyone his DMs were open, fishing for whistleblowers. It all sounded like spy novel tactics to Mike.

Mike couldn't help but feel a little useless. "So, what do I do?" he asked, his voice betraying a hint of helplessness.

Sarah offered a straightforward and practical solution. "You can't go back to your apartment. Come stay in my spare room," she said.

Mike, slightly taken aback but feeling grateful, just smiled and nodded.

As they wrapped up their strategy, Silas emphasized the importance of caution and secure communication. "Remember, don't trust anyone outside of this RV. If everyone agrees, I will make some copies, keep them safe, and bring the original USB stick back and get it analyzed," he said.

They all nodded their agreement.

Henry, trying to lighten the mood, quipped, "OK folks, stay frosty," leaving Mike puzzled. "Just something we used to say in my combat days," Henry explained.

Did he wink? Mike sat there, absorbing everything. The reality of the situation fully dawned on him now. He was no longer just a bystander in his own story; he was right in the middle of something potentially world-changing, dangerous, and surreal.

CHAPTER 21

As Sarah maneuvered her car through the streets, her mind had blown up a cyclone of thoughts and concerns. Beside her, Silas, ever the coolheaded investigator, broke the silence. "Are they going to be OK?" he asked.

Sarah's grip on the steering wheel tightened slightly. "I don't know—honestly, I hardly know them. Henry's tough, but Mike? He's why I'm worried." She glanced briefly at Silas, her face etched with concern. "He seems fragile," she added, thinking about how Mike's life had been turned upside down and inside out in such a short period.

Silas nodded, understanding. "Well, I guess his life just exploded, so we should maybe cut him some slack?" he suggested, sounding empathetic.

Sarah sighed as she thought about what they were dealing with. "The crash itself is hard for him to handle, let alone all this other stuff. I'm worried."

As they pulled into the hotel parking lot, Silas's advice was simple. "Just monitor him; make sure he doesn't do anything stupid. Stay out of sight until the rats are in the open, scurrying for cover."

As Sarah pulled to a halt at the entrance, Silas turned to her, a hint of weariness in his eyes. "You not coming in? I could use a stiff drink," he said, grinning.

Sarah paused and glanced at the hotel entrance, then back at Silas, her thoughts momentarily clouded by their shared history. She gave a quick nod. "OK, just one. You grab your things and get checked in, and I'll park and meet you in the bar." Watching Silas smile and exit the car, she felt trepidation and a hint of excitement.

Later Sarah watched Silas as he walked into the bar, relaxed yet attentive. Two Moscow mules, his favorite, sat on the table in front of her. Silas's smile widened as he approached. "You remembered!"

"Yup, your favorite, right?" Sarah replied, managing a big smile despite the storm of thoughts swirling in her head.

They sat in silence for a moment, the tangy taste of the cocktails providing a brief respite. "Great working with you again," Silas said, finally breaking the silence, raising his drink in a toast.

Sarah took a thoughtful sip, her gaze fixed on her drink. "I wish it were under less horrifying circumstances, but it feels good. Not going to lie."

Silas spoke enthusiastically. "I feel energized by this story. I'm so glad you thought of me. This is the big one. Pulitzer stuff."

"Are you not scared?" Sarah asked, her voice edged with concern.

"Of course, it's terrifying. Big stories shouldn't be a walk in the park," Silas replied, his confidence unwavering.

Sarah leaned back, absorbing his words. "This is another level, Silas. This is mass murder. It's beyond the pale. It's evil. Don't you feel it?" she whispered, leaning forward again.

"It's all those things, and that's why it needs the daylight we will provide," Silas said, his determination coming through loud and clear.

Sarah couldn't help but notice the fire in Silas's eyes. "You're loving this."

"I was born for this story," he stated, his conviction clear.

She finished her drink and sat back, a range of emotions playing across her face. "What's up, petal?" he asked.

Sarah sighed, feeling overwhelmed. "I don't know. It's all happening so fast. Still getting my head around the implications, I guess."

"We're a team; worry not. Another mule?" Silas asked playfully.

"I said just one," Sarah replied with a half-hearted smirk that betrayed her inner turmoil.

"I know what you said, petal," Silas said, grinning.

The next morning, Sarah woke to find Silas on the balcony, a cigarette in hand. "Morning, petal. Coffee?" he offered as she stirred.

"Uh, what time is it?" Sarah asked, her voice groggy, her head throbbing from the previous night's indulgence.

"Ten a.m.; you were out like a light. I hope I didn't wake you. My flight leaves just before one, the earliest one I could find, United via Newark. I'll be back in Blighty early tomorrow, ready to start work," Silas said with a grin, his energy contrasting starkly with her lethargy.

"What just happened?" Sarah asked, her memory hazy.

"I think they call it a 'rekindling'? Something like that. Any regrets?" Silas inquired, a playful glint in his eyes.

Sarah felt a whirlwind of emotions as she sat across from Silas at the breakfast table later. Her head still throbbed slightly. She sipped her coffee slowly, trying to ground herself in the familiar bitterness. "That mule kicks hard. How come you're so chipper?" she asked, her voice a curious blend of admiration and envy.

Silas shrugged. "I don't know, tolerance? Or adrenaline. Bit of both, I suspect." His infectious energy contrasted with Sarah's demeanor; she struggled to match it, weighed down by the enormity of their situation and a sizeable hangover.

As Silas excitedly loaded his plate with a hearty breakfast, Sarah could only manage to nurse her coffee. The room seemed too bright and loud, and she donned her sunglasses to shield herself from the sensory overload. Silas noticed. "The hangover is that bad?"

Sarah sighed. "I'm just not used to it. I haven't let loose in a long time. All I seem to do is work." Her confession went beyond the hangover.

Silas's question about her dating life only added to her introspection. "Well, no, just work. You used the word 'rekindling' earlier, but we should leave it at a 'reconnection,' Silas. The reasons we broke up before still exist, don't they?" Her confession acknowledged the consuming nature of their jobs.

Understanding yet hopeful, Silas responded, "Look, petal, it's been wonderful to see you again. I understand what you're saying. The story gets all my energy and focus until the truth is out. Let's see what happens afterward?"

Sarah pondered the enormity of the task ahead. "If work took up all my time before, I don't know what the next few months will look like. It's scary and exciting, but maybe more the former than the latter right now," she admitted, her eyes fixed on her half-empty coffee mug.

After breakfast, their farewell at the airport blended professional resolve with personal warmth. "Stay strong, Sarah. We'll get through this together, and on the other side, we'll write that book together," Silas said, his embrace comforting.

Sarah, her heart lifted by the thought, replied with a smile. "OK, call me when you're back at the office. Remember, everything goes through the Signal app. Security is paramount."

As Silas disappeared into the security area, Sarah felt a strong determination and noticed a tinge of pleasure from their brief reconnection.

As she navigated her car from the airport, the mixed emotions from her encounter with Silas gave way to a sharp focus on the daunting task ahead. The familiar fear, always lurking in the background of her investigative work, surfaced like a shark near the beach. Yet the excitement and satisfaction of seeing Silas again tempered it, offering a brief respite from the intense pressure of their new mission.

Driving back to the RV, her thoughts drifted to the winding path of her journalism career. Sarah had come a long way from her humble beginnings at the *Quincy Sun*, where her parents had proudly displayed her first byline about a bear sighting. Those early days had planted the seeds of her tenacity and commitment to uncovering the truth.

As a junior reporter at the *Examiner* in Boston, she had carved out a name for herself, delving into stories with the depth and rigor that set her apart. Her work there, especially her exposé on local political corruption, had brought about real change and cemented her reputation as a fearless journalist.

Going freelance had been a leap of faith, propelling her into the big leagues of journalism. The Senator Connelly story, a highlight of her career, had demonstrated her ability to navigate complex, high-stakes investigations, earning her both respect and a comfortable lakeside home in Indiana. The house that Connelly built, she called it.

She reflected on the path ahead as she steered toward her biggest story yet. This went beyond being just another scoop; it represented a battle against a faceless evil, a force that callously prioritized profit over hundreds of lives. Sarah's resolve hardened. The skills and connections she had honed over the years weren't just tools for her career anymore; they were weapons in a fight for justice.

As the RV appeared in front of her, Sarah steeled herself for the challenges ahead. This story, the Vivair crash, was not just another headline; it was a clarion call for accountability, a chance to shine a light on the darkest corners of corporate and political power. The thought of the lives lost, and the families shattered by greed fueled her determination. She would stop at nothing to ensure the truth came out and those responsible paid for their heinous actions. For Sarah, this meant more than journalism; it had become a personal crusade for justice.

CHAPTER 22

As Jibril steered the Land Cruiser off the dirt path from his mother's farmhouse, the evening sky deepened into twilight. He glanced in the rearview mirror, alerting him to the two black SUVs parked where he remembered. No sooner had he merged onto the main road than the SUVs roared to life, blatantly tailing him. Their lack of subtlety, the arrogance of their pursuit, scared him. It delivered a clear warning: they weren't merely observing now but closing in.

Jibril drove the Land Cruiser toward the presidential palace, which loomed ahead. Just shy of nine o'clock, he carefully exited the vehicle, moving deliberately and cautiously. He slipped through the rear entrance, silently offering a prayer of thanks once more. Inside the spacious sitting room, he found his wife, Nia, seated on the edge of the couch. Her eyes, typically warm, now reflected the storm of thoughts in his mind. Their eyes met, and they exchanged nods, conveying an unspoken understanding. The time had now come to act, to put their escape plan into motion. The enormity of that simple, silent agreement pressed upon Jibril as he advanced further into the room, each step marking a silent countdown to an uncertain future.

Jibril watched Nia retreat from the room, her steps measured but heavy with the burden of their impending departure. He settled himself at the writing desk, his fingers instinctively brushing against the phone in his left pocket. It had transformed into more than just a device; it now served as their lifeline. He withdrew his regular phone from his right pocket and set it on the desk; its presence reminded him of the role he would soon abandon.

A restless energy propelled him to the bedroom, where he found Nia seated on the edge of the bed, a picture of vulnerability. He approached her, his heart aching at her distress. "Nia, do not cry," he implored softly, his voice comforting and commanding. He longed to offer more than words, to shield her from the turmoil of their lives.

Jibril watched Nia dab at her tears with a tissue, her sniffles punctuating the tense silence of the room. Guilt scratched away at him as he gazed at her, his heart aching with the realization that his actions had led them here. Nia had been his steadfast support throughout their life together, yet now she had to face this tumultuous upheaval. He couldn't afford to wallow in self-reproach. Their escape and survival were paramount.

Jibril gestured for silence and reached for a notepad to maintain their precarious secrecy. His pen moved quickly across the paper, scribbling a crucial reminder:

Ensure the children are ready for Ezekial's arrival at dawn.

He handed the note to Nia. Her eyes scanned the message, and a faint smile touched her lips as she jotted a reply. She handed it back to him. His eyes traced her words:

I said goodbye to Amara. It was so sad. I don't know if I'll see her again.

Her straightforward, poignant words palpably conveyed the sorrow of potentially never seeing her friend again. Jibril felt her sadness, the emotional toll of their imminent escape.

In Jibril's eyes, Amara wasn't just his wife's assistant; she had become a dear friend to Nia, and their relationship had grown into something profound and heartfelt. Witnessing Nia's grief over potentially losing this cherished connection tugged painfully at his heart. He offered her a supportive nod, a silent acknowledgment of their shared sorrow, and quickly scribbled another note, a hopeful assurance:

We will be back, I promise you.

When he showed her the note, Nia's fragile and faint smile clearly indicated the uncertainty clouding their future. Jibril yearned to bolster her spirits, to bring back the confidence and joy that had once radiated from her, but his hands were tied by their grim reality. He silently destroyed the note in the bathroom, ensuring no trace of their plans remained. No trace of a promise he didn't think he could keep.

Back in the bedroom, he lay on the bed, a tumult of unspoken fears racing through his mind as he stared blankly at the ceiling. Beside him, Nia mirrored his anxiety, her gaze fixed on the void above. A paralyzing dread enveloped Jibril as he questioned their escape's success, his family's safety, and the looming uncertainty of his fate. He knew, deep down, that his chances of leaving Njala alive were slim.

But he couldn't afford to entertain these fears. His family's safety took precedence, and any display of weakness on his part could unravel their carefully laid plans. He resolved to stay strong, to be the steadfast anchor they needed in these turbulent times. He would have to postpone his fate; for now, he could only focus on the safety of his loved ones.

Time seemed to stretch endlessly in the tense silence of the room. Jibril's glance repeatedly fell on his watch, each tick echoing the urgency of their situation. Finally, the appointed hour arrived. Turning toward Nia, he gently nudged her, a silent signal. Her immediate response spoke volumes about her inner turmoil, a storm of anxiety she bravely contained for the sake of their children. Wordlessly, she slipped out to ready their young ones for the journey ahead.

Jibril swiftly donned his shoes, a sense of purpose steadying his movements. He soon joined his family in the hallway, where his children's wide-eyed stares met him. Fear replaced their usual vibrancy, instilling a stillness in them. An intuitive understanding of the seriousness of the situation made them unusually compliant.

Together, they traversed the palace's corridors, their swift footsteps echoing softly under the dimmed lights. The opulence around them felt surreal, a static contrast to the urgency of their escape. Dawn's first light filtered through, casting a gentle glow on the marble, adding an ethereal quality to their flight.

Nia's lingering gaze swept over the familiar grandeur, a silent farewell to the palace she had grown to love. Jibril noticed the sorrow in her eyes, a poignant reminder of what they were leaving behind. He would carry this sight with him, considering it a symbol of the sacrifices they made to pursue safety and a new beginning.

The crisp night air enveloped Jibril as he stepped outside, its tropical scent briefly suspending his peril. He led his family through the gardens, their hushed footsteps brushing against the meticulously kept grounds.

At the edge of the palace grounds, two black SUVs idled, their engines humming softly in the stillness of the predawn hour. Ezekiel, the architect of their escape, stood resolute by the lead vehicle. With their children in tow, Nia quickly climbed into the back seat. Jibril caught Ezekiel's eye, seeing the same fierce determination reflected in his gaze before Ezekiel slid into the driver's seat. Jibril sat in the second car, his mind in overdrive with thoughts of their perilous journey ahead.

As the convoy pulled away from the palace, a chill of foreboding crept over Jibril. He peered through the windshield at the vehicle ahead, carrying its precious cargo, his world. Doubts nagged at him, whispering fears of unseen threats lurking on the empty road. He couldn't shake off the sense of being watched, of not being as alone as the road suggested. He repeatedly glanced over his shoulder, searching for the ghostly glow of headlights in pursuit, but found none. Could their early departure have given them an edge? His heart rate steadied as the SUV continued unchallenged toward Mkumbwa Airfield, the landscape passing by in a hazy blur.

Jibril's heart raced as he watched the lead SUV skillfully swerve around a sharp bend, only to be confronted with an unexpected barricade strewn across the road. With the poise of a seasoned driver, Ezekiel executed a nerve-wracking maneuver, narrowly squeezing the vehicle through the small opening, tires perilously close to the road's edge. Jibril's grip tightened on the door handle in the second car, his muscles tensing. His mind raced with questions. The road had been clear the previous night; there had been no storms, nothing that could explain this sudden obstacle.

It dawned on him—someone had tracked them and was attempting to thwart their escape. Panic momentarily gripped him.

Quickly reacting, his driver slammed on the brakes and reversed sharply. He then accelerated through the gap, following closely behind Ezekiel's SUV. Jibril peered anxiously through the window, searching for any hint of pursuit or ambush. He could only see the expansive countryside, serene and undisturbed. His grip loosened as he considered the possibility it was a mere coincidence, perhaps the work of the forestry division clearing debris for fire prevention. But the timing felt too perfect, the placement too strategic. Deep down, Jibril couldn't dismiss the sensation that this went beyond mere happenstance.

Jibril's presidential phone vibrated abruptly, breaking the

tense silence in the SUV. Glancing at the screen, he spotted a cryptic message, a coded warning that someone had unveiled their escape plan. His heart sank, a chill coursing through him. Rampton's men were on their tail, much closer than Jibril had anticipated.

Peering nervously through the rear window, his worst fears materialized. In the distance, two large SUVs weaved through traffic, rapidly gaining on them. Quickly, he fished out his burner phone and dialed Ezekial. "We're being followed," he hissed into the phone. "We will lead them away. Ensure my family reaches the plane safely."

Ezekial's voice, steady yet urgent, came through. "Your driver knows what to do. You are the diversion, brother. May God protect you."

Jibril turned to his driver, his voice firm with resolve. "Let them get closer, then make a break for it." The driver nodded, easing off the accelerator, allowing the ominous SUVs to close in.

As their pursuers neared, the driver suddenly jerked the wheel, veering down a narrow alleyway in the shantytown, dust billowing in their wake. The SUV swerved left and right as it navigated the intricate maze of streets, the driver's detailed knowledge of the city obvious.

The chase intensified, with the pursuers doggedly tailing Jibril's vehicle. They hurtled down an alley that seemed to lead nowhere. At the last second, their SUV sharply turned into another alley, narrowly escaping a dead end. Jibril braced himself, straining against his seatbelt as the vehicle swayed violently, barely managing to stay on course.

Behind him, he saw their pursuers overshoot the turn, their momentum carrying them past the hidden alley. His driver took advantage of their mistake, accelerating down a long, straight stretch of road. Jibril scanned the road behind them. One, two, three checks, and only the empty road greeted him each time. The diversion had worked, for now.

He breathed a sigh of relief but knew the danger had not yet passed. The realization that they had been so close to being caught sent a wave of cold dread. The next few hours would be crucial.

Jibril looked over his shoulder again at the road behind just as the pursuing vehicles came once more into view. Dust clouds rose as they gunned their accelerators to resume the chase. With swift precision, his driver made a sharp left, then two rapid rights. The SUV surged and lunged left to right as it sped down a long, deserted road, the landscape opening up around them.

Jibril nodded, leaning back in his seat, allowing himself a deep, measured breath. The close call had rattled him; they had nearly been caught. But his quick thinking prevailed. Suddenly, a thought struck him, chilling him to the bone—his phone, they were tracking him. He couldn't believe that such a stupid mistake, so mundane, could be his undoing.

Without hesitation, he rolled down the window and flung his government-issued phone out. He watched it bounce off the rugged terrain and vanish into the undergrowth, severing his last ties with the presidency he had now left behind.

Jibril's gaze returned repeatedly to the road behind them. Each time, only the undulating hills and dusty roads of the Njalian countryside met his view. Relief washed over him as he realized they had successfully shaken off their pursuers.

"We've lost them, sir," his driver announced with a note of triumph.

As the SUV journeyed toward Kivuli, Jibril tried to find solace in the success of their escape. The drive to the safe house that Ezekial had arranged would be long. He'd set up a secluded farmhouse overlooking the town's hills. He wouldn't arrive until late afternoon, leaving him with hours to ponder the events and the uncertain path ahead.

After a time, the vibration of the burner phone in his pocket snapped him back to the present. He pulled out the device and read the message on the screen. His wife, Nia, and their children were safe, and they were in flight on their way to a new life.

Overcome with emotion, tears welled up in his eyes as he clutched the phone to his chest. They were safe, and he didn't care about anything else.

CHAPTER 23

Silas Knox, illuminated by the late-night glow of his computer screen, scrutinized the draft of his tweet. His dingy office remained silent, with only the soft tapping of keys and the occasional flick of a lighter breaking the quiet. The ashtray on his desk brimmed with cigarette butts.

The words on the screen read like the plot of a conspiracy thriller. "Njala's Mysterious Tale . . . Viktor Malaba's untimely end . . . Corporate colonization . . . Government in exile . . . Vivair crash . . ." The narrative wove a complex web with provocative phrases, each sentence crafted to stir the pot of public opinion and elicit a response.

Leaning back, Silas lit another cigarette, a wry smile forming as he exhaled a stream of smoke. The stakes were high. His heart raced with excitement and apprehension as he contemplated the potential fallout his words might create. He opened the bottom drawer of his desk and retrieved a bottle of Louis XIII Cognac, an expensive gift from his benefactor, Lord Jonathan Worthington. Tonight warranted the indulgence.

He had a clear rationale: cast a wide net with bold statements and wait for anyone with inside knowledge to bite. His half-

million followers on Twitter, combined with the allure of contro-
versy, would surely draw out someone with critical information.
The risk of exposure certainly existed, but Silas had always
thrived on the edge.

He clicked "Post" with a sense of irrevocable commitment.
Silas watched, waiting for the one message to make it all
worthwhile.

Almost immediately, the notifications started pinging, likes
and retweets, and soon, he hoped, direct messages.

A few minutes later, his Signal app notified him of an
incoming video call. It was Sarah. *Boy, that was quick.*

Silas connected, and Sarah's face appeared on the screen. She
did not look happy.

"Silas, what the fuck have you done?" she asked, her anger
obvious.

"Relax, petal, I—"

"I thought we agreed to be subtle? That was about as subtle
as a brick through the fucking window. Do you know what
you're doing?" Silas thought her expression seemed more
worried than angry.

"I have thought about this; it's the only way. It has just the
right balance. We're only asking questions, that's all. Why would
it raise any suspicions?"

"Fucking hell, that's exactly what it's going to do! Won't they
be curious about what we know? Jesus, Silas, I don't know what
to say."

"Please don't worry. I knew you'd react like this, so I didn't
tell you what I planned. We must draw the bad guys out into the
open; it's the only way."

"I'm not sure Mike will see the logic, Silas. If these people
connect the dots, Jesus, we know what they're capable of."

"How would they? We've put distance between all of us.
Unless they have a mole, which is impossible, then we are OK.
Honestly, relax."

"Stop fucking telling me to relax. They will have seen the video and seen what happened. They'll be looking for Mike, who is staying with me, for fuck's sake. I don't want them knocking my door down."

"OK, sorry. I get it, but it has to be this way; please trust me."

"You tell me anything good or bad as soon as you get any messages. Do you hear me?"

"Of course, I—"

"Never do this again without telling me."

She disconnected.

Silas expected a backlash, but the ferocity of Sarah's reaction had surprised him.

Notifications were still pinging, but no messages yet. He hoped he'd have his first lead by the morning.

The desk phone rang.

Silas hesitated before answering the phone. *Who the hell is ringing the office landline at midnight?*

"Silas, old boy, I knew you'd still be at the office."

"Good evening, Your Lordship; where are you, a strip club?" Silas's smile returned.

"Not quite, but pretty close to it."

"Why are you ringing so late? Is it urgent?"

"Well, like I said, I knew where you'd be, and I have just seen your tweet. I have a bit of gossip to pass on."

"Gossip?" Silas repeated, raising an eyebrow.

"OK, not gossip, just insider info. Anything to help, my dear friend."

Silas could tell Jonathan had been drinking. He must be on his third or fourth large cognac by now. "Oh, yes? Sounds intriguing. Spill the beans, then."

"Well, I am on the board of the Njala Mining Co. I bet you didn't know that, did you?"

"No, Jonathan, I didn't. I do not keep a dossier on all your business dealings."

Silas's forehead creased as a faint alarm bell started ringing in his head. *Njala?*

"I have tales to tell. It's a non-exec position, only one day a month, but we get to see some interesting facts and figures. Come to Cleargrove on Friday night; I'm having a little soiree. I'll fill you in."

"Sounds good, Jonathan. See you then."

"Cheerio."

Jonathan disconnected.

Once animated with a mischievous grin, Silas's face was now blank; the earlier vibrancy drained away. His entire demeanor had shifted from one of triumphant audacity to sobering apprehension.

How much did he know about Jonathan's business dealings? Why had he never dug into them? Was he willing to accept money without question? To him, Jonathan was a friend, off-limits. He swallowed something hard.

He opened the web browser on his laptop and searched for Njala Mining Co. The first result displayed a company profile page from Bloomberg: "Njala Mining Co. is a subsidiary of Alithia Mining and Commodities Inc., which has a controlling interest."

"Fuck," he said under his breath.

Jonathan knew all about the hurried trip to Chicago. He'd even paid for it. Then, as soon as Silas was back, he tweeted about Njala. Shit, maybe Sarah had been right. He felt panicked and stupid. This carried significant risk. To what extent was Jonathan involved? Who did he know at Alithia? How much had he already mentioned? Shit, shit, shit!

He drank the cognac, closed his laptop, and left the office.

Silas had difficulty sleeping that night. Too much coffee, nicotine, and cognac. Too many thoughts.

He gave up trying to sleep as soon as it started getting light and got up.

He paced around his flat, trying to think. He knew contacting Jonathan before noon had become an exercise in abject futility. How could he phrase it without setting off alarm bells? Jonathan was smart. He would put two and two together—a quick trip to Chicago and back. Then, Silas sent out contentious tweets about Njala. Jonathan would know they had something cooking. But how immersed was Jonathan in the business? A one-day-a-month non-exec role? *It's a prestige thing.* They could publicize that they had His Lordship Jonathan Worthington on the board as a marketing tool. He doubted whether Jonathan was involved in anything meaningful. It still sent shivers down his spine when he contemplated how close everything had come to his doorstep and how potentially foolish he might have been.

Silas picked up his phone and checked his Twitter notifications once again.

A lone direct message from a user named Njalion, a play on words. It read:

Mr. Knox, I have information that will interest you; I am sure of it. Please advise, as I have to be very careful.

Silas replied immediately.

Thank you. Elaborate if you can.

Then, another message appeared instantly:

Let's just say I'm a voice from the land where truth is buried. A friend of truth, and this puts me in grave peril. This Njalian lion needs your help to roar, Mr. Knox. The daylight must shine on the terrible darkness they are responsible for.

He thought someone could be horsing around until he received the third and final message.

Viktor's legacy haunts us. They are hunting me, so I have to be careful. Danger looms, but secrets must find the sun — the secrets of Vivair. I know the truth, and so must you.

The last message and the dark reference to Vivair made Silas's blood run cold.

CHAPTER 24

Dalton sat in his office at Alithia headquarters in Los Angeles, the clock ticking past midnight. His expression revealed nothing, betraying none of the thoughts marching through his head. He reclined in his chair, his feet casually propped on the table. The recent call from his operatives in Njala played over in his mind; they had allowed President Abena and his family to slip away, and Tyler Rampton no longer controlled events. Picking up the phone with a steady hand, Dalton dialed a number, his demeanor calm but his mind moving forward with plans and contingencies.

Dalton's voice remained steady as he initiated the call. "Tyler, it's Dalton."

An irritated voice answered: "Do you know what time it is?"

Dalton remained unfazed. "You're not at home."

"Well, no, but it's late."

"It's important. We have a problem," Dalton continued, his tone smooth and even.

"What is it?" Tyler sounded concerned.

"Abena has flown," Dalton stated matter-of-factly.

"What?" Tyler's voice spiked with surprise.

Dalton repeated, "Abena has flown."

Tyler's frustration emanated clearly as he spoke. "I heard you. I just—"

Dalton continued, undeterred. "They fled the palace. He had help. His current location is unknown. We don't know what he has."

"Fuck!" Tyler said, his rising an octave. "How has this happened? I thought . . ."

"You asked me to have him monitored. That's what we did."

"And, what? Nothing?"

"We detected nothing unusual."

Tyler accused, "So, he outwitted you, is that it?"

Dalton's voice remained calm. "As I said, he had help."

"Now what?"

"We are looking for him."

"I was told your team was the best, Dalton, the very best."

Dalton's face remained stoic, though a muscle twitched in his jaw.

"We are on it. We will find him."

Rampton issued a cold and definitive command: "Find and eliminate him. Do it swiftly."

The line went dead as Rampton hung up. Dalton placed the phone back on the desk, a smirk creeping across his face despite the news he'd just given Rampton.

Dalton's office was shrouded in darkness, the only light emanating from the laptop he'd just powered up. The light from the screen radiated an eerie glow across his face, lending him a ghoulish look as he settled into his chair. He delved into his email inbox, eyes scanning the influx of new messages. His attention zeroed in on the multiple alerts from the monitoring app—all triggered by mentions of Njala across various media platforms. He was on high alert, knowing the sensitivity of the situation.

Then, he found a tweet from Silas Knox that was causing a stir. Dalton's history with Knox went back to the fallout from the Connelly affair—another life, another assignment. His mental

Rolodex pulled out Knox's ties to Lord Jonathan Worthington, a pawn on Alithia Mining Co.'s chessboard and, conveniently, an employee under his indirect control. The contents of Knox's tweet narrowed Dalton's eyes in calculation; it was evident someone knew something.

He glanced at his watch, calculating the time difference. Morning in the UK. Perfect timing to leverage his hold on Worthington. Dalton's mind methodically assessed the possibilities. He had enough dirt on Worthington to coerce him into compliance. The right pressure on Worthington could be the key to reeling in Knox, perhaps even making him a pawn in Alithia's wider game.

He reached for his phone, scrolling through his contacts with a purposeful tap. Sending a barrage of messages, he soon secured Worthington's contact details. His first attempt, a call to Worthington's cell, led to voice mail. Undeterred, he tried the landline at Worthington's residence, but again, there was no answer. Dalton leaned back, a plan forming in his head. Worthington would be his gateway to Knox, and he stood ready to play his cards ruthlessly. The leverage he held over Worthington had a potency—enough to bend even a lord to his will.

Dalton's fingers moved with purpose as he composed a text message and sent it to Worthington's cell. His next move, dialing the local police station in Ascot, Berkshire, had a strategic purpose. The phone rang, and he prepared his approach, knowing exactly how to spin the situation.

"Hello, is this the police?" Dalton's voice remained controlled, his tone even.

"Yes, can we help you, sir?" came the measured response from the other end.

"Yes, I think something might have happened at the Cleargrove estate. Lord Worthington was supposed to attend an important meeting, and we can't get hold of him. We are very concerned, as he has not been well of late. Would it be possible for one of your officers to perform a welfare check?" Dalton's tone feigned concern, concealing the calculated intent.

"Cleargrove? Yes, of course. We'll send somebody along," the voice replied, sounding concerned.

"I would appreciate that. Thank you," Dalton said, oozing sincerity.

He ended the call, a sense of satisfaction settling in. Dalton knew the leverage he held over Worthington: financial irregularities, dubious dealings, and troubling accusations made to go away—not far enough. Dalton smirked. He thought he had enough information to ruin his lordship's reputation. He intended to use this to manipulate Worthington, to bend him to his will. And through him, he would get to Silas Knox. It resembled a chess game, and Dalton poised himself for his next move. He reclined in his chair, awaiting the alignment of pieces, prepared to wield his influence and dictate the narrative.

CHAPTER 25

The knocks on the door were becoming more insistent. Jonathan looked at the bedside clock with bleary eyes. It read: 8:20.

"For heaven's sake," he said, getting out of bed and putting on his robe.

His housekeeper, Janice, had gone on vacation, and the fill-in he'd hired as an assistant didn't start until nine, so he reluctantly padded out of the bedroom, along the landing, and down the ornate staircase.

"Alright, I'm coming!" he bellowed at the incessant knocks.

As he swung open the heavy front door, his annoyance appeared carved into his features, and his angry gaze settled on the two police officers standing on his doorstep.

"Hello, Lord Worthington, it's nothing to be concerned about," said the taller officer, trying to assuage Jonathan.

"They asked us to perform a welfare check. Someone has been trying to reach you. They were concerned you were unresponsive," the officer continued, unaware of the irritation bubbling inside Jonathan.

"Unresponsive? I should bloody well think I was unresponsive. I was fast asleep. Do you know what time it is?" Jonathan's tone sounded riven with indignation and disbelief.

"Apologies, we'll leave you in peace now," the officer said, sensing the rising tension.

"Hang on. Who was trying to get ahold of me?" Jonathan's curiosity was piqued despite his irritation.

"We don't know, sir, just that you had an important meeting," replied the officer, unable to provide the clarity Jonathan sought.

"At eight a.m.? I have never had a meeting before noon in my entire life!" Jonathan scoffed, his frustration evident.

After the officers left, Jonathan retreated to his study, his mind doing cartwheels and his brow furrowing as he picked up his mobile phone from the desk. It revealed a message from an unknown number in the United States.

My name is Dalton, Alithia Corp, LA. Call me as soon as you read this message.

With concern and more than a hint of curiosity, he dialed the number.

"Dalton," came the reply after three rings.

"Ah, yes, Mr. Dalton. You left a somewhat enigmatic message for me to call you. I assume you may have had something to do with a rather unwelcome visit from His Majesty's constabulary that I just received at a rather ungodly hour," Jonathan said in plummy tones.

There followed a long pause before the person on the other end spoke.

"What?"

"Can I help you, Mr. Dalton?"

"Yes. I am head of security for Alithia, and I want to talk with you about Silas Knox and luke-817.org," Dalton said with authority.

"Oh, yes? Why do you need to speak with me about Silas?"

"Just due diligence. As our employee, you know of our extensive interests in Njala. Your associate has made some . . . I think we can call them . . . accusations?"

"I think he was just asking a few questions. I see nothing wrong —"

"Why?"

"What?" Jonathan screwed up his face, confusion as well as concern settling in.

"Why is he asking questions?"

"I don't know. Maybe you should ask him?" Jonathan swallowed. He didn't like this at all.

"You bankroll his operation. I am asking you."

This kind of integration was unfamiliar to him, making him uncomfortable. The tone of this Dalton character held more than a hint of menace. But he also felt annoyed. He'd been woken up early, startled by the police, and now somebody on the other side of the world dared to try and interrogate him in his own home.

"Look, if you have any questions about Silas, I suggest you direct them to him. I do not have time —"

"Be very careful, Your Lordship."

"I beg your pardon!"

"Does the name Millicent McKay mean anything to you? I'm guessing it does?"

Jonathan swallowed hard. He suddenly felt ridiculously hot and thought he might faint.

"Your Lordship, are you still there?" Dalton replied with a cold, even tone.

"Um, yes . . . I'm . . ."

"Good, so, you were saying?"

"Look, I know nothing at all about what he does. I just—"

"Pay for everything?"

"Well, yes, I help where I can with travel expenses. You know, I even do the filing and —"

"Where has he been?"

"What?"

"Where has he been recently? You said you pay for his travel, so where has he been?"

"Well, nowhere until recently, just this week. Sue, that's his assistant. She told me he had a call from an American lady and asked if I would pay for a ticket to Chicago ASAP. Nothing fancy, just economy class, poor fellow, and—"

"Who?"

"Sorry?"

"You said an American lady. Who was it?"

"I think Sue mentioned her name was Sarah. Honestly, that's all I know. I . . ." Jonathan's eyes were darting left and right.

"OK, thank you. You've been accommodating."

"Look, you won't, you know, I mean . . ."

Dalton had disconnected.

Jonathan put the phone back on the desk and had to lean against the wall for support. He took a few deep breaths and slumped in the green leather desk chair, staring straight ahead. *What just happened? Who the hell was that man? How did he know these things about me? What danger am I in? What danger is Silas in?*

He let out a long breath. He felt too jittery to return to bed. He would shower and dress. But, for now, he just sat, stunned, staring into space.

Jonathan had guests over that evening, just a few people, and he'd invited Silas to tag along. He'd tell him about the mysterious Dalton character then. *Maybe he'd heard of him?* Jonathan would not travel to London today. He'd had an unpleasant start to the day and did not enjoy having his pulse elevated by unwelcome events. He would take a long lunch in Ascot and maybe rest in the afternoon. He didn't think he had anything pressing to attend to that couldn't wait.

With that, he padded back up the staircase, still in a state of shock.

CHAPTER 26

Silas Knox sat at a table outside Caffè Nero on Frith Street, Soho, nursing his morning coffee. Normally, this would be a moment of tranquility, a chance to ease into the day while observing the bustling London scene. But today, the warm autumn air and the gentle hum of the city couldn't dispel the unease that clung to him.

Two concerns chewed away at his thoughts, disrupting his equilibrium. The impending visit to see Jonathan at the Cleargrove estate troubled him. He had a lot of questions, too many questions, swirling in his head, and a nagging worry about how deeply his old friend might be entangled with Alithia. He needed clarity, assurances that Jonathan wasn't in over his head, that their friendship wouldn't drag them both into peril.

Then there were the Twitter messages. Cryptic, almost enigmatic in their wording, they had made the hairs on the back of his neck stand the moment he'd deciphered their meaning. The implications appeared vast, and the potential dangers were clear. Whoever lay behind those messages possessed some deep, dark knowledge, placing Silas in a precarious position.

His coffee felt warm against his lips, but it didn't help to clear the cloud of worry. He'd replied to the last message with his phone number, imploring the sender to contact him urgently. Now, waiting for the enigmatic Njalion to call him, he felt like he stood on the edge of a precipice.

Silas Knox returned to his office, his usual calm demeanor replaced by a restless energy. He had no room for relaxation or an appetite beyond coffee and cigarettes. He greeted Sue with a brief "morning" and retreated to his office. The tension of his situation felt tangible in the air.

He settled into his chair, booted up his laptop, and delved straight into Twitter. A slew of messages greeted him, but only one held his attention—the cryptic message that had set this whole chain of events into motion. His mobile phone lay on the table. He'd cranked the ringer volume to maximum and set his notifications to alert him of any developments. He couldn't afford to miss a thing.

He needed to send Sarah a quick message. He informed her about the potential lead, his fingers hesitating slightly as he typed. Her response, a terse "OK," confirmed his suspicion: Sarah was still pissed at him. Could he blame her? The risks were high, and his recent decisions hadn't made things any easier.

Jonathan worried him. They needed to talk, and it had to happen before their meeting at Cleargrove that evening. *What approach should I take with Jonathan?* A confrontation that aimed to ensure he exercised caution in his conversations with others, or a more oblique tactic to keep him off-balance? The problem bore down on him. He had one clear priority: make sure Jonathan knew enough to be careful but not enough to put him in danger.

Checking the time, ten a.m., Silas hesitated, then decided to take the plunge and call Jonathan's mobile. To his surprise, the call connected after only two rings.

"Silas!" Jonathan's voice sounded unexpectedly alert, especially for a man rarely reached before noon.

Taken aback by Jonathan's brisk greeting, Silas steadied his voice. "Jonathan, how are you doing?"

"I'm doing very well, considering. I had a rather early start this morning, two constables on the doorstep, so not a great commencement to proceedings, I have to say." Jonathan recounted matter of factly.

Silas sat tensely in his office chair, phone pressed against his ear, listening intently to Jonathan's voice. He tried to keep his tone casual, but his mind raced ahead.

"The police? What did they want?" He probed, masking his growing concern, alarm bells faintly ringing in his head.

"Oh, it was what they call a welfare check, just checking up on me. Apparently, someone from America was trying to get a hold of me urgently and went to extraordinary lengths to involve the police. Can you imagine? Anyway, I gave them short shrift; I mean, they obviously don't know me very well; before noon? I ask you—"

"America? Who was trying to reach you?" Silas asked, his pulse quickening; the information only heightened his anxiety.

"Well, it was someone from the parent company, the head of security or something. Said his name was Dalton. Frankly, I didn't much care for his tone."

Silas felt a knot form in his stomach as Jonathan spoke. This was all too close for comfort. He remained silent, his mind churning, working, trying to gauge the extent of the problem.

"Silas, are you still there?" Jonathan's voice broke through his thoughts.

Snapping back to the conversation, Silas pressed, "Yes, sorry. What did you tell this person?" He tried to keep his voice steady, but inside, he felt anything but calm.

"Well, I couldn't tell him much because I don't know much, of course. He seemed interested in you, though specifically."

"Me? What did he say?" Silas swallowed hard.

"He wanted to know about my relationship with you and Luke. He knew of my financial help. I mean, it's not a secret, something about due diligence, probably my employment as a non-exec or—"

"Due diligence? What else did you tell him?" Silas could feel the panic rising in his chest as he spoke.

"He asked what sort of help I gave you, and, well, I have no reason to conceal anything from these people, so I just said I help with expenses. Travel and the like. I said I even do some filing and—"

"Travel? Were you specific about anything?" Silas could no longer mask the urgency in his voice.

Jonathan's reassurance turned into confusion. "Are you OK, Silas? You sound troubled."

Silas's vocal cords became taut as he went on: "What did you say? Jonathan, it's important."

"Look, Silas, what's all this about?" Jonathan's concern was growing stronger.

"What did you say?" Silas could feel his voice rise an octave, his heart pounding.

"All I said was that you had made no trips recently until this past week when you had to fly to Chicago in a hurry to meet a mysterious American lady called Sarah. I said you were in economy class, and I pitied—"

"Shit," Silas muttered, a wave of realization crashing over him.

"Sorry, what?" Jonathan's voice echoed with confusion.

"I have to go. I can't make it tonight, sorry." Silas abruptly ended the call, his mind clouded with thoughts about the implications of Jonathan's revelations.

He stared at the phone, now lying inert on the desk, as if it were a harbinger of impending disaster. The revelation that Jonathan had inadvertently exposed his recent movements to a security head at Alithia seemed more than just a breach of privacy; it lay as a direct threat to the delicate web of secrecy they had woven. Silas knew the stakes were high, and now they had just skyrocketed.

As he sat motionless in his cluttered office, the morning light filtering through the blinds, he cradled his phone, his thoughts a

storm of regret and fear. His impulsive pursuit, fueled by adrenaline and excitement, had been reckless—now the impending
repercussions hung ominously over him like a threatening storm
cloud, gray and plump with rain. His bold move with the tweet,
meant to draw out information, had instead potentially exposed
them all to danger.

Picking up the phone, he dialed Sarah, his heart pounding
with dread and urgency—the call connected.

"Hi, Silas."

"Hey, petal, how's things?" He said, trying to sound
nonchalant.

"It's going OK. Mike has settled into the guest annex. He still
seems paranoid, but he might loosen up."

"That's good. Listen, petal, we have got a bit of a problem."

Concern rose in Sarah's voice. "What problem?"

Silas took a deep breath, his voice thick with remorse. "I
fucked up. That post, you were right. I got a good lead but may
have inadvertently led Alithia to us."

"For fuck's sake, Silas, I told you—"

He cut her off, his voice tinged with frustration and a hint of
panic. "Look, it wasn't the tweet exactly; it was Jonathan."

"Jonathan? Do you mean your friend, the lord? Why?"

"Please don't freak out, but he works for them."

"What the fuck! He does what?"

Silas recounted the chain of events, his words tumbling out in
a rush. Jonathan's unwitting disclosure of Silas's recent trip to
Chicago and the tweet about Njala had connected too many dots
for Alithia's liking.

In response to each new revelation, Sarah seemed engulfed
by a wave of shock and fury that resonated in her voice. "Shit,
Silas. And it won't take a genius to work out who the fuck Sarah
is when they put our two names together, will it?"

"No," Silas admitted, feeling the consequences of his mistake.

"So, what's the plan, Einstein?"

"I'm working on it. Just lie low for a few days; don't draw

attention. My guess is they will just watch you... but I don't know. Be prepared. Think about where you might head to in a hurry."

"Great. What do I tell Mike?"

"Don't tell him anything for now."

After filling Sarah in on the cryptic messages, her agreement that they were onto something significant appeared to be the only silver lining in this dark cloud of anxiety and fear.

"Silas, keep me updated, OK? I hope whoever this is contacts you soon because we don't have much time. The sooner we can get this out in the open, the safer we'll all be."

"I'm so sorry, Sarah. I should have checked everything. I feel like a newbie."

"Before doing anything like that again, please check with me first?"

"Understood. Sorry."

"OK, I've got to go. Call me as soon as you have something."

Silas hung up, feeling a hint of relief, but mostly fear. He knew they were treading on thin ice, and his mistake had only made it thinner.

He sat back in his chair. Jonathan, having unknowingly spilled everything to Alithia, made the situation a clusterfuck, but at least he no longer needed to worry about what Jonathan might do or say; the cat was well and truly out of the bag. He closed his eyes, aware of their capabilities, trying to predict Alithia's next steps. The thought of an organization bringing down commercial jets petrified him. This was no ordinary adversary.

He had no illusions about the assurances he'd given Sarah. Their situation extended beyond mere surveillance. Alithia knew they were onto something, and they wouldn't just back off. For the first time in his career, Silas was genuinely afraid for his life and Sarah's.

Picking up his notepad, he began jotting down the chain of events: Alithia's reaction to his tweet, the discovery of his connection to Jonathan, and his sudden trip to Chicago. It tied together too neatly. But they didn't know the crucial details about Chloe's files. They must have seen the handoff to Mike, so he must also be in grave danger. If they found Sarah, they would get him. Buy one, get one free. *Shit.*

Silas thought if he were in their shoes, he would either seek the information source or eliminate the threat. Silas's hand trembled slightly as he considered these options. He destroyed his notes methodically, first burning them, then ensuring their remnants were flushed away, erasing any trace of his thoughts.

Back at his desk, he questioned his paranoia but couldn't shake the feeling of being watched. He walked to the small window in his office, eyes searching the street below for anything unusual. He knew, however, that pros would be observing him, and if he saw them, it would already be too late.

His phone rang suddenly, making him jump. Snatching it up, he braced himself for what might come next. He hoped that Njalion, whoever they might be, would provide some much-needed answers quickly. Time, he feared, would soon run out.

CHAPTER 27

Jibril Abena, once the president of Njala, now sat incognito in a modest farmhouse on the outskirts of Kivuli. The blunt contrast between his surroundings and the presidential palace could not have been clearer. Dressed plainly and now with an unshaven face, he still felt exposed, fully aware that his presidential image remained familiar to everyone.

Ezekial, his loyal ally, had stressed the precariousness of the situation. "You must remain unseen, Jibril. Your face is on billboards everywhere. We move under the cover of darkness, and when you're ready, we must act swiftly to leave Njala." Ezekial's words echoed in his mind, urging him to expedite his departure.

In his current hideout, Jibril reflected on the crucial information he had extracted, information that could overturn the current state of affairs in Njala. His years as a government fixer had taught him the art of leveraging contacts and situations. He'd used this expertise to gather intelligence against Field Marshal Diallo, exploiting a security service operative with a vendetta against Diallo.

The data he'd obtained had been alarming: discussions of assassination plots, detailed plans of subterfuge, and chilling indifference to human life. Diallo's boldness in his communication with Dalton and Rampton had laid bare the extent of their machinations. It had been Dalton's methodical, almost detached responses that had initially caught Jibril's attention. But Rampton's less cautious, emotive replies revealed their true intentions —and their underestimation of the exiled government's resolve and resources.

Jibril's contact had helped him capture crucial communications, which they exchanged through a shared webmail account, always using draft messages and borrowed devices to maintain secrecy. The content was explosive: Diallo's disdain for Viktor and his allies, Rampton's assurance of a "perfect plan" to eliminate any threat, and the real story behind the Vivair crash. Jibril realized he held potentially the most significant leverage against his adversaries.

Ezekial had shown him Silas Knox's tweets, a beacon of hope in his desperate situation. Together, they crafted messages to reach out to Silas with a plan to expose the truth and set his country on a path to freedom.

He picked up the disposable phone, the one that had ensured his family's safety, and dialed the number Silas had provided. The phone rang twice before a voice, urgent and slightly out of breath, answered.

"Hello, this is Silas Knox," came the voice on the other end.

Jibril steadied himself, knowing full well the implications of the conversation they were about to have. Here stood his chance to make a difference, to strike back against those who had wronged his nation and its people.

"Mr. Knox, I believe I have information that could be vital to you," he stated. His voice had a firmness, the residue of the authority he once wielded leading a nation. But as he spoke, there manifested a subtle tremor of urgency that even his practiced confidence couldn't fully mask. It served as a reminder of the dangerous tightrope he now walked.

The conversation that followed would set in motion events that could change the fate of Njala forever. Or so Jibril hoped.

CHAPTER 28

Silas gripped his mobile phone delicately between his finger and thumb as if it were an ancient relic capable of disintegrating at the slightest touch. His heart pounded in his chest. The voice on the other end, laden with urgency, a deep baritone, held his complete attention.

"I don't need your name, but I'm curious about your knowledge of recent events," Silas ventured cautiously, his voice steady despite the whirlwind of thoughts.

"I cannot reveal my name. It is impossible," the caller responded, their tone veiling deep-seated fear.

Silas took a moment, processing the serious nature of the request. "Of course, I understand," he replied respectfully, despite his curiosity.

"As I alluded to in my messages to you, I have information," the voice continued. Each word sounded laden with mystery.

"Yes, I am keen to learn what you know," Silas responded, his journalistic instincts kicking in, sensing a slight reticence with his caller.

The voice on the other end grew more grave. "My country is infested, overrun. Our people are subjects of a foreign entity, a colonial power capable of enormous wrongdoing." The caller paused, and Silas felt the air thicken with tension. "I will tell you this: I suspect you are already in very grave danger."

Silas felt a sudden surge of panic. He swallowed hard, feeling the dryness in his throat. He could hear his heart pounding in his ears. The caller's words resonated with a foreboding truth he couldn't ignore. The visceral reality of the danger he faced now felt like a slap across the face.

Silas Knox's fingers tightly gripped his mobile phone, trying to maintain a calm exterior.

"I have already taken many great risks, more than you can imagine," the voice on the other end said solemnly. "But I know what has been done and by whom. These people do not care about the sanctity of human life; they care only for money and power, nothing else. When I was alerted to your messages, it was as if Almighty God had intervened."

"What evidence do you have?" Silas asked his instincts on full alert. "Now is the time to share."

"I have emails and other messages and files in my possession that show direct communication between Field Marshal Diallo, leader of the Njalian Armed Forces, and senior executives of the Alithia Corporation," the caller revealed, each word landing like a punch. "I cannot say how these communications came into my possession, as it would reveal my identity, but you can see them for yourself. I will provide the login details to a webmail account where I have saved all the attachments in drafts. When you log in, you will see them. Then you must download all of them. Keep them safe."

"What do they say?" Silas pressed, eager for more concrete details.

The caller's voice grew heavier with emotion. "You suspect the crash of Vivair 002 may not be all that it seems, which is correct. They killed Viktor Malaba in the same way. I heard them speak about how they would do it. My biggest burden is that I did not warn him about what would happen. Now, I must live with that burden. Please read the documents and see for yourself."

Silas's phone pinged, interrupting the conversation. He pulled it away from his ear to check the screen. It was a message from the caller with the webmail access details.

"I will call again in thirty minutes."

The call disconnected.

Silas's gaze lingered on his phone, his fingers trembling as he set it on his desk. A sense of urgency propelled him to flip open his laptop and hastily navigate to the webmail address provided by Njalion. His heart pounded in his chest as he keyed in the login details.

The drafts folder burst open on his screen, revealing hundreds of emails with attachments. Silas's eyes widened in disbelief as he clicked through the messages, recognizing many sent from the name Jonathan had mentioned. His hand instinctively covered his mouth, a physical barrier against the shock, as he delved into the incriminating exchanges. He quickly plugged in a thumb drive, downloading every piece of evidence he could find.

Once the download had been completed, Silas leaned back, and the magnitude of what he had just unearthed hit him like a hammer blow. This was the irrefutable evidence they needed, coupled with the data on Chloe's USB stick. His thoughts were interrupted by the shrill ring and vibration of his phone.

Without hesitation, he answered, and the deep voice on the other end started speaking immediately. "Do you have it all?" the voice asked with conspicuous urgency.

"Yes," Silas responded, barely able to catch his breath.

"I will delete everything and close the account. I cannot speak to you again; this phone will be destroyed. May God be with you," the voice said, and before Silas could reply, the line went dead.

Silas's hands were still shaking as he pocketed the thumb drive. He walked over to the window, peering into the street, searching for any abnormality. His pulse raced uncontrollably. Finding nothing amiss, he lit a cigarette, the smoke curling up as he inhaled deeply, trying to calm his nerves.

He retrieved Chloe's USB stick and copied it onto the new thumb drive, so all the data was together. When it had finished copying, he let out a long, faltering breath.

He knew he had to inform Sarah. She picked up almost immediately.

"Do you have anything?" she asked, breathless with anticipation.

"I have it all," Silas replied, his voice trembling.

He recounted the phone call and shared snippets of the earth-shattering information he had just uncovered, including details about this Dalton character.

"Shit, this is real, isn't it? Oh my God," Sarah responded, her voice filled with shock and realization.

Grasping his mobile phone as if it were a lifeline, Silas's pulse raced with urgency. He looked at Sarah through the screen, his eyes intense and determined.

"Looks that way," he confirmed. "Listen, I don't think they will monitor us. I hate to say this, but I think they will act. These people are evil."

Sarah's voice trembled slightly. "Silas, you're scaring me."

"Frankly, we should be scared. We need to get this published as soon as possible, but we have to do it right; I need to verify a few things because we'll only get one shot at this. We can't make a mistake."

"I thought you said we don't have much time?" Silas could hear the anxiety in her voice.

"Look, I know I acted in haste with the Njala tweet, and I should have checked everything, but now that we have this, I must be meticulous. We must verify the authenticity of this stuff before publishing it."

"So, how can we protect ourselves in the meantime?"

"We have to keep moving. Don't stay at home. Go somewhere they will have to work hard to find. Do not wait for them to show up."

"What about Mike? Have you forgotten about him?"

"You'll have to take him with you. Sarah, this is serious, but in forty-eight hours, it should be out in the open."

"OK, understood."

"But we must also protect the story, Sarah. This has to come out, whatever happens."

"OK," she agreed, her voice firm.

Silas nodded, even though she couldn't see him. "Kill switch."

"What?"

"We set up a kill switch. If anything happens to us, all of it gets published. Chloe's files and all the emails. Then, notifications will be sent to all the relevant authorities. We ensure that everyone on their payroll is spooked by what we have. Now they know who we are and that we know something, they will try to silence us. We can't let that happen."

"Damn straight, we can't let that happen."

"OK, let me get to work."

"I'm going to get moving. We don't want to be sitting ducks. Whatever you need to do, do it fast, OK?"

"Forty-eight hours, I promise. I need to call Alex."

"Who's Alex?"

"Alex Mercer, my cybersecurity expert, specializes in digital forensics. I need him to check the files, make sure they're genuine."

"OK, tell him to hurry the fuck up."

Sarah's call ended abruptly, and Silas dialed Alex's number.

"Alex Mercer."

"Hi, Alex, it's Silas."

"Hi, Silas, how are—"

"Alex, I need a favor, massive favor. It's big, life or death," Silas said breathlessly.

"Whoa! OK, what do you need?"

"Alex, I have a ton of stuff, email exchanges, and attachments that I need you to go through for me. This is very hush-hush, super urgent, and deadly serious."

"OK, sounds intriguing."

"I need you to do the works: metadata, headers, and all the other technical wizardry you do to confirm accuracy. It's urgent, Alex. I need a forty-eight-hour turnaround—sooner if you can?"

"No problem. How do you want to get it to me?"

"Let's meet, but I must be careful. I'm probably being watched."

"Jesus, Silas, what have you got mixed up in?"

"You'll find out soon enough—and prepare to be shocked, mate."

"OK, let me know when and where."

"Will do. There are a few things I need to do, but I will call you back via the app ASAP. Stand by, and thanks, mate."

"*De nada*. Speak soon."

The call ended, and Silas's gaze drifted to the window, eyes scanning the street below. A white van parked across the road caught his attention. "Just another white van," he muttered, shaking off the creeping paranoia. But in the back of his mind, Silas knew they were in deep water, and, now more than ever, caution was their best ally.

Silas methodically transferred the contents of the thumb drive to his laptop, each file a heavy responsibility he couldn't afford to mishandle. He created a password-protected zip file, the virtual equivalent of a locked safe, and uploaded it to a newly created email draft. He repeated the process with Chloe's data, a digital dance of drag, drop, and secure.

As he unplugged the thumb drive and slipped it into his pocket, Silas leaned back in his chair, his gaze lost in the void of his thoughts. He had always imagined the adrenaline rush of being at the center of a groundbreaking story, but the reality meant a cocktail of exhilaration and terror.

The initial thrill of uncovering Chloe's files in Big Bertha had given way to a creeping dread. His thoughts, once dominated by dreams of recognition and glory, now circled the brutal truth of his adversaries' capabilities. The realization that his life could be a negligible obstacle compared to their agenda frightened him. He could almost feel the shadow of their ruthlessness enveloping him, his significance diminishing in its wake.

With a heavy sigh, Silas ran a hand over his face, a gesture of weariness and resolve. It was time to think like his adversaries, to anticipate their moves. Staying in his office or returning home meant danger. He needed to be unpredictable and elusive.

The urgency to deliver the data to Alex made his pulse quicken. Emailing the files or sharing the email account crossed his mind, but the dangerous circumstances certainly called for something more tangible. Handing over the USB stick in person seemed like the only way to ensure the data's safety. In this high-stakes game of digital espionage, the physical exchange of information felt almost archaic, yet profoundly secure.

Determined, Silas mapped out his next move. He would meet Alex, hand over the USB stick, and then create a diversion. The plan seemed simple yet fraught with peril. It meant more risk, but he had to take it. He had to navigate through the shadowy corridors of danger for the truth to emerge, and he felt ready to do just that.

CHAPTER 29

Dalton leaned into his desk, eyes scanning Sarah Reynolds' Wikipedia page. Her career as an investigative reporter had been dotted with high-profile stories, each illustrating her skill and tenacity. The connection between Silas Knox, Sarah, and Chicago looked crystal clear. *But why?* What had prompted Knox to fly to Chicago urgently, only to return the next day and immediately tweet about Njala? These weren't random events but connected dots that led to a bigger picture.

Dalton's research on Sarah had yielded nothing significant. However, he couldn't ignore Chicago's significance: the departure point for the doomed Vivair 002, a haven for Njala's government in exile, and the suspected pass-off in the video. Knox's visit to Chicago had not been a mere coincidence. It had to have been a calculated move that demanded immediate action.

Realizing the urgency, Dalton picked up his phone to update Rampton. Despite being early, they couldn't afford to waste more time. Rampton's groggy voice came through after three rings.

"You need to be aware of some developments," Dalton stated, cutting to the chase.

"Abena?" Rampton's voice sounded hopeful and weary at the same time.

"No, he is still in the wind," Dalton replied, keeping his tone even.

"OK, fuck. What is it?" Rampton's frustration boiled over.

Dalton explained, "An individual named Silas Knox, with half a million followers on social media, has posted a tweet relating to Njala and our interests. I just emailed you a link. You should go read it and call me straight back."

Rampton ended the call abruptly, without a word. Dalton put the phone on his desk and waited patiently, knowing the considerable spanner in the works would return Rampton to the phone soon.

Ten minutes later, Rampton returned, his voice alert and focused. "Just what the fuck is going on? What do we know about this Knox person?"

Dalton dove into the details. "Silas Knox runs a whistleblower site called Juke-817.org. He's an investigative journalist. He traveled to Chicago two days ago. He dropped everything to meet with another journalist named Sarah Reynolds. He flew back to London the next day and sent his tweet that evening. I guess that there was an information exchange between them. I'm guessing it has something to do with whatever was passed to the drunk passenger in the video, but we're still trying to break it down."

Silence fell as Rampton processed the information. "Tyler?" Dalton prompted, breaking the brief stillness.

"Yes, yes, I'm thinking," Rampton finally said.

Dalton remained silent, giving Rampton the space to digest the news.

"How do you know all this, his movements?" Rampton's question cut through the call, sharp and demanding. Dalton felt surprised at the sudden edge in his voice, contrasting with the earlier calm.

"His friend and benefactor, Lord Jonathan Worthington, is an employee of Njala Mining Co." Dalton's response was matter-of-fact.

"What? So how are they linked?" The confusion in Rampton's voice was unmistakable.

"Old friends. Worthington bankrolls the site. I called him, applied some leverage, and he told me about the hastily arranged travel plans," Dalton explained with precision.

"OK, apply more pressure on him. Find out what else he knows," Rampton ordered.

"Already on it," Dalton assured, his tone confident and controlled.

"Good. OK. This tweet looks like a fishing exercise by this Knox individual. But something prompted the fishing trip. Chicago bothers me. It's the epicenter. What is your take?" There was a noticeable shift in Rampton's voice, now tinged with concern.

Dalton detailed his proactive steps: "We know Reynolds contacted Knox in London. Whatever she told him made him rush to Chicago. I have sent two operatives to the Reynolds' residence for recognizance. They will report back today. I also have two operatives on Knox. I'll have a report by tonight PST."

"This is deeply troubling. Abena, and now this. We need to clean up fast," Rampton stated urgently.

"Understood. I'll know more later and will call you back," Dalton reassured, sounding ready to take whatever action was necessary.

"It goes without saying what needs to be done, right?" Rampton's voice carried more than a hint of menace.

"We will do whatever is necessary," Dalton confirmed, his words cold and final.

"With this Knox guy, make it look like a particularly unpleasant act of onanism. Autoerotic asphyxiation—that's it, I think. Dress him up as a woman and inject him with street drugs. Let that be his legacy. If you can't get to his intel, we should discredit him entirely," Rampton's voice cut through, harsh and unyielding, his instructions chilling.

Dalton raised an eyebrow as he listened to Rampton's increasingly drastic measures. "Roger that," he replied, attempting to mask his contempt.

The call ended, and Dalton leaned back in his chair, already strategizing his next move. The day ahead would be long and demanding, but Dalton was prepared.

He stood in his office, scanning the room's contours—a fortress inside a fortress. The need for security dominated here; only a few trusted individuals, verified by an iris scanner, could access the atrium outside his office. It required his palm print and iris scan to enter his inner sanctum, where he now stood. Gaining entry meant surpassing Dalton's lifeless body, his eyes and right hand taken as trophies.

His attention settled on the large safe nestled in the corner. Over his years with Tyler Rampton, this safe had become a repository for kompromat—a collection of secrets and scandals involving the powerful and influential, the great and the bad. Tyler often joked about it being his get-out-of-jail-free card. In Dalton's eyes, it meant more than that; it served as a testament to their influence, a catalog of control over those who governed and judged.

This cache of kompromat blended illicitly gathered information, surveillance records, financial misdemeanors, and tales of personal misconduct. He had dirt on judges, lawyers, law enforcement, congress members, and senators—a gallery of the compromised and corruptible. Rampton could access this safe, the only other soul with that privilege, the only one with an override to Dalton's sanctum.

In the safe was Dalton's most potent weapon. He had evidence of undisclosed offshore accounts, shady business dealings, and illegal campaign financing, each a potential career-ender. Personal indiscretions ranging from extramarital affairs to drug abuse and sexual depravity could destroy carefully culti-vated public images and careers in a heartbeat. His incriminating emails and messages revealed unethical and politically damaging discussions. He had evidence of ties to criminal orga-nizations and the sharing of classified information with unautho-rized parties, which could compromise national security. His evidence of tax evasion and breaches of lobbying laws could lead to prosecutions.

To Dalton, this collection was a masterpiece, a melding of artistry in leverage and control. It matched his idea of a collabo-ration with Picasso, Van Gogh, and Leonardo da Vinci in beauty, power, and scope.

As he contemplated his next steps, Dalton awaited reports from his field teams—two operatives in Chicago surveilling Reynolds and two in London on Knox. He didn't expect their findings to alter the trajectory of events, but he remained eager to gather as much intelligence as possible. Neutralizing Knox and Reynolds would be futile if they had already disseminated their knowledge. Rampton often saw elimination as the solution, but Dalton knew better.

Dalton felt skeptical about Knox possessing concrete evidence, yet he couldn't dismiss the possibility. And what, if anything, had been passed to the drunk guy on the plane? They still hadn't tracked him down; he'd gone AWOL from his resi-dence. That element acted like a splinter in his big toe, constantly irritating him. *Is it connected to Knox and Reynolds?* There were too many questions, and he didn't like it. But someone seemed to be talking, and Dalton felt it was his job to silence that voice. He surmised that Lord Jonathan Worthington had to be the likely conduit, vulnerable to exploitation because of the skele-tons in his closet. Regarding Reynolds, she presented a more challenging target, as Dalton had no dirt on her. She would require a more direct approach, and Dalton had acquainted himself well with the brutal necessities of his trade.

As he stood in his office, Dalton weighed up the decisions to come, the machinations of power playing out in the shadows. The day ahead would be long and full of critical choices, but Dalton had chosen this life—a life navigated by manipulating secrets and wielding unseen influence—a life in the shadows, a darkness that would soon envelop him once more.

CHAPTER 30

Silas checked his watch and saw that lunchtime had long passed. However, his stomach wasn't complaining; the past two sleepless nights had taken away his appetite. He leaned heavily against the cool exterior of Charing Cross tube station, a static, silent observer amid the constant bustle of humanity. He remembered the white van parked directly opposite his office earlier. He'd walked to the station and kept his wits about him, but if he had a tail, they were skilled enough to remain unseen.

He had been at the station for about five minutes now, a second USB stick containing the full complement of Njala files securely tucked in his inner pocket, encased in a small padded envelope.

Silas acutely understood that his every action had to be under surveillance. The importance of getting the USB stick to Alex Mercer, his trusted confidant and cybersecurity expert, made him breathless. They needed to act swiftly and stay one step ahead of those who might wish to stop them at all costs.

He chose RetroBean, a quaint, 1950s-style café in Covent Garden's heart, for the drop-off. He often visited with Alex and planned to leave the USB stick hidden in plain sight. The café provided the perfect cover with its vintage charm and bustling lunchtime crowd.

Earlier, amid the clatter of dishes and the chatter of patrons, Silas discreetly made his way to the café's old jukebox. This vintage piece, a relic rarely touched or inspected, held a secret he had discovered during his previous visits—a hollowed-out compartment, the perfect hiding spot. The simple act of transferring crucial information undetected would now be the difference between life and death.

Silas casually slid the USB stick into its secret compartment as the café owner busied himself elsewhere. To avoid raising suspicion, he selected a Chet Baker song, "I Fall in Love Too Easily," on the jukebox and then settled in at a table with his coffee. His appearance remained calm, but his stomach churned with anxiety.

Silas knew the significance of what he had just done, the risk, and the potential fallout it could cause. But he needed to take this step, as it could change the course of their investigation and perhaps even their lives.

He had carefully crafted an encrypted email for Alex Mercer, embedding it with instructions only Alex could decipher. The message subtly directed him to the café, guiding him toward the jukebox and ultimately to the concealed USB stick.

After finishing his coffee, Silas exited the café and melted into a crowd gathered around a street magician. From this vantage point, he could monitor the café's entrance, observing the patrons entering and exiting. The waiting became tense, testing his cunning and Alex's ability to follow the trail he had laid out.

His tension eased slightly when he spotted Alex arriving about fifteen minutes later. Silas watched from his spot in the crowd as Alex ordered coffee, then moved to the jukebox and punched in a song code. Moments later, Alex appeared back at his table, casually sipping his coffee, the USB stick hopefully now in his possession.

Silas walked away from Covent Garden, his thoughts now a

whirlwind of hope and concern. Someone who could validate its authenticity now held the crucial data. If the information were verified, the world would soon know the explosive truth he had uncovered.

Now standing outside Charing Cross station under the August sun, Silas contemplated his next step. He could feel the envelope pressed against his side. He had put some stamps on it, opting for second-class mail, and addressed it to his former boss at the BBC. The envelope contained a note explaining the contents and instructions on what to do if something happened to him. It would be risky to send the data without verifying its authenticity. Still, he believed disseminating the information among trusted contacts would decrease the chances of it being suppressed or destroyed.

In Silas's mind, this approach maximized the likelihood of the truth emerging. Such high-stakes scenarios demanded redundancy. He played a strategic game, ensuring backups were in place in case one channel got compromised. This effort aimed to do more than break a story; it focused on ensuring that the truth, however dangerous or desperately hidden, would come to light.

Amid London's bustle, Silas Knox's thoughts swirled with strategies for survival. He had meticulously set up a kill switch system. This digital tripwire would unleash a cascade of sensitive information onto multiple secure servers across the globe, ensuring the truth's survival, regardless of his fate. This served as his safety net, a plan B if Alex Mercer, his digital forensics expert, couldn't contact him after verifying the files. Despite this precaution, lingering anxiety clung to him. In less than two days, the villains behind the Njala conspiracy could be exposed, scrambling in the wake of the impending leak. But first, he had to mail a crucial package without drawing attention.

As he observed the crowd of pedestrians, his gaze landed on a young woman laden with letters and parcels, likely headed to the post office—a plan formed in his mind—a chance to send the package incognito. Silas covertly slipped the manila envelope with the USB up his jacket sleeve, timing his move.

As the woman approached, Silas feigned hailing a taxi, his arm sweeping out grandly. In a perfectly timed accident, his arm collided with her bundle, sending letters and parcels tumbling to the sidewalk. The young woman let out a startled shriek as Silas swiftly turned, his manila envelope discreetly joining the fallen mail.

"I'm so sorry," Silas apologized, crouching to assist her with the scattered items. They worked together, amid a sea of passing legs, to gather the items.

"That's OK; it just gave me a shock. I was miles away," the young woman said, slightly rattled but forgiving.

Silas handed her the collected items with a well-practiced smile, ensuring his package remained among them. "Sorry, I'll be more careful in the future," he offered amiably.

The young woman returned his smile and continued on her way, unwittingly carrying Silas's vital package to its destination. Silas watched her disappear into the crowd, a crucial part of his plan now set in motion. He knew the next forty-eight hours were crucial—a tightrope walk.

Silas leaned against the station wall, drawing in a deep, steadying breath. The time had come to test his theory about Jonathan. His fingers hovered over his phone, locating Jonathan's contact info. He pressed call, and the phone rang briefly before Jonathan's voice came through.

"Silas!" Jonathan said, sounding chipper despite Silas's assumption he was hungover.

"Hi, Jonathan, how's things?" Silas asked, his voice neutral.

"You missed an absolute humdinger of a soiree last night. I'm feeling a little fragile today, Silas. I will not lie," Jonathan replied, his tone light but tired.

"Sounds like you had a good time," Silas responded, his mind racing ahead, planning.

"Yes, it was a pity you couldn't make it. What happened?"

"Something came up. A story I'm working on. It's big," Silas said, a bit distracted.

"Is that the Chicago thing?" Jonathan inquired with curiosity.

"Yes, well, there's a lot of moving parts. It needs my full focus," Silas explained, carefully veiling his true intent.

"I see. Well, I'm in town tomorrow. I can come over and—" Jonathan offered.

"I'm not using the office currently, and I'm not staying home. It's complicated, but this story, let's say some people won't be too happy when it's published, and I need to keep a low profile for now," Silas elaborated.

"Of course, I understand. Where are you staying?" Jonathan asked, concern evident in his tone.

"A hotel south of the river, Battersea," Silas lied, weaving his web.

"South of the river? Are you sure, Silas? I mean, is it safe?" Jonathan's worry infused his voice.

"Yes, it's safe, Jonathan."

"OK, give me the details. I'll pop along and see you tomorrow night?"

"It's just a Travelodge. I am checked in under the name of Tim Clarke. Room 414," Silas continued, his voice steady despite internally cringing at the deceit.

"Bloody hell, Silas, that's all a bit cloak-and-dagger, isn't it?"

"Needs must, Jonathan. Room 414."

"OK, understood. I'll see you tomorrow, then."

Jonathan hung up, the lie leaving a bitter taste in Silas's mouth. But he had a plan. He'd set up a digital booby trap at the Battersea Travelodge, complete with surveillance equipment, in room 414. Alex, his contact, had checked in as Tim Clarke and prepped everything. Silas's phone would alert him to any movement in the room. This test aimed to uncover if someone was monitoring Jonathan's calls or if he was acting as a mole. It was that straightforward.

Blending into the crowd, Silas moved toward the station,

descending into the Northern line. He boarded the first train, alighting at Leicester Square after just one stop. He watched the passengers disperse, confirming he hadn't been followed. Satisfied, he moved toward the westbound Piccadilly line platform, his destination Heathrow Airport. He needed to keep moving, stay ahead, and protect the story at all costs.

CHAPTER 31

Sarah knocked gently on the guest annex door, then said softly, "Mike, are you awake?"

The door eventually swung open, revealing Mike Anderson, disheveled and sporting her silk kimono. The sight, under normal circumstances, would have looked comical, but their situation wasn't funny. At eight a.m. on Saturday, Sarah, already dressed and ready for action, wasted no time.

"We have to leave. I'll tell you everything when we're in the car. Sorry, please grab your things, and let's get going," she urged, her voice urgent and apologetic.

"Wait, what?" Mike's voice was tinged with unmistakable confusion, contrasting with the urgency pulsing through Sarah's veins. She heard the bewilderment in his tone, but they didn't have the time for lengthy explanations. Every second counted, and patience was a luxury she couldn't afford.

Fifteen minutes later, they were speeding away in her car. Mike, still disoriented, had managed to dress himself hurriedly, his T-shirt on backward and his hair in disarray.

"What's going on?" Mike's tone matched his disheveled appearance.

"We have to move. Silas published some info about Njala, questions, mainly, but it's brought some heat; we're playing it safe. Just keep moving. That's what Silas said to do, and I agreed. So, that's what we're doing: moving," Sarah explained, her eyes focused on the road, her mind on unseen threats.

"Are these people after us or something? You're freaking me out," Mike said, his anxiety increasing.

"No, it's precautionary. Look, let me concentrate on driving. We'll find a place to stop, and I will tell you what's happening," Sarah said, trying to pacify him while navigating the traffic.

"What about Henry?" Mike asked with clear concern for their friend.

"We'll loop him in later. Get some sleep. You look shattered; I'll wake you up when I find someplace, OK?"

"Not sure I can sleep. That was quite a rude awakening, Sarah."

"Sorry, Mike, but—" Sarah began apologizing, but Mike interrupted her.

"I didn't mean you were rude; it's just an expression. I think it means—"

"It's OK, Mike. I know what it means," Sarah cut in, a half-smile gracing her lips despite the tension.

Sarah maintained her focus on the road, occasionally glancing at Mike, who seemed lost in his thoughts. He turned to look at her. "So, you were in situations like this before? All this on-the-run stuff?" His question hung in the air.

"Well, it got pretty heated when I was working on the story about the senator," Sarah began, her voice steady but tinged with apprehension. "These sorts of people don't take kindly to journalists sniffing around, so, you know, threats were made. Just had to watch my back."

"That's what we're doing now? Watching our backs?" Mike replied, sounding concerned.

"I guess. This is on another level; I won't lie to you. We both know what the people behind all this are capable of," Sarah admitted, her eyes briefly meeting Mike's in a sideways glance.

"Mass murder?" Mike's voice barely rose above a whisper.

"Well, yes."

"What about Henry? Shouldn't he find someplace to hide?" Mike asked.

"We figure he's safe. There's nothing to tie him to me, you, or Silas. We need to be wise when we communicate with him. The less he knows, the safer he is," Sarah explained, confident in their plan.

"What do you think about Henry?" Mike asked, sounding curious.

"Tough old boot, I reckon. He's been around the block. I think he has a military background or something," Sarah speculated, a hint of respect in her voice.

"Yeah, I thought that, too. Tried to make out he worked in sewage." Mike chuckled.

"I somehow doubt that," Sarah replied, sharing a brief smile with him.

Mike's gaze shifted to the countryside beyond the window. "You wouldn't know it, not now, not to look at me, but I was a highflier in the marketing world a couple of years ago. Sharp suits, nice car, house by the lake, beautiful girlfriend. They ground me down at work and spat me out. The trip to London, the Vivair flight, was one of my last days of gainful employment. My career is finished. I don't know what I'm going to do. All this shit that's going on, the plane crash, the things we discovered, has changed everything."

Sarah listened, Mike's words sinking in. The road ahead looked unclear, literally and figuratively, but she knew one thing: they were in this together, and somehow, they had to find a way through.

Sarah's fingers gripped the steering wheel tighter as Mike opened up about his feelings. She glanced at him, noticing the exhaustion etched on his face.

"Come on, Mike, you—" she started, but he cut her off, his voice laced with a resignation that tugged at her heartstrings.

"Henry said all this stuff we're involved in would offer me redemption. He said, plain and simple, that I was finished—washed up—without it."

"I don't think he meant—" Sarah began, hoping to offer reassurance.

"No, he's right. I'll never get a job doing what I was trained to do, what I was good at. That's over for me now. I'm the drunk plane crash guy. But this story you and Silas are working on changes everything. If they crashed that plane deliberately and I am wildly involved in exposing that truth, it will redeem me. Henry is right. Nobody will care that they kicked me off that flight," Mike said, his words filled with despair and a flicker of hope.

Sarah sighed softly. "Maybe you're right, Mike, maybe Henry was right, but honestly, sleep if you can."

She watched as Mike leaned his head against the window, closing his eyes, the lines of fatigue and worry smoothing out slightly as he tried to rest.

Sarah's thoughts drifted as she navigated the car. She had recognized the signs in Mike, the telltale behaviors of someone struggling with alcohol. Each night at her place in Porter, Indiana, he'd drowned his sorrows, his demeanor fluctuating between sorrow and numbing indifference. Sarah knew he was battling his demons, grappling with the enormity of what had happened to him. Her heart went out to him; she could only imagine how she might cope in similar circumstances. She resolved that once this nightmare had concluded, she'd ensure Mike got the help he needed. Right now, though, their priority was to stay safe, which meant to keep moving.

As Sarah navigated the car smoothly westward out of Chicago, she thought about how things might play out. She had booked two rooms at a Hilton in Omaha for the night. The drive to Scottsbluff, Nebraska, awaited them the following day. Sarah had arranged a stay at an old college friend's holiday rental there, driven by the need to be far from potential danger yet close enough to maintain a semblance of normality.

When Sarah called the previous night, Daisy, her college friend, had readily offered for her to stay at a vacant holiday home. Sarah had masked the urgency in her voice, casually claiming a need for fresh country air. She anticipated the inevitable conversation when she showed up with a man, aware that it would stir Daisy's curiosity and that she would potentially share the gossip with others.

The thought of resting in Scottsbluff brought a sense of temporary relief. Since the story with Silas had unfolded, her home had transformed into a place of anxiety and paranoia. Every creak and rustle had amplified her edginess, painting scenarios in her mind where faceless threats lurked, ready to pounce.

On the road, her eyes flicked to the rearview mirror more often than necessary. She half expected to spot the cliché of a suspicious black sedan, its occupants resembling characters straight out of a spy thriller, but the road behind her remained innocuously normal. Despite this, an unsettling thought lingered —the real professionals tracking her would likely be invisible until the very last, unavoidable moment. This realization sent an involuntary shiver through her, a reminder of the dangerous game they were now a part of.

As Sarah maneuvered the car off the interstate and into the parking lot of the Sunshine Family Restaurant in Flagg, she glanced at Mike, slumped in his seat, fast asleep with his mouth agape. The sight tugged at her, and she thought about the turmoil he had been thrust into.

The simplicity of the days before the crash, when her biggest concern was giving a story the justice it deserved, seemed a world away. Here they were, both unwitting players in a deadly chase orchestrated by a cabal capable of unspeakable horrors. She shook her head in disbelief; life, indeed, had a way of blindsiding you with its swift, unforgiving twists.

Drawing the car to a stop, Sarah exhaled deeply. They needed a break for physical rest and for Sarah to collect her thoughts. The journey stretched ahead, and the unknowns they faced loomed large. She glanced again at Mike, a physical embodiment of how quickly and drastically life could change.

The clock in Sarah's Audi A4 showed just past ten a.m. "Brunch and then Omaha," she whispered, formulating a plan for the day. She gently nudged Mike awake.

"Mike." Her voice was soft but firm.

He stirred, a groggy "Uh?" escaping his lips.

"Wanna grab some brunch?" Sarah suggested, hoping the thought of food would offer him some semblance of normalcy.

Mike, still tired, agreed with a simple: "Um, OK."

Exiting the car, they walked toward the bustling restaurant. Sarah's gaze darted around the parking lot, her journalist's instinct scanning for anything unusual, though she wasn't quite sure what that might be.

Inside, the Saturday morning crowd filled the place with a comforting buzz. They paused at the "Please Wait to be Seated" sign, and a cheery server soon greeted them. "Good morning, folks," she chirped.

"Hi, table for two, please," Sarah responded, slipping her sunglasses atop her head.

They were led to a cozy two-seater by the window. Sarah chose the seat facing the entrance, strategically positioning herself to monitor the door and the parking lot. Settling into her seat, she felt temporary relief amid the constant tension of the past few days.

Turning to Mike, she asked, "What'll you have?"

"Just a coffee, I think," he replied, his appetite seemingly absent.

Concerned, Sarah pressed, "Aren't you hungry? It's a long drive ahead; you should eat something."

His face contorted slightly at the mention of the drive's length. "How long?" he asked, a hint of worry in his voice.

"About eight hours, more or less," she answered, trying to sound nonchalant. Seeing his discomfort, she reassured him, "Don't worry, you can sleep through it."

Mike's eyes met hers. "Could we, like, stop at the liquor store, you know, just for something to help me sleep?"

Sarah nodded, understanding his need for a crutch, even if it was alcohol. "Sure, but eat something first."

After a moment's thought, Mike decided on pancakes and bacon. Sarah ordered the same.

The server briskly set down two large tumblers of iced water and coffee mugs on their table, stirring Sarah and Mike from their tense bubble. After giving their breakfast order and watching the server walk away, Mike's gaze lifted to meet Sarah's again.

"So, are you going to tell me what's happening?" Mike's tone sounded curious and more than a little concerned.

Sarah leaned in, her voice dropping to a whisper. "Silas tweeted to fish for info on Njala, hinting he knew they were up to no good. It was a bit much. I warned him."

"And?" Mike prodded, his eyebrows arching in anticipation.

Sarah's expression grew more serious. "The problem is, Silas didn't know that Jonathan, the UK lord funding his site, is connected to Alithia. Jonathan got a call from Alithia's head of security and revealed Silas's urgent trip to Chicago."

Mike's face paled. "Shit, that's . . . not good."

"Exactly. Now they know we're onto them, and given what they're capable of, I know we're targets," Sarah said, her voice betraying her fear.

"Fuck," Mike muttered, reality sinking in.

"But there's good news," Sarah added quickly, trying to inject a sliver of hope into the bleak scenario.

"Really?" Mike's voice wavered.

Sarah nodded. "A Njala whistleblower with loads of files contacted Silas. They implicate Alithia in Malaba's death and the Vivair crash. It's real, all of it."

Mike's eyes widened with disbelief and realization. "It's real? Henry was right . . . Holy shit."

Sarah continued. "Silas thinks his contact might be in military intelligence. He's handed all the data and Chloe's files to his cybersecurity expert. He's verifying it now. Once that's done, we publish. And Silas set up a kill switch."

"A what?"

"It's a fail-safe. If something happens to any of us, everything gets published anyway," Sarah explained, though she knew the implication sounded grim.

"You mean, if we get killed?" Mike's voice didn't rise above a whisper.

"Yes, that's exactly what it means," Sarah confirmed somberly.

Mike fell silent, absorbing the information, his face contorted with fear and resolve. Sarah felt a pang of guilt, but knew honesty remained vital.

"We'll be OK, Mike. We'll be in Nebraska. No one knows where we are. It'll all be over soon," Sarah reassured, trying to believe her words as much as she wanted Mike to.

Their conversation paused as the server returned with their pancakes, asking if they'd like more coffee. Both agreed gratefully.

After a few bites, Mike broke the silence again.

"Is Silas safe?" he asked, concern etched in his eyes.

"Yes, he's moving around too. In two days, we should be clear, and then it'll be their turn to run," Sarah replied, her voice steady.

"And Henry?" Mike inquired.

"I'll call him. Henry's after justice for his granddaughter and is close to getting it. We can all visit him once this blows over," Sarah said, trying to paint a picture of a hopeful future.

"Sounds good," Mike said, a genuine smile briefly crossing his face at the thought of seeing Henry again.

Silence enveloped their table as they ate, with Sarah's gaze intermittently lifting to monitor the entrance and the parking lot outside. Her vigilance remained high, but nothing out of the ordinary caught her eye, assuring her that their low-key brunch at the Sunshine Family Diner still appeared under the radar. She found herself enjoying the pancakes, a small respite.

"These are good," she commented, her words slightly muffled by a mouthful of pancake as she gestured with her fork toward her plate.

"I guess," Mike replied, lacking enthusiasm.

Observing him, Sarah could see that he had barely touched his food and was nudging it around on the plate. His attention seemed more focused on his coffee, which he finished swiftly. She watched him scan the area for the server, his movements sluggish.

Sarah's concern for Mike deepened. She sensed his approach to the brink, his fragility becoming more apparent with each passing moment. The thought of him spiraling into a meltdown loomed in her mind, a scenario she knew she wasn't equipped to handle, especially given the risk of drawing unwanted attention. Despite her reservations, Sarah recognized that keeping him calm with alcohol, though not ideal, seemed a necessity for the moment. A pragmatic, albeit temporary, solution to maintain their low profile.

The server, noticing Mike's empty cup, promptly came over to refill it. Sarah offered a grateful smile as she watched Mike wrap his hands around the warm mug, the coffee seemingly his sole source of comfort. She hoped the warmth of the drink might offer him some solace, even if just for a brief moment.

"Hey, Mike, go easy. You'll have trouble sleeping after all that coffee," she warned, her tone tinged with a hint of maternal concern.

"I'll be OK. I feel shattered, if I'm honest. It's been a rough few days, and I'm finding it difficult to see the light at the end of the tunnel. I know you said all this will be over soon, but for me, at least, it feels like a shit chapter in my life is just beginning," Mike confessed, his voice carrying a weariness that seemed to emanate from his very bones.

Sarah nodded, her gaze sympathetic. "I understand, but first, you must care for yourself. You need help to come to terms with all this. Remember the doctor who interviewed you after, you know, what happened? Maybe you can reach out to her when we're through this? It would be a good place to start."

"I still have her card. She was nice, you know, calm and friendly," Mike mused, a faint glimmer of hope in his eyes.

"OK, well, that's something positive. Sounds like a plan?" Sarah suggested, trying to instill a sense of optimism in him.

"Sure," Mike replied, his gaze fixed on the table.

Sarah could tell this journey to recovery would be challenging for him. After finishing their meal, she signaled the server to bring the check.

"OK, I'll settle up, and we can get back on the road. Need the restroom?" she asked, preparing to leave.

"Yeah, sure. Tell me something," Mike said, pausing for a moment.

"Sure, what?" she responded.

"Are we going to nail these murdering bastards?" His voice now contained a tinge of determination.

"Yes," Sarah affirmed, meeting his gaze with steely resolve.

"Good," Mike said, standing up to head toward the restroom.

As Sarah waited for the check, her eyes drifted to the parking lot. A silver Lincoln Navigator parked close to her car caught her attention. Two figures in the front seats seemed to be watching the diner intently. Her heart rate sped up. *Am I being paranoid?* The sight was unnerving.

When Mike returned, Sarah hastily left money on the table, and they headed outside, only to find the silver SUV gone. Relief washed over her, along with a lingering sense of unease. She inhaled deeply, savoring the fresh morning air, trying to convince herself it was just paranoia. She thought briefly about ditching the Audi. If they were on the run, they should do it properly. She took a breath. No, they weren't being followed. It was just paranoia.

CHAPTER 32

Tethered to his desk, Dalton had remained there throughout the night. Despite the extended hours, he stayed wide awake, artificially boosting his alertness with stimulants. Critical decisions hung in the balance, and Dalton stood ready to make them. Loose ends needed tying up, and he was just the man to do it.

His attention sharpened as the first report about Knox came in. The intel was clear: Knox was holed up in a Travelodge in Battersea, London, room 414. Dalton issued orders to his team with crisp efficiency: "Go to the room, detain Knox. Sweep the room, his office, his residence. I want a list of all his recent contacts."

Simultaneously, another team was tracking Sarah Reynolds from a distance. They had discretely planted a tracking device on her car, now parked at a diner in Flagg, west of Chicago. Dalton's hypothesis seemed confirmed when the team reported that Reynolds was accompanied by the same man who had been ejected from the Vivair flight, now her traveling companion. Dalton surmised they had acquired critical information passed on during the flight.

"Take out the vehicle at the earliest safe opportunity, then secure Reynolds," Dalton instructed, his voice steely. "And the man with her, bring him in. I want to know what he knows."

As Dalton leaned back, he tested strategies in his head. He believed that Knox and Reynolds had safety measures in place for whatever information they possessed. He had confidence that their secrets would come to light, whether alive or dead. His priority rested on gaining leverage over Knox, and then he would pivot to address the subsequent developments.

In the back of his mind, Dalton knew Tyler Rampton's come-uppance approached. This outcome was something Dalton had long anticipated and prepared for, employing his fail-safe measures. The only surprise was the rapid pace at which events were unfolding, yet Dalton remained unfazed. While accelerating, he had mastered control, and this situation was nothing exceptional.

Dalton's interest was piqued as he mulled over Mike Anderson's involvement. Watching the video of his fortunate escape from the Vivair flight, Dalton couldn't help but smile at the odd turn of events that had saved Anderson's life.

The thought crossed Dalton's mind that Anderson's luck was about to run out. They'd soon discover what he knew, and Dalton doubted it would be a pleasant experience for him.

Dalton glanced again at the message he had received earlier, a single word: *Exit*. It represented a clear sign that his association with Alithia and Rampton was drawing to a close. The endgame had been set; there was no turning back from this point. For Dalton, this whole debacle served as nothing more than a mere checkpoint in his journey, a transition to whatever came next.

Despite his professional demeanor, Dalton harbored a deep-seated disdain for Rampton. Yet, he had always maintained a veneer of professionalism in their interactions. To his mind, their objectives had been achieved, and Dalton rationalized them as serving the greater good. He rarely dwelled on the morality of his actions. A soldier at heart, he considered obedience to orders paramount.

Dalton viewed the sabotaged flight control systems as an essential step, a necessity for the regime change they aimed to achieve. He understood the grave consequences and collateral damage but saw them as unavoidable in pursuing their goals.

Where others might struggle with the morality of such operations, Dalton found it easy to justify his actions. He believed in the righteousness of the outcome, a conviction that the ends justified the means, even at the cost of innocent lives. In Dalton's world, innocence seemed like a rare commodity, and most people, in his eyes, were far from it.

Dalton leaned back in his chair, his mind working through the dark, turbulent waters of political intrigue he swam in. His ambition had become a driving force, positioning him as a pivotal player in the grand chessboard of global politics. Yet, he knew the limitations of his understanding. The broader motivations and the actual machinations behind his orders remained shrouded in mystery beyond his clearance level.

He had long accepted the inevitable revelation of Alithia's misdeeds. The demise of the organization as he knew it loomed on the horizon. However, Dalton's primary concern had to be to direct the fallout squarely at Alithia's doorstep, shielding himself and his superiors from any collateral damage. The whole truth had to remain buried.

The possibility that Knox and Reynolds might possess information extending beyond Alithia's conspiracy set off alarm bells in Dalton's mind. They posed a significant risk, potentially exposing him or, even more dangerously, those above him. Such exposure threatened to unravel the entire fabric of his meticulously orchestrated covert operations.

Navigating the complex network of relationships and clandestine maneuvering required finesse, something Dalton excelled at. But the investigative forays of Knox and Reynolds posed a threat. They risked unearthing the delicate connections Dalton had so carefully cultivated and maintained. Any leak leading back to him or hinting at the broader context of his actions could unravel years of work and put him in grave danger.

For Dalton, the mission had been clear and straightforward: ascertain the extent of Knox's and Reynolds's knowledge and ensure it led only to Alithia. He knew he had to act swiftly and decisively to contain any potential breach.

Amid all this, Dalton contemplated his alias with distaste. The name "Dalton" had been another layer in his complex identity, one he looked forward to discarding as soon as circumstances allowed.

He longed for the day when he could cast off this persona and start a new chapter, far from the unsavory world he was currently navigating, one where the distasteful residue of Rampton's greed and bloodlust stuck to his skin like an oily mist.

CHAPTER 33

Sarah settled into the driver's seat of her car, fingers deftly manipulating the satnav. "We've got a solid four hundred miles to Omaha," she mused aloud, calculating the journey. "If we're lucky with traffic, we'll make it by around six. It's going to be a stretch. Maybe you should try to get some sleep. You can relax out in the back if you'd like?"

Mike interrupted her train of thought. "The liquor store?" he asked hesitantly.

"The what?" Sarah replied, looking confused.

"You mentioned we could stop for . . . you know, something to help me sleep?"

"Oh, right," Sarah remembered, a hint of reluctance in her voice. "Yeah, there's a grocery store just across the street. Why don't you pop in? I'll hang back and plan our route."

Mike's expression looked grateful and embarrassed at the same time. "Um, do you have any spare . . ." He trailed off awkwardly.

Without a word, Sarah handed him a fifty-dollar bill, trying to mask her concern.

"I'll pay you back. It's just—" Mike began, but Sarah cut him off.

"It's fine, Mike. Just get what you need, and let's get going," she said, a sense of urgency in her voice.

"Need anything from the store?" Mike asked, already halfway out of the car.

"No, thanks," Sarah replied, her mind already moving on to the journey ahead.

Sarah's gaze lingered on the intersection as Mike disappeared into the store—a silver SUV, eerily familiar, cruised past. A cold wave of unease moved through her. *Is my overworked mind playing tricks, or is there more to it?* She tried to dismiss the thought, shaking her head as if to dislodge her growing anxiety physically.

Fifteen minutes later, Mike reappeared, lugging two grocery bags filled to the brim. He settled in the back seat, and Sarah saw his haul in the rearview mirror. The fifty dollars she had handed him had been well spent.

"I'm just going to crack open a beer," Mike said, his voice slightly muffled, as he pulled a can from one of the bags and opened it with a hiss.

Sarah's thoughts flicked to the practicalities of their journey. If Mike started on his stash now, they'd have to stop more frequently than planned. She eyed the bags again, suspecting a bottle of Jack Daniel's nestled within. The road to Omaha suddenly felt a lot longer.

Sarah's hands gripped the steering wheel, the leather cool beneath her tense fingers. "We're all set?" she asked, shifting the car into drive with a decisive movement.

In the rearview mirror, Mike's reflection gave a lethargic thumbs-up, his hand loosely clutching a beer can. They smoothly exited the restaurant parking lot, merging onto the main road leading them to I-80 West. The streets, bathed in the calm of a quiet morning, offered a temporary respite, allowing Sarah to focus on the road stretching before them.

Sarah felt a sense of progress as they drove, the miles adding a buffer between them and their troubles. Mike, already on his second beer, seemed increasingly distant. Sarah glanced at him occasionally, observing his descent into inebriation with concern and resignation. The inevitable task of managing him upon reaching Omaha loomed in her mind, a nagging reminder of their fragile situation.

The drive seemed smooth, the interstate welcoming them with open lanes. However, Sarah's sense of calm was shattered after about two hours. The same silver SUV she had noticed earlier reappeared in her rearview mirror, a ghostly presence that seemed to materialize and vanish at will. Each sighting sent a jolt of adrenaline through her, heightening her senses. She swallowed hard, now regretting not switching to a rental car.

Always maintaining a discreet distance, the SUV appeared like a shadow, never too close yet ever-present. Sarah's mind sped up as she tried to convince herself the sightings were coincidental, but the persistent appearances of the SUV gnawed at her intuition.

Amid the bright afternoon sunshine, the landscape shifted to open rural spaces. Mike had fallen asleep. He'd made a significant dent in the bottle of Jack Daniel's, and he now bobbed in the back seat like a cheap marionette. She decided to pull off the freeway—a test to see if they were being followed. If the silver SUV disappeared, she'd sigh with relief and pick up I-80 again, but if not? She frowned as she pulled off the interstate.

The asphalt looked weathered, and the surroundings suddenly seemed bleak and desolate. As Sarah maneuvered the car along meandering bends, the world seemed quiet, as if holding its breath in anticipation. Behind them, the silver SUV swung around the bend she'd just negotiated. Her eyes widened as they flicked from the road ahead to the rearview and back again.

Sarah's heart raced, each beat echoing the urgency of their escape. She pushed the car faster, feeling it lurch beneath her, an unspoken fear gripping her. Mike, jarred from his drunken stupor, slid across the back seat, his head thudding against the window.

"What's going on?" His voice, muddled with alcohol and confusion, broke the silence.

"We've got company," Sarah replied, her voice tinged with fear.

Once a path to safety, the road now felt like a trap. Every twist and turn of the asphalt brought the silver SUV closer, its presence an ominous shadow in pursuit. Sarah's eyes flicked to the rearview mirror, catching a glimpse of Mike's pale, wide-eyed expression as he peered over his shoulder at their pursuer.

Sarah's driving pushed the limits of her skill, the car accelerating beyond her comfort zone. Her heart pounded against her ribs, a frantic drumbeat urging her to flee, to escape the nightmare unfolding behind them. The thought of stopping, of confronting what followed, sent waves of terror through her. She regretted leaving the safety of the interstate, cursing herself for the decision that had exposed them to this peril.

Her hands, gripping the steering wheel with white-knuckled intensity, were the only anchors in a world that had suddenly turned hostile. The road ahead, no longer a familiar path but a twisting serpent, seemed to challenge her at every curve. Each turn presented a gamble, a desperate bid to outrun the malevolent force inching ever closer. In this high-speed chase, Sarah found herself cast in a role she never wished to play, racing against an unknown enemy on a road that offered no refuge.

Sarah's foot slammed down on the accelerator, the engine howling in response. The pursuing car clung to their tail, an unshakable specter in the rearview mirror. Her efforts to evade it seemed futile, and a sob escaped her, a sound of desperation and fear.

"Sarah, what are we going to . . ." Mike trailed off, filled with alarm.

Sarah screamed, and there followed a cacophony of screeching metal that shattered the illusion of survival, a chilling crescendo that marked the climax of this grim ballet. Their car, once a vessel of hope, was quickly transformed into a wreck, thrown off the road by the force of impact. It collided with a tree with a bone-jarring thud, a grim punctuation to their flight.

Dazed and disoriented, Mike sat up, clutching his head, his mind struggling to grasp the reality of their situation. He'd been jolted awake from a nightmarish slumber only to find himself in a new living nightmare. Through the spider-webbed rear window, his eyes tried to make sense of the chaos outside. He turned toward Sarah, her still form slumped in the driver's seat, a trickle of blood staining her face.

Suddenly, the back door swung open, revealing a masked figure who gestured for silence. Mike's fear petrified him, his heart pounding in his chest. Another figure appeared at Sarah's door, swiftly unbuckling her and dragging her limp body out with alarming ease. Mike heard the gravel crunch under her weight, followed by a soft thud.

Mike looked up at the masked man, his gaze locking with cold, emotionless eyes. Fear paralyzed him as the other door opened, and he felt hands gripping him, dragging him out. His eyes darted in panic, searching for any sign of help, but they were alone in the desolate stillness.

He heard one of the men speak, a command filled with ominous finality.

"Give him a shot."

A sharp pain pierced his leg, and then darkness enveloped him, swallowing him whole.

CHAPTER 34

Dalton lay back in his chair, feet on his desk, as a voice crackled over the radio. "We've got them, Reynolds and that douchebag," it announced confidently.

"OK," Dalton responded, his voice firm and controlled, "bring them to the warehouse. I'll meet you there. Take the plane. I sent it to Council Bluffs Municipal Airport, west of Omaha. It's waiting for you, hurry."

"Roger that," came the crisp reply.

The recent call from Dalton's London team played back in his mind. They'd reported that the operation at the Travelodge in Battersea hadn't gone as planned. Knox had eluded them, a clever setup leaving them grasping at shadows. Dalton wasn't pleased. However, he already had a plan in motion to lure Knox out.

As he mulled over the situation, Dalton felt something shifting. Events were spiraling, becoming increasingly challenging to steer. But with Reynolds and the Vivair guy now in his grip, he knew he'd extract whatever they knew soon enough.

Dalton possessed enough experience to recognize the momentum of such situations. Savvy as he appeared, Knox would have prepared for every eventuality, ensuring the release of the information regardless of what happened to him or his associates. Dalton acknowledged Knox's foresight, especially the Travelodge ploy. But it hardly mattered to him. His role now neared its end. Soon, it would be someone else's job to clean up the mess. For Dalton, the endgame appeared to already be in sight.

Now up on the roof, his eyes tracked the sleek black Alithia Corp helicopter as it whirred to life on the helipad. The day had started unfolding into the late morning in Los Angeles. He had decided to forgo updating Rampton until he had concrete information to share.

Striding purposefully toward the helicopter, Dalton felt the anticipation of the day's events. He acknowledged the pilots with a casual hand raise and hustled to the passenger door, ducking under the rotor wash. The helicopter, a Sikorsky S-92, gleamed under the sun, its immaculate condition a testament to Alithia's wealth. This machine, valued at over $20 million with customized luxuries, now served as his ride to Sacramento.

Settling into the plush confines of the back seat, Dalton felt a sense of finality. Today, he was the helicopter's sole passenger, a rare occurrence. The door shut firmly behind him, sealing him inside with the growing hum of the engines. His hand reached the drinks cabinet and pulled out a bottle of high-end cognac. Pouring himself a generous serving, Dalton lifted his glass in a solitary toast as the helicopter began its ascent.

He reclined in his seat, the cognac cradled in his hand and gazed out at the sprawling city below. A breathtaking view of Los Angeles unfurled below him, presenting a sprawling canvas of life and movement. But this flight felt different for Dalton, almost like a final farewell to a lifestyle he was leaving behind. He recognized that the coming hours held crucial significance with an uncertain outcome. But one thing remained clear—his path was shifting, and the days of executive luxuries like this were limited.

Ninety minutes later, Dalton's gaze swept across the expansive central warehouse of the Alithia Security Division facility in Sacramento. The vast, sprawling space functioned as a hub for covert operations and contained numerous small offices and a heavily restricted basement area. This remained his domain, where his technology team operated in the depths and where rooms, euphemistically labeled as "one-to-ones," served as spaces for the darker purposes of interrogations and secret meetings.

As he stood in the sterile corridor, Dalton contemplated his next steps. He awaited the arrival of Reynolds and Anderson, brought in from Omaha by his most trusted operative, Douglas, and Bryce, the less competent son of a family friend of Rampton's. Dalton had little faith in Bryce, viewing him as not much more than a thug but sometimes useful. His plan involved having Bryce attempt to extract information from Anderson in one of the interrogation rooms. Dalton didn't expect much; he doubted Anderson had anything of value to say, but he still might provide some answers about what they were up to. Reynolds had to be the real target, the key to drawing out Knox. He envisioned a strategic interrogation with Douglas, a psychological game he relished.

Descending to his private office in the basement, a place only he could access, Dalton settled in to wait. He received a message from Douglas; they were about an hour away. Dalton had spent the past months methodically winding down operations in Sacramento, moving personnel and equipment, and erasing any incriminating evidence. Once bustling with activity, this facility now felt like a ghost of its former self.

Instructing the remaining staff to depart for the day under the guise of a security sweep, Dalton ensured the building would be deserted except for the imminent arrival of his guests. He favored operating in isolation, especially considering what might happen next.

At four p.m., the sound of the warehouse shutters announced their arrival. Dalton ascended to the ground floor, his steps echoing in the empty space. He watched Douglas and Bryce approach, each pushing a wheelchair. Reynolds and Anderson, unconscious and hooded, were slumped over, their heads lolling to one side.

"They still out?" Dalton asked.

"Yup. The female banged her head during the stop, but it didn't look too bad. Gave them both a shot. Shouldn't be out too much longer," Douglas replied.

"OK, bring them down. Take the elevator. Douglas, take the female to room 40. I'll see you there. Bryce, take the male to room 48 and make a start. We'll catch up with you later," Dalton instructed, his voice carrying the weight of authority.

"Roger that," they responded in unison.

Returning to the stairwell, Dalton felt a sense of urgency. He had to send a message to Knox, and time was of the essence. Back in his office, he powered up his laptop, ready to set his plan in motion. The game was escalating, and Dalton was prepared to make his move.

CHAPTER 35

As Mike sat, bound and disoriented, a mocking voice cut through the darkness. "Glad you could make it." The words, incongruously genial, were spoken in a tone devoid of any warmth. Mike, defiant despite his vulnerable state, remained silent.

The deliberate footsteps approaching him, echoing ominously in the space, sounded like a scene from a movie playing out. Mike's heart pounded, and he took a deep breath of the musty odor inside the hood, making his stomach churn.

Abruptly, the man ripped the hood from his head, flooding Mike's vision with harsh light. He winced, his eyes rebelling against the sudden, sharp brightness. "What is this? Where am I? Where's Sarah?" he demanded, his voice bouncing off the concrete walls of the room.

"She's OK. She was a bit more busted up than you, but she'll be fine," came the reply. As Mike's vision adjusted, he saw the figure of a large man dressed in dark military-style clothing, his surroundings now clear: a windowless room with oppressive gray walls, plastic sheeting on the floor, and a chillingly familiar metal table.

"Are you a cop?" Mike's voice wavered slightly.

"Nope," the man answered, his voice cold.

"Why am I here?" Mike pressed, trying to mask his growing fear.

"My boss thinks you know something, and he's asked me to find out what that might be," the man replied.

Mike felt scared by the man's sinister tone. "Know something about what? Listen, if you let me go, I won't call the cops," he bargained. He doubted it would sway his captor, but he was buying time.

"No, you're not going anywhere. Well, only when you tell me what we need to know. Then we'll see. You will not get out in one piece if you don't tell me. You have my word on that," the man said, spit irrigating his words.

Mike's heart sank as he realized the precarious position he now found himself in. "I'm not saying jack until I know Sarah's OK," he retorted, his eyes swiveling left and right.

"I told you she's OK," the man insisted. "You are not in control of events. I am. So start telling me what you know."

Mike watched in horror as the man picked up a hammer from a steel bench against the wall. "Fuck, what are you going to do with that?" Mike's voice shook with fear.

"I don't know. Start hitting you with it until you talk. How's that sound?" the man replied with a hideous grin.

His captor sat opposite Mike on a white plastic chair, the hammer resting ominously in his lap. Mike's gaze fell on the polythene sheeting beneath his chair, his stomach turning as he realized its purpose.

"You've seen it in the movies . . . the hard way or the easy way? What will it be?" the man asked, a sadistic glint in his eye. *He was enjoying this.*

Mike's pulse thundered in his ears as he desperately searched for a way out. He snorted out a hollow laugh.

"What the fuck are you laughing at, you moron?" the man barked.

"It just dawned on me what the press called me after the

plane crash," Mike replied, his tone tinged with bitterness despite the terror.

"The Vivair crash?" the man asked. "Yes, I know, you're that guy—the drunk who got dragged off the flight. Humiliating," the man acknowledged, shaking his head with contempt.

"Yeah, I'm that guy. I thought it was funny, but whatever this is, it doesn't feel like luck had a hand in it," Mike said, displaying a grim acceptance, his jaw set.

"No. You've got that right. You're not lucky. You're one unlucky son of a bitch, and I'm done with the small talk," the man concluded, his patience wearing thin.

Trapped in a room that seemed to shrink with each passing second, Mike found himself at the mercy of someone who didn't know the word's meaning. The walls, dark and menacing, amplified his sense of entrapment. Despite a part of him yearning to surrender, a newfound resilience began to stir within him. He knew he had to somehow manipulate this dire situation in his favor.

He watched the captor, whose smirk seemed as chilling as the hammer he nonchalantly rested on his lap. This must be the same man who had silenced him in the back of Sarah's car. Mike knew it. His build and those lifeless, dark eyes were unmistakable.

"So, what's it going to be, jerk? Easy or hard?" the captor taunted.

Mike desperately needed time. He sought to engage the man in conversation, hoping to divert him from the looming brutality. It seemed like the ultimate pitch, but this time, for his life. "I always wondered how this scene would play out in real life," Mike said, trying to sound braver than he felt.

"What?" the man responded, his brow furrowing in confusion.

"The hammer and all. Classic move," Mike replied, acknowledging the chosen tool of torture.

The captor seemed thrown off by Mike's unusual response.

Seizing this unexpected advantage, however slight, Mike continued. "You must have watched your fair share of action movies, right?"

"What are you talking about?" The captor's words sliced through the air, each syllable edged with a distinct, sharp irritation. His voice now betrayed a hint of annoyance, as if the question was an unwelcome interruption to his thoughts.

"You wanted me to talk, so I'm talking, right?" Mike's voice wavered, but he pressed on. "I bet you're into those 'bad guy' characters—the ones who meet their end most dramatically."

The captor's expression shifted to anger, but Mike didn't relent. "So, how's your script going? Will you impress the boss or end up as a tragic footnote?"

Mike noticed the captor's hands tighten around the hammer, veins bulging on the back of his hands. *Am I breaking through, or am I just infuriating the man more, which will lead to a more painful outcome?*

But Mike couldn't stop now. He couldn't help but feel a rising tide of anger toward these ruthless individuals. He forced a smile.

"Enough of this, you freak." The captor stood up, his patience gone.

Mike played his final card. "In those movies, the villain always underestimates the hero. They think they've got all the power. But in the end, they get outsmarted. Happens every time."

The captor looked visibly perplexed, as if he'd been thrown off-balance by Mike's defiance and unexpected analysis. Like cat and mouse, Mike had chosen his role, clinging to the slim hope that, like in the movies, the underdog, or mouse, might save the day.

In a desperate bid for survival, Mike played a dangerous game, poking at his captor's ego and trying to undermine his need for control. His mind had gone to another place to plot the next move while his arms flexed against the bindings, testing their limits.

The captor's confusion morphed into fury, and he raised the hammer menacingly. "Dumb shit, stop talking," he snarled.

"I thought you wanted—" Mike began, but as the hammer descended, he acted. Summoning every ounce of strength, Mike lunged forward, his arms breaking free from the chair, his head colliding with the captor's chest. The force threw the man off-balance, and he slipped on the plastic, his head striking the concrete floor with a gruesome crack as his large bulk fell.

He lunged for the hammer, which was now lying on the floor. With a swift, twisting motion, he wielded it over his body and drove it into the center of his captor's chest. A guttural sigh escaped the man as the hammer made impact. Mike, still partially bound to the chair, struck again, this time catching the man squarely on the chin, sending a plume of blood arcing through the air.

Breathing heavily, Mike kneeled there, his heart racing. The only sounds were his own labored breaths and the hideous gasps of his captor. Beneath the man, a dark-red pool of blood expanded ominously. Mike held a hand to his mouth in disbelief. *How the fuck did that happen?* Maybe luck might be on his side after all.

The captor's breaths became more sporadic, resembling angry snores. In the eerie silence of the room, he noted longer gaps between snorts. Mike realized the man was probably dead or soon would be. He checked his feelings, searching for any reaction within himself, but found no remorse, nothing.

What now? He knew he needed to plan his next steps carefully, with his legs still shackled to a chair in a room with the lifeless body of a man he'd just killed. The urgency of escape pressed down on him. Yet, he felt momentarily frozen, the proverbial deer in the headlights processing what had just happened and the reality of his dire situation.

Mike's raging thoughts jostled for position as he scooted the chair toward the workbench, his gaze fixed on the sinister array of tools and weapons, remnants of his captor's intentions. His fingers found a small knife, and with a few swift cuts, he freed his legs from their bindings. Standing, he took in the room again, his heart still hammering against his rib cage.

In the corner, two bags caught his attention. One was a small backpack, and the other was a large holdall. His legs felt foreign as he walked toward them, adrenaline still coursing through his veins. Rifling through the backpack, he found their belongings untouched: clothes and toiletries. He checked the front pockets and found both his and Sarah's wallets. He slung it over his shoulder, then turned his attention to the holdall.

Unzipping it, Mike's eyes widened. Inside lay an arsenal of automatic weapons and stacks of cash. *What the hell is this place?* He grabbed two stacks of cash, stuffing them into his bag—more money than he had ever seen. He considered taking a weapon but opted against it. The added weight would only slow him down, and he knew he couldn't use it effectively. Instead, he pocketed a knife from the workbench, its presence a small comfort.

He scanned the room one last time, noting the eerie silence now that the man's labored breathing had ceased. His eyes caught the blinking red light of a camera—*time to move.*

Approaching the door, Mike listened for any sound beyond it. Hearing nothing, he tried the handle, his breath catching as the door unlocked with a click. He didn't know the time, but the quiet suggested it had to be late. Stepping into the dim corridor, with its stark gray walls and a white stripe running the entire length, he paused, straining to hear beyond the thick walls.

Mike's heart pounded as he hesitated in the dim corridor, muffled voices echoing hauntingly in the distance. The urge to rush back, grab a weapon, and play the hero for Sarah seemed compelling. But reality bit him hard; this wasn't a scene from an action flick. A misstep could be fatal for both of them.

Yet, the thought of abandoning Sarah gnawed at him. What

would leaving her behind make him? *So much for redemption.* With a heavy heart that raced again, he retraced his steps back to the interrogation room, each footfall echoing in the deserted corridor.

The gruesome sight that greeted him made his stomach churn—the expanding crimson pool of blood oozing from his captor's head, forming a slick pool reflecting the harsh lights. Mike winced, his stomach churning. He approached the holdall again, his gaze lingering over the lethal array of firearms. He silently hoped they were loaded; he wouldn't know how to do it himself. Selecting the simplest weapon to handle, he gripped it with uncertain hands and returned to the corridor's threshold.

His decision made, Mike stood in the doorway, weapon in hand, ready to face whatever lay ahead. He knew the risks but also knew he couldn't leave Sarah behind. He stepped forward with a deep, steadying breath, determined to do whatever he could.

He edged his way down the hallway toward the distant voices, his heart thudding in his ears. As he moved forward, his back to the wall, he discovered a small nook shrouded in darkness. He ducked into the space and crouched down, wincing as the butt of his automatic weapon hit the concrete, and a loud crack echoed in the emptiness.

He waited, trying to calm his breathing. *What am I going to do? Just kick the door open and start shooting? What the fuck?* He decided to wait and see what happened, then seize any opportunity. *Maybe I'm still lucky?* Mike's gaze darted up and down the corridor, his pulse a drumbeat in his ears. Left or right? Indecision gripped him momentarily before he chose a direction propelled by fear, urgency, and a faint glimmer of hope.

CHAPTER 36

Sarah Reynolds sat awake and alert in a windowless room, her restraints painfully digging into her skin. Opposite her, two large men, clad in combat fatigues, were leaning against a table, staring at her. She returned their stares with a defiant glare.

The slightly shorter one broke the silence. "So, I sent a brief message to your buddy Silas Knox. I wanted to trade. And you know what?"

"What?" Sarah retorted, her voice dripping with contempt.

"He didn't reply. Not a word. Any thoughts on that, Ms. Reynolds?"

"I don't know," Sarah responded, her voice steady, betraying none of her inner turmoil.

The man leaned forward. "I think he's cut you loose. He has no further use for you. So, whatever you gave him, that's all he cares about now."

Sarah scoffed. "Whatever."

His voice hardened. "You need to think about your situation. Don't expect a heroic rescue. Start talking, or you'll be useless to us, too." He leaned back, observing her reaction.

Sarah, though inwardly shaken, maintained her stoic exterior.

"What are you guys, anyway? Not cops, not soldiers. Just, like, dudes playing dress-up?"

"We make our own rules," he replied, his eyes unyielding.

Sarah's gaze didn't falter. "Your friend, the one who crashed into my car, is he even capable of handling a vehicle?"

The other man screwed up his face at her accusation. "What?"

"You heard me. Whoever was driving was a complete moron."

The first man's patience snapped. "Enough about the damn car!"

Sarah persisted, mocking their driving skills. Her defiance was met with a sudden, stinging slap from the second man. He glared at her, his hand still raised. "This is not a game!"

The first man, who she figured had to be the boss, exchanged a brief look with his companion, then turned back to Sarah, whose ear rang painfully from the blow. But she refused to back down, her gaze unwavering, even as her face burned from the assault.

"Check on Bryce. See if Anderson has started talking yet," the boss said.

Sarah sat, immobilized in the windowless room, listening to the man's fading footsteps. The intense gaze of the boss bore into her. She taunted him, "You need to train that guy."

"You're going to talk, and it won't be about your car," he retorted.

Sarah smirked. "We'll see."

As they exchanged terse words, urgent footsteps broke the silence. The other man burst in, his face etched with shock. "You better come and see this," he urged.

The boss narrowed his eyes at Sarah. "Think about your position. I want answers when I return." He left swiftly, following the other man.

Alone, Sarah exhaled deeply, her mind racing, her ear still

stinging. *What happened to Mike? Did this Bryce oaf overstep?* Her thoughts darkened as she considered the possibilities, the dangers Mike faced, and what he might have disclosed under duress.

Time served as her ally, yet it was slipping away. She clung to the hope of delaying them, buying time for the truth to emerge. With every passing minute, she marked a victory, a step closer to the possibility of Silas triggering the kill switch. She preferred not to think about how the publication might affect her fate. Would they be more or less likely to kill her? She swallowed hard. *How long have I been unconscious? Where am I, and what day is it?*

Fear nibbled away at her as she considered the next move, war-gaming scenarios in her feverish mind. Would they flee or silence her if they learned about Silas and the kill switch? Her heart raced at the thought.

The room seemed eerily quiet, heightening her anxiety. No voices, no footsteps, no noise. Just silence and uncertainty. She tried to gauge the time in order to piece together the events that led her to this terrible place, but the quietness made her nervous. The emptiness had become eerie and unsettling, leaving her thoughts to fill the vacuum.

Sarah's eyes narrowed as the man who had caused her crash reappeared alone. His boss had vanished, leaving only this thug who had struck her earlier.

"There's been a change of plans," he announced bluntly.

Sarah, seething, managed a sharp retort. "What?"

"We're going on a little trip. Sit tight."

His attempt at humor didn't amuse her. She glared back, trapped in her wheelchair, her body tensing at his every move.

"Oh, yeah, you're strapped in. Just stay calm. I'll put the hood back on, and then we'll be on the move." He spoke with a voice devoid of any empathy.

Sarah's mind boiled over with anxiety. "What's going on? What have you done to Mike?" she demanded, but her question received no response as the hood was lowered over her head, plunging her back into darkness.

Encased in the hood's musty confinement, Sarah's thoughts spun. The abrupt change in their plans hinted at something gone awry. *Was Mike the cause?* She shuddered at the thought, trying to focus on her immediate situation. She sensed the man's hurried movements as he wheeled her forward, her thoughts careering with possibilities and fears.

She experienced a brief interlude during the elevator's ascent before she was quickly transitioned into a vehicle. The swift removal of her straps from the wheelchair made her disorientated. Before she could react or attempt an escape, her arms were yanked back, and she felt zip ties pinching her wrists. Then she was unceremoniously shoved into the back seat of a vehicle, a heavy door slamming shut beside her.

Lying motionless, Sarah focused on her breathing, trying to calm her racing heart. She could hear the front door open and the sound of a helicopter fading away in the distance.

"Keep your head down," the man ordered.

Sarah complied while her mind churned with thoughts of escape, Mike's fate, and what lay ahead. Her world had become only fear and anxiety. She lay on the back seat for a while, wondering why they weren't moving. Then she heard a burst of gunfire, and her heart jumped in her throat. It was close. *What the fuck is going on?*

CHAPTER 37

Mike, still crouched in the shadows of the alcove, heard the door down the corridor open. His heart started racing again as he waited to see what would happen. *I'm a deer in the fucking headlights.* He held his breath as a man dressed in the same military attire as the guy he'd just killed marched down the hall straight past him. He heard another door open and assumed it was the room he had been in. *OK, this is coming to a head; keep breathing.* An eerie silence prevailed, followed by heavy footsteps running from the room, passing him again, and returning to where he assumed they were holding Sarah. This time, he could hear the words spoken.

"You better come and see this," the man said.

Huddled in the alcove's dimness, Mike's senses were on high alert as two sets of footsteps echoed in the corridor. *The boss is here.* He stayed out of sight, eavesdropping on their conversation at the doorway of his former holding room.

"Bryce is dead," declared the first man, his voice sounding matter-of-fact in the hallway.

"Yeah, I can fucking see that. What the hell happened?" The boss spoke with a terse and cold voice.

"No idea. Want me to check the camera?" the first man asked, his tone suggesting routine procedure.

"They're not recording. This is a clusterfuck," the boss snapped, his anger mounting. "I'm heading back to LA. We'll send in a cleanup team, shut everything down."

Mike experienced a jolt of fear as they mentioned a cleanup team, but their following exchange chilled him to the bone.

"What about the prisoner? What should we do with him?" the first man inquired.

"Fuck him. We don't have time for a wild-goose chase," the boss dismissed, his voice cold and unfeeling. "Just clean up. But if you find him, kill him."

Mike's heart raced at the casual order for his execution. He listened intently as they discussed Sarah's fate.

"What about the female?" the first man asked.

"Take her to the safe house. Wait for my instructions. I have plans for her."

"Understood," came the reply.

The boss's footsteps receded down the hall, his departure echoing ominously. Mike knew time was running out. He had to act quickly to save Sarah and himself. He took a few deep breaths.

Mike's heart pounded as he crouched in the shadows, his ears straining to catch every sound. The solitary man's footsteps echoed in the hallway. Mike realized the time to act had come. He couldn't allow this man to transport Sarah, and he knew he had to be the one to prevent it. He needed to create a diversion to distract the man and give himself the chance to intervene.

Mike's pulse raced as he watched the captor wheel Sarah, hooded and vulnerable, down the corridor. He seized the moment as they disappeared around the corner, darting across the hallway to follow at a safe distance. The sound of the elevator dinging shut propelled him into action. He raced to the stairwell, taking the steps two at a time, his heart pounding.

Emerging into the vastness of the hangar, Mike's eyes

quickly scanned the area—the SUV, sitting ominously by the large doors. He spotted a door in a corner with keys dangling from the lock. He darted toward it, slipping inside just as the elevator opened and Sarah and her captor emerged into the hangar.

Hiding in the janitor's closet, the acrid smell of chemicals stung his nostrils. Through a sliver of an opening, he watched in desperation as the man roughly transferred Sarah into the SUV. Adrenaline surged through him. He knew he had to act. He looked down at his weapon and then back at the SUV.

As the man turned to get into the driver's seat, Mike slid out of the closet and hid behind racking on the door's left-hand side. *This was it.* He aimed the gun at the ceiling and squeezed the trigger. The sudden blast sent a jolt through his body, the noise hurting his ears and the recoil slamming into his shoulder. His heart hammered against his ribs, panic rising in his chest.

As the captor spun around, weapon drawn, Mike realized the folly of attempting a confrontation. Thinking quickly, he snatched a spent shell casing from the floor and lobbed it into the janitor's closet. The casing rattled against the walls, echoing in the enclosed space. The captor, now alert to the location, cautiously approached the closet.

Mike held his breath, his entire body tensed for the next move. As the captor peered into the closet, poking his gun muzzle into the gap and prizing it open, Mike seized his chance. He burst from his hiding spot and rammed his shoulder into the man's back, sending him sprawling forward. He then slammed the closet door shut and locked it with a swift turn of the key. The captor's muffled curses and pounding fists echoed behind the door.

Wasting no time, Mike sprinted to the SUV. Pulling open the door, he quickly removed Sarah's hood and cut the zip ties binding her wrists. Her eyes, wide with shock and confusion, met his. "No time to talk. I will explain later," he said as he closed the back door and hopped in the driver's seat.

Mike's plan, though haphazard, had been working well until this pivotal moment.

"Shit," he cursed under his breath, a sinking realization hitting him.

"What is it?" Sarah's voice, hoarse with fear and tension, cut through his thoughts.

"The keys," he blurted out. The SUV, their only means of a quick escape, was now just a useless hunk of metal.

Sarah echoed his sentiment: "Shit. Where's the guy? Did you . . ."

"No, I locked him in the janitor's closet; he's got the keys."

"Shit," she said again.

With an urgent, desperate tone, Mike said, "Come on, let's get out of here. I've got no idea if that guy can shoot his way out of that closet. But I sure don't want to stick around to find out."

Adrenaline fueling their steps, they bolted from the building, Mike dropping the gun, which clattered onto the concrete, glad to be rid of it, not thinking if he might still need it. Their feet pounded against the ground, leaving behind the muffled sounds of their captor's frustrated bangs.

CHAPTER 38

Silas Knox found himself in an unforeseen predicament, detained in the grim confines of a detention center at Rome's Leonardo da Vinci International Airport. Shackled to a table leg in a room reeking of stale sweat, cigarette smoke, and an unidentified but distinctly off-putting odor, he brooded over his recent missteps.

His decision to flee to Italy after his decoy play at the Battersea Travelodge now haunted him. He'd flown to Rome seeking refuge in a safe house his old friend Giorgio provided, thinking it a perfect hideout. The city's bustling anonymity promised a brief respite, a chance to regroup while the storm of events he'd set in motion blew over. But an unexpected arrest warrant for "violating state secrets" had upended his plans. The details, muddled by the arresting officer's vague explanation, left him chained in a dingy room, a far cry from the control he'd once exercised over his fate.

As he sat there, Silas's thoughts turned to the contingency plan—the kill switch. If Alex couldn't reach him, the protocol stated he should try to contact Sarah for a final confirmation before releasing the data to the public. A simple press of a metaphorical big red button could set everything in motion without his oversight. His plan for a controlled, strategic release of the information, warning Jonathan, and priming his media contacts now seemed like a distant dream. The current situation felt haphazard, a chaotic battle against time.

Silas's frustration increased with each passing minute. Stripped of his possessions, including his sneakers, he couldn't even distract himself by checking the time. He rested his head on the cold table, exhaled a long breath, and grappled with the harsh reality of his predicament, feeling far removed from the control and influence he had been accustomed to wielding.

The door opened, and two men walked in. Silas assumed they were detectives and sat up straight. The older of the two, the one with a no-nonsense demeanor, sat opposite Silas.

"Good evening, Mr. Knox. My name is Detective Marco Coretti, and they have assigned me this case; this is my colleague, Alessandro Carbone," Coretti began, his voice rising on the word "case," his tone stern and authoritative.

Silas looked at the detectives. Coretti was middle-aged, stocky, with thinning black hair and a rugged face, while Carbone, younger and sharply dressed, stood silently by.

Coretti placed a green folder on the desk, his palm pressing down on it. "This file contains a lot of interesting information about you. It seems clear that you are not a friend of Italy," he said, his tone implying a predetermined judgment.

"I wouldn't say that. I—" Silas started, but Coretti interrupted him.

"No, you do not speak now, just me. You can speak later when your lawyer gets here. For now, you must listen," Coretti instructed, pulling out a pack of cigarettes.

He offered one to Silas, who accepted it after a moment's hesitation. Coretti lit their cigarettes, casually remarking, "There are laws, Mr. Knox. They say we cannot do this. But some laws can sometimes be ignored, can't they?" His question hung in the air, heavy with implication.

Silas, on the verge of responding, got cut off once more. "It was a *domanda retorica*, a rhetorical question. Your input is not required."

Coretti had a commanding presence, and his experience showed. "This file is bad news for you, and I regret to inform you of this. Let's have a look, shall we?"

Silas felt increasingly trapped and realized this was less about gathering information and more about asserting authority. He braced himself for what Coretti would reveal next, his mind mechanically trying to find a way out of this increasingly desperate situation.

Silas eyed the detective as he thumbed through the folder, his heart pounding. The room's stifling atmosphere felt like a crushing weight, intensifying the stress of his situation.

"Well, what have we got here? Let's see. So, there is espionage first. That's a strong and ugly word. It involves the unauthorized gathering, transmission, or receipt of sensitive or classified information intending to benefit a foreign government or entity. Heavy stuff," the detective said, his tone underlining the seriousness of the charge.

"Look, I—" Silas began, his voice blending frustration with disbelief.

"No, Mr. Knox, remember, you are listening, not speaking. Next, we have the unauthorized disclosure of classified information and the unauthorized access to computer systems. Plus, incitement to unlawful activity and conspiracy. We'll stop there for now, but there's more. I think you have been very busy," the detective continued, not allowing Silas to defend himself.

Silas remained silent, trying to make sense of the accusations. The detective's words felt like heavy blows, each adding to his sense of entrapment.

"This is grave, Mr. Knox. You'll likely be in prison for a long time," the detective said, closing the file with a thump that echoed in the small room.

Silas could only stare back, his thoughts swirling. He tried to discern the true motive behind these allegations. *Is this an attempt to extract information about my Italian sources?* Over the years, Silas had unearthed a wealth of corruption within Italian politics. *But why now?* He had not touched Italian politics for years, and the political landscape had significantly changed since then.

"Can I speak now?" Silas finally asked, his voice steady but containing a tinge of defiance.

The detective responded with an open-armed gesture as if granting Silas a favor. Silas took a deep breath, preparing to navigate this intricate game of *gatto e topo.*

Silas shackled to the table, stared boldly at the detective. "I won't go to prison. Several others went to jail after I uncovered what they had been doing. It wouldn't be a good look for your government to imprison me: the whistleblower," he asserted, his voice ringing with confidence and challenge.

The detective, seemingly unimpressed, leisurely blew smoke toward the ceiling. "Mr. Knox, I am a police officer, and you broke many laws. I must investigate when people commit crimes," he responded, his tone casual.

"Of course, but in this case, I believe your activities may be misguided," Silas retorted, trying to maintain composure despite the tightening knot of anxiety in his stomach.

The detective smiled, stood up, and collected the folder. "I will be back later, Mr. Knox. Make yourself comfortable, but given your surroundings, I do not think it possible," he said with a hint of irony.

As the detectives exited and closed the door behind them, Silas muttered a frustrated "Fuck it" under his breath. He knew that it would be a long, arduous night, trapped in his thoughts in a room that reeked of stale sweat and uncertainty, among other things.

CHAPTER 39

Dalton sat in the helicopter's rear, listening to the rhythmic whir of the overhead blades. Below, the rolling mountains gave way to the busy streets of Los Angeles. He glanced at his phone—three missed calls from Rampton. With Anderson in the wind, things were escalating. Incredible. *How the hell did that happen, anyway?*

Bryce had been duped and killed. *It's as simple as that.* What else did Dalton need to know? The facility had been compromised. Thankfully, he'd cleared everyone out.

He'd ordered some of his guys to shut it down and dispose of Bryce's body and everything else. En route to Alithia HQ, he considered Anderson's next move. He believed he'd go to the cops and shout about what had happened to him, so Dalton had shut everything down. He couldn't take the risk.

Dalton reflected on the operation's disastrous turn. Knox had eluded their trap, and Bryce, foolishly outsmarted, lay dead at the hands of Anderson, who had somehow managed to flee. Now, he only had Reynolds, who at least offered Dalton some leverage if he could only get to Knox. He knew well that these efforts merely postponed an inevitable outcome. His imminent departure marked the mission's conclusion, solution delivered, albeit not as flawlessly as he had hoped.

He retrieved his phone, composing a concise message to Rampton:

On chopper. I am heading back to HQ. Everything is under control. Speak soon.

His next move needed to be calculated; it had to buy him the necessary time to implement his exit strategy.

As he pocketed his phone, it vibrated with an incoming response. Dalton glanced at the screen, revealing Rampton's terse reply:

Good. No more fuckups.

A smirk crossed Dalton's face. "Good luck with that," he muttered, aware of the chaos that now enveloped Rampton's carefully laid plans.

He flung the phone at the seat opposite him, the handset bouncing off the seat back and landing on the cushion.

He let out a long breath and turned his gaze to the window.

Dalton, a seasoned operative, found himself mired in the complexities of a mission spiraling out of control. A sense of weariness had begun to settle in the deep recesses of his mind. The number of mistakes stacking up in this operation was unlike anything he had encountered during his extensive career. The Sacramento fiasco represented the latest in a series of blunders that seemed to mock his expertise. He longed for reassignment, a fresh start away from the mounting errors and the haunting shadows of his current predicament. His experience informed him that every operation had its life span, and he could see this one drawing to a close, not with a triumphant crescendo but with a series of dissonant chords.

His phone vibrated on the seat beside him. Dalton stared at it, disgusted. *What now?* He retrieved it and looked at the screen.

Now, all he could do was laugh.

The latest message from his cleanup revealed the second operative on the ground at the Sacramento facility, Douglas, had been discovered absurdly locked in a closet. Worse, Sarah Reynolds and Anderson, the drunk fool from the Vivair flight, had escaped. This wasn't merely a setback but a glaring testament to the operation's unraveling.

The message served as a salient reminder of the reality he faced: a carefully orchestrated plan, now crumbling under the sheer weight of its own complexity. Dalton's mind grappled with the implications, the potential fallout, and how the chance to rectify the situation had now slipped from his grasp. Amid this chaos, a part of him couldn't wait for his reassignment, a chance to escape the mission's web of missteps.

Dalton mused over Rampton's ignorance of the impending storm. He visualized Rampton issuing orders with smug satisfaction, sometimes blatantly, sometimes subtly, suggesting people be eliminated. Yet, he remained oblivious to the looming consequences of his actions.

Dalton's gaze swept over the cabin's luxurious interior as the sleek black Alithia chopper neared the equally imposing Alithia HQ. He pondered the fate of such extravagant amenities in the face of the unraveling situation. Shaking his head, he dismissed these thoughts as trivial compared to what lay ahead.

Back on the ground, he swiftly made his way to his office, ensuring he locked the door securely behind him, his actions precise and methodical.

After an hour passed, Dalton was gone. Like a shadow in the night, he had vanished, leaving behind the chaos of a plan that had spiraled beyond his control.

CHAPTER 40

Gasping for air, Mike leaned against the chain-link fence, his chest heaving from the frantic escape. He squinted back at the building they had just fled from—an ordinary warehouse that masked its sinister purpose. Mike's mind briefly entertained the thought of his unexpected heroics. He hadn't seen himself as capable of overpowering his captors, but desperation had brought something out of him, something hitherto hidden.

Sarah's voice broke his train of thought. "Well, I have to say, I didn't think you had it in you," she said, her smile reaching her eyes as she playfully clapped him on the back.

Still catching his breath, Mike turned to her with a puzzled expression. "Huh?"

"Rescuing the damsel in distress is impressive." Her tone was amused and carried genuine admiration.

Mike managed a weak smile. "Well, I had a bit of a hangover, to be honest—not sure if it was the drugs they knocked me out with or the booze," he said, rubbing his temple as he reflected on the ordeal.

Sarah's laughter rang out, a sound that seemed out of place in their current predicament, however welcome. "Even more impressive, then." She chuckled, her laughter easing some tension from their harrowing escape.

As Sarah set her sights on the distant fence, Mike trudged behind her, a heavy fog of exhaustion cloaking his thoughts. "I think walking along the roadway to the exit is far too risky," Sarah said, voicing her concerns as she gestured down the road. "I think we should try to get through the fence here and walk across that wasteland." Overwhelmed by recent events, Mike could only muster a nod in agreement.

Sarah's curiosity about the backpack's contents broke him out of his trance. "It's our stuff; it was in the room with me," he told her. "It's got our wallets and clothes. No phones, though, and I am not going back to look for them," Mike explained, his voice tinged with fatigue and determination.

"I'm with you on that," Sarah agreed.

Mike then revealed another find. "Picked up some cash from the other bag, the one with the guns." He unzipped the backpack, showcasing two stacks of cash to Sarah.

"Wow, that's a lot of money. Are those hundred-dollar bills?" The astonishment in Sarah's voice was unmistakable, her words colored with disbelief and curiosity.

"Yup," Mike replied, a hint of pride creeping into his voice despite the surreal situation. He zipped up the backpack and slung it over his shoulder.

Confronted with a fence too tall to climb, Mike's survival instincts kicked in. He remembered the knife in his bag, retrieved it, and began digging a crawl space beneath the fence. After about five minutes of relentless effort, he had carved out an escape route. He shoved the backpack through the gap, took a deep, steadying breath, and slithered through the opening like a desperate fugitive. He stood up on the other side and felt a rush of relief as he helped Sarah through. The fence now stood as a physical barrier between them and the horrors they had left behind.

Mike squinted into the distance, grappling with uncertainty.

They could be anywhere. His gaze fixed on the vast, empty expanse stretching before them. The wasteland, sloping uphill, offered no clues, only a view of a distant skyline marked by towering structures. He nudged Sarah, and together, they decided to head toward the cityscape.

As they descended the other side of the incline, the hum of a busy road reached Mike's ears. The darkness of the night provided no hint of the hour.

Continuing their descent, a car parked precariously at the edge of the wasteland, half on the sidewalk, half off, drew Mike's attention. He noticed the small Toyota bearing California license plates. "So, maybe we're in California," he speculated, recalling conversations about Alithia's headquarters in Los Angeles. But something felt off. "Is this LA?" he asked Sarah, uncertainty tingeing his voice.

"No, it's not LA," she responded with certainty, squinting at their surroundings.

Reaching the road, they turned toward the city's heart. They hadn't walked far when a yellow taxi approached from the opposite direction like a beacon in the night. Mike instinctively raised his arm, hailing it. The taxi complied, executing a smooth U-turn before pulling up in front of them. Mike and Sarah exchanged a quick, wide-eyed glance before stepping toward the vehicle, each step a mix of caution and relief.

As they slid into the back seat of the taxi, a sense of fortune washed over Mike. He experienced an odd feeling of exhaustion and exhilaration, as if he were riding on the edge of luck itself.

With a deep Latino accent, the taxi driver asked, "Where to?" His voice carried a hint of weariness.

Mike hesitated. "Um, if you can tell us where we are, we'll tell you where to go." His voice wavered slightly.

The driver glanced at them through the rearview mirror, his eyes narrowing, sizing them up. "You are in Sacramento," he stated flatly, his voice devoid of warmth.

Mike cringed inwardly as he realized how disheveled and

suspicious they must look. His face probably bore the marks of their recent ordeal, broadcasting their plight to the world.

"OK, sorry," Mike responded quickly, trying to sound casual. "We've been walking for a while. Can you take us to the airport?"

"Sure," the driver replied, shifting the taxi into gear.

The vehicle lurched forward, tires screeching against the pavement as they sped away. Mike's eyes drifted to the taxi's digital clock. It read 9:45 p.m.—confirming how time had slipped away from them.

Thirty minutes later, they arrived at Sacramento International Airport. Mike handed the driver a generous amount of cash from his recently acquired stash, insisting he keep the change. Together, he and Sarah hurried into the terminal.

Once inside, Sarah turned to him with a look of determination. "What's the plan?"

Mike paused, his mind racing ahead. "A plan? How about Chicago, and then we find Henry?"

Sarah nodded decisively. "OK, let's do it." They had set their course, and their resolve remained firm. Despite the chaos, they could still think straight.

"There's a Chicago flight at eleven ten," Sarah said, pointing at the departures board that loomed large above them.

Mike's heart raced as they approached the United ticket desk. "Hi, we need to be on the next Chicago flight. It's urgent. We have cash," he stated, trying not to sound desperate.

The ticketing agent eyed them, her fingers poised over the keyboard. "Chicago is at eleven ten. We're full in coach, but first-class seats are available."

Mike couldn't help but smile. "We'll take two, thank you."

The agent hesitated, squinting at him. "Are you . . . ?"

"Sorry?" Mike feigned confusion.

"You look familiar. Hey, are you that guy from Vivair?"

Mike chuckled wryly. "Oh, that guy? No, it's not me. What a

loser. I don't even drink." He watched as the agent smiled, seemingly convinced. Sarah could barely contain her laughter.

"That will be sixteen hundred dollars, please. Cash, you said?" The agent now spoke in a businesslike tone.

Mike nodded and counted out sixteen crisp $100 bills, handing them to her.

"ID?" she asked.

Mike paused, concern washing over him. Would she recognize his name? He took their wallets from the backpack, handing Sarah's to her. They both presented their driver's licenses.

The agent's puzzled gaze lingered on his ID, then she tapped something into her keyboard and handed it back with a knowing smile. Mike knew she recognized him, but they both ignored the unspoken acknowledgment.

"Any bags to check?" she asked.

Mike held up his backpack. "Nope, traveling light."

"Here are your boarding passes and receipt. Gate A15, your flight is boarding. Have a pleasant trip."

They thanked her and turned toward security. But, suddenly, Mike froze. The knife. The money. He grappled with the potential consequences.

"What's wrong?" Sarah replied, sounding worried.

"I still have the knife on me and all this cash. What if they pull me out in security?"

"You'll have to ditch the knife, obviously," Sarah replied, pragmatic despite the tension. "But keep the cash. We don't know if they can trace our movements if we use cards."

Mike nodded, a plan forming. "Wait here." He turned on his heel, heading to find a place to dispose of the knife. He contemplated the risk of carrying so much cash, but they had no choice. They needed it, especially now when their every move might be watched.

Mike swiftly pivoted and made a beeline for the restroom, his steps purposeful. As he passed by a Hispanic cleaning lady lingering near her cart, he offered her a brief, inconspicuous nod before slipping into a stall. The door locked with a definitive click. He set his backpack on the toilet seat and extracted the knife, delicately placing it on the cistern.

Methodically, he began distributing the cash he'd retrieved from the bag. Bills tucked neatly into his wallet, some stashed in his jeans, and a few found their way into his sock in a spur of cautious creativity. He estimated he had redistributed about $4,000, and satisfied with the concealment, Mike pocketed the remaining cash in his hoodie. He emerged from the stall, approaching the sink with a heavy heart. Staring into the mirror, he scarcely recognized his weary, battered reflection. A tender bruise adorned his forehead, a memento of the night's ordeal. A splash of cold water offered a fleeting respite.

Digging through his backpack, he fished out a baseball cap and sunglasses, adjusting them to mask his bruised appearance. Satisfied, albeit marginally, he exited the restroom.

Passing the cleaning lady once more, he paused and doubled back. With a gentle smile, he offered her the cash from his hoodie. *"Feliz Navidad,"* he uttered, the only Spanish he knew. Her stunned silence spoke volumes as she gazed at the unexpected windfall.

Turning back to rejoin Sarah, Mike felt both relief and anticipation. They needed to navigate security, but he felt an inexplicable sense of good fortune. As they approached the checkpoint, he glanced at Sarah and nodded, ready to face whatever came next.

Mike strode confidently through security, his gut telling him they would face no obstacles. His instincts proved correct; the metal detector remained silent, and the security personnel seemed disengaged, not bothering with a pat down. The operator at the X-ray machine seemed to be asleep or well on the way. Mike felt a fleeting pang of regret for not bringing more of the money with him, but he quickly dismissed it, the image of the cleaning lady's astonished face bringing a sense of satisfaction.

Without delay, they headed to Gate A15, joining the queue for boarding. As Mike stepped onto the air bridge, a shiver ran through him as a horrific flashback of his last plane journey flooded him. He recalled the faces and voices of those who had shared the bridge with him on that fateful flight—all now silenced. A surge of anger rose within him, fueled by the senseless loss. Those people were gone, all for the sake of money.

His mind then flashed to the man he'd left behind in the warehouse, his head gruesomely crushed. Mike wrestled with the memory, convincing himself it had been self-defense, not murder. The man had intended to torture and kill him; Mike had had no choice. He pushed away any thought of remorse, focusing instead on their current mission.

Mike felt a bizarre collection of emotions as he and Sarah silently made their way onto the plane. Boarding another plane was surreal, almost like he was now living a different life. His last conscious flight, even though he'd never left the ground, seemed like a distant memory.

Greeted by a smiling flight attendant, Mike couldn't help but think of Joy. The attendant's professional, welcoming demeanor felt strangely comforting, even though he knew it was just her job.

"Welcome aboard," she greeted cheerily.

"Hello," Mike responded, his voice steadier than he felt, showing his boarding pass.

"2B, right there," she directed, pointing to a window seat near the bulkhead. "Have a pleasant flight."

She then assisted Sarah to seat 2A. As they settled into their seats, exhaustion started to settle in. Mike stowed his bag beneath the seat ahead, then leaned back, letting his eyelids fall shut, seeking respite.

"Would you care for a preflight beverage?" The question cut through his brief solace.

He opened his eyes to find a flight attendant offering a tray of drinks. Parched from their recent trials, Sarah eagerly accepted an orange juice.

The attendant turned to Mike, her tone professional yet warm. "Champagne, juice, or sparkling water, sir?"

"Water, please," Mike heard himself respond, a choice that surprised him as if his subconscious had taken the helm. He silently acknowledged it had been the right call, considering the journey ahead and the clarity they needed.

Accepting the glass of water, Mike's eyes met Sarah's. She offered him a knowing smile, an unspoken acknowledgment of their shared ordeal and determination. Their glasses met in a quiet toast.

Upon arrival in Chicago in the early morning, their first task would be to rent a car, preferably one equipped with satnav. Mike reasoned that Sheboygan Falls, the quaintly named town where Henry resided, couldn't be too large or complex to navigate. Yet, without an address or any means to contact Henry, the task felt daunting. In Mike's mind, it was just another challenge to overcome in his new game of life.

CHAPTER 41

M ike maneuvered their rented Ford Focus through the streets of Sheboygan Falls, a sense of uncertainty settling over him. After three hours on the road since landing in Chicago, the town's size came as a surprise. He eased the car to the curb, turning to Sarah with bewilderment.

"You're an investigative journalist, right?" he asked, a touch of hope in his voice.

"Yes," Sarah replied, her tone reticent.

Mike gestured vaguely toward the bustling town. "Do you think you could figure out where to find Henry? I imagined Sheboygan Falls as a quaint little place, but it's not quite what I expected."

Sarah's eyes narrowed. "What do we know about Henry?" she asked, looking back at Mike.

Mike leaned back, his gaze drifting to look out the window. "There's a lot I don't know, like where he lives or his contact details," he admitted with a shrug.

Sarah's investigative instincts kicked in. "But we know about Chloe, his granddaughter, and his RV, right?" she prodded.

"Big Bertha," Mike replied, his eyes still on the view outside.

"And don't forget his boat," Sarah added, an idea dawning. "It was the USB stick password, remember?"

Mike's attention snapped back to her. "Oh, yeah, the boat," he said, a grin breaking through as the realization hit him like a eureka moment. He snapped his fingers.

Sarah leaned forward, her mind working things through. "Why don't we try the harbor? We could look for the boat or ask around. Someone might know him."

Mike looked at her, admiration shining in his eyes. "You're brilliant," he said, genuinely impressed. "*Serenity Seeker*, wasn't it?"

"That's the one. Let's go," Sarah said, her voice firm.

Mike steered the rental car into the modest harbor parking lot, his gaze sweeping over the many boats lined up along the quayside. Exiting the car, he and Sarah set off toward the docks.

Splitting up seemed the best strategy to cover more ground. Mike veered left, eyes scanning the names emblazoned on each boat. *Serenity Seeker* wasn't anywhere to be seen. With a heavy sigh, he continued his search, realizing a big town would have a big harbor.

An older man in worn dungarees and a frayed trucker cap approached him. The man had a steady gait and curious eyes.

"You seem a bit lost, son. Need help?" the old man asked, closing the distance between them.

Mike turned to him, hope flickering in his chest. "Yeah, I'm looking for a boat, or rather, its owner."

"What's the boat's name?"

Caught off guard, Mike blinked. "Uh, *Serenity Seeker*. It belongs to a guy named Henry."

"Henry Mitchell?"

"That's him! Do you know him?"

The old man nodded, his eyes squinting slightly. "What's your business with him?"

Mike hesitated, aware of how odd his request sounded. "I'm a friend, but I don't have his address."

The old man's gaze sharpened. "You a cop?"

"No, just a friend," Mike replied, feeling furtive.

"And your name?" The old man said, folding his arms across his chest.

"Mike . . . Mike Anderson." His name sounded uncertain, even to him.

The man's eyes widened with recognition.

"You're that guy, aren't you? The one from the plane crash!"

Mike's face flushed, "Could you maybe call Henry for me?"

"It's early for a Sunday."

Mike insisted, "Henry's an early riser. Please, it's important."

The man seemed to weigh his options before nodding reluctantly. "Alright, stay here. I'll be back."

As the old man walked away, Mike watched him go. He hoped he would soon be reunited with Henry but felt anxious; his Luckiest Man Alive nickname seemed to follow him around like a bad smell.

Leaning against the rail, he gazed over Lake Michigan, its tranquil expanse soothing his frazzled nerves. In his mind's eye, he pictured Henry and Chloe sailing across these waters, the boat slicing through the cold lake with a gentle rhythm. But his reverie disappeared and was quickly overshadowed by the haunting memory of his nightmare, where bodies thudded against a boat's hull in a macabre dance. Mike shuddered, trying to shake off the image, and took several deep, calming breaths.

"Henry vouched for you," the man said, cutting through Mike's thoughts and causing him to startle.

Opening his eyes, he found the man standing before him with a matter-of-fact expression.

"Thanks," Mike replied, relieved.

"He'll be here soon. Look for Bertha in the parking lot," the man added before leaving, his wave casual yet final.

Mike signaled Sarah, who now approached them an inquisitive look on her face.

"Found Henry. He's coming for us," Mike explained a hint of pride in his voice.

Sarah's eyes sparkled with amusement. "Impressive. It seems there's no end to what you can do," she teased, winking at him.

Mike lugged the backpack from the trunk of the rented Ford, his eyes catching the arrival of Big Bertha in the parking area. At the wheel, Henry offered a mini-salute, a hint of a smile playing on his lips.

Henry parked next to their rental. "Sarah, Mike, good to see you. What brings you here?" he asked with a curious tone.

"Hi, Henry. Things have escalated. We need to catch you up and contact Silas," Sarah explained, her voice tinged with urgency.

Henry's demeanor shifted swiftly. "OK, hop in, we'll go to my house."

Sarah slid into the passenger seat, followed by Mike. The door thudded shut.

Henry's house soon loomed into view, a picturesque double-fronted property with impeccably manicured lawns. Its light-blue timber, accented by white frames and a gray slate roof, spoke of a comfortable, well-earned retirement. As Mike followed Henry and Sarah inside, his eyes were drawn to the photographs adorning the walls. One in particular, featuring Henry and a beaming Chloe aboard the *Serenity Seeker*, captivated him.

The aroma of fresh coffee filled the polished oak-floored kitchen as they settled around the large table. Henry, acting the gracious host, brought over three steaming cups.

"Alright, let's hear it. What's happened?" Henry urged, settling in his chair with a serious gaze fixed on Mike and Sarah.

As Sarah detailed their harrowing journey to Omaha, the ambush, their kidnapping, and subsequent drugging, Mike felt Henry's gaze as he then took over, recounting the harrowing details of his encounter with the captor, his daring rescue of

Sarah, and their escape with a substantial amount of cash, all the way to the airport in Sacramento.

Henry absorbed their story, his expression full of surprise and admiration. "Glad you're safe, but we're not in the clear yet," he said, eyes scanning the verdant garden through the large window.

"I'm going to call Silas," Sarah said. "Can I use your phone? We lost ours."

Henry unlocked his phone and slid it across the table to Sarah.

She opened up the secure messaging app, found the right contact, and put the phone to her ear.

"No answer," Sarah said after a few moments, looking downcast. Henry had a worried expression on his face as he looked at Sarah. "I hope he's OK. I don't know what will happen with Silas out of the picture. We need—"

"I do," Mike interrupted.

"What?" Henry looked puzzled.

"I know what's going to happen," Mike continued.

"Would you mind enlightening me?" Henry asked.

"The kill switch," Sarah interjected.

"The what?" Henry replied.

"Kill switch, it's what they use when—" Mike started.

"I know what a kill switch is, Mike," Henry said calmly.

"Well, we have one. Silas ensured that if anything happened to either of us, the kill switch would be activated, and all the files, Chloe's info, and the data Silas received would all be published everywhere, all at once." Sarah said.

"I would guess that's pretty goddam imminent, then," Henry said.

"Affirmative."

"In that case, we need to go on a trip," he said.

"Where are we going?" Mike said warily.

"Las Vegas."

"What?"

"I'll tell you about it on the way to the airport. Grab your things, let's go."

Mike's heart raced as he stood up, his body responding to the sudden adrenaline rush. He glanced at Sarah, who looked determined, seemingly happy to go along with Henry. *He has that effect on people.*

They quickly returned to Henry's RV, speeding down I-43 toward the Milwaukee International Airport.

Henry handed Mike his unlocked phone. "Find us the next flight to Vegas," he instructed.

Mike's fingers danced over the screen, inputting flight details. The clock read 7:30 a.m. They were an hour away from the airport. Mike's brow furrowed as he sifted through the options.

"We're coming back, right?" he asked, his voice tinged with uncertainty.

"I sure hope so," Henry replied.

Mike found a Southwest flight leaving at three and arriving in Las Vegas at five. But it wasn't soon enough. He then stumbled upon a Delta flight leaving at 9:15 a.m., with a layover in Minneapolis, that arrived just before one.

"We might not make that one," Mike cautioned.

Henry pressed harder on the accelerator. "Book it. We'll make it," he declared confidently.

Mike hesitated for a moment. "I need your credit card, Henry."

Without a word, Henry reached into his jacket and handed over his wallet. As he opened the wallet, Mike noticed a US Department of Defense ID card and cast a quick glance at Sarah. He swiftly booked three tickets on the Delta flight. He felt slightly disappointed at the ample coach availability, hoping for a reason to book First, but brushed it aside.

They arrived at the airport with forty-five minutes to spare and left Big Bertha in the parking garage. With no luggage, they breezed through to their gate, arriving twenty minutes before their flight.

Throughout the rush, Mike realized Henry hadn't explained why they were heading to Las Vegas. "Why are we going to Vegas?" he asked, almost apologetically.

Henry's response was brief. "I'll tell you on the plane."

Mike looked at Sarah. She shrugged. *Good enough for me.*

Mike leaned against the wall near the boarding gate, his thoughts a complex tapestry. The past events felt surreal, like jigsaw puzzle pieces that refused to fit together. He recalled the days before this chaos when his world revolved around petty grievances and self-absorption. His biggest concern had been the indignity of flying economy. How trivial those concerns seemed now.

He remembered the fateful day of his flight to London, the culmination of all his frustrations and alcohol-fueled anger that led to his embarrassing outburst on Vivair 002. That episode had led to his ejection from the flight, an act that had ironically saved his life. Those passengers, he now understood, hadn't just died; they had been murdered.

In the days that followed, Mike had felt isolated, cut off from the world, until Sarah and Henry found him and dragged him into a far more complex and dangerous reality than he could have ever imagined. The knowledge of the conspiracy he'd stumbled into had only driven him deeper into the bottle.

Mike shivered as he recalled the terror of their car being forced off the road, the sheer panic that enveloped him. The memory of his captor, the hammer-wielding man whose life he had ended in a desperate struggle for survival, sent a cold wave of fear washing over him. The grotesque sounds of the man's final moments echoed in his mind, followed by the haunting stillness and the image of the spreading pool of blood.

Now, here he stood, about to board a flight to Las Vegas, of all places. A wry smile touched his lips at the thought of the air miles he could be racking up. Milwaukee to Las Vegas after a whirlwind of unexpected travel. He glanced at Henry, who sat silently, his thoughts inscrutable. Mike knew better than to press him for answers in the middle of an airport. The reason behind their trip to Vegas remained a mystery that Henry would reveal when he deemed it appropriate.

Mike couldn't help but speculate. What awaited them in Vegas? Alithia's headquarters were in Los Angeles, and they had just escaped from their facility in Sacramento. But Vegas? The connection eluded him. For now, he could only wait and see what the next chapter of this bizarre journey held.

Mike handed the attendant his boarding pass, feeling relieved as she scanned it without a hint of recognition. The sound of the beep was almost comforting. He followed Henry down the narrow aisle of the aircraft, Sarah trailing behind. Their seats were near the rear, away from prying eyes and eavesdropping ears. Henry claimed the window seat, leaving Mike sandwiched in the middle and Sarah in the aisle seat.

The cabin fell silent as an announcement declared boarding complete. Glancing around, Mike noted the sparsity of passengers. Henry seemed to be waiting for the right moment to speak, his expression unreadable.

Mike's mind ran through a tornado of questions and scenarios. *How much longer will this turmoil last?* His old life felt like a distant memory, almost like it belonged to someone else.

As the plane ascended, Henry's demeanor shifted. He scanned the cabin with a practiced eye, ensuring their relative privacy. Once satisfied, he leaned forward, retrieving a Moleskine notebook from his jacket. His movements were deliberate and calculated. Mike watched intently.

Henry laid the notebook on the tray table, tapping it with a finger, his gaze shifting between Mike and Sarah. "I've been doing some digging while you two were in the thick of it," he began, his voice low but clear. "Everything I've found out is in here."

Sarah leaned in, her eyes narrowing in interest. "And what exactly have you discovered?"

Henry's expression hardened. "I've identified the man at the top of Alithia—Tyler Rampton. He's the architect of this whole thing. He's a bad hombre."

Sarah's face darkened at the mention of the name. "That's an understatement," she murmured, shaking her head in disgust.

Henry continued, his voice growing more serious. "If this kill switch is activated, and I have no reason to doubt it, Rampton's world will implode. He won't stick around to face the consequences."

Mike cut in, his voice trembling slightly with anxiety. "So he'll run. But what are we doing?"

Henry's eyes gleamed with determination and resolve. "We're going to make sure he doesn't get away. He won't have a chance to escape."

Mike felt a twinge of apprehension. Yes, he'd been lucky so far, but this seemed like a whole different level of risk. "And why Vegas?" he asked, his curiosity overcoming his trepidation.

Henry flipped open the notebook, revealing pages of notes and scribbles. "His escape plan involves a plane—a private jet. That's where we come in."

Sarah and Mike exchanged a glance; what they were embarking on sinking in. They were no longer fleeing or surviving but actively stepping into the lion's den. The reality of their mission appeared daunting, but they knew there was no turning back. The stakes were too high, and they were in too deep. As the plane cut through the skies, heading toward the neon lights of Las Vegas, Mike braced himself for what lay ahead.

"His plane is in Vegas?" Mike echoed, trying to grasp what they were up against.

"Well, one of them. Like I said, I've been researching and asked myself, if he runs, where will he go?"

Sarah chimed in, her tone reflecting both her knowledge and

the urgency: "Njala." Mike noted the certainty in her voice; she seemed to be piecing the puzzle together as rapidly as he was.

"Right again, Njala. Now, a regular business jet couldn't make a trip of over seven thousand miles nonstop. Takes a special type of business jet. The company owns three jets, and Rampton himself owns two. He gets to choose from five jets, all based out of different airfields, but only one can fly to Njala nonstop. And it has to be nonstop. This asshole can't risk making a refueling stop in a country with an extradition treaty. So he will take the Gulfstream G650ER, which he keeps at Las Vegas International."

Mike's brow furrowed, his thoughts swirling. "So, how do we stop him?" The enormity of their task was starting to dawn on him.

"We'll be waiting. Don't worry. I have a plan, and the less you know about it, the better."

Mike's heart pounded. "You're not going to . . . ?" He trailed off, not sure if he wanted to hear the answer.

Henry's expression softened slightly, reassuringly. "No, Mike, no killing. But I want to be there when he's caught, see the realization dawn on his face."

"If he even gets that far," Mike added, thinking out loud. The likelihood of their plan succeeding hinged on numerous variables, each as unpredictable as the next.

Henry's confidence seemed unshaken. "Oh, he's resourceful, no doubt. But we'll be his unwelcome surprise. Consider it an insurance policy."

Sarah interjected, her tone skeptical: "Henry, how are we supposed to get close to his plane? And even if we do, then what?"

Henry tapped the Moleskine notebook again, his gaze fixed. "Perfect planning. That's how we'll do it."

Mike sat back, trying to process it all. They were diving into uncharted waters, chasing after one of the most powerful men in the shadowy world of Alithia, armed with nothing but a plan sketched out in a notebook. He believed the risk to be immense, but so were the stakes. Mike felt a strange cocktail of fear, excitement, and determination brewing within him. As the plane soared toward Las Vegas, he couldn't help but wonder what awaited them on the ground. This was no longer just about survival but about confronting the heart of darkness they had been pitched against.

CHAPTER 42

Silas sat in the semi-dark interrogation room, his mind exploding with thoughts of escape. His only connection to the outside world was the dim light that filtered through the frosted glass above the door, presumably from an office down the hallway. He mused bleakly about his fate if that light were to go out.

He had dozed off earlier, caught in a restless state between wakefulness and sleep. His captors had brought him a sandwich that tasted like it had been salvaged from an airport bin. Despite its sorry state, he ate the salami, Emmental, and mayonnaise sandwich. He had requested coffee but received none, making him wonder if he had been forgotten.

Listening intently, Silas tried to discern any signs of life outside his confinement. He thought he heard voices, a distant murmur of activity. Then, finally, footsteps approached. A wave of relief and apprehension washed over him as he braced for what might come next.

The light in the hallway snapped on, and the door swung open. Detective Coretti entered, carrying the familiar green file. As the overhead light flooded the room, Silas squinted, trying to adjust his eyes to the sudden brightness.

"Mr. Knox," Coretti began apologetically, "I'm sorry for the delay. This file"—he gestured to the dossier in his hands—"is extensive. There are many aspects to investigate, many calls to make."

Silas exhaled deeply, a hint of resignation in his breath. "Thank you, I—"

Coretti continued, cutting him off. "We're moving you to the cell complex for now. It's not right to keep you here while we work through this. You'll be more comfortable there—a shower, fresh clothes, hot meals. I've arranged for your lawyer to meet you back here tomorrow."

"But, wait, you don't understand; I have to—" Silas began to protest, a sense of urgency creeping into his voice.

"There's nothing more to discuss, Mr. Knox." Coretti's words sounded final, leaving no room for negotiation. The detective's demeanor seemed professional yet detached, making Silas feel helpless and frustrated. As Coretti gave him a nod, Silas realized the fix he was in. He was at the mercy of a system that seemed indifferent to his plight.

Silas sat at the table, his wrists sore from the chains, eyes locked with Detective Coretti, silently pleading for a reprieve, looking for a hint that this was all a ruse. But the reality was stark and unyielding as two uniformed officers entered, flanked him, and lifted him to his feet; they released the cuffs and, with a firm grip, escorted him out of the interrogation room.

Silas found himself in the minimal comforts of a prison cell an hour later. A stiff mattress on a metal bunk, a gray sweatshirt, matching pants neatly folded at the foot of the bed, and a corner toilet were his only conveniences. He'd noted the time—four a.m.—as they passed the front desk. Now, lying back, hands cushioning his head, he resigned himself to the situation. He believed this ordeal must be just a procedural hiccup, a delay before being sent back to London. There would be no sightseeing in Rome for him; he knew that much.

His mind wandered to the outside world, Alex, and the kill

switch. If he remained unreachable twelve hours from now, Alex would activate it. Soon, the world would know the truth.

The raucous symphony of prison life woke him the next day —the shouts, clangs, and bangs of an institution coming to life. The light filtering through the small window suggested it was still early. A tray slid onto the shelf as the hatch in his door opened. He stretched, approaching the tray with mild curiosity.

The tray held a beaker of dark coffee, a rice pudding-like concoction, and a round bread roll, complete with a pat of butter and a slice of cheese, all wrapped in plastic. *Italian cuisine at its finest*. His hunger won out over his skepticism. Sitting back on his bunk, he dug into the rice pudding with a plastic spoon, pleasantly surprised by its palatability. The coffee tasted strong and rich, and the roll and cheese were satisfactory. He returned the empty tray, feeling surprisingly upbeat.

In the relative safety of his cell, Silas awaited the evening, knowing it would usher in a world transformed by the truth.

CHAPTER 43

Tyler Rampton's irritation spiked as his phone buzzed with a message from Laura, his assistant. It was Sunday, his sacrosanct day of leisure, and here she was, intruding with an insistence that he watch the news. He sat on his patio, immersed in the tranquil harmony of Mozart's Quartet in G Major, no. 3, the music echoing through the spacious garden from his high-end Bang & Olufsen speakers. The rhythmic dance of the sprinklers, synchronized with the music, had been his focus, alongside the tangy zest of his freshly squeezed orange juice.

As Rampton's leisurely brunch had been abruptly interrupted, his previously calm demeanor shifted to annoyance. His brow furrowed, lips curling in displeasure. His thoughts churned with irritation, and he contemplated calling her to reprimand her sharply for this disruption. He could hear himself, stern and authoritative, reminding her of the sanctity of his Sundays. But instead of making the call, he pushed away his annoyance and left his serene outdoor setup in a huff.

Striding into his study with a sense of urgency, he briskly turned off the music, cutting short the classical strains that had soothed him moments before. He grabbed the TV remote with a swift, decisive motion and powered on the large TV. Flicking through the channels, he settled on CNN, his curiosity piqued and his frustration simmering beneath a facade of composure. What could be so important?

Rampton stood frozen, the remote control slipping from his hand and hitting the floor as the news anchor's words reverberated through the room, each syllable striking him like a physical blow. His heart pounded in his chest, a rapid drumbeat echoing the shock and disbelief coursing through him. The TV screen, usually a portal to the outside world, now seemed like a harbinger of doom, his carefully curated plans unraveling in public.

The anchor's voice continued, each word a hammer striking at the integrity of his empire.

Classified documents had been leaked online, linking the tragic Vivair Flight 002 crash to high-ranking officials and US executives—his world collapsing in real-time. The allegations of deliberate tampering, the manipulation of political landscapes in Njala, and the intricate web of corruption were all laid bare for the world to scrutinize.

He could hardly believe what he was hearing. The situation was overwhelming, the implications far-reaching and catastrophic. It felt like witnessing a car crash in slow motion, except he was the unwilling protagonist behind the wheel.

Staring open-mouthed at the screen, Tyler felt a surreal detachment, as if this couldn't be his reality. He glanced up at the portraits of his grandfather and father on the wall, their stoic faces now seeming to gaze back at him with disgust. *Is this a nightmare? Am I dreaming?* The bitter realization that this was all too real hit him like a tidal wave, washing away any remnants of denial.

His thoughts raged, crashing against one another in a chaotic disarray. The world as he knew it, the empire he had built, was crumbling before his eyes, disintegrating into dust. The news continued to play in the background, a grim soundtrack to his rapidly deteriorating situation. In that moment, Tyler Rampton realized the full extent of the catastrophe he faced—a personal and professional disaster of monumental proportions.

He sank into the armchair, his gaze locked on the TV screen. Though the news hadn't named Alithia explicitly, a gnawing certainty told him it was only a matter of time. He thought the only thing in his favor was the timing, assuming everyone, including law enforcement, was discovering this simultaneously. He snatched up the phone, his hands unsteady, and dialed Dalton's number—and the response he got chilled him to the bone.

"The number you have dialed is not in service . . ." echoed the automated message. Confusion clouded his thoughts. He yanked the phone away, scrutinizing it like an alien object. This had to be a mistake, a temporary glitch in the system. He redialed, only to be greeted by the same cold, impersonal message.

Realization dawned on him bitterly like a rusty penny clanking as it hit the bottom of a jar. Dalton had gone—unreachable, cut off. Panic surged through Rampton as he bolted from the armchair, his mind cartwheeling with fear and urgency. He rushed outside, his eyes sweeping over the fleet of cars in the garage. He needed to move quickly.

He dashed back inside, his forehead beading with sweat. His office became a blur as he frantically gathered his essentials— laptop, passport, stacks of cash. He stuffed them into his bag with trembling hands.

"Where are the fucking car keys!" he bellowed, his voice echoing through the expansive lobby of his opulent home. His housemaid, startled, emerged from the kitchen, offering to call his driver, Enrique.

"No, I want the keys. I haven't got time," he snapped, his tone desperate and furious. The housemaid hurried away, and Rampton paced like a caged animal. His grandfather's portrait at the top of the staircase overlooked the scene with a stern gaze that seemed to pierce through him.

"Come on!" Rampton urged, his impatience mounting. The

maid reappeared, her hand extended with the keys to his Porsche. Without a word of thanks, he snatched them and spun on his heel, sprinting toward the garage.

In those frantic moments, Tyler Rampton's world had contracted to a single imperative—escape. The empire he had built, the legacy he had crafted, crumbled around him, and he could only run.

His pulse raced as he ignited the engine of his silver Porsche 911. Gravel sprayed behind him like shrapnel as he sped down the driveway, the roar of his vehicle slicing through the neighborhood's tranquility. He would now live the life of a fugitive, fleeing like a common thief caught in the act.

As he navigated toward Alithia HQ, his fingers fumbled to redial Dalton, only to be greeted by the same frustrating message. Anger overtook him, and he screamed, the sound lost in the engine's roar.

He tried to quell the panic eating at him from inside and forced himself to take deep, measured breaths. He needed to think strategically, use his influence to buy time, and stave off the impending chaos. It was time to play his hand and utilize the leverage he had carefully amassed over the years.

His thoughts turned to his escape plan—the private jet in Vegas. His lakeside house in Njala flashed in his mind, a sanctuary where he could reign supreme, untouchable. He dialed Laura.

"Laura, it's Tyler," he said, his voice urgent.

"Hello, Mr. Rampton, did you watch the—"

"I haven't got time for that. I need the plane ready in Vegas. I need it refueled and two pilots ASAP. Understood?"

"Yes, Mr. Rampton, but—"

"Just do it, Laura, now!"

He cut off the call with a sharp jab, cranking up the air-conditioning as sweat cascaded down his face.

Tyler cursed Dalton's absence. The loyalty he had bought seemed to evaporate just when he needed it most. He zoomed through the unusually light Sunday traffic, his mind crafting a plan.

He would start with his media contacts, leverage his influence to twist the narrative, and discredit the leaks. Then, he would activate his connections in the Department of Justice, those who owed him and would want to work with him to keep his secrets hidden.

Reaching the office, he planned to mobilize Laura and the PR team and put them to work on damage control. If only Dalton were here, they could unleash their cyber team and scrub the internet clean of any mention linking Alithia to the Njala affair.

He clung to a thread of hope that his name hadn't been sullied in the reports. Maybe they knew better than to cross him. As he sped toward the heart of his crumbling empire, Tyler Rampton clung to this faint glimmer of hope amid the encroaching darkness.

His sense of hope flickered as he navigated his Porsche into Alithia HQ's underground garage. He briskly parked beside his private entrance, using his badge to scan himself into the building with a practiced motion. His clear destination: Dalton's office, hidden in the depths of the basement.

The offices stood eerily silent, the usual corporate buzz replaced by the solitary greeting of a security guard, which Rampton ignored. His footsteps echoed off the marble floors, each step amplifying his urgency. He rapidly pressed the elevator button multiple times before descending to the lower basement, where secrets were kept and strategies were crafted.

Entering Dalton's office, a chill of foreboding crept over him. The door to Dalton's inner sanctum stood ajar, an unusual sight. He called out, "Dalton? You there?" But only silence answered.

The scene that met his eyes confirmed his worst fears. The safe, usually a fortress of secrets, gaped open, its shelves hollow and barren. The office looked scoured, devoid of any sign of Dalton's presence. The smell of disinfectant hung in the air, sharply contrasting the room's usual aura of intrigue.

Panic clawed at Rampton's chest, his heart pounding in a frantic rhythm. The realization hit him like a physical blow— Dalton had vanished, wiped his existence clean from this sanctuary of covert operations. Rampton stood alone, now exposed to the vultures he had once controlled.

The thought of all those he had manipulated and blackmailed sent his stomach into a lurch. He had reveled in their hatred, basking in the power of knowing their darkest secrets. Those same people would be sharpening their knives, eager for their turn at retribution.

Adrenaline coursed through his veins, fueling a desperate need to flee. Alithia HQ would be the first target of any raid, and he needed to be miles away. The helicopter might be an option, but the logistics on a Sunday were impractical, not to mention the glaring visibility.

He swiftly decided to ditch his conspicuous Porsche with its vanity plates. A low-profile escape seemed crucial. A town car— that should do it. Unremarkable and anonymous, it had to be the perfect vehicle for a man desperately trying to vanish into thin air. Rampton's mind raced with plans, his survival instinct in overdrive as he prepared to navigate the treacherous waters he had once ruled.

His gaze lingered on the gaping maw of the empty safe, the starkness of its emptiness mirroring the sudden unraveling of his carefully laid plans. The realization of Dalton's betrayal quietly nibbled at his insides, a bitter pill to swallow. Yet, amid the chaos, a sliver of hope flickered—Njala. It could be his haven, a place to regroup and reassert control. Not everything had been lost, not yet.

With a newfound resolve, he turned on his heel, exiting the basement complex to return to the surface. He navigated the silent corridors of Alithia HQ, his steps resolute as he made his way to the transport room. There, he snatched a set of keys for a nondescript town car, a substantial downgrade from his usual flashy Porsche.

In the garage, he clicked the key fob repeatedly, striding among the row of black Lincoln town cars. He heard a chirp and saw a flash of rear lights; he'd located his escape vehicle. He flung his bag onto the passenger seat, started the engine, and programmed the satellite navigation for Las Vegas. A four-hour drive lay ahead—a journey demanding discretion over speed. A glance at the fuel gauge showed a full tank; he gave a slight nod to the efficiency of his transportation team. A commendation, perhaps, from the seclusion of his Njala lakeside retreat? He smiled at the thought, but it quickly faded, crushed under the overwhelming intensity of his dire situation. Despite his intention to be cautious, his foot pressed harder on the accelerator, urgency seeping into his driving.

As the town car ate up the miles, Rampton's thoughts turned to the Gulfstream awaiting him at Harry Reid International Airport. His phone ringing broke the silence, and when he answered, Laura's voice sounded urgent.

"Mr. Rampton, the plane . . ." she began, outlining the logistical challenges of arranging a last-minute international flight.

"Just me, no bags. Jalaka, Njala," he snapped, curt and decisive.

Laura's voice wavered, revealing the tension of the situation. "They're saying it's short notice and—"

"Double the pay, whatever it costs. No delays. I'll be there in four hours." His words sounded sharp as a blade, cutting through any hesitation.

Ending the call with a jab of frustration, he glanced at the dashboard clock. One p.m.—he had a strict timeline. By five, he needed to be airborne, leaving behind the crumbling empire he had built. Anything less could spell disaster.

CHAPTER 44

Henry, Mike, and Sarah touched down in Las Vegas just after one p.m. A dark determination hung around them as they walked among the holidaymakers and gamblers. The flight from Minneapolis had passed in a contemplative silence, each absorbed in their thoughts, united by an unspoken resolve. Mike had questioned Henry's reticence about detailing his plan to confront Rampton. However, knowing less, in this case, felt safer and easier. He wanted to calm down, take a back seat, and avoid danger if possible. Henry took charge, and Mike was happy about that.

Aboard the plane, Mike's mind had wandered through the recent timeline. The changes in his life had arrived at a dizzying pace. He mulled over the idea of being a part of bringing down the villains in such an earth-shattering drama—it might indeed be a shot at redemption for the drunk plane crash dude or whatever they were calling him these days. But the shadow of the skirmish in Sacramento lingered. The life he had taken. *Am I a murderer now?* He'd had no choice but to defend himself, kill or be killed. *Justifiable homicide; yes, that's what it was.* He thought about the man he'd killed, and surprisingly, he found that he felt no remorse whatsoever. He'd toyed with the idea of shooting through the closet door and killing the other guy, too. He felt his pulse quicken and took a few deep breaths. *Maybe the guy is still in there? Good, leave the past behind.*

His mind meandered to thoughts of writing a book when everything had ended. A smile appeared and then disappeared quickly, and he admonished himself. When would this chapter of his life conclude, and what would follow? His old life felt distant, belonging to someone else. He remembered the days with his then-girlfriend Juanita before she left him in the depths of his all-consuming work struggles. The simmering anger toward Cooper and the satisfaction of throwing the visitor's pass at his head, even though he'd missed. If only he had acted sooner. Instead, his fate had twisted on the day of the flight. He closed his eyes as he realized the enormous repercussions of his decision to get drunk. Now, he was en route to a confrontation in Vegas, his role in this overwhelming, bizarre narrative far from over.

Exiting the airport, Henry decisively announced, "We'll rent a car."

Mike, perplexed, glanced back at Henry. "We're here, aren't we?"

"We need to head over to the business jet area," Henry explained, pointing across the airport to the other side of the runway. "I ain't walking."

The trio hopped onto the courtesy bus, bound for the rental car area. Sarah sat quietly beside Mike, her thoughts seemingly miles away. She looked at Mike. "You OK?" she asked.

"Never better," he lied, but he felt something like resolve, excitement, fear, and something else he couldn't measure or name. "What about you?" he said to Sarah, turning in his seat.

"Well, I'm not sure I signed up for this, but I'm looking forward to the truth coming out and for those bastards to face justice," she said.

As the bus rumbled slowly to their destination, Mike thought for a moment, then asked, "You know that place they took us? It was weird, wasn't it? Just those guys and a ton of weapons. I mean, it looked like the operation, whatever it was supposed to be, was winding down. Do you think they knew the game was up or something?"

Sarah met his gaze. "Yeah, something was up for sure. The guy in charge, whatever his name was, just disappeared, like he definitely had someplace better to be."

"Do you think that guy is still in the closet?" Mike laughed, and Sarah joined in.

"Yeah, I hope so; maybe he doesn't have the guts to tell his parents." They both started laughing. Henry, seated in front of them, turned around with a distinctly unamused look on his face. "We should probably stay focused," he said. They both fell silent after each giving a sideways glance at the other, like scolded kids.

Once they picked up another Ford Focus, Henry took the wheel, and the radio burst to life as soon as the engine started. The car's speakers blared out the latest news headlines, vividly depicting the startling events tied to Vivair Flight 002. Words like "conspiracy," "sabotage," and "murder" filled the air.

Henry glanced at Mike, then at Sarah in the rearview mirror. Their gazes locked, silently exchanging an understanding filled with a somber realization. "It's on," Henry said with gravitas. Pressing the accelerator, he steered out of the compound, each bracing for the uncertain challenges ahead. As they ventured onto the road, they headed straight into the unknown.

"I hope Silas is OK," Mike said.

"I think he'll show up; he's a survivor," Sarah replied. Mike thought her expression didn't look as confident as the words she'd chosen.

As they drove around the airport's perimeter, they listened silently to the rest of the news report. Henry eventually pulled into a layby outside an entrance to some hangars and killed the engine, which turned the radio off.

"Well, we know the kill switch worked," Henry said after a period of silence.

"Can we call it something else?" Mike replied. His lips twisted involuntarily, a sharp tug at the corners, as a wave of discomfort rippled across his face.

"What do you suggest?" replied Henry.

Sarah interjected, "All we know is either Alex couldn't get a hold of Silas or Silas is behind the release, and we can't get a hold of him. Henry, can we try calling Silas again? Maybe he was hiding out, incognito, until they released it?"

"Who is Alex?" Henry asked, a puzzled look on his face.

"He's Silas's cyber guy; he sent him all the files to validate. He told Alex what to do if he couldn't reach him after verification."

"I see. Here," Henry said, handing his phone to Sarah.

Sarah jabbed at the screen and then put the phone to her ear. Mike and Henry had turned their heads and were looking at her intently as she let the phone slip away from her ear, whispering, "Shit," as she did so.

"OK, let's get this guy," Henry said in a clear, loud voice, and Sarah and Mike adjusted in their seats.

When nothing happened, Mike turned to Henry, an apologetic smile forming on his face.

Henry just looked at Mike with one eyebrow raised.

"What happens next? Can you tell us the plan?" Mike said softly.

Sarah leaned forward. "This guy's a cornered animal. He's probably dangerous. He most likely has bodyguards with him or something. You're not planning on a shoot-out, Wild West style, are you?"

"No. I am going to make sure he doesn't escape justice. Putting a bullet in his forehead would be too nice. No easy way out for this asshole. He doesn't get to escape, either on his plane or by a bullet. Mine, his, or anyone else's."

"You sound confident," said Mike.

"There's only one way this ends, believe me," he replied, stone-faced.

"OK, what now?" Sarah said.

"We wait."

"What are we waiting for?" she insisted.

"Movement," Henry replied.

"Henry, can we quit with the twenty questions?" Sarah said, sounding frustrated.

"We are waiting for the hangar doors to open and for a Gulf-stream G650ER with the registration number 'N650TR' to emerge. When that happens, we know things are in play. We then move to phase two of the operation."

"What do you mean by 'in play'?" Mike asked.

"He's called it in. He's told them to prepare the aircraft," Sarah replied for Henry.

"Got it," Henry said.

"Phase two?" Mike asked.

Henry just gave Mike a sideways glance.

"OK, OK," Mike said, holding his hand up.

Glancing at his watch, he saw that it was almost two. He gestured for Sarah to hand him the phone. His thoughts raced as he browsed the news. Reports of the Njala files' leak had hit the web around 10:30 a.m. Four hours. That's how long Rampton had had to begin his escape. Mike figured Rampton, a man of contingency plans, probably had an "evil CEO" go-bag ready at all times.

A sly grin crossed Mike's face at the thought. His mind worked overtime, piecing together Rampton's possible moves. *Helicopter escape?* It sounded flashy but feasible. Mike cracked the window open slightly, letting in the warm air.

"What are you doing?" Henry asked.

"I was thinking, maybe he's coming by chopper? Just cracking the window see if I can hear one approaching, you know—"

"Good point."

"It's a bit of a 'look at me' statement, though, isn't it?" Sarah said. "I'm guessing he wants to travel under the radar, and a chopper in company livery is too showy. But who knows?" Sarah shrugged.

"I'll watch the road, and you keep an eye up there," Henry told Mike.

"Do you think he'll have protection with him? You know, armed guards? Sarah, you mentioned bodyguards before?" Mike turned to Sarah. "What do you think?"

"I don't know. Honestly, it's hard to say. He'll be in a hurry, so I don't think he'll have the time to organize the chopper, as it's Sunday. I think he'll be driving, and he'll be alone. If I were in his shoes, I'd want to be agile. Having a car full of heavies with guns will slow him down and cause him other problems. This guy may be a psychopath, but I reckon, like a lot of them, he's smart. He's smart enough to think on his feet. He'll have thought things through and figured this is his best shot to escape. Think about it. All he has to do is get the plane ready, get to Vegas, and take off. That's it."

Henry paused before saying, "That doesn't mean he won't be carrying a firearm, of course."

Mike stayed quiet for a while, staring straight ahead. Henry joined him.

Sarah leaned back in the middle of the rear seat, staring out through the windshield. They sat like this for ten minutes, and then Sarah finally spoke.

"Those hangar doors are opening."

The white doors of the bigger of the two hangars, the light-green one, started to move slowly apart.

The hangars were about a hundred yards in front of them and had the name "AirGuard Secure Storage" in prominent red and black signage.

"This could be it," Henry muttered, his eyes fixed on the widening gap. "If the records are right, we're looking for a black plane."

Time stretched out as Mike watched the hangar doors laboriously open, his heart thudding. Every creak and groan of the metal seemed amplified, and the process agonizingly slow, like a slow-motion replay.

With a final clang that reverberated out in the open space, the doors reached their full extension. Sitting in their rental car a few yards away, the trio could hear the distinct sound clearly. Yet, nothing else stirred, the hangar sitting eerily still as if holding its breath.

Henry pulled out a telescope with a distinctly military look to it. Mike watched him intently as he adjusted the zoom, trying to peer into the darkness beyond the hangar doors.

"Anything?" Mike asked.

"I can see a nose cone. It's black. There's movement around the jet. Yeah, this is it, I'm certain. OK, we'll move to phase two."

"Um, OK. Are you able to let us know what phase two is now?" Mike asked sheepishly.

"Yes. We'll sweet-talk ourselves onto that plane and wait for the guest of honor."

Mike turned and looked at Henry, then back at Sarah.

"Just like that?" Sarah said.

"Trust me, I've done my research. There will be two security guards on duty. Here's what we'll do: Mike, you're with me. Just stay quiet and follow my lead. Sarah, you'll engage the other security guard in conversation. Once Mike and I are on board with the first guard, he'll call his partner to bring you aboard. Then, we wait for our target. Everyone clear on that?"

Sarah raised an eyebrow. "And if things go south?"

"We don't entertain failure," Henry responded, his gaze fixed forward.

"So, what's my role?" Mike said, a note of exasperation in his tone.

"You just keep quiet. Oh, and I'm your dad," Henry replied without a hint of a smile.

"What?" Mike said, his eyebrows knitting in confusion.

"You'll see. Remember, be quiet," Henry said as he started the engine and put the car in drive.

As they parked behind the AirGuard hangars, the tension felt thick. Henry led the way, with Mike and Sarah following. The intense heat outside the car made Mike's neck slick with sweat. His heart raced as sensations of anxiety and anticipation surged through him.

Approaching the security door, Henry pressed the intercom button, and a burst of static filled the air before a voice responded, "AirGuard."

Sarah's eyes darted around, taking in every detail of their surroundings. She noticed a CCTV camera angled toward them and gave Mike a subtle nod, signaling him to stand in a way that partially obscured their faces. Her journalistic instincts kicked in: she memorized the layout of the parking lot, the number of vehicles, and any potential escape routes. Her focus snapped back when Henry started speaking.

"Hello. My name is Henry Mitchell. I wondered if I may speak with William Turner?"

"This is Bill. Hello, Henry, you made it! I'll buzz you in," squawked the reply.

Sarah glanced at Mike, raising one eyebrow. Mike responded with half a smile and a shrug.

They heard a buzzing sound, and Henry pushed on the door, which made a reassuring click as it opened. Mike and Sarah followed behind.

As they entered the small office, an older man stood smiling.

"Hi, Henry; I didn't think you'd show up so soon. Couldn't wait, eh?"

"Something like that. This is my daughter, Sarah, and my son, Mike. Kids, this is Bill."

"Well, hi, folks, how are you?"

Sarah and Mike smiled and nodded, unsure what to say, not having been given a script.

"Your pop and I served together in Vietnam. He reached out

online. We were in the same platoon. I had no idea," Bill, the security guard, said.

"That's awesome," said Mike.

"Turns out we have a shared love of aircraft," Bill said, smiling broadly.

"You've got the perfect job for a plane spotter," Sarah said, joining in.

"Sure do," he replied before turning back to Henry. "So, what brings you down to Vegas?"

"An Airbus A320," Henry replied.

They both laughed. After a brief pause, Mike and Sarah joined in a little awkwardly.

"Well, my kids came for a visit, and I told them, hey, fancy a trip to Vegas to do some plane spotting? Mike's always loved planes, so he jumped at the chance. I told him I knew someone down here who could get us up real close, and, well, he almost wet himself at the thought," Henry said, and they laughed again.

Bill turned to Sarah. "What about you, miss?"

"Shopping and blackjack?" she said with a smile, sounding unsure.

"Hey, son, check out the Gulfstream outside. It's a sight to see." Henry's casual directive snapped Mike back to the moment.

Bill, playing the hospitable host, chimed in with directions. "Just head out and turn right twice. Can't miss it." His voice carried a note of enthusiasm, the kind reserved for sharing something special.

Mike didn't hesitate. He darted out as instructed, leaving Henry and Bill to their conversation. From the corner of his eye, he noticed Sarah peering at him through the window with a worried expression.

CHAPTER 45

Sarah watched as Henry and Bill chatted like old friends. She felt slightly uneasy at how Henry had slipped so easily into this deception. *He's definitely done this before.*

"Hey, Bill, thanks for this. You know Mike is, well, not all there, if you know what I mean? This means a lot."

"Oh, it's nothing, Henry; we'll do the full tour later. Hey, your Mike looks familiar. Do I know him from somewhere?"

"Don't think so, unless he's won the Powerball and not told me."

They both laughed again.

Sarah looked at Henry, frowning; he seemed quick-witted for his age, agile and practiced. Her gaze quickly returned to watching Mike through the window.

"It was great to find you online, Henry; not many of us vets are left standing. A fellow of the 1st Cavalry to boot. Proper combat!"

"Absolutely. Well, at least I'm retired; you're still working for a living."

"What, this? I don't consider this working, Henry." Bill chuckled.

"It was good of you to invite us down. As I said, it means a lot."

"It's nothing; vets need to stick together."

"I appreciate it, honestly." Henry's expression appeared full of earnest sincerity.

"Please, think nothing of it," Bill responded, spreading his arms wide in a palms-open gesture.

Henry continued. "Listen, I have another favor to ask Bill. You know about Mike, right? Well, he would be bowled over if he could get a look around one of these planes, you know, close up—that Gulfstream, for example, would make his day, hell, his year!"

"I'm not sure. I mean, there are protocols and stuff. I don't think . . ." Bill said, a pensive expression spreading across his features.

"It's just that he's been through so much recently, I just . . ." Henry looked wistful as he averted his gaze.

There followed a brief pause in the conversation before Bill spoke once more.

"Listen, they are just going to refuel the Gulfstream; it's off on a long-haul trip someplace. Pilots are due here in an hour. We can do a walk-around, don't see the harm."

"That's great, Bill; I appreciate that. We're in town for a couple of days. Dinner's on me, OK?" Henry smiled broadly again.

"That's not necessary, but thank you, I'd like that. You two go and get Mike and meet me at the rear entrance to the hangar. I'll get you some passes."

"Thanks. Will do." Henry clapped Bill on the back.

Sarah watched Henry and shook her head slightly, half in disbelief, half in admiration.

Henry and Sarah returned outside and walked up to Mike, who watched the Gulfstream through the fence as instructed.

"What's going on?" Mike asked, turning around.

"We're going on a little tour. Oh, and keep quiet," Henry said, all business now.

"Well, I haven't a clue what's going on, so . . ."

"No, he means, really, act like you don't know what's going on. He told them you were, you know, a bit simple," Sarah said, shrugging apologetically.

"You did what?" Mike asked, his mouth hanging open in disbelief.

"Listen, I had to say something to get us on that plane. I wanted him to feel sorry for us. Look, acting like you're not that smart is easy. Just smile and don't say anything—nothing to remember. You don't need to worry about saying the wrong thing. You'll work it out. If he asks you anything, just one-word answers, OK?"

Sarah turned to Henry. "Were you really in Vietnam together?" she asked, one eyebrow raised.

"Well, we were both in Vietnam; that much is true. Just the together bit is somewhat of a stretch. Anyway, don't worry about that. Follow me," Henry replied, before turning back toward the entrance.

They all walked around to the main hangar entrance at the rear, off the car park, and waited by the door.

"Remember, keep your mouth shut," Henry whispered to Mike.

"OK, I get it," Mike replied, flustered.

Sarah looked once again at Henry as they waited by the entrance. *Is Henry actually enjoying this?*

Bill reappeared at the window of the door in the wall next to the hangar shutters. He held up three lanyards with a big smile, opened the door wide, and made a sweeping motion with his arm.

"Lady and Gentleman, please walk this way," he said.

Henry went in first, followed by Sarah and Mike. If Henry felt wrong about duping this guy, Sarah thought he was doing a great job concealing it.

As they stood in the vast hangar, Sarah remembered her role. "Bill, you know the plane thing? Well, it's for the boys, really. Do you mind if I grab a coffee and wait it out?"

Bill turned around to look at her. "Oh, yes, of course, I figured that was the case," he said, chuckling. "My colleague Jason will fix you a coffee and get you comfortable in our VIP lounge; how does that sound?"

Sarah gave him a broad smile and a thumbs-up.

CHAPTER 46

Under the harsh Las Vegas sun, Mike squinted as he and Henry stood next to the shimmering wingtip of the Gulfstream. The heat radiated off the tarmac, but Mike focused on Bill's animated explanation as they walked around the aircraft.

Holding a clipboard firmly, Bill seemed in his element, passionately detailing the process. "This Gulfstream's a beauty, set for a long haul soon. We'll do our walk-around and show you what the pilots look for."

Mike listened, feeling out of his depth yet intrigued. He watched Bill gesture toward the plane, emphasizing each point with a wave of his clipboard. The walk-around, Bill explained, required a meticulous visual inspection to ensure the aircraft's airworthiness, checking everything from tires to wings, engines to control surfaces.

Mike glanced at Henry, who absorbed every word with a seriousness that belied the charade. Mike himself tried to appear interested yet clueless, hoping his facade of ignorance remained convincing.

Bill continued, his voice carrying an air of authority. "The walk-around is vital. It's a religious practice for pilots. Safety is paramount. Skipping this? That's asking for trouble."

Henry's solemn nod reflected his understanding of the importance of the procedure. They edged closer to the sleek black jet, its surface gleaming under the sun. Mike followed, thinking hard about what lay ahead, wondering what the next step in Henry's plan would be.

Standing on the sun-soaked tarmac next to the Gulfstream, Mike's attention shifted as Henry played his part perfectly, feigning tourist-like excitement. "Can we take a peek inside? Mike's dying to see it, aren't you, Mike?"

Caught off guard, Mike managed a clumsy, "I sure would," his voice betraying his discomfort with the ruse.

"Well, I really shouldn't, but we have time. The principal, that's what we call the VIP, isn't due for a couple of hours. You'll need to wear shoe covers, though. They have some fancy carpeting in there."

Mike's eyes caught the glint of metal—a gun holstered at Bill's side. His eyes widened as a chill of realization ran down his spine. He glanced at Henry, who returned a knowing look with a subtle nod, a silent message that they were treading in dangerous waters.

Bill deftly unlocked the plane's cabin door, letting it swing open with practiced ease. The steps, adorned with elegant red carpet inlays, lowered gracefully. Mike marveled at the attention to detail, a luxury so far removed from his world.

"Put these on," Bill said, handing over blue plastic shoe covers. They clumsily slipped the covers over their shoes, trying to maintain the facade of wide-eyed tourists.

"Follow me," Bill beckoned, leading the way into the jet's luxurious embrace. Mike's heart raced as he stepped onto the plane, each movement calculated yet colored with an undercurrent of fear and anticipation.

Stepping up into the Gulfstream, Mike's senses were immediately greeted by an unexpectedly fresh citrus scent, a welcome change to the typical, musty odors of commercial flights. The air inside felt cleaner, more refined.

Bill stood confidently, a gatekeeper to this world of luxury. "Gentlemen, the cockpit's right here." He gestured to his right. The cockpit looked like a symphony of advanced technology, a setup that made flying seem like an art form reserved for the highly skilled.

Henry peered into the cockpit, his expression one of playful bewilderment. "Looks like you'd need a PhD to fly this thing." He chuckled, his eyes scanning the many buttons and screens.

Bill's voice carried a note of pride. "It's all about making flying smoother these days," he explained.

Curiosity drew Mike's gaze to the opposite side. "Is this where the food magic happens?" he inquired, eyeing the galley.

Bill nodded. "The galley, yes. Fully equipped for any culinary challenge." Mike stepped closer, his eyes tracing the sleek lines of mahogany, chrome, and glass. He pulled open the fridge, revealing a lineup of twelve bottles of Dom Perignon Champagne—a testament to the lavish lifestyle of the jet's usual passengers.

Mike then turned his attention to the main cabin. It felt like stepping into a different world. The spacious area was lined with wide white leather seats. The dark blue carpet underfoot, woven with gold threads, gave off a sense of luxury. The seats were arranged around polished mahogany tables, each edge detailed with gold. Beyond this setup, a large sofa faced a state-of-the-art flat-screen TV.

In this cabin, every detail whispered of luxury, and Mike couldn't help but be momentarily captivated by the extravagance surrounding him.

Navigating the cabin, Mike followed Bill toward the rear. With a smooth slide of the door, they stepped into a private area that felt like a high-end hotel suite. A large flat-screen TV dominated one wall, opposite a plush sofa that, Bill noted, could transform into a six-foot-long bed. The space exuded opulence and privacy, unlike any aircraft Mike had experienced.

His curiosity piqued, Mike couldn't help but ask, "Who owns

this incredible jet?" He casually picked up a silk cushion bearing the distinct Alithia logo.

Bill's face briefly registered discomfort, a flicker of embarrassment that didn't go unnoticed by Mike. Alithia seemed a sensitive topic, perhaps a secret everyone knew but never discussed. Mike speculated silently that Alithia Corp.'s days of power and influence were numbered.

Shifting the focus, Henry chimed in with a lighthearted query. "Owning a jet like this must cost a fortune, right, Bill?"

Bill's response carried a hint of humor. "Well, it's one of those things: if you need to ask the price, it's probably out of reach."

Henry pointed to a door at the end of the private cabin. "Is there a private bathroom or something behind that door there?" Henry said, looking quizzical.

As Bill turned, Henry's actions caught Mike off guard. In a swift and fluid motion, Henry disarmed Bill, smoothly extracting the gun from his holster while simultaneously detaching the radio from his belt. The suddenness of Henry's movements left Mike momentarily stunned.

Bill's face mirrored Mike's astonishment. He gaped at the firearm now firmly in Henry's grasp, aimed steadily at him. The confusion and disbelief in Bill's eyes were unmistakable.

"Henry, what . . ." Bill trailed off, sounding bewildered, his voice containing more than a hint of fear.

Henry's words came out calm yet firm. "It's OK, Bill. We're not here to hurt you." The reassurance did little to alleviate the tension in the air.

Bill glanced nervously between Henry and Mike. Mike could feel the cabin walls closing in, his heart pounding.

Gesturing with the gun, Henry directed, "Bill, just take it easy and sit in that seat." He indicated the plush chair facing the large TV.

Bill hesitated momentarily before complying, slowly sinking into the seat, his eyes never leaving the gun.

Henry's voice took on a more serious tone. "Bill, this is a long story, and you deserve to hear it. But first, you need to understand something. This plane isn't going anywhere today. When your principal arrives, he'll think he's off to Africa. Instead, we'll be handing him over to the FBI."

Bill's expression shifted from confusion to shock as Henry's words sank in. His mouth hung open slightly, disbelief and concern etched across his face. Mike could sense the tension ratcheting up a notch as they stood in the luxurious cabin, the situation growing more surreal by the second.

CHAPTER 47

Henry sat at one of the mahogany tables and rested the gun on his lap. He looked up at Mike.

"Mike, close the door," he said; it wasn't a request but an order.

"The aircraft door? I don't know how. I mean, I've never . . ." Mike stammered his response.

"It's easy," Bill said flatly, shell-shocked. "Select 'close' on the panel by the door, just one button," he continued.

"Thanks, Bill," said Henry, giving the ashen-faced man a nod of appreciation.

As Mike returned to the main cabin to deal with the door, Henry switched his gaze to Bill on the big sofa.

"Have you seen the news today, Bill?" he asked in a no-nonsense tone.

"Well, not really. I was at work early, had a ton of stuff to do . . ." Bill trailed off, his eyes dropping to the carpeting as if his mind was elsewhere.

"So, you won't have heard about the predicament the owner of this wonderful aircraft now finds himself in?" Henry continued.

Bill looked up, starting at Henry, a quizzical look on his pale features. "I guess not. I am sensing it isn't good. Hence, you know . . ." Bill trailed off again, nodding at the gun Henry still had in his lap.

"Well, yes. I needed to get on board and lie in wait. Call it a personal crusade. That son of a bitch killed my granddaughter. I'm not sure you can get more personal than that, can you, Bill?" Henry said matter-of-factly.

Henry explained to a traumatized Bill what had happened, how they were involved in publishing the Njala files, and how Tyler Rampton would soon be public enemy number one.

Bill looked back at Henry blankly, shaking his head in disbelief. After a long pause, he began to speak.

"I don't know what to say. I don't. But this is not the way, you know. Couldn't you leave it to the professionals? What will you do when he gets here, the gun and all?" Bill asked, looking scared.

"I'm not going to shoot him, Bill. That's too kind for this asshole. The gun here is to inform him that the game is up, and he will not travel today. Not until the FBI gets here and takes him into custody."

Bill looked a little relieved.

"So, have you called the FBI?" Bill asked, running his hand through his receding gray hair and blowing out an unsteady breath.

"Not yet. I want him here first. I suspect they will be on the lookout for him right about now, though."

Henry watched as Mike, looking slightly flustered, returned to his seat beside him. Mike's fumbling with the door's controls had not gone unnoticed, but he had eventually closed it, sealing them inside the Gulfstream. The reassuring sound of it locking into place had given Henry a sense of control over the unfolding situation. He had been through scenarios like this before, where precision and swift action were paramount. Disarming Bill had been second nature to him, a reflex from his years of training and experience.

Observing Bill, Henry could see the resignation in the man's eyes. "Henry, I'm sure you've thought this through," Bill began, his voice tinged with uncertainty. "But my colleagues are going to wonder what's going on."

Henry casually held up the radio. "You're going to tell them everything's fine. Say you're catching up on paperwork or something," he instructed, his tone leaving no room for argument. "And make sure they send Sarah up here. Tell them I want her to see this jet."

Bill nodded hesitantly as Henry continued. "Let the pilots do their checks when they arrive. We must keep everything normal. so Rampton doesn't get spooked."

Bill seemed to shrink slightly in his seat, overwhelmed by the events. Henry could tell that the last thing Bill desired was to be part of this drama. But he required Bill's cooperation, and it appeared he had it.

Turning to Mike, he commanded, "Pull up the news story on my phone. I want Bill to see it." Mike quickly complied, then handed the phone to Bill, who scanned the screen with growing disbelief.

"Jesus," Bill muttered, his voice barely above a whisper as he handed the phone back to Henry, who slipped it into his pocket.

"Pretty spectacular, isn't it?" Mike chimed in, trying to lighten the mood.

Bill just shook his head. "Not sure I'd use that word."

Henry, sensing the time, passed the radio back to Bill. "You can make the call now," he said, eyes locking onto Bill's, ensuring there was no misunderstanding. "We good?" he asked, seeking confirmation.

Though visibly unsettled, Bill nodded and brought the radio to life with a click. The plan moved to the next phase, and Henry felt a familiar adrenaline rush. This was where he thrived: amid chaos, bringing order and control. The stakes were high, and Henry stood ready.

"Jason, it's Bill. Over."

A squawk and some static preceded a voice coming through.

"Hey, Bill, what are you up to?"

"I'm on board the Gulfstream, just handling some paper-work. It will probably take a while. Listen, when our principal arrives, send him straight across, OK? Over."

"Sure thing, Bill."

"And, Jason, Sarah's pop wants her to come on board and have a quick look around. Says she'll love it and that she shouldn't miss the opportunity. Over."

"OK, I'll let her know," Jason replied.

"OK, thanks. Out."

Bill reluctantly handed the radio back to Henry, and there was a subtle shift in the air. Henry noticed that Bill, with his military precision, adhered strictly to the radio protocols, a world away from the more laid-back approach of Jason on the other end. It was clear to Henry that Bill's old-school military training had been ingrained in him, while Jason seemed more like a rookie, unaware of the unusual situation unfolding.

Henry didn't miss the fact that Jason wasn't armed. In his experience, details like that could make all the difference. The sudden crackle of the radio momentarily heightened the tension in the cabin. A brief "Roger" echoed through the space, and then silence returned, thickening the already charged atmosphere. Bill rolled his eyes, a silent communication that spoke volumes to Henry about the professionalism of his backup.

Amidst this, Mike, perhaps seeking a momentary escape from the intensifying situation, stood up and headed toward the galley. "Bill, mind if I grab a water?" he asked, to which Bill responded with a nonchalant shrug. Mike offered drinks to the others, but both declined. Henry watched as Mike, alone in the galley, paused momentarily, his gaze lingering on the fridge's contents. He leaned in, grabbed a water bottle, and returned to the cabin. Henry wondered if the champagne had tempted Mike, but didn't say anything.

Mike settled into one of the plush cabin seats and hit the

recline button. The smooth motion of his legs rising briefly trans-fixed Henry. He watched as Mike unscrewed the bottle cap and took a long drink.

The time ticked past three on Henry's watch. The waiting game had begun, and Henry could sense the tension. They were all in a holding pattern, each playing their part, waiting for the next move. Henry's gaze shifted back to Bill with the silent, unspoken understanding that they were all bound to the unfolding events in one way or another.

CHAPTER 48

In the VIP lounge of the private hangar, the air-conditioning hummed, and the air it chilled seemed to exude understated luxury. Sarah sat on a plush black leather sofa, her gaze casually sweeping the room. Outwardly, she appeared completely relaxed, but her thoughts raced as she wondered how this would unfold. With each passing second, she felt increasingly anxious, waiting for her cue, her signal to act. But this all felt like improvisation; there was no script.

Jason, the junior of the two AirGuard security personnel, approached with a friendly demeanor, carrying two steaming cups of coffee. "Here you go, miss. Bill said you might like a nice cup of coffee while you wait," he said, offering her a cup and saucer with a polite smile.

Sarah accepted the coffee with a gracious nod, her smile masking the adrenaline coursing through her veins. Jason sat opposite her, and she initiated small talk, weaving a tapestry of words designed to engage Jason and keep him anchored in conversation. They discussed innocuous topics—the weather, recent sports events, and the city's bustling energy. She believed he hadn't seen the news, as he would have likely mentioned it, so she avoided referencing recent events involving Vivair and

Alithia Corporation. Instead, she artfully steered the conversation to other topics, ensuring Jason remained oblivious to their true intentions.

As they chatted, Sarah divided her attention. One part of her mind focused on Jason, while the other strained for any sign from Henry and Mike. She occasionally glanced out of the big picture window to the gleaming black jet on the apron, knowing they were aboard Tyler Rampton's private plane. A bold move, if ever there was one. Henry continued to surprise her. She wondered what she'd do if she heard a gunshot or saw the flash of a muzzle through one of the jet windows. She knew Henry and Mike had to subdue the guard on board somehow, and the genuine danger they faced increased with each passing second.

Jason's radio squawked. He glanced at the walkie-talkie and then back at Sarah, a nervous smile forming. Sarah smiled back as they both listened.

"Jason, it's Bill. Over."

There was a squawk and some static before Jason answered. "Hey, Bill, what are you up to?"

"I'm on board the Gulfstream, just handling some paperwork. It will probably take a while. Listen, when our principal arrives, send him straight across, OK? Over."

"Sure thing, Bill."

"And, Jason, Sarah's pop wants her to come on board and have a quick look around. Says she'll love it and that she shouldn't miss the opportunity. Over."

"OK, I'll let her know." Jason smiled at Sarah as he spoke.

"OK, thanks. Out."

Jason took another glance at Sarah and waited, seemingly thinking about something, and then confirmed receipt with a simple: "Roger?" He made it sound like a question.

After clipping the radio back on his belt, he looked at Sarah. "Well, miss, it doesn't look like you're going to be able to avoid the tour altogether," he said, smiling broadly.

Sarah's heart leaped, but she maintained her composure. She

stood, brushing imaginary specks from her jeans, and offered Jason a polite smile. "Thank you, Jason. OK, let's take a look at this jet the boys seem so enamored with," she said, returning his warm smile.

As they walked toward the jet, Sarah's thoughts went into overdrive. She had to hand it to Henry. His plan appeared to be in motion and seemed to be working. *So far, so good.*

Jason activated the door mechanism from outside and asked Sarah to remove her shoes, which she did. The stairs unfolded in the hot, dry air, and Sarah ascended. Jason stood at the bottom, watching her climb. Sarah heard him say, "Have fun," as she disappeared through the entrance, carrying her shoes by her side.

CHAPTER 49

Tyler Rampton easily navigated the sparse Sunday afternoon traffic, his Lincoln cutting a swift path on I-15. The clock nudged closer to four as he sped past the Seven Magic Mountains, an art installation he found utterly absurd. Brightly colored rocks stacked into giant totems offered a striking contrast against the desert backdrop, but they represented nothing more than idiotic frivolity to Rampton.

His eyes flicked to the satnav, and he calculated the remaining distance to Harry Reid—only twenty minutes to the security of his jet. The thought injected a surge of adrenaline into his veins, sharpening his focus on the escape that lay tantalizingly close.

In the early stages of his drive, Rampton had been on edge, his gaze darting to the rearview mirror every few seconds. The possibility of being followed loomed large in his mind, casting a shadow of unease over him. But as the miles rolled by, his tension eased. He reassured himself with the thought that law enforcement rarely moved quickly, especially in cases shrouded in ambiguity like this.

He envisioned the luxurious interior of his jet, the clink of a champagne glass, and the rich taste of lobster. These indulgences awaited him, promises of relaxation and a respite from the mounting stress. Each mile he covered brought him closer to that sanctuary in the sky, where all his worries would dissolve into the clouds below.

With each mile closer to the airport, he strategized his next moves like a rarified to-do list. As soon as he boarded his aircraft, a flurry of financial maneuvers awaited his command. He planned to shuffle funds and switch assets, ensuring ample liquidity upon landing in Njala. The future of his US operations hung in a precarious balance and, though he harbored a fleeting hope for it all to blow over, the sheer scale of the crisis left little room for such optimism. He had lost all his carefully curated leverage, which cornered him into a flight he hadn't ever anticipated.

Dealing with hard facts, Rampton always found firm footing. He thrived in the concrete, the tangible. Speculations and what-ifs unsettled him and took him off his game. And now, Dalton's sudden disappearance sat at the forefront of his thoughts, an unmistakable red flag whipping violently in a storm of suspected betrayal. Mulling over Dalton's motives, Rampton's unease solidified into a cold realization—he might very well have been set up. Other explanations seemed feeble in comparison. He tensed, grimacing at the unwelcome thought.

Determined, Rampton resolved to extract whatever advantage he could from this situation. He navigated his car onto the airport perimeter road, his eyes following the signs to the private aviation center. As he pulled into the parking lot behind the AirGuard buildings, the sight of his Gulfstream jet on the apron accelerated his pulse. There it stood, his ticket to freedom, a stunning silhouette against the sunlight. Spotting the pilots in the cockpit, busy with preflight preparations, Rampton felt a surge of reassurance. They were on schedule, and so was his escape.

Rampton swung the Lincoln into a VIP parking spot and stepped out swiftly, leaving the keys in the ignition. He leaned back into the car, grabbed his bag with a practiced motion, and made a beeline for the reception door. The door buzzed open at his approach, an apparent acknowledgment of his urgency.

Inside, an AirGuard operative greeted him with the usual pleasantries, offering to escort him to the VIP waiting area, but Rampton cut him off. "I'm in a hurry. I need to get going. Is the jet ready?" His words were crisp, brooking no delay.

The AirGuard employee, seemingly untroubled by his brusqueness, assured him that they were conducting final checks on the jet, with a colleague already aboard handling paperwork. Rampton's impatience appeared obvious. "Get me on board," he insisted, his tone leaving no room for further discussion.

Without hesitation, the operative reached for his radio, informing a colleague, the employee on the jet, of Rampton's arrival. The brief exchange over the radio ended with a concise: "Roger that. Out." Rampton barely registered the conversation, his focus singularly on the jet.

Sensing Rampton's urgency, the employee led him through the hangar's side door and out onto the apron. The Gulfstream jet loomed ahead, its stairs unfurled elegantly. Chrome guardrails caught the sunlight, shimmering invitingly, while LED lights along the steps flickered faintly in the bright sunshine.

At the base of the stairs, the employee stepped aside to let Rampton pass. Rampton ascended the stairs with purpose, each step reinforcing his resolve to leave everything behind. He didn't glance back or acknowledge the employee's courteous wish for a pleasant flight, his mind already soaring ahead, aligning with the freedom that awaited him in the skies.

Rampton stepped into the cabin, his senses on high alert. He glanced left at the pilots engrossed in their instrument checks, then right toward the galley and the cabin beyond. Striding through the galley, he settled into the main cabin, tossing his bag onto the seat opposite him with a sense of finality. A long breath escaped him—he had made it.

Surveying his surroundings, Rampton noted the absence of the usual flight attendants. He attributed this to the short notice of his departure. Pouring his own champagne seemed a minor inconvenience, a triviality in the grander scheme of things. He allowed himself a small, self-deprecating smile at the thought of facing such "hardships."

As he contemplated contacting his son, Dexter, to let him know he was leaving, the idea sparked a brief internal struggle. He quickly dismissed the prospect of enduring a conflict with Dexter today. It could wait, he decided. *A few days won't make much difference.*

The sound of the private cabin door opening abruptly interrupted his train of thought. Without turning, Rampton assumed the ground crew member he'd been expecting had emerged. His gaze remained fixed on the cockpit, visible through the galley.

The sudden appearance of a pistol's muzzle in his peripheral vision jolted him. He swiveled his head to meet the stern gaze of an older man holding the gun. "Take it easy," the man commanded, settling across the aisle with the weapon casually resting on his lap.

"What the fuck . . ." Rampton started, his voice edged with disbelief and growing alarm.

"Take it easy," the old man repeated firmly, then called out: "Mike, come down here, please."

A younger man joined the old man, his eyes locked on Rampton. Following the old man's instruction, Mike approached the cockpit and soon returned with the senior pilot.

"There has been a change of plans," the old man declared, looking up at the pilot, his voice steady and commanding.

"Excuse me?" Rampton's confusion mingled with a growing dread as he tried to interject.

"I canceled this flight. Please vacate the aircraft," the old man stated unequivocally at the slightly incredulous pilot.

The old man subtly revealed the gun in his lap to the pilot, cutting short Rampton's protest. The pilot, clearly understanding what was happening and the seriousness of the situation, quickly relayed a message to his copilot and then vacated the aircraft, leaving Rampton to confront his drastically altered circumstances alone.

His heart pounded fiercely, a rapid drumbeat keeping pace with his mounting panic. Confusion swirled within him as he faced the unexpected intruders. *What the fuck is happening? Who are these people?* His thoughts raced, his mind urgently plotting a way to regain control, to get the pilots back and the plane airborne.

"Look, I don't know what this is, but this plane has to leave this afternoon; it's imperative that—" he started, his voice clinging to authority but with a hint of desperation.

The old man cut him off. "Shut the fuck up. We canceled this flight," he said, his words sharp and unwavering.

Rampton's bewilderment deepened. "Who are you? What do you want?" he demanded, his voice becoming shrill. "Those pilots, they'll call the police and—"

"Good," the older man said before passing a slip of paper to the younger one, maintaining eye contact with Rampton. "Mike, call this number and ask for Agent Rapinski. Tell him we have Tyler Rampton in custody and give him our location." The old man's methodical and calm response only added to Rampton's unease.

"The feds? You've been speaking with them? I thought—" the younger man responded.

"It's OK, Mike. Research, remember? The news is out there now and can't be suppressed. I will fill you in later, but I trust this guy. Please make the call." Mike hovered, looking at Rampton and back at the old man.

"I need a phone?" he said, smiling weakly.

The old man grimaced, fished into his pocket, and handed over his phone.

"Here," he said, passing the phone to Mike, who walked to the far end of the cabin to make the call.

Rampton's thoughts reeled, the situation spiraling further from his grasp, and yet these people seemed to be improvising. *Just what the fuck is going on?* His mind grappled with the unfolding scenario, every revelation tightening the knot of dread in his stomach.

After a pause where Rampton could only hear the sound of his escalating heartbeat in his ears, the older man spoke once more.

"My name is Henry Mitchell, and you murdered my granddaughter." The accusation hit Rampton first like a strong wave, slapping him, then full force, like a physical blow, as the adrenaline kicked in.

"I . . . what?" Rampton stuttered, disbelief tangling with a creeping sense of dread.

Henry's calm demeanor contrasted sharply with Rampton's growing agitation. Rampton's attempts to negotiate, to bring the confrontation back under his control, at least near his orbit, were met with unwavering resolve from this Henry.

"You heard me. You are responsible for bringing down Vivair Flight 002, and you are going to jail."

"Look, calm down, let's disembark and chat. Man to man." Rampton desperately tried not to sound desperate.

"I'm calm. Mike's calm. You? Well, you don't look so calm."

"Listen, we can—"

"Bill, you can come up here now, buddy," the old man shouted to the back of the aircraft while Rampton tried to speak. Another old man then appeared in a security guard's uniform and trudged up the aisle, followed by an attractive woman.

What the hell is this? Rampton thought.

The security guard glanced at Rampton but said nothing.

"Feds will soon be here, Bill; just hang tight, OK?" Henry, the man with the gun, said as he passed.

As the man in the security guard uniform settled on the sofa, *my fucking sofa*, Rampton saw a glimmer of opportunity, a chance to turn the tide. He tried to stand.

"Sit the fuck down," the old man said, and Rampton complied.

Rampton noticed Henry's sweat, suggesting that his insistence on being calm might be a facade. Clinging to this sliver of hope, Rampton strategized. If he could just get everyone back on the ground, maybe he could salvage the situation, reach the pilots, and involve the other security guards.

He tried once more, trying to sound persuasive but coming across as desperate. "Let's just sit in the office and talk this through. I'm sure we can work this out, whatever it is." His plea hung in the air, a last-ditch effort to regain control in a situation rapidly slipping from his hands.

The young woman sat in the vacant seat directly opposite Rampton, staring at him for a long moment. Rampton shifted in his seat and then looked directly at her.

"And who the fuck are you?" he sneered.

"Oh, just someone you tried to torture and kill, nobody special," she replied.

CHAPTER 50

Rampton's gaze shifted from Sarah back to Henry.
"We'll just wait here," said Henry, meeting his gaze.
"Money? Is that it? How much do you want? Get those pilots back, and I'll make you rich. Just do it." Rampton had reached the bargaining phase.

"It's all about money with you. You think everyone's the same. Either money solves the problem or murder. It's over. Get used to that notion," Henry barked.

"Look, old man, I have my guys coming. They will be here soon, and we arm them to the fucking teeth. If you want a shoot-out, I'll give you one. Bullet in the back of your head. Is that what you want?" Rampton snarled, his composure long gone.

Henry watched him unravel, his poise fraying into snarls and spit. But Henry remained unmoved, his experience grounding him. "Nobody's coming to rescue you, Rampton. What security detail arrives after their principal? You're finished. Accept it like a man. Your grandpa would say that, right?" he countered, his tone sounding contemptuous.

"Fuck you. You're not fit to shine my grandfather's fucking shoes," Rampton spat.

"Neither are you, by the looks of it. He must be so proud of you for all the destruction you've caused. He was no saint, but at least he was subtle," Sarah said, her words reinforcing the contrast between Rampton and the legacy he so poorly represented. Henry felt a grim satisfaction in seeing Rampton so thoroughly dismantled, not by physical force but by the unvarnished truth.

Henry Mitchell observed the unfolding scene with a calculated calm. Mike, seated across from him, matched his composed demeanor. Rampton's eyes flitted between them and Sarah, his once arrogant facade now marred by creeping desperation. He directed a desperate plea at Mike, offering a life-changing sum in exchange for betrayal. "What about you? Ditch this old man. He doesn't have enough time to spend the money I will give you. Get those fucking pilots back. You'll never work again. What do you say?" Rampton's voice quivered with urgency, his plea bordering on pathetic.

Mike responded immediately, his words laced with contempt. "Nope. I don't want your filthy money, you prick. I know you would have killed me if the people you employed to do it weren't so fucking dumb." His words were sharp, a verbal dagger thrust at Rampton's desperation.

Rampton's face twisted into a contortion of shock and realization as he recognized Mike. "You're the guy! You're that fucking guy on the plane! Fuck, what a loser," he jeered, his laughter cold and joyless.

"Am I the loser when you're going to spend the rest of your sorry life in prison?" Mike shot back, his retort slicing through Rampton's mockery.

Henry, still as a statue, idly toyed with Bill's gun in his lap, symbolizing their control over the situation. "Be careful with that, old man," Rampton snarled, desperate for any semblance of power.

In the tense cabin, each word and glance became a battle of wills. Henry remained stoic, his experience and resolve contrasting with Rampton's fraying composure. He prepared himself for whatever Rampton might throw at him next.

Then, with a composed, practiced demeanor, Henry lifted the gun in a two-handed grip, aiming it squarely at Rampton's face. Rampton, his bravado crumbling, raised his hands instinctively, his eyes widening in a silent acknowledgment of the threat. Henry held his arms steady, his gaze unflinching, until Rampton, unable to maintain eye contact, looked away. Their arms lowered simultaneously, a silent dance of power and submission.

Turning to Mike, Henry said, in a steady voice loaded with urgency, "What did the agent say?"

Mike's attempt at casualness fell flat as he admitted, "Um, I left a voicemail."

For the first time, exasperation seeped into Henry's voice. "You're kidding me?" The words were edged with evident frustration, a departure from his usual composure. It was as if his patience had finally reached its limit.

Mike, striving to sound reassuring, offered, "I guess he's busy?"

Rampton's laughter, devoid of humor, cut through the tension. "You guys are real pros, aren't you? The FBI is not interested. It's a civil matter, that's all. Get the pilots so I can go."

Ignoring Rampton's taunts, Henry instructed Mike through gritted teeth, "Can you try calling him again, please?"

"Sure," Mike replied, retreating to the far end of the cabin once more. Meanwhile, Henry's gaze stayed on Rampton, unyielding, a manifestation of quiet fury. Rampton, now unfazed, responded with a smirk, his arrogance still showing despite the circumstances.

Mike returned through the cabin. "Um, voice mail again, sorry. I left another message and told them it's urgent." Henry's features drew tighter.

Eager to help, Mike suggested, "Is there someone else I can try?"

Henry, weighing his words carefully, responded, "I have been in contact with this guy, Agent Rapinski. He has the complete story. I don't want to repeat it to someone else. I trust this guy."

Seizing the opportunity, Rampton sneered dismissively, "Your agent isn't interested. Like I said, this is going nowhere. You'll land yourselves in big trouble."

Amid this escalating situation, Henry remained focused and resolute, his mind calculating ways to counter the uncertainty and Rampton's continuous provocations.

Henry set his jaw and said, "This plane is going nowhere. You got that right." His stance remained resolute.

Rampton, ever the manipulator, tried to sow doubt with his words. "Straightforward false arrest. That's a felony charge right there. Hijacking an aircraft? Whoa, they'll throw the fucking book at you for that one. If I were you, I'd cut my losses. I'll be gone, and there will be nobody to file a complaint unless that other guy is upset about what you did; anything crops up, I'll make all the problems go away for you; you have my word," he said, nodding toward the hangar.

Henry replied immediately, "I couldn't care less what happens to me."

"Me neither," Mike chimed in, his voice firm.

"That makes three of us," Sarah added, her tone equally steadfast.

Rampton let out a long sigh, shifting in his seat. He attempted to deflect. "That news report? Well, you know they have it all wrong, don't you? It had nothing to do with me, I—"

"Save it for your lawyer. We're not interested," Henry snapped, cutting him off.

Suddenly, the phone in Mike's pocket buzzed, drawing everyone's attention. Pulling it out, Mike saw the incoming call from the number Henry had given him. He jabbed the speaker-phone icon and answered, "Hello, this is Mike Anderson."

"Hello, this is Agent Rapinski. I just received your voicemail. Is Henry with you? Can I speak with him?" the voice on the other end inquired.

"Sure." Mike handed the phone to Henry, who never broke his intense gaze on Rampton, ready to speak, his expression a mask, prepared for the next phase of their confrontation.

Henry addressed Agent Rapinski with the urgency and confidence of a man who had taken control of an impossible situation. "Agent Rapinski, this is Henry Mitchell. Have you seen the news?"

The agent's response, detailing their efforts, came through the phone, but Henry cut straight to the heart of the matter. "I got the head of the snake."

"You've got what?" the agent asked, confusion evident in his tone.

"Rampton. I have him in custody. Come and get him. He's stinking the place up," Henry said, the disdain clear in his voice. "We're at Harry Reid, Las Vegas, at AirGuard Secure Storage. We're on his jet. Oh, and his pilots will probably call the cops as we just kicked them off, so you may want the locals to back off before you get here."

"OK, don't do anything stupid. We're on our way."

They disconnected, and a satisfied grin spread across Henry's face.

Rampton's complexion drained of color, his face etched with panic. Henry, unflinching, declared, "It's over."

For the next twenty minutes, a heavy silence hung in the cabin. Henry's gaze never left Rampton, who stared vacantly ahead, seemingly lost in his thoughts of defeat. The tension was palpable, but the situation was different outside the plane.

Henry quietly informed Bill about their intention to detain Rampton until the FBI arrived. He instructed Bill to radio Jason and tell him everything was OK. Jason panicked and asked Bill what was happening as the pilots called the cops. Bill just told Jason not to worry; everything was under control.

As dusk crept in, the first signs of external activity began. Mike noticed the flashing red and blue lights painting Rampton's face first, followed by the cacophony of noise and shouting from the approaching police and FBI agents.

Having been informed of the situation by Henry, the FBI had seemingly taken charge of the operation to ensure that Rampton was apprehended without unnecessary complications or risks.

When law enforcement stormed the plane, Henry calmly placed the firearm on the table and raised his hands. Mike and Sarah were made to kneel and then lie down in the aisle, one in front of the other, and were unceremoniously cuffed. Officers rapidly thwarted Rampton's desperate lunge for the gun, pinning him down with his face pressed against the expensive carpet, right over one of the Alithia logos, as if eating it. Henry didn't feel threatened by the action and believed that Rampton would have only used the gun on himself.

The police officers cuffed Rampton and marched him back down the steps with his head bowed. Mike, watching Rampton's undignified exit from his prone position, couldn't help smiling.

Agent Rapinski removed everyone from the plane as the authorities sorted through the chaos. He asked his colleagues to release the handcuffs and approached Henry, Sarah, and Mike, his expression stern. "Look, I appreciate what you've done here, but I can't ignore your methods. Taking the law into your own hands, taking hostages, for Christ's sake, stealing guns, this is serious. We'll need to take you in for questioning, and there will be a full investigation into your actions." Mike and Sarah nodded, reality dawning on them. Henry just stared straight ahead, his gaze fixed. Although they had caught Rampton, their unconventional methods would have legal consequences they couldn't escape.

The trio joined Bill on the apron, their faces illuminated by the patrol cars' blue and red flashing lights.

Henry extended a hand to Bill in a gesture of reconciliation. "No hard feelings, Bill?"

Bill shook his head, relief and exhaustion etched into his face. "The boys will return the plane to the hangar. FBI said it's a federal crime scene, so we have to preserve it until they come back."

Bill accepted the handshake, but his grip was tense, "What happened here... it was reckless and terrifying. I was held at gunpoint at my place of work. I'm sorry, but I need to process this. You deceived me; it made me look like an old fool. Dammit, you endangered lives." His voice was strained, reflecting the turmoil of his experience. Henry nodded in understanding; he knew they had crossed lines that couldn't be ignored.

"I hope you'll see one day that the ends justified the means," Henry replied, his face expressionless.

Henry, Sarah, and Mike were eventually escorted to two SUVs: Henry and Mike in one and Sarah in the other. Mike was worried about Sarah being isolated and glanced at Henry as the panic in him started to rise, and this new predicament dawned on him. Henry looked serene, however, utterly unfazed; it gave Mike a crumb of comfort as the cars pulled away. Rampton was long gone.

After hours of questioning at the local FBI field office, Henry, Sarah, and Mike were finally released. Agent Rapinski, while handing back their personal belongings, remarked, "We're letting you go for now, but this isn't over. Your actions today, while they did lead to Rampton's capture, have legal consequences. You'll be contacted for further inquiries. Stay available, and don't leave town."

Exhausted, the trio stepped out into the cool evening air. Despite their temporary freedom, potential legal repercussions hung over them. Sarah broke the silence, her voice weary, "We did what we thought was right, but we're not out of the woods yet. We should probably look into getting a lawyer." Mike nodded in agreement, his mind already racing with the implications of their actions and how he could afford a lawyer.

"We'll be fine, trust me."

Mike and Sarah both turned to look at Henry, who was

staring impassively into the middle distance. He did not appear troubled in the slightest.

"Henry, I don't think—" Sarah started to say before Henry cut her off.

"I said trust me."

Sarah and Mike looked at each other, and Mike shrugged, giving Sarah a small, sheepish smile.

They took an Uber back to the Airguard parking lot, and as they walked towards their car, the reality of their situation began to sink in. They had entered a complex legal and moral grey area that wouldn't be easily resolved. The night ahead offered a brief respite, but the coming days promised new challenges.

Looking back at the Airguard hangar where Rampton's jet now sat once more, Mike added, "I guess we should rest tonight and regroup tomorrow. Work out what we're going to do?"

Sarah looked at him, a hint of a smile forming. "Screw that, we're in Vegas." The night ahead promised a well-deserved respite from the day's drama.

CHAPTER 51

Silas Knox navigated the airport, flanked by two watchful, uniformed police officers. His flight to London had started boarding, its passenger call echoing in the busy terminal. Though free, he felt a sense of confinement. The officers, still holding his personal belongings in a bag, represented his lack of control. Desperate for information, particularly about Alex's activation of the kill switch, Silas thought through the unsettling possibilities.

He scanned the terminal, searching for any hint of news—a broadcast, a newspaper headline, anything that could illuminate the situation. But the bustling Monday morning crowd offered no clues, leaving him in an unnerving vacuum.

As they approached the desk for his 8:05 a.m. British Airways flight to London, one of the officers handed him his bag. "Your things," the officer stated, his expression unreadable.

"Thanks," Silas replied, offering a smile not reciprocated by the grim-faced officer.

At the desk, the officers handed Silas's documents to the ground crew. The familiar beep of the boarding pass scanner seemed to break the tension.

As they proceeded toward the plane, one of the officers

shouted something in Italian. The crowd ahead, previously absorbed in their travel routines, shifted aside, creating a clear path for them as the non-Italian-speaking passengers cottoned on. Silas walked through the parted queue, acutely aware of the curious eyes on him. This public spectacle had become a mortifying final chapter to his frustrating interlude.

Silas confronted the officer, his voice edged with frustration and doubt. "Is this necessary?" The officer's indifferent shrug in response did little to alleviate Silas's frustration.

"We have to put you on this plane. It is the order of the court. You are an enemy of Italy," the officer declared, his tone matter of fact.

This accusation struck Silas with a jolt of disbelief. An enemy of Italy? *For fuck's sake.* The very notion seemed absurd to him. He had only sought to assist, not hinder. But arguing seemed futile, a pointless expenditure of energy against the rigid walls of Italian bureaucracy.

As they reached the forward door of the aircraft, the officers handed Silas his passport and boarding pass, then left abruptly, their departure as silent as their escort had been. Silas watched them retreat down the air bridge, their figures diminishing with each step.

Turning to face the flight attendant with a wry smile, Silas remarked, "I'm a VIP," his tone sarcastic, his attempt to inject some humor into the surreal and embarrassing situation.

The flight attendant responded warmly, "Certainly looks like it. Welcome aboard," which offered momentary respite from the tension.

Seizing the opportunity to catch up on the news, Silas asked, "Could I be cheeky and ask for a newspaper?"

"Certainly, sir, we have the *Daily Mail*, *The Times*, *The Guardian* . . ." she offered.

"*The Times*, please—that today's?" Silas asked, hoping for the latest updates.

"Yes, it is, fresh this morning," the flight attendant confirmed.

"Thank you." As he took the newspaper, he felt a sense of anticipation mingled with apprehension. Unfolding the news within those pages was vital to understanding the true breadth of his predicament.

With the newspaper in hand, Silas's heart raced as he made his way to the back of the plane. He rummaged for his phone, stowed his bag above, and settled into his seat. Unfurling the newspaper, his eyes fixated on the front page. The headline screamed at him, confirming everything.

VIVAIR CONSPIRACY REVEALED—Sabotage, conspiracy, and cover-ups alleged in the tragic crash of Vivair Flight 002.

The enormity of the story sprawled out before him. He leaned back and exhaled deeply, his thoughts cycling. The great unraveling was now the mundane unfolding.

Pulling out his phone, he dialed Alex Mercer. Alex answered with a relieved exclamation: "Silas! Fuck me sideways, you're alive!" His sentiment echoed Silas's sense of surreal survival.

"Sure am," Silas replied, recounting his arrest and the absurd accusation of being an enemy of Italy. His tone mixed disbelief with a hint of dark humor. He inquired about the operation, needing confirmation that all had gone as planned.

Alex's response reassured him. "Yes, all are legit. I tried to get a hold of you all day yesterday, but last night I thought, fuck it, and flicked the switch. You were right, dude; the world's gone crazy."

Silas's laugh, loud and unexpected, turned heads in the cabin. He waved an apologetic hand to the other passengers. "Thanks, Alex. I'll buy you a beer when I'm back."

The conversation ended, leaving Silas staring out the window at the bustling activity on the tarmac. Despite the turmoil, a faint sense of relief flickered within him. The switch had been flipped, the truth had been revealed, and he was on his way home.

Curious, Silas Knox scrolled through his phone to contact

Sarah. His call went straight to voice mail, which was unsurprising, he concluded, as she likely remained in the mountains, cut off from a steady signal. He pondered whether she might be missing out on the unfolding drama.

As he delved into the front-page article of the *Times*, his phone buzzed insistently in his pocket. Pulling it out, Silas saw Henry's number on the screen and answered immediately.

"Henry! How are you?" he greeted, only to be taken aback by Sarah's voice responding from the other end. Her incredulous tone conveyed her shock.

"Fucking hell, you're alive?"

Silas couldn't help but chuckle at her reaction. "Of course, I'm alive, petal! I'm just reading *The Times*. Fuck me, we did it!" His voice sounded triumphant and full of relief.

As Sarah inquired about his whereabouts, Silas briefly explained his situation. "Rome. I'm sitting on a plane waiting to fly back to London. They've deported me. It's a long story. I spent the last two days incommunicado in detention."

"Learned some Italian, too, by the sounds of it."

Sarah's attempt at humor about his newfound linguistic skills made Silas smile. "Spanish," he corrected her gently. "*Incommunicado* is Spanish."

"Oh, yeah, of course," Sarah replied, slightly embarrassed. "Anyway. Well, it has all been happening."

Silas, his excitement barely contained, pressed for details. "Yeah, I can see that. It's amazing. How have you been holding up? Getting some good mountain air? Where's your phone?"

Sarah then dropped a bombshell. "My phone is long gone, and we never reached the mountains. They tracked us down and ran us off the road en route to Omaha. Fucking totaled my car and kidnapped me and Mike."

Silas's laughter rang out again, loud and skeptical. "You're kidding, right?"

"No, Silas, I am not fucking kidding. They drugged us and

took us to some facility they were running in Sacramento. We assume they flew us. No idea."

"What the fuck?" Silas said, the smile diminishing.

"It gets worse."

Silas Knox's expression contorted in disbelief, fading from joy to concern as Sarah relayed her harrowing experience. "Fucking hell, Sarah." His face twisted as if he were trying to extract juice from a bitter lemon, his mind reeling from her words.

"They split us up. When I came to, Mike was nowhere to be seen. I was freaking out but trying to keep it together. These guys were fucking hard asses. You know the type: vast shoulders, shaved heads, and dressed as soldiers," Sarah explained, her tense voice betraying the strain of the ordeal.

Just then, an announcement echoed through the cabin. Boarding had been completed, the doors were closed, and the plane would soon take off. Silas's mind struggled to keep pace with the unfolding narrative.

"Shit, you must have been petrified. Poor Mike, he didn't sign up for this—" Silas began.

"Mike? Don't worry about him, he escaped," Sarah interjected.

"He what?" His surprise was evident in his tone.

"Mike . . ." Sarah paused, searching for the right words to convey what had happened.

Silas listened intently, his heart pounding, as Sarah continued. "He overpowered the guy interrogating him. I still don't know how. The other guy didn't make it, Silas, that's all I know. Anyway, he escaped and then rescued me. We left with stolen cash, went to the airport, and flew back to Chicago. Then we drove up to Sheboygan Falls to meet with Henry."

"What the fuck? That's quite something. I didn't have him pegged as a man of action. Shit, that's amazing!" Silas exclaimed, shaking his head.

"It gets better . . ." Sarah began as a flight attendant tapped Silas's shoulder.

"Please, sir, can you finish your call? The captain has asked that all electronic devices be switched off or put into airplane mode as we are about to depart," she said politely.

Silas gave her a smile and a nod.

"Shit, just getting to the juicy part, but we're about to take off," Silas said into the phone. "I'll call you back when we land, petal."

Silas disconnected the call, his mind still swirling with Sarah's revelations. He exhaled a long sigh, releasing the mental and emotional whirlwind he had been through. This entire saga had morphed into an adventure far beyond his expectations, and the whole picture still eluded him. While relieved everyone was safe, the fate of their adversaries remained a mystery to him. The newspaper article had not mentioned arrests, investigations, or sealed indictments—too soon, he imagined. He resolved to piece together the complete story once back in London. He followed the cabin supervisor's advice and relaxed for the remainder of the flight.

The in-flight breakfast sandwich and the peculiarly flavored coffee were less than remarkable, yet he consumed them both, driven by utilitarian need rather than culinary pleasure. Reclining his seat, he closed his eyes, not expecting sleep to come easily after such an adrenaline-fueled period. Surprisingly, exhaustion took over, and he dozed off, his body succumbing to the intense weariness of his recent hardships.

Waking up as the plane began its descent into Heathrow, Silas felt a bit disheveled, with drool at the corner of his mouth. He quickly freshened up using the moistened tissues provided earlier. With no one aware of his arrival except Sarah and Alex, he anticipated a quiet reentry into London, expecting to be able to blend in. Once through immigration, he planned to reconnect with Sarah for the rest of the story over a decent coffee.

The irony of his situation didn't escape him. The man behind the biggest story in recent times was about to slip back into the city unnoticed, anonymous among the throngs of travelers. Part of him, where his ego resided, bristled at this anonymity, but the rational side, the planner in him, found solace in it. A bit of normalcy would be welcome after the recent tumult of fear and excitement.

Landing and navigating his way to Caffè Nero in the arrivals hall took less than thirty minutes, which was impressively quick, in Silas's estimation. He ordered a large Americano and a ham-and-cheese croissant, choosing a table near the entrance, where the tiles met the wooden floors of Caffè Nero. As he sat, the juxtaposition of his current humdrum calm surroundings and the recent chaos of his life struck him profoundly. He was back in London, ready to face whatever came next.

He dialed Henry's number, his anticipation building for the continuation of Sarah's story. "Hey." Sarah's voice came through softly, a subtle undertone of exhaustion beneath her words.

"Hi, petal, I'm back in London. I grabbed a coffee and a croissant, and I'm all ears," Silas responded, his tone light despite his eagerness to hear the unfolding tale.

Sarah hesitated, then resumed her narrative. "Yeah, well, anyway, we escaped to Chicago—"

Silas interjected, his voice tinged with disbelief. "Wait, so, Mike,"—Silas looked around to make sure nobody was close enough to hear him and whispered—"iced the dude?"

"Yup, stone cold." Sarah's stark confirmation startled him.

Silas sighed, "Well, thank God it's all over. Let's hope arrests will—"

Sarah cut him off. "Oh, I haven't finished."

Silas looked around him and whispered, "What, you mean there's more?"

"Yes, you haven't asked me where I am."

"I thought you said you were in Chicago?"

"I was in Chicago. Now I'm in Vegas with Henry and Mike."

"What?" The word burst out of Silas.

"Las Vegas, baby!" Sarah said, giggling.

"Why are you all there, and, more importantly, why aren't I?" Silas asked, half joking.

"What's stopping you?" Sarah countered playfully.

Silas paused, then made an impulsive decision. "I'll call you right back. I want to hear the rest of this!"

After a quick flight search, he called Sarah back.

"What time is it there, petal?"

"Two thirty, we're still up celebrating," she replied, her voice cheerful.

Silas could sense her high spirits. "I booked a flight. I'll be there later, around six tomorrow night. You can fill in all the details in person."

"Great, I look forward to it. We'll have a Big Bertha reunion. I'll tell the guys. By the way, we're at the Wynn on the Strip."

"OK, I'll book a room."

"Well, you don't have to, you know?"

"See you soon, petal." They disconnected, and Silas smiled at the thought of their impending reunion.

Checking his watch, Silas noted he had an hour before his Delta flight via LA. As he contemplated the journey ahead, a fleeting thought crossed his mind about the Alithia HQ and its proximity to the flight path. He hoped for a glimpse of it from the air, a symbolic view of the saga they were now part of.

CHAPTER 52

Stepping into the opulent lobby of the Wynn Hotel on the Las Vegas Strip, Silas scanned the area and quickly landed on Sarah. As she rushed toward him, he set down his bag, and they embraced warmly, sharing a tangible sense of relief and accomplishment.

"We did it, petal," Silas whispered, his tone triumphant, his face a portrait of happiness.

"I haven't quite forgiven you yet," Sarah replied, tone light yet pointed.

"Fair enough, I suppose," Silas conceded with a chuckle, acknowledging the complexity of their situation.

They approached Henry and Mike, who lounged in the lobby area. "Gentlemen," Silas greeted them, his smile wide and genuine.

"Hello, Silas. We assumed you were dead, so it's excellent to see you," Henry remarked, his tone dry but warm.

"Still life in the old dog yet," Silas quipped, his laughter booming through the lobby.

Turning to Mike, Silas addressed him with curiosity and admiration. "I hear you are now officially a man of action?"

Mike shrugged, a look of disbelief on his face. "I don't know about that. Honestly, it's like it never happened. Like I saw it happen in a movie. People would think I was making it up. I just saw an opportunity and ran at him; I had nothing else. He slipped, you know, and well. There haven't been any follow-ups and no questions. It feels surreal. I don't know what happened to the guy."

Trying to lighten the mood, Silas joked, "I wouldn't worry— he's probably been disposed of somewhere. Maybe a barrel of acid or out in the desert or something."

"Yeah, that doesn't help," Mike responded.

Sensing the need for a change in topic, Sarah suggested, "Let's go eat."

"Good, I could eat a scabby cat between two bread vans," Silas exclaimed, laughing again.

"You could what? That's gross," Sarah replied, her face wrinkling in disgust.

"The food on the plane was fucking awful, so, yeah, I'm starving. Let's eat," Silas explained.

"You in coach?" Mike inquired a hint of surprise in his voice.

"Sure was, as I was paying. I felt like throwing up a stink, but we were already airborne by then," Silas responded with a wry smile, acknowledging his less-than-luxurious flight.

Mike raised his palms in a gesture of understanding, ready to move on to a more pleasant experience—a hearty meal with friends. The group, united by extraordinary circumstances, prepared to celebrate their hard-won victory.

As they settled into the congratulatory atmosphere, Silas Knox asked his burning question: "OK, folks, what are we doing in Vegas? I'm assuming it has something to do with a certain T. Rampton, who was arrested in the vicinity?" he asked, his tone even.

Sarah, beaming with admiration, pointed to Henry. "Well, it all comes down to Henry," she said. "He made sure Rampton didn't escape. He knew exactly where he'd be and when after the news broke. He also made sure the feds arrived just in time. I have to hand it to him."

Henry received a congratulatory pat on the back from Sarah, who responded with a modest smile directed at Silas. "I did it for Chloe," he said, his voice tinged with sadness and pride.

Silas opened his mouth to respond, but words failed him. What could he say?

"The only problem is we're in trouble with the feds about the way we detained Rampton. I'm trying not to think about it, but they were pretty angry. I think they want to throw the book at us." Sarah said, the smile fading.

Henry looked up, his gaze fixed on Sarah.

"Nothing will happen to us; you have my word. Relax, enjoy yourself." He said impassively.

The rest of the evening flowed with toasts and laughter, a much-needed release after the tension of recent events.

As the evening wound down, Mike, clear-eyed from drinking water all night, posed a reflective question to the group. "What now?"

"We have a book to write, don't we, petal?" Silas replied, turning to Sarah with a knowing look.

Sarah nodded, her gaze fixed on Silas. "Sure do, and you will be in demand when you resurface," she said, raising her glass in a toast.

Silas couldn't hide his eagerness. "Yeah, I won't lie. I'm looking forward to the attention. It's been a while."

Mike, who had been quietly contemplating his next steps, spoke up. "I'm going to write a book, too," he announced, his voice steady, betraying a newfound sense of purpose.

The group turned to him, surprised. Mike's decision to embrace sobriety had instilled in him a sense of clarity and determination. He felt a profound shift within himself since the kidnapping and the violent events that had followed. "It feels as if maybe two people died in that warehouse: the old Mike and the other guy. I've been learning a lot about myself and think I might have a future," he confessed, his voice earnest.

Silas raised his glass in support. "Good for you, Mike. And on you writing a book, I'd say you certainly have a story to tell. I can help you with that, for sure."

Mike, appreciative, replied, "Silas, I know you might be drunk, but I'm going to hold you to that."

Attention then shifted to Henry. Curious, Sarah asked, "What about you, Henry?"

Henry pondered for a moment. "Me? I don't know. I feel I have a shot at justice for Chloe and all those other poor people, but I won't relax until they convict and sentence that son of a bitch Rampton and everyone else involved in what they did."

Sarah prodded further into Henry's mysterious past, but he remained tight-lipped. "Can't say, won't say. That's all there is."

An awkward silence ensued, broken eventually by Sarah's understanding nod. "OK, I respect that," she said.

Silas raised his glass once more. "To Henry," he toasted, and the others joined in, clinking glasses in solidarity. Silas caught the fleeting smile on Henry's face, a rare glimpse of satisfaction, before it vanished, leaving behind the stoic demeanor of a man seemingly still on a mission.

CHAPTER 53

A few days later, Henry, Mike, and Sarah were back in one of the Las Vegas FBI field office meeting rooms, waiting to hear their fate. Seated with them under the harsh lighting was a lawyer Henry had contacted, someone he knew evidently, given how they greeted each other. Mike couldn't help but notice Henry's usual stern demeanor softened momentarily as he shook hands with the lawyer, a shared history subtly implied in the brief exchange of smiles.

The lawyer, a man of poised confidence with a hint of gray at his temples, had an air of seasoned experience. His sharp, observant eyes flicked between the trio before settling on Henry, with whom he shared a quiet, almost conspiratorial conversation. Mike watched, intrigued but unable to catch their words spoken in low, discreet tones. The familiarity between them was evident: the way Henry leaned in slightly, the lawyer's occasional nod, and the brief, knowing glances they exchanged. It was clear to Mike that their relationship was built on more than just professional grounds; there was mutual respect and understanding, the kind that was forged over time and shared experiences.

Henry's voice, usually so commanding, took on a softer cadence as he spoke with the lawyer, suggesting a level of comfort and trust that Mike hadn't often seen in him. It made him wonder once again about Henry's past: the stories and battles behind the stoic facade of the man they had come to know under such extraordinary circumstances.

As their conversation drew to a close, the lawyer turned his attention to the rest of them, his expression shifting to one of professional focus. Mike leaned back in his chair, trying to shake off his curiosity about the nature of Henry's connection with the lawyer. Right now, what mattered was the here and now, the outcome of this meeting, and what it meant for their future.

Their lawyer turned to them, his expression a blend of seriousness and reassurance. "I've had a word with the federal prosecutor," he began, folding his hands on the table. "Given the unique circumstances of this case, they're inclined to be lenient."

Henry nodded, echoing the lawyer's sentiment. The lawyer continued, "As I suspected. The FBI's discretion, the weight of Rampton's crimes, and the public attention this case has garnered have all played in our favor. While legally questionable, your actions ultimately led to a significant criminal's capture."

Sarah leaned forward, her eyes reflecting both anxiety and hope. "So, what does that mean for us?" she asked, her voice tinged with concern.

The lawyer paused before responding, choosing his words carefully. "The prosecutor is willing to offer a deal. No jail time, but you'll be under probation and required to complete community service. There will also be a formal reprimand for taking the law into your own hands. I believe it's a fair outcome, all things considered."

Mike let out a breath he didn't realize he'd been holding. "That's... better than I expected," he admitted, relief washing over him.

"And it's the right decision," Henry added, his voice steady. "We did what was necessary but must also respect the law. This outcome is a reminder of that balance. I am happy with it, and so should you be."

Sarah nodded in agreement, a small smile breaking through her apprehension. "It's over, then. We can finally move on from this."

As they left the FBI office, the specter of jail time and the anxiety of the past days lifted from their shoulders. They had stepped into a legal and ethical grey area, but now, with the resolution of their case, they could look to the future. The sun was setting over the Las Vegas skyline, casting a warm glow that felt like a promise of new beginnings. Henry, Mike, and Sarah walked together, united by their experience, ready to face whatever lay ahead.

"I told you to trust me." Henry said, looking straight ahead.

EPILOGUE

In Njala, Field Marshal Diallo seized power effortlessly, his soldiers occupying key locations without firing a shot. Internationally, there were calls for democratic elections, but privately, Diallo garnered support from the United States and other Western nations, eager to maintain their regional interests. Despite his involvement in the Njala files, Diallo, now untouchable within his country, ruled with military might, aligning with the United States to keep Chinese influence at bay. For the CIA and the elusive Dalton, this marked a successful mission.

Jibril Abena, now residing in Geneva, faced an uncertain future. His dreams of returning to Njala as president were dashed, torn apart by his illegitimacy and the revelation of his corrupt rise to power. His once unlimited funds dwindled, and with Diallo pursuing legal action against him, Abena contemplated a new life under a new identity, far from Geneva's high cost of living.

Chicago O'Hare International Airport erected a memorial for Vivair Flight 002 victims, a solemn reminder of the destructive intersection of greed, power, ego, and politics.

Silas Knox and Sara collaborated on a book, *Greed, Corruption, and Mass Murder: The Full Story of Alithia, Njala, and Vivair Flight 002*, and later began another project on the Senator Connelly scandal. Their relationship remained strictly professional, with Silas continuing to run luke-817.org with Lord Jonathan Worthington's assistance.

True to his promise, Mike authored *Lucky Guy: My Part in the Downfall of Alithia*, a bestseller that catapulted him into the spotlight. His book tour offered a form of redemption, a chance to fade into obscurity with enough earnings. Henry, ever resourceful, hinted at helping Mike with a new identity.

Henry was still full of surprises.

The federal government took action to dissolve Alithia because of the criminal activities that had benefited the corporation. The government seized all assets believed to have been gained illegally, which essentially meant everything.

The court order stated that the assets seized through civil forfeiture were to compensate victims and fund government programs to prevent similar crimes.

After proving that Alithia's continued existence threatened public interest or safety, they eventually dissolved the company.

Some media outlets expressed concerns that civil asset forfeiture might adversely affect innocent parties with legitimate claims to the assets. Legal processes aimed to balance the recovery of unlawfully acquired assets with the protection of rights for individuals or entities uninvolved in criminal activities. Despite this, the public's clamor for retribution engulfed anyone associated with Alithia, drawing them into legal turmoil and expelling them without mercy. Legal cases sprang up everywhere, and experts predicted that litigation involving Alithia's wrongdoing and the repercussions of civil asset forfeiture would likely persist for decades.

The court convicted Tyler Rampton and sentenced him to life in prison without the possibility of parole for the sabotage leading to the deaths on Vivair Flight 002. For each life lost on that tragic flight, he received an additional life sentence. The case stood out for the tragedy's scale and the intentional nature of the act. Despite heavily investing in his defense, Rampton couldn't shake off Dalton's shadow, a figure his team couldn't prove existed. Essentially, Rampton had hired a ghost, with the prosecution arguing that he was merely a straw man. Former employees testified about Dalton's employment, yet efforts to locate him yielded no results. Frustration marred Rampton's demeanor throughout the trial, especially when he insisted that Dalton had orchestrated the sabotage of the flight control systems. His outbursts in court captured nightly news headlines, painting him as a pantomime villain. At the verdict, a cheer erupted in the packed courtroom as they found him guilty on all counts.

Rampton watched a documentary about Alithia's downfall from his cell at ADX Florence Federal Prison. The documentary depicted employees emptying Alithia's headquarters. In one of the final scenes, four employees slung his grandfather's massive portrait onto the back of a truck. The camera zoomed in on this symbolic image, capturing Randolph's stony face staring back at the viewer.

Seeing that image, Rampton fully grasped the enormity of the events. The burden felt so crushing that he thought it might overwhelm him. He longed for death as an escape, but the prison system denied him that option. He expressed remorse to his prison counselor, not for his victims but for his grandfather. The counselor frequently suspected Rampton of being a psychopath, though this never became an official diagnosis.

Rampton sat on the bunk in his cell, his back against the wall. He had a book open on his lap, a self-help book by some spiritual guru. He wasn't reading, just staring blankly at the opposite wall, which had a poster of an African lake bathed in sunlight with lush foliage surrounding the water.

Rampton heard footsteps approaching, echoing. They stopped when they got to his cell door.

"Rampton, you have a visitor," the guard said.

Rampton screwed his face up. *God, I hope it's not Dexter.* "Who is it?" he snapped.

"I have the name Dalton on my list."

ABOUT THE AUTHOR

Iain Ronayne's journey from the bustling heart of London to the thrilling pages of his debut novel, "The Luckiest Man Alive," is a story of passion, curiosity, and the enduring love for storytelling. His early fascination with technology led him through a vibrant career in IT, globetrotting and absorbing diverse cultures, enriching his narrative palette, experiences that broadened his horizons and fueled his imagination.

Visit his website: https://theluckiestmana.live/
Join him on X: https://twitter.com/IFR65

Printed in Great Britain
by Amazon